SIZE 12
AND READY
TO ROCK

By Meg Cabot

Overbite
Insatiable
Ransom My Heart (with Mia Thermopolis)
Queen of Babble series
Heather Wells series
The Boy series
She Went All the Way
The Princess Diaries series
The Mediator series
The 1-800-WHERE-R-YOU series
All-American Girl series
Nicola and the Viscount
Victoria and the Rogue
Jinx
How to Be Popular
Pants on Fire
Avalon High series
The Airhead series
Allie Finkle's Rules for Girls series
The Abandon series

SIZE 12

AND READY
TO ROCK

MEG
CABOT

WILLIAM MORROW

An Imprint of HarperCollins*Publishers*

P.S.™ is a trademark of HarperCollins Publishers.

SIZE 12 AND READY TO ROCK. Copyright © 2012 by Meg Cabot, LLC. All rights reserved. Printed in the United States of America. No part of this book may be used or reproduced in any manner whatsoever without written permission except in the case of brief quotations embodied in critical articles and reviews. For information address HarperCollins Publishers, 10 East 53rd Street, New York, NY 10022.

HarperCollins books may be purchased for educational, business, or sales promotional use. For information please write: Special Markets Department, HarperCollins Publishers, 10 East 53rd Street, New York, NY 10022.

Designed by Diahann Sturge

Library of Congress Cataloging-in-Publication Data has been applied for.

ISBN 978-0-06-173478-6

12 13 14 15 16   OV/RRD   10 9 8 7 6 5 4 3

Many thanks to:

Beth Ader, Nancy Bender, Jennifer Brown, Benjamin Egnatz, Jason Egnatz, Carrie Feron, Michele Jaffe, Lynn Langdale, Laura J. Langlie, Ann Larson, Michael Sohn, Pamela Spengler-Jaffee, Tessa Woodward, and most especially, all of Heather Wells's amazingly supportive fans . . . rock on!

SIZE 12

AND READY
TO ROCK

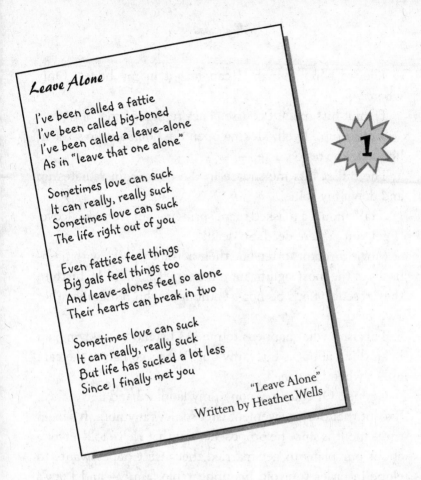

Leave Alone

I've been called a fattie
I've been called big-boned
I've been called a leave-alone
As in "leave that one alone"

Sometimes love can suck
It can really, really suck
Sometimes love can suck
The life right out of you

Even fatties feel things
Big gals feel things too
And leave-alones feel so alone
Their hearts can break in two

Sometimes love can suck
It can really, really suck
But life has sucked a lot less
Since I finally met you

"Leave Alone"
Written by Heather Wells

Racing up the stairs to the second floor, my heart pounding—
I'm a walker, not a runner. I try not to race anywhere unless
it's an emergency, and according to the call I received, that's
what this is—I find the corridor dark and deserted. I can't
see anything except the bloodred glow of the EXIT sign at the
end of the hall. I can't hear anything but the sound of my
own heavy breathing.

They're here, though. I can feel it in my bones. Only where?

Then it hits me. Of course. They're behind me.

"Give it up," I yell, kicking open the doors to the student library. "You're so busted—"

The bullet hits me square in the back. Pain radiates up and down my spine.

"Ha!" shouts a masked man, springing out from an alcove. "I got you! You're dead. So dead!"

Movie directors often cue their heroine's death with flashbacks of the most significant moments from her life, birth to the present. (Let's be honest, though: who remembers her own birth?)

This isn't what happens to me. As I stand there dying, all I can think about is Lucy, my dog. Who's going to take care of her when I'm gone?

Cooper. Of course, Cooper, my landlord and new fiancé. Except that our engagement isn't so new anymore. It's been three months since he proposed—not that we've told anyone about our plans to get married, because Cooper wants to elope in order to avoid his unbearable family—and Lucy's grown so accustomed to finding him in my bed that she goes straight to *him* for her breakfast and morning walk, since he's such an early riser, and I'm . . . not.

Actually, Lucy goes straight to Cooper for everything now because Cooper often works from home and spends all day with her while I'm here at Fischer Hall. To tell the truth, Lucy seems to like Cooper better than she likes me. Lucy's a little bit of a traitor.

Lucy's going to be so well taken care of after I'm dead

that she probably won't even notice I'm not there anymore. This is disheartening enough—or maybe encouraging enough—that my thoughts flicker irrationally to my doll collection. It's mortifying that someone who is almost thirty owns enough dolls to form a collection. But I do, over two dozen of them, one from each of the countries in which I performed back when I was an embarrassingly overproduced teen pop singer for Cartwright Records. Since I wasn't in any particular country long enough to sightsee—only to go on all the morning news shows, then give a concert, usually as the opening act for Easy Street, one of the most popular boy bands of all time—my mom got me a souvenir doll (wearing the country's national costume) from each airport gift shop. She said this was better than seeing the koalas in Australia, or the Buddhist temples in Japan, or the volcanoes in Iceland, or the elephants in South Africa, and so on, because it saved time.

All this, of course, was before Dad got arrested for tax evasion, and Mom conveniently hooked up with my manager and then fled the country, taking with her the entire contents of my savings account.

"You poor kid." That's what Cooper said about the dolls the first time he spent the night in my room and noticed them staring down at him from the built-in shelves overhead. When I explained where they'd come from, and why I'd hung on to them for all these years—they're all I have left of my shattered career and family, though Dad and I have been trying to reconnect since he got out of prison—Cooper had just shaken his head. "You poor, poor kid."

I can't die, I suddenly realize. Even if Cooper does take care of Lucy, he won't know what to do with my dolls. I have to live, at least long enough to make sure my dolls go to someone who will appreciate them. Maybe someone from the Heather Wells Fan Club Facebook page. It has close to ten thousand likes.

Before I have a chance to figure out how I'm going to do this, however, another masked figure jumps out at me from behind a couch.

"Oh no!" she cries, shoving her protective eye shield to the top of her head. I'm more than a little surprised to see that it's a student, Jamie Price. She looks horrified. "Gavin, it's Heather. You shot Heather! Heather, I'm so sorry. We didn't realize it was you."

"Heather?" Gavin raises his own face mask, then lowers his gun. "Oh shit. My bad."

I gather from his "my bad" that he means it's his mistake that I'm dying from the large-caliber bullet he's shot into my back. I feel a little bit badly for him because I know how much I meant to him, maybe even more than his own girlfriend, Jamie. Gavin's probably going to require years of therapy to get over accidentally murdering me. He always seemed to relish his role in the May-December romance he imagined between us, even though our love was never going to happen. Gavin's an undergrad film major, I'm the assistant director of his residence hall, and I'm in love with Cooper Cartwright . . . besides which, it's against New York College policy for administrators to sleep with students.

Now, of course, our romance is *definitely* never going to happen, since Gavin's shot me. I can feel the blood gushing from the wound in my back.

I'm not even sure how I'm still able to stand, given the size of the bloodstain and the fact that my spine is most likely severed. It's a bit hard to see how deep the wound is, since the room—along with the rest of the second-floor library—is in darkness, except for what light is spilling in from the once-elegant casement windows overlooking Washington Square Park's chess circle, two stories below.

"Gavin," I say in a voice clogged with pain, "would you make sure my dolls go to someone who—"

Wait a minute.

"Is this *paint?*" I demand, bringing my fingers to my face so I can examine them more closely.

"We're so sorry," Jamie says sheepishly. "It says on the box that it washes easily out of most material."

"You're playing paintball *inside?*" I do not feel sorry for Gavin anymore. In fact, I'm getting really pissed at Gavin. "And you think I'm worried about my *clothes?*"

Although truthfully, this shirt does happen to be one of my favorites. It's loose over the parts I don't necessarily want to show off (without making me look pregnant), while drawing attention to the areas I do want people to notice (boobs—mine are excellent). These are extremely rare qualities in a shirt. Jamie had better be right about the paint being washable.

"Jesus Christ, you guys. You could put someone's eye out!"

I don't care that I sound like the kid's mom from that Christmas movie. I'm really annoyed. I'd been on the verge of asking *Gavin McGoren* to take care of my collection of dolls from many nations.

"Aw, c'mon," Gavin says, regarding me wide-eyed. "You've

been shot at before with live ammo, Heather. You can't take a little paintball?"

"I never *chose* to put myself in a position where I could be shot at with live ammo," I point out to him. "It isn't part of my job description. It simply seems to happen to me a lot. Now would you please explain to me why Protection Services called me at home on a *Sunday night* to say there's been a complaint about an unauthorized party—at which they claim someone has allegedly passed out—going on in a building that's supposed to be *empty* for renovations for the summer, except for student staff workers?"

Gavin looks insulted. "It's not a party," he says. "It's a paint-ball war." He holds up his rifle as if it explains everything. "Fischer Hall desk and RA staff against the student paint crew. Here." He disappears for a moment behind the couch, then reappears to pile a spare paintball gun, face shield, coveralls—doubtless stolen from the student paint crew—along with various other pieces of equipment into my arms. "Now that you're here, you can be on the desk staff team."

"Wait. *This* is what you guys did with the programming money I gave you?" I'm barely able to hide my disgust. I know from the class I've enrolled in this summer that it takes the human brain until the midtwenties to reach full maturation and structural development, which is why the young often make such questionable decisions.

But playing paintball *inside* a residence hall? This is a boneheaded move, even for Gavin McGoren.

I throw the paintball stuff back down on the couch.

"That money was supposed to go toward a *pizza party*," I say. "Because you said all the dining halls are closed on

Sunday nights and you never have enough money for anything to eat. Remember?"

"Oh no, no," Jamie assures me. For a big girl, her voice can sound awfully babyish sometimes, maybe because she often ends her sentences on an up-note, like she's asking a question even when she's not. "We didn't spend the money on paintball equipment, we checked it out free from the student sports center? I didn't even know they *had* paintball equipment you could check out—probably because it's always checked out during the school year when there're so many people around?—but they do. All you have to do is leave your ID."

"Of course," I grumble. Why *wouldn't* the college's wealthy alumni have donated money to purchase paintball equipment for the students to check out for free? God forbid they'd donate it for something useful, like a science lab.

"Yeah," Gavin says. "We *did* use the money on pizza. And beverages." He holds up the remaining three cans of beer, dangling from the plastic rings of what was once a six-pack. "You wants? Only the best American-style lager for my womenz."

I feel a burning sensation. It has nothing to do with the paintball with which I was recently shot. "*Beer*? You bought *beer* with money I gave you for pizza?"

"It's Pabst Blue Ribbon," Gavin says, looking confused. "I thought cool girl singer-songwriters were supposed to love the PBR."

Perhaps because she's noticed the anger sizzling in my eyes, Jamie walks over to give me a hug.

"Thanks so much for letting me stay here for the summer,

Heather," she says. "If I'd have had to spend it at home with my parents in Rock Ridge, I'd have died? Really. You have no idea what you've done for me. You've given me the wings I needed to fly. You're the best boss ever, Heather."

I have a pretty good idea what I've given Jamie, and it's not wings. It's free room and board for twelve weeks in exchange for twenty hours of work a week forwarding the mail of the residents who've gone home for the summer. Now, instead of having to commute into the city to see Gavin in secret (her parents don't approve of him, since they think their daughter can do better than a scruffy-looking film major), Jamie can simply open her door, since he's living right down the hall from her, as I've given him (unwisely, I've now decided) the same sweet deal.

"I'm pretty sure your parents wouldn't agree I'm the best boss ever," I say, resisting her hug. "I'm equally certain that if anyone in the Housing Office finds out about the paintball— and the beer—I'm not going to be anyone's boss anymore."

"What can they do to you?" Gavin asks indignantly. "We're in a building that's shut down for the summer, that's going to be completely painted anyway, and we're all over twenty-one. No one's doing anything illegal."

"Sure," I say, sarcastically. "That's why I got a call from Protection, because no one's doing anything illegal."

Gavin makes a face that looks particularly ghoulish with the protective shield still pushed back over his hair. "Was it Sarah?" he asks. "She's the one who called in the complaint, wasn't she? She's always telling us to shut up because she's trying to get her thesis finished, or whatever. I *knew* she wasn't going to be cool with this."

I don't comment. I have no idea who ratted them out to the campus police. It could easily have been Sarah Rosenberg, Fischer Hall's live-in graduate assistant assigned to respond to overnight emergencies and assist the hall director with nightly operations. Unfortunately, since the last one's untimely demise, there's no director of Fischer Hall for Sarah to assist. She's been helping me supervise the student skeleton staff and waiting until Housing decides who our new hall director is going to be. I've already left one message for her—it's weird that Sarah didn't pick up, because she's taking classes this summer and so is usually in her room. She has nothing to do but study, although she did acquire, around the time that I got secretly engaged, her first ever serious boyfriend.

"Look," I say, taking out my cell phone to call Sarah again, "I didn't give you guys that money for beer, and you know it. If there really is someone passed out, we need to find them right away and make sure they're all right—"

"Oh, definitely," Jamie says, looking worried. "But they can't be passed out from drinking. We only bought two six-packs—"

"Well, the basketball team bought a bottle of vodka," Gavin admits sheepishly.

"Gavin!" Jamie cries.

I feel as if I really *have* been shot, only this time in the head, not the spine, and with a real bullet. That's the size of the migraine blooming behind my left eyeball. *"What?"* I say.

"Well, it's not like I could stop 'em." Gavin's voice goes up an octave. "Have you seen how big they are? That one Russian kid, Magnus, is nearly seven feet tall. What was I going to say, 'nyetski on the vodkaski'?"

Jamie thinks about this. "Wouldn't it be 'nyet'? And 'vodka'? I think those are Russian words."

"Fantastic," I say, ignoring them as I press redial and call Sarah's number again. "If any of those guys is the one who's passed out, we're not even going to be able to lift him onto a gurney. So where's the basketball team right now?"

Gavin looks excited. He takes something from a pocket of his coveralls and goes to one of the casement windows. In the glow from the streetlamps outside, I see that he's unfolding a floor plan of the building. It's covered in mysterious notations made with red marker, presumably a plan for tonight's battle. My headache stabs me even harder. I should be home having Chinese takeout and watching *Freaky Eaters* with my boy-friend, our Sunday-night tradition, although for some reason Cooper fails to see the brilliance of *Freaky Eaters*, preferring to watch *60 Minutes*, or as I like to call it, "The Show That Is Never About Freaky Eaters."

"We'll probably need to split up to find them," Gavin says, lifting his beer and taking a swift sip before pointing at a location on the floor plan. "We set up a bunker in the library because we can hear anybody coming up the stairs from the lobby or taking the service elevator. We estimate Team Paint Crew is holing up somewhere on the first floor, most likely the cafeteria. But they could be in the basement, possibly the game room. My idea is, we get down there, then take out *all* of them at once, and win the whole game—"

"Wait," Jamie says. "Did you hear that?"

"I didn't hear anything," Gavin says. "So here's the plan.

Jamie, you go down the back stairwell to the caf. Heather, you go down the front stairwell and see if anyone is hiding out in the basement."

"You've been breathing too many chemicals in the darkroom at your summer film classes," I say. Sarah's phone has gone to voice mail again. Frustrated, I hang up without leaving another message. "And anyway, I'm not playing."

"Heather, Heather, Heather," Gavin says, chidingly. "Film is all digital now, no one uses darkrooms or chemicals. And you most certainly are playing. We killed you, so you're our prisoner. You have to do what we say."

"Seriously," Jamie says. "Didn't you guys hear that?"

"If you killed me, that means I'm dead," I say. "So I shouldn't have to play."

"Those aren't the rules," Gavin says. "The way we'll take them is, we go in through the dining office, then hide behind the salad bar—"

"McGoren," a deep, masculine voice says from the darkness of the hallway.

Gavin looks up.

"Nobody shoots Heather," my fiancé, Cooper, emerges from the shadows to say, "and gets away with it."

Then he fires.

Once in a While

Once in a while you regret the road not taken
Start giving up on the plans you made

Once in a while you feel so forsaken
Wondering why so many took, not gave

Once in a while you ask, how could this happen?
How did I end up in these shoes?

But once in a while you meet a special someone
Someone who chose the same path as you

And suddenly it stops feeling so lonely
Out on that road that you just had to choose

And that's when you know it all was worth it
Because once in a while dreams do come true

"Once in a While"
Written by Heather Wells

"I told you I heard something," Jamie says, laughing at
Gavin's stupefied expression as he stares down at the bright
green paint splotch on the front of his white coveralls.

"Uncool, man," Gavin says forlornly. "You aren't even on
an official team."

"Where'd you get that paintball gun?" I ask as Cooper
comes over to wrap an arm around my neck.

"A nice young man at the front desk handed it to me when I asked where you were," he says. "He told me I was going to need it in order to defend myself."

I realize belatedly that Mark, the resident assistant working at the front desk, was calling out to me as I raced up the stairs. I'd been in too much of a hurry to listen.

"What are you doing here?" I ask Cooper as he kisses the top of my head. "I told you I'd be right back."

"Yes, that's what you say every time you get dragged over here on a weekend," Cooper says drily. "Then it's three hours before I see you again. I figured this time I'd hurry things along. You don't make enough money at this job to be at their beck and call twenty-four hours a day, Heather."

"Don't I know it," I say. My annual salary as an assistant resident hall director actually puts me at the U.S. poverty level, after the IRS and NYS take their cuts. Fortunately, New York City College's health care and benefits package is excellent, and I pay zero rent thanks to my second job doing data entry for my landlord, who's untwined his arm from around my neck and is reloading his paint gun.

I'm not going to lie: though I disapprove of gunplay in residence halls, the effect is undeniably sexy. Of course, Cooper had to familiarize himself with firearms in order to pass the New York State Private Investigator Exam. He doesn't actually own a gun, however, and has assured me that in real life being a private detective is nothing like it is on TV shows and movies. When he isn't home looking stuff up online, he mostly sits around in his car taking photos of people who are cheating on their spouses.

It's a relief to know this, since I'd worry if I thought he was out there getting shot at and then returning fire.

"This time it's serious," I tell him. "Campus police got a report of an unauthorized party—"

"You don't say," Cooper says, eyeing the beer.

"—*and* someone unconscious," I add. "No one seems to know who called in the report. Sarah isn't picking up, and everybody else is spread out across the building, playing paintball war." I don't want to seem ineffectual at my job in front of the residents, but the truth is, I'm not entirely sure how to handle the situation. I'm only an *assistant* residence hall director, after all.

Cooper has no such reservations.

"Fine," he says and levels his paint gun at Gavin and Jamie. "New game plan. You're all my prisoners, which means you have to do what I say."

I can't help letting out a tiny gasp. I used to fantasize about becoming Cooper Cartwright's prisoner and him forcing me to do what he said. Full confession: wrist restraints were involved.

Now my fantasy is coming true! Well, sort of. It's typical of my luck lately that there are a bunch of undergraduates hanging around, ruining it.

"Let's go round up the rest of the players," Cooper says, "and make sure they're all accounted for. Then I'll take anyone who's interested out for Thai food."

Gavin and Jamie groan, which I think is quite rude, considering my boyfriend has offered to buy them dinner. What is wrong with kids today? Who would rather run around shooting at one another with paint than eat delicious pad thai?

"Are you serious?" Gavin demands. "Right when we were about to demolish the basketball team?"

"Yes, I can see you were mere moments from accomplishing that," Cooper says, one corner of his mouth sloping up sarcastically. "But my understanding is that Heather likes this job, and I don't think she should get herself fired for fraternizing after work hours with students firing paintball rifles while intoxicated."

I stare at my husband-to-be in the half-light. I think I've just fallen in love with him a little bit more. Maybe he *would* have known what to do with my dolls.

I'm turning back to my cell phone—really, where *is* Sarah? It's completely unlike her not to call me back right away— thinking about how I'm going to repay Cooper as soon as we get home (wrist restraints will *definitely* be involved), when we hear footsteps in the hallway. From the sound of them, they're masculine. And insistent.

"That's them," Gavin whispers. He grabs his reloader. "The *pansies*. . . ."

He isn't being offensive. The Pansies are the name of New York College's basketball team. Once known as the Cougars, a cheating scandal in the 1950s resulted in their being demoted from Division I, the highest college ranking, to Division III, the lowest, and their being renamed after a flower.

One would think this would have taught the college a lesson, but no. Just this past spring "Page Six" got hold of a memo from the office of the president of New York Col-

lege, Phillip Allington, written to my boss, Stan Jessup, head
of the Housing Department, telling Stan to make sure that
each of the school's basketball team players received free
room and board for the summer, as some of the Pansies lived
as far away as Soviet Georgia and the cost of the flight home
was too crushing an expense for their families to bear.

That's how Fischer Hall ended up with a dozen Pansy
"painters" living here for the summer.

Since current NCAA regulations strictly forbid providing
players with cash or gifts—and Division III players in particular from receiving athletic scholarships of any kind—this
memo from President Allington's office launched what had
become known as Pansygate . . . though personally I don't
see how exchanging free room and board for painting nearly
three hundred dorm rooms can be considered a "gift."

"Those bonehead jocks can't have figured out we're in
here," Gavin whispers. "Please lemme shoot 'em."

Jamie adds a heartfelt *"Please?"*

Cooper shakes his head. *"No—"*

It's too late. As the door to the library swings open, Gavin
lifts his paintball gun and shoots at . . .

. . . Simon Hague, the director of Wasser Hall, Fischer
Hall's bitterest rival, and my own personal workplace
nemesis.

Simon shrieks at the Day-Glo burst that's appeared
on the front of his stylish black polo. His companion—a
campus protection officer, from the outline of his hat—
doesn't appear too happy about the bright yellow paint that's
splashed onto the front of his blue uniform either.

Jamie, realizing her boyfriend's mistake first, gasps in horror, then says almost the exact same thing to them that she'd said to me: "It comes out in warm water!"

A part of me wants to burst out laughing. Another part longs to disappear on the spot. Simon, I remember belatedly, is the residence hall director on duty this weekend, which means he must have gotten the same message I did about the unauthorized party and unconscious student.

If I wasn't dead before, I am now, at least career-wise.

"What," Simon demands, fumbling along the wood panel-ing for a light switch, "is going on here?"

Hide the beer, I silently pray. *Someone hide the beer, quick.*

"Hi," I say, stepping forward. "Simon, it's me, Heather. We were just doing a team-building exercise. I'm so sorry about this—"

"Team-building exercise?" Simon sputters, still trying to find the light switch. "This building is supposed to be *empty* for the summer. What kind of team could you possibly be building, and on a Sunday night?"

"Well, we're not really empty," I say. I hear movement behind me and am relieved to notice out of the corner of my eye that Gavin is discreetly shifting the six-packs of PBR behind the couch. "Dr. Jessup wanted us to keep the front desk open, so of course there's the student desk staff and the mail-forwarding staff and a few resident assistants, because of the—"

—*basketball team,* I was going to say. Conscious that the college president's favorite students were living in the build-ing for the summer, the head of Housing had asked me to make sure that the team—who are, after all, students first, athletes second—had plenty of supervision, so I'd provided it, in the form of seven RAs, who were also receiving free housing for the summer in exchange for working a few hours in my office or at the desk, but also keeping an eye on the Pansies.

Simon cuts me off before I can finish. "Mail-forwarding staff?" He sounds incensed. I remember belatedly that during one staff meeting at which we were asked to brainstorm ways the college might save money, Simon had suggested cutting all the assistant residence hall director positions—*my* position.

He finally finds the light switch, and suddenly we're bathed in a harsh fluorescent glow.

Simon doesn't look so good. I can't imagine I look any better, though. Then I recognize the campus protection officer, who looks the worst of all three of us.

"Oh," I say, surprised. "Hi, Pete. You're working night shifts now?"

Pete, who normally mans Fischer Hall's security desk, is trying to wipe the Day-Glo off his silver badge.

"Yeah," he says glumly. "I picked up a few extra shifts. The girls are going to sleepaway camp this summer. Those places are expensive. The good ones anyway."

It's clear from Pete's expression that he's regretting his decision to take on the extra shifts.

"You have students living here for free in exchange for *forwarding the mail?*" Simon demands, a dog with a bone he refuses to drop.

Wasser Hall is across the park, in a different zip code than Fischer Hall, and serviced by a different post office. They're also in a new building where they don't have to worry about asbestos being exposed and the ceiling of the room below collapsing whenever a toilet floods.

"Yeah," I say. "Our post office won't forward Fischer Hall's mail, because it considers dormitories transient housing. So that's what Jamie and Gavin are doing in exchange for free housing, in addition to shifts at the desk."

I'll admit I've been playing pretty fast and loose with the rules, basically running the building like—as Cooper refers to it—my own "Island of Misfit Toys," thanks to the kids I've hired to staff it all having nowhere else to go, due to either financial or family pressures. I'm pretty sure *nothing* I've been doing would meet with Simon's approval, and that if he knew the full extent of it, it would only confirm his conviction that I *and* my job should both be eliminated immediately.

"Free housing," Simon echoes in a cold voice. Outside, a distant siren begins to sound much closer. The casement windows are cranked as far open as they can go—which is only two inches, thanks to the mandatory window-"guard" policy that the college instituted after a few too many Fischer Hall students were pushed to their deaths this past year—so every catcall and car horn can be heard with perfect clarity. Although Fischer Hall has air-conditioning, the system is antiquated.

"Free housing in exchange for forwarding the mail?" Simon's face is a perfect mask of incredulity. "And you're conducting *team-building* exercises for these mail-forwarders? At *night*?"

"Um," I say. "Yes." Out of all the hall directors who could have been on call the night I found my summer staff misbehaving so badly, why did *Simon* have to be the one on duty? Anyone else—Tom Snelling, for instance, who runs Waverly Hall, which houses the fraternities—would have confiscated the beer and paintball guns and kept quiet to the administration.

But no, it had to be fussy, overbearing Simon. Could things possibly get any worse?

Yes. Because I'm standing close enough to the casement windows to determine that the siren I heard belongs to an ambulance, and I can see it turning onto Washington Square West.

Of course, Fischer Hall is one of many buildings along Washington Square. The ambulance could be going to any one of them.

But what are the chances?

Simon glares at Cooper. "And who's *this*?" he demands with a sneer. "Surely he's a little old to be one of your *mail-forwarding staff.*"

"Cooper Cartwright," Cooper says, stepping forward with his right hand extended. I'm relieved to see that he's hidden the paintball gun. "Safety consultant. Heather asked me to be here to make sure all the necessary security precautions were in place for tonight's team-building exercise."

Safety consultant? I feel my stomach sink. No way is Simon going to fall for that one.

"I wasn't aware," Simon says, shaking Cooper's hand, "Fischer Hall had enough money in its budget to hire a safety consultant—"

"Well," Cooper says, giving Simon a knowing wink, "what with all the tragedies that occurred here this past year, I was more than happy to waive my fee. We can't have kids calling this place Death Dorm forever, can we?"

I see Simon's face change. Although normally I hate it when anyone says the words "Death Dorm," Cooper made the right call bringing it up. Fischer Hall had the highest number of deaths of any residence hall in the entire nation last year, including a semester-at-sea cruise ship that experienced a freak norovirus outbreak, killing three. (Only one was a student. The other two were faculty. No one in residence life cares about faculty, really, but technically their deaths do count.)

Still, the number of students entering New York College as freshmen who asked for a transfer to "anything other than Death Dorm" after finding out they'd been assigned there has been quite high . . . nearly 97 percent. That's part of the reason why Fischer Hall is being shut down for the summer for a makeover, so the kids who don't get their requested transfer—which will be all of them, there being no other halls to transfer them to because all the savvy entering freshmen requested Wasser Hall—will at least have nice white walls when they check in to their room at Death Dorm.

It's starting to look like our longest streak at being accident-free is coming to an end: the ambulance outside pulls up in front of Fischer Hall.

I am in a perfect position to see not only the ambulance but also the person who darts through Fischer Hall's front doors—directly beneath the proudly waving blue-and-gold New York College banners above those doors—to greet the ambulance.

It isn't anyone on the Fischer Hall staff, but it *is* someone with whom I'm more than a little familiar, *and* someone who I'm certain wouldn't want Simon Hague poking into his business.

Simon is standing too close to the second-floor library door to see out the windows, and all his attention is focused on what's happening inside, not outside. He seems to have softened a bit since Cooper brought up the Death Dorm thing. Simon is, after all, in this for the children, as he points out so frequently during staff meetings that Tom and I have begun keeping a running tally.

"I understand," he says, raising his voice so he can be heard over the siren—so ubiquitous in this neighborhood that he doesn't even pause to ask what it is or wonder if it might have anything to do with our current situation—"but if this is a programming activity, what's with this report Protection received about an unauthorized party with an unconscious student?"

"That's a good question," I say. Though it's one I completely understand now that I recognize the tall, lanky frame and handsome features of the person speaking with the EMTs in the bright security lights that flood the front entrance. "Maybe it has something to do with the basketball team?"

Simon goes pale behind his neatly trimmed mustache. "You mean . . . *the Pansies*?" His voice falls into a hushed whisper. Since the siren has been abruptly shut off, his next words sound absurdly loud. "You think *they're* involved?"

"I can't think who else it could be." I keep my gaze averted from Cooper's as he crosses the room to stand beside me, even when I see him glancing curiously out the window. "The paintball war is student desk staff against the student paint staff . . . the basketball team. I thought I mentioned that before—"

"You didn't," Simon interrupts, tersely. "Where are they?"

"The Pansies are in the cafeteria." Gavin is suddenly being very helpful . . . not because he thinks any of the basketball players are in trouble, but because he's seen a way for his paintball game to continue. "Want us to show you?"

"Yes, of course," Simon replies, spinning toward the door. "It's nice that *someone* around here knows what's going on. . . ."

Gavin throws me a mischievous smile; then he and Jamie follow Simon toward the door. Since Simon's back is to Gavin, he doesn't see the paintball rifle in Gavin's hand.

But Pete does. He snatches the guns from both Gavin's and Jamie's hands, giving them each a baleful look as he does so. They slink out, looking disappointed. As soon as they're safely out of earshot, Pete glares at me.

"Really?" he asks. "I'm supposed to follow those knuckle-heads down there and let myself get sprayed a second time?"

"Well," Cooper says, "you're armed now. Just spray them back."

"The ballplayers are good guys," I say quickly, seeing the look Pete throws my boyfriend. "They'll put down their weapons if they hear you say you're with campus police."

Pete tosses the paint guns onto the couch, not seeming very reassured. "Who they loading into the meat wagon?" he asks, nodding toward the windows.

I'm not surprised he's figured out that the siren belonged to an ambulance and that the ambulance has stopped in front of Fischer Hall. Pete's worked for New York College a long time. His intention is to stay until he can collect his benefits package and retire to his family's casita in Puerto Rico.

"Someone from the penthouse," I say.

Pete looks even more displeased. "What're *they* doing here? I thought they spend summers at their place in the Hamptons. That way she can get soused on Long Island iced teas without everyone on campus knowing about it."

Pete's right: Mrs. Allington, President Allington's wife, is a woman who has been known to over-imbibe. This has made living in the penthouse of a building in which they have to take the same elevator as seven hundred undergraduates an occasional challenge.

Mrs. Allington is also a woman who keeps a cool head in emergencies . . . enough so that she once saved my life. Not that she's recognized me ever since. Still, there are few things I wouldn't do in order to preserve her privacy and reputation.

This, however, is one occasion when she has no need of my discretion.

"I don't think it's Mrs. Allington this time," I say.

Pete looks puzzled. "The president came into the city without her? That's not like him."

"No," I say. "I'm pretty sure the Allingtons aren't the ones having the unauthorized party."

"Then who is?" Cooper asks.

"Their son."

Bank Card Lover

In the club, bodies tight
Think I may, think I might
See your face across the floor
That's when you tell me the score

Late at night, lobby light
Press my code, away we go
Hours pass, you make it last,
Just so long as I've got the cash

He's a bank card lover
Girls warned me about him
Just a bank card lover
Don't let him under your skin

Club is closed, money's tight
I'm going home alone tonight
I don't even know his name
But I'm not feeling any shame

I know he's just a bank card lover
The other girls were right
Just a bank card lover
Gave me the ride of my life
(Dance break, repeat)

"Bank Card Lover"
Performed by Tania Trace
Written by Larson/Sohn
So Sue Me album
Cartwright Records
Three consecutive weeks
in the Top 10 Billboard Hot 100

"Why are we doing this again?" Cooper asks.

We're alone in one of Fischer Hall's ancient elevators as it wheezes its way to the penthouse. Pete's left us to go make sure Simon doesn't get completely soaked under a hail of paintballs.

"Because Christopher Allington hasn't exercised the best judgment in the past," I explain. "I want to make sure he's not up to his old tricks. That ambulance better be for his mom and not some young girl he roofied."

Cooper shakes his head. "You always think the best about people, don't you? That's what I love most about you, your boundless optimism and faith in the goodness of mankind."

I narrow my eyes at him . . . but I can't deny it. There are few people I've met since coming to work at Fischer Hall—a job I lucked into after getting kicked off the Cartwright Records label, and then out of my former boyfriend's bed—whom I *haven't* suspected of murder. It's surprising how often I've been right.

Possibly this is an instinct I honed during the years I spent working in the entertainment business. Not that a lot of musicians are murderers, but many of them *are* damaged in one way or another. Maybe this is what draws them to the profession in the first place. Sex, drugs, and rock 'n' roll are all ways to exorcise your inner demons . . .

Which is how I ended up moving in with Cooper Cartwright. After I found my live-in boyfriend, Jordan—Cooper's brother and lead singer of Easy Street—exorcising some of his inner demons with Cartwright Records' newest rising star, Tania Trace, in our bed, I had nowhere else to go.

Cooper and I came to a very businesslike arrangement: He rented me a floor of his downtown brownstone in exchange for my doing his client billing.

How we managed to keep it businesslike for nearly a year, I have no idea, especially given that in the past three months since we revealed our true feelings to each another we've managed to boink in every room of the house too many times to count (except for the basement, due to spiders).

"Well," I say, in my own defense, "the last time he and I talked, Christopher said he was starting a dance club or nightclub or something. Isn't that what guys like him do? Roofie girls' drinks?"

The son of the college president and I are not friends, to say the least, mostly because for a while he was not only *actually* sleeping with every Fischer Hall resident he could lure into his bed, I also suspected him of murdering them. The fact that he was proved to be innocent of the latter is beside the point. The former is still true.

"Why would a budding nightclub mogul who likes to sleep with young girls live with his parents?" Cooper asks.

"I'm pretty sure Christopher's got his own place in Williamsburg," I say. "He only crashes here when his parents aren't in town."

Or so I've inferred when I've seen him slinking from the elevator across from my office early in the morning to sign out an overnight guest. It's always highly noticeable when anyone in Fischer Hall steps off the elevators before ten, since very few students at New York College schedule their classes prior to eleven, but it's especially noticeable when it's the president's son and a blond woman in her late twenties wearing business attire, Louboutins, and a $20,000 gold Rolex. Although I suppose it's nice that Christopher's found a friend his own age for a change.

"Williamsburg," Cooper says with a grunt. "Of course. Where else would any self-respecting young roofier be residing these days but the current hub for indie rock and hipster culture?"

I give him a sour look. "Considering they've all been priced out of the Village by this college, celebrities, and trust fund babies like you," I say pointedly, as the numbers on the dial above our heads reach 20, "where else are they supposed to live?"

"Touché," he says with a grin. "But all I inherited was the brownstone, not a trust fund. *You're* the only celebrity in this neighborhood. What I wonder is why—"

The doors slide open before he can finish his question or I can protest—I was a celebrity back when the Taco Bell Chihuahua was popular, and I'm about as widely recognized now as that deceased canine—and we see that the EMTs are in the hallway outside the Allingtons' penthouse.

Christopher Allington is standing in his parents' doorway, holding a clipboard and a pen and saying, "Sorry to be such a pain, but if you guys could just sign these waivers before you come in, that'd be super."

The two uniformed ambulance attendants, holding their heavy kits beneath their arms, are looking pissed off.

"What kind of waiver?" the female EMT wants to know.

"It's a quick release stating that we can use your—" Christopher breaks off when he sees me and Cooper in the hallway. "Oh hey," he says, his expression going from one of cordial welcome to one of complete disdain.

Then, just as quickly, the cordiality is back again. But there's an undeniable coldness in his voice as he stares at us. Who can blame him for being touchy, really, considering the murder thing?

"What brings you folks up here?" he asks.

"The ambulance parked in front of my building," I say just as coldly.

"*Your* building?" I can tell that Christopher means for his laugh to sound casual, but there's a hard edge to it. "I believe this building belongs to New York College, of which my father is the president. So it's not really *your* building, is it?"

Christopher is wearing a blue dress shirt, white trousers, and a white jacket. He's sweated profusely through the shirt. I won't deny that it's hot in the hallway, which, unlike the rest of the building, is elegantly carpeted and painted a subtle olive green, in deference to the floor's high-prestige—and only—residents. There's a gilt-frame mirror across from the elevators in which I can see my reflection. I'm perspiring too, enough so that tendrils from my blond ponytail are sticking to the back of my neck. But I can feel cold air coming from the apartment behind Christopher. He's got the air conditioning on full blast in there.

Skipping the niceties, Cooper asks, "What's that all over your suit?" He doesn't mean the sweat stains either. Christopher has dark brown flecks all over his otherwise pure white linen suit. I know I'm not one to talk, with the big glob of

Day-Glo paint I have on my back. So far as I know, Christopher wasn't on either of the paintball war teams downstairs.

"Oh, this?" he says, swiping at some of the larger stains on his jacket, smiling like it's nothing. "Well, yes, this is from an unfortunate situation that arose earlier in the evening, but I can assure you that everything is—"

The female ambulance attendant turns to me and Cooper. "I know when I see blood, and that's blood," she says flatly. "Either one of you in charge? 'Cause we got a call about an unconscious woman at this address. This gentleman"—she uses the word "gentleman" sarcastically—"says she's conscious now, but he's denying us entry unless we sign some kind of waiver."

"Well," I say, because between the spots on Christopher's suit and the EMT's mention of a woman being unconscious, I'm ready to take *total* charge. Roofies is all I can think. Roofies and blood. "I'm the assistant director of this building. This man doesn't even live here. He has no authority to require anyone to sign anything. So I say you can go on in."

A male voice calls my name from a room in the apartment behind Christopher, apparently having overheard my little speech.

"Heather? Is that you?"

Cooper is past the EMTs like a gunshot, shoving Christopher roughly out of the doorway. "*Jordan?*" he says in a tone of disbelief.

I don't blame him. Cooper's little brother Jordan is one of the last people I'd expect to find in a New York College residence hall, even in the president's cushy apartment, and *especially* one in which roofies and blood are apparently present. Cooper and Jordan have never exactly been close, and not only because Cooper, unlike Jordan, refused to become a member of Easy Street when their father, Grant Cartwright, CEO of Cartwright Records, thought it up. There's also the fact that Cooper's extremely wealthy—and equally eccentric—grandfather, Arthur Cartwright, left Cooper his pink townhouse in the West Village, now estimated to be worth in the high seven figures.

The way Jordan broke up with me could also be a contributing factor to Cooper's dislike of him, but I don't want to make assumptions.

Still, Cooper practically flattens Christopher in his effort to come to what he believes is his brother's aid. It's touching, really, although not everyone finds it so.

"Do you mind?" Christopher calls testily after Cooper, adjusting his lapels. "This suit is Armani. And this is private property. I could call the cops."

"Go ahead," I say to Christopher as I lead the EMTs past him. "I'll tell them you're trespassing. Your parents aren't here, are they?"

"They're in the Hamptons," Christopher replies sullenly. "But seriously, you guys are disrupting a very important scene. They can check her afterward. She's feeling better now anyway."

"Scene?" I echo, my heart sinking. An unconscious woman, blood, and *cameras?* Has Christopher talked Jordan into making a *porno?* The sad part is, it wouldn't surprise me.

As I turn the corner from the penthouse's elegant foyer, I

see exactly what Christopher means by *scene*, however, and also why Cooper has stopped short so abruptly in front of me that I run right into him.

"Cooper?" Jordan Cartwright is sitting on an overstuffed couch clutching the hand of his new—and extremely pretty—young wife, best-selling recording artist of the year Tania Trace. Jordan looks even more astonished to see us than we are to see him, and that's saying a lot. "What on earth are *you* doing here?"

"What am *I* doing here?" Cooper stares at his brother, then broadens his gaze to include the group gathered around his brother and the couch on which his brother is sitting under the glow of two enormous lights set on tripods. "I think the more appropriate question is, what are *you* doing here? And why are you covered in blood?"

"Am I?" Jordan looks down at himself, surprised. He's dressed similarly to Christopher, only his suit is a pale beige, and his shirt is pink. Like Christopher, he's sweating profusely. And like Christopher, there are droplets of blood flecked all over him. "Oh shit, I didn't notice. Why didn't you guys tell me?" Jordan glares at the film crew, all of whom are dressed in cargo shorts and T-shirts with various band logos emblazoned across them, though Easy Street is not one of them. Even though the air conditioning is on full blast, the lights make it blazingly hot in the room, so they're all sweating too.

"The blood's good. It makes it more real, man," a guy with a pair of headphones, holding a boom—one of those long microphones with a fuzzy thing over the end—assures Jordan.

The guy holding the camera says, peering through the lens, "Blood's barely tracking because it's so dark in here. Could somebody adjust that scrim like I asked, or am I talking to myself here?"

A young woman with her hair tucked into tiny braids to keep it off her neck hurries over to one of the tripods and pulls a mesh screen from in front of the light bank. A second later, the white-hot glare on Jordan and Tania increases about a hundredfold and the temperature in the Allingtons' living room seems to go up another ten degrees.

"Perfect," the cameraman says in a satisfied voice. "*Now* I can see the blood."

Tania, who's wearing a metallic gold minidress—and I use the word "mini" loosely, since the dress is barely large enough to cover her nipples and lower extremities—lifts a limp brown arm over her eyes, turning her exquisitely featured face away from the searing light.

"I can't do this," she murmurs weakly.

"Sure you can, Tania honey," says a woman I haven't noticed before. She's standing off to the side in the shadows, but not deep enough into the shadows that I can't see her Louboutins or the glint of gold around her wrist. It's the woman I've noticed so often lately exiting the elevator in the morning with Christopher. "Put your arm down and tell us how it felt when you saw a man get shot right in front of you."

"I don't want to." Tania keeps her arm where it is. From what little I can see of it, her face seems to have gone as olive green as the walls in the hallway outside the elevator.

"Keep it together, baby," Jordan says, putting his own arm around his wife's diminutive frame and looking down at her tenderly, though the only part of her he can possibly see from where he's sitting is her elbow and maybe her knees. "I know what we went through tonight was ugly. But you heard what they said at the ER. With time and our prayers, Bear's going to be all right. And until then, *I'll* protect you. And the baby too, when she comes. I'll never let anything happen to either of you, I swear it. Not while there's a breath left in my body."

I can hardly believe what I'm hearing. Someone named Bear was shot in front of Tania? And they're making her talk about it on camera, in the penthouse of Fischer Hall? *Why?*

"That's good, Jordan," Gold Rolex says, from the shadows. I can see by the glint of her watch that she's holding a cell phone to her ear. "But can you do it again, and this time, Tania, can you take your arm down and look at Jordan?"

The bulbs in both tripods go out, plunging the room into darkness. Someone screams.

The room isn't plunged into *total* darkness. Numerous Tiffany lamps belonging to Mrs. Allington continue to blaze on side tables, and there are fairy lights sparkling outside on the terrace, so there is *some* light to see by.

But the sudden contrast in lighting is startling, and it takes a moment for everyone's vision to adjust.

"What the—" cries Christopher.

"I thought that take was really good," Jordan says, commenting on his own performance in front of the camera. "Are you guys going to be able to use any of it?"

No one is paying any attention to him. Everyone is running around, trying to figure out what happened. The production assistant is swearing at the camera operator.

"I told you we should've gone with the softbox," she says. "These light banks throw a fuse every time in these crappy old buildings."

"Excuse me," I say, again and again, my voice rising in pitch and volume until finally I have the full attention of everyone present. Then I hold up the extension cord I've pulled from the wall outlet. "It wasn't the fuse. It was me. I believe the appropriate phrase is . . . cut."

Tania Be Me

I ain't Christina, wagging my thing
I ain't Beyoncé, flashing my ring

Who am I? You want to know?
Who am I? Just watch the show

I ain't no Katy, bouncing my bling
I ain't no Fergie, flinging my fling

Who am I? You want to know?
Who am I? Just watch the show

Who am I? Just wait and see
Who am I?
Tania be me

"Tania Be Me"
Written by Larson/Sohn
Cartwright Records Television
Theme song to *Jordan Loves Tania*

4

"In order to ensure the safety and privacy of all residents," I say, "filming is not permitted in any New York College residence hall without proper authorization."

Surprisingly, this is a sentence I utter several times a week, most often to Gavin, who is an aspiring Quentin Tarantino. But the policy on not filming in the building has nothing to do with privacy issues. I've actually been called to more smoke-filled floors because of gel filters left on too long over onboard flashes (whatever those are) than I can count. And don't even get me started on the number of students trying to pay their way through college making amateur pornography films.

"Well?" I ask when everyone simply stares at me. "Does anyone here have proper authorization? Because I didn't see any paperwork about this . . . this . . . what *is* this exactly?"

Everyone begins speaking at once—everyone except Tania, who's lowered her arm now that no more lights are glaring into her face and is looking at me as if she's never seen me before . . . which is ironic, since I walked in on her once with her face in my ex-boyfriend's crotch.

Hard as it was after that—having to move out, find a new place to live, and start over, not to mention the endless sleepless nights questioning how I could ever have been so stupid since, after all, I was with Jordan for *ten years*—Tania actually did me a big favor that day: she freed me to find my new life . . . and Cooper.

Of course, neither she nor Jordan knows this, because Cooper and I haven't exactly announced to his family the fact that we're dating, much less getting married.

Now doesn't seem like the best time.

"Hold it," Cooper shouts over the general din, glaring from his brother to Christopher and back again. "How do you two even know each other? Who's the ambulance for? *Who got shot?*"

It's the woman with the expensive gold wristwatch who answers, letting out an extremely colorful expletive as she comes striding toward us, her Louboutins clicking noisily on the parquet.

"Excuse me, but who are you?" she demands, her eyes shooting angry sparks at us. "I'll have you know you're interrupting a very important shoot for CRT—"

"Stephanie, it's all right," Christopher says, seeming resigned to the situation. "This is Jordan's brother."

The woman in the gold Rolex halts in her tracks. "His brother?" Her eyes widen as she stares at Cooper. "Wait . . . you can't be *Cooper* Cartwright?"

"The one who wouldn't join Easy Street," Cooper says. He's looking extremely annoyed. "Yes, I am. I don't do pimple cure commercials or teen mass hysteria. So maybe now someone can explain to me how exactly my brother got someone else's blood all over him? And what the hell is CRT?"

"Oh my God," Stephanie says, her demeanor completely changing. Besides the wristwatch—which looks enormous because her wrist, like Tania's, is so bony—and the Louboutins, she has on a sleeveless red sheath dress that is so tight in the skirt that she hobbles awkwardly over the cables strung across the floor to get to us. Still, she manages, every inch of her being the harried television exec, from the vein that's begun suddenly to throb in the middle of her forehead (her chin-length bob has been swept back with a tortoiseshell barrette, so the vein's easy to spot) to the BlackBerry she has clutched in her left hand.

"Stephanie Brewer," she says, holding out her right hand to shake Cooper's. "Executive producer, Cartwright Records Television. I can't tell you what an honor this is. Cooper Cartwright, the one Cartwright I haven't met! I've heard so much about you."

"I can only imagine." Cooper barely glances at Stephanie as she pumps his hand. "Dad bought a *television network?*" he asks Jordan.

"Cable," Jordan says with a shrug. "We didn't sign either Adele or Gaga, so Mom told him we needed to do something."

"Mom's idea," Cooper says, with an eye roll. "Figures."

"I want you to know how much I adore working with your father," Stephanie Brewer is gushing. "He's one of the reasons I chose Harvard for my MBA. I wanted to walk in the footsteps of the great Grant Cartwright."

"I'll try not to hold it against you," Cooper says drily.

Stephanie's smile wavers only slightly. "Thanks," she says, blinking with confusion.

"So who got shot?" Cooper asks.

"Oh, of course," Stephanie says, finally dropping his hand. "I'm so sorry. It was Tania's bodyguard. He was taken to Beth Israel for stitches and X-rays after he was struck by a bullet earlier this evening—completely at random—as we were filming in front of Christopher's club on Varick Street. He's expected to make a full and complete recovery—"

"And the cops let all of you leave? They didn't hold any of you for questioning?" Cooper is shocked.

"Of course they questioned us," says the girl with the braids. I was guessing from her clipboard that she was the production assistant. "At the scene. What could we tell them? One minute Bear was standing next to us, and the next he was on the ground, and Jordan and Chris had his blood all over them."

"Exactly. The thing about a *random shooting* is that it's *random*," Christopher says. "None of us saw anything. It wasn't a drive-by. The shot seemed to come out of nowhere."

"The police think it might have been teenagers," Stephanie explains, "playing with a gun on a nearby rooftop. So far they haven't found anyone."

"It's not like any of *us* shot him," Jordan protests. "Bear's our friend."

"I can tell." Cooper is scowling. "Such good friends that you stuck around the hospital to make sure he's all right."

"Jared, our field producer, stayed with him," the camera operator says.

"Yeah," grunts the guy with the boom. "With the assistant camera operator to get footage of them putting in the stitches."

"Bear's *fine*." Stephanie cuts everyone else off. "His injury did create some unwanted attention from the press and has also put us way behind schedule, in addition to upsetting Tania, as you can see. So now that all this nonsense about not being allowed to film in the building is cleared up, could we please—"

I'm not listening to her anymore, though. Tania—who was named one of *People* magazine's fifty most beautiful people—looks terrible. Her painfully thin shoulders are slumped inward, her hands limp in her lap, her bony knees knocked. Her normally cappuccino-colored skin tone is yellowed, though whether this is a reflection from the gold of her dress, the suddenly insufficient lighting, or what she's been through, it's hard to tell.

I do know jaundice is never a good look for a pop star. It's especially worrisome for one who should be glowing. Tania's going into her second trimester. The cover of *Us Weekly* recently crowed that she and Jordan are expecting a little girl.

The baby makes me feel especially protective of Tania, even if its mother has always treated me like crap.

"You still can't film in here," I say flatly. "In fact, I need everyone to leave in order to give Tania some privacy while the EMTs take a look at her."

Stephanie narrows her eyes. "*Excuse me?*" she says.

"Someone called an ambulance," I remind her. "I'm assuming that wasn't done to add drama to your show, because it's unlawful to place a call to emergency services for any reason other than to report an actual emergency—"

The ambulance attendants have been watching our exchange like spectators at a tennis match. "That's true," the female EMT says. "What's this show called anyway?"

The vein in the middle of Stephanie's forehead has begun to throb again. "*Jordan Loves Tania,*" she says. "We're hoping it's going to be CRT's first hit, and next season's number-one-rated husband-and-wife-themed reality show. That's why we certainly didn't place any unlawful calls to emergency services. We can't allow any scenes to roll off camera. Jordan's and Tania's fans are going to want to share this emotional moment—"

Jordan, still on the couch with his arm around Tania, looks uncomfortable.

"I know you wanted to film them examining her, Steph, but I think Tania would rather—"

Jordan is doing something I've never see him do before: putting another human being's best interests before his own. It's sort of sweet, especially the way Tania is looking up at him with her humongous brown eyes so weepy and trusting.

Too bad "Steph" has to ruin the moment by interrupting him, waspishly. "Jordan, that wasn't the agreement you signed. Nothing off camera. That's what we said. That's what your *father* said."

Jordan looks dejected. "Right," he says. "No, of course, you're right."

I see Tania's gaze drop to the floor in defeat. I'm not surprised that Jordan has failed to stand up for his wife's rights. Unlike Cooper, Jordan has always done whatever his father told him to—including getting rid of me—and Stephanie has clearly figured this out. All she has to do, apparently, is say the words, "That's what your father said," and Jordan snaps to it. I glance at Cooper, and see that he looks as disgusted with his brother as I feel.

Before Cooper can say anything, however, I come to Tania's rescue. I don't really want to. I certainly don't owe either her or Jordan anything. But I can't help it. Fischer Hall is my island—of misfit toys, as Cooper pointed out—and I don't like seeing people pushed around on my island.

"Well, once again, too bad," I say, "because *there's no filming allowed in the building.*"

Tania lifts her heavy layer of false eyelashes, and I'm reminded of why she's such a popular performer. It's not only because she has such a great voice—she does—or looks so great in her skimpy costumes—that's true too. It's because her face conveys such a wealth of emotion in a single glance . . . or seems to at least. Right now it's conveying overwhelming gratitude toward me.

I'm a little confused. Tania Trace has sold more than 20 million albums, topped the charts in over thirty countries, won four Grammy Awards, and now she has a baby on the way with Jordan Cartwright, who's produced a record number of hits of his own (with his dad's help, of course). The two of them have their own TV show. She's a diva. Why she can't tell Stephanie Brewer *no* herself is beyond me.

"And we ain't signing no waivers," the male EMT says loudly as he and his partner cross the living room to Tania's side.

Stephanie's vein begins to throb so wildly, I'm scared it's going to burst.

Cooper must have noticed the same thing, since he says, "Maybe we should go outside. Isn't that a terrace out there? It might be a little cooler."

Cooper's being polite. He knows perfectly well that there is a terrace outside the Allingtons' apartment. I was almost murdered on it once.

"Yes, great idea," Christopher says quickly. He claps his hands. "Okay, hey, everyone, let's take five and give our star some privacy while she gets checked out by these nice, er, ambulance people. Drinks in the fridge in the kitchen if anyone wants them—"

"Guarana?" asks the sound mixer in a hopeful voice as he drops the boom and strips off his earphones.

"Guarana for Marcos," Christopher says. "Red Bull for everyone else. You guys want anything?" He looks at Cooper and me and without waiting for an answer says, "Hey, Lauren, grab us all some bottled waters—"

The film crew stampedes for the Allingtons' kitchen as Christopher throws open the French doors that lead to the wraparound terrace off the dining and living area of his parents' penthouse. Instantly a cool breeze hits us. The air this high up—we're twenty floors from the street—seems fresher and cleaner than the air below. You can barely hear the traffic, but through some acoustical trick you *can* occasionally hear the sound of the fountain jets in Washington Square Park. The 360-degree views of Manhattan are stunning— the twinkling city lights and even, on a clear night like this one, the moon and a few stars.

It's out on this terrace that the Allingtons do most of their entertaining when they're in town, catered affairs with professional waitstaff in black-and-white uniforms. It's out on this terrace that I also once almost lost my life. I try never to think about this, however. The professor of the class I'm taking this summer session (Psych 101) says that this is called disassociation and that it almost always comes back to haunt people.

I'm willing to take my chances.

"Who *are* you anyway?" Stephanie Brewer turns to ask me as we step toward a set of green-and-white-striped settees. "I think President Allington will be interested to hear how unhelpful you were during all of this. He and his wife are big fans of CRT, for your information."

Cooper, who has overheard this, looks angry. "I'm sorry," he says to Stephanie, though he doesn't appear sorry at all. "Did I forget to introduce—"

"Heather," I interrupt. I can see what Cooper's about to do. He doesn't like the way Stephanie is treating me—as if I'm some kind of underling—and he wants to let her know that I'm someone special.

But I get sneered at and spoken down to by people like Stephanie every single day. Like millions of administrators and service industry workers, I've gotten used to it, though I don't think I'll ever understand it. It might make sense if I wasn't good at my job, like Simon, but I am. Stephanie shouldn't treat *anyone* the way she's been treating me, though . . .

Which is why I don't want Cooper pointing out to her that I used to be famous. And he *definitely* shouldn't give away the secret we've been guarding so closely for so many months—that I'm dating her boss's son—just to teach her an etiquette lesson.

"I'm the Fischer Hall assistant director," I say to her. "When you complain to President Allington about me, be sure to get the name right. My last name is Wells." I spell it for her.

"Tell my dad too," Cooper says as he pulls one of the green-and-white-striped lounge chairs out for me to sit on. "I'm sure Grant will get a kick out of hearing how you met Heather, Stephanie."

I shoot him a dirty look since he's spoiled my plan, but he only frowns at me. Cooper doesn't like it when I "diminish my extraordinary accomplishments," as he puts it, by not introducing myself as *the* Heather Wells, youngest artist ever to top the Billboard charts with a debut album, and the first female to have both an album and a single simultaneously at number one (*Sugar Rush*).

Honestly, though, what person who is practically thirty goes around reminding people of something they did when they were fifteen? That's like using a picture of yourself as your high school's quarterback or homecoming queen as your Facebook photo.

I can see in the glow of the terrace's fairy lights, however, that it's too late. Stephanie's already figured it out, thanks to Cooper's hint. I can tell the exact moment I go from being the shrewish college administrator in Stephanie's eyes to Heather Wells, former pop teen sensation, and one of her boss's biggest success stories . . . until I gained a few pounds, insisted on writing my own songs, and suddenly wasn't so successful anymore.

I can't hold it against Cooper, though, because Stephanie realizes she's put her size 7 foot in it, and it's amusing to watch her backpedal.

"Oh, *that's* why you look so familiar," Stephanie says, graciously holding her perfectly manicured hand out to me across the glass table between our two chairs. "'Don't tell me stay on my diet, you have simply got to try it,'" she sings, perfectly on pitch. "God, I can't tell you how many times I must have listened to 'Sugar Rush' when I was younger. It was my favorite song. You know, before we all moved away from pop and on to real music?"

I keep my own smile frozen on my face. Real music? I hate that so much. Some people seem to forget that "pop" is short for "popular." The Beatles were considered pop musicians. So were the Rolling Stones. Stephanie seems to be forgetting pop music pays her salary, and the salaries of everyone working for Cartwright Records. Give me a break.

"Right," I say as Stephanie crushes my fingers in her own. She must do Pilates. Or press diamonds out of coal with her bare hands.

"I can't believe I didn't recognize you right away," Stephanie gushes. "It's been a while, hasn't it? Still, you look great. So healthy. Your skin is glowing."

When skinny girls say that you look healthy and your skin is glowing, what they mean is that they think you look fat and you're sweating. Cooper and Christopher are sitting there, completely oblivious to the fact that Stephanie has insulted me to my face.

I know it, but I'm going to let it go, because I'm the bigger person. Not just literally but metaphorically as well. I believe what you put out into the universe comes back to you times three, which is why I try only to say good things, except of course when it comes to Simon.

"Wow, thanks," I say in the kindest voice I can muster.

Some of the members of the film crew are drifting out onto the terrace. All of them are holding cold drinks from the Allingtons' refrigerator. Most of them are clutching cell phones to their ears, using their break to call friends or significant others to make plans for later, from the snatches of conversation I can hear floating toward us. The production assistant, Lauren, brings us each a bottle of cold mineral water, though neither Cooper nor I asked for one.

"Thanks," I say to Lauren, again in my incredibly kind voice. So much goodness is going to come back from the universe, it's amazing. I'm going to find the most beautiful dress to marry Cooper in, and all the students are going to behave like angels for the rest of the summer.

"You kinda disappeared off the face of the earth for a while there, didn't you?" Stephanie says as she opens her bottle of water. Her smile is beatific. She clearly Botoxes. Too bad she can't Botox her personality. Or that vein in her forehead. "So *this* is what you're doing now?" she asks, gesturing around the Allingtons' terrace. "Running a *dorm?*"

"Residence hall," I correct her automatically. "But you probably know that already. It's written at the top of the sign-in log."

Stephanie looks blank. "The what?"

"The sign-in log," I say. "You know, the one you're required to sign whenever Christopher checks you in and out of the building?" I try not to make it sound like I know how many times she's spent the night here, even though I do, or that I think it's weird she sleeps over so much in her boyfriend's parents' apartment. "It says Fischer Hall is a college residence hall right across the top. You must have noticed that we require your signature and a valid form of photo ID every time you stay, so that if you break a housing regulation while you're here—such as filming without authorization—we can hold you accountable for your actions."

Stephanie stares at me across the glass patio table. "You're serious," she says in disbelief. "This is really what you do for a living."

"Why not?" I ask, making my voice light with effort.

"Obviously I heard that your mother took off with all your savings," she says. "But surely you still earn enough royalties from your songs that—"

I can't help letting out a snort. Stephanie glances from me to Cooper in bafflement. "What?" she asks.

"You're a Harvard MBA, Stephanie," Cooper says, his tone mildly amused. "You should be familiar with how record companies—particularly your employer—cook their books."

"I still get royalty statements from Cartwright Records claiming they haven't earned back what they spent on the billboards advertising concerts I gave in Thailand ten years ago," I explain to her, "so they feel they don't owe me any money."

Even in the fairy lights, I can see that Stephanie's turned a little pink, embarrassed for her employer.

"I see," she says.

"But things are good," I hasten to assure her. "As part of the benefits package for working here, I can go to school for free to get my degree—"

"Oh," Stephanie says knowingly. "So *that's* what you're doing, working here, getting your law degree so you can sue your mom . . . and Cartwright Records too, I presume?"

I put as much confidence as I can into the smile I give her.

"Not exactly," I say.

The truth is that I don't even have a bachelor's degree. When everyone else my age was going to college, I was singing to packed malls and sold-out sports arenas.

I could still sue Cartwright Records, of course, but I've been assured by various legal experts that such a suit would take years, cost more than I'd ever win, and likely result only in a bad case of acid reflux . . . my own. Same thing with going after my mom.

"I've got . . . different priorities," I explain to her. "Right now I'm taking classes toward a BA in criminal justice."

"Criminal . . . justice?" she repeats slowly.

"Uh-huh," I say. The incredulous look on her face is making me rethink my choice of majors. Is there a degree in advanced butt-kicking? If so, I'm signing up for it, and starting with hers.

"Heather Wells," she says, shaking her head. "Heather

Wells is working in a New York College dorm and getting a degree in *criminal justice*."

I raise my fist only to have Cooper reach out to grasp it beneath the glass tabletop.

"New York College is lucky to have Heather," Cooper says calmly, his gaze on Stephanie's. "And so are the students who live in this residence hall. And I think Christopher might know a thing or two about how good Heather is at mitigating crime and upholding social justice. Don't you, Chris?"

Christopher looks uncomfortable. "I might have heard a few things," he mutters.

Stephanie glances curiously at Christopher. "Christopher, what on earth is he talking about?"

"In fact," Cooper goes on, giving my hand a comforting squeeze, "it's lucky for you, Stephanie, that it was Heather, and not someone else, who found you up here. She's very good in a crisis. That's one of the many reasons I'm marrying her."

I stare at Cooper from across the Allingtons' table. He's just told someone that we're getting married. He's never admitted this out loud before to *anyone*. It's supposed to be a secret. And now he's announced it to the producer of his brother's reality TV show.

What is he thinking?

Christopher Allington and Stephanie Brewer look about as shocked as I am.

"Fiancée, huh?" Christopher finds his voice first. "Wow. That's great."

His expression indicates that what he actually means is, *Your funeral, buddy.*

Stephanie can barely formulate a sentence.

"I . . . I had no idea. I thought . . . I understood you were friends, but I never imagined—"

"I believe the word you're searching for, Ms. Brewer," Cooper says, giving my hand a final squeeze before letting it go, "is 'congratulations.'"

"Oh, of course," Stephanie says. She smiles, but the gesture is more like a snarl. "It's so great."

I see Stephanie's gaze drop to the ring finger of my left hand. It's bare, of course.

As if he's read her mind, Cooper says, "We're eloping, so it's a secret. If either of you tells anyone—including my brother or Tania—I'll have no choice but to kill you."

More of Stephanie's teeth are exposed. She laughs, and it sounds like a horse's whinny.

"I'm serious," Cooper says, and Stephanie stops laughing.

"That's cool," Christopher says. "I hate big weddings."

"Me too," I say. "Aren't they the worst? Who needs another Crock-Pot?"

"About the shooting," Cooper says. "The man who was shot, Bear—"

Stephanie and Christopher look startled by the sudden change of subject.

"Bear? Great guy," Christopher says. "Really, really could not feel worse about what happened to him. His nickname is so right-on. He's a big cuddly teddy bear."

"A big cuddly teddy bear who happens to be a bodyguard," Cooper says.

"Well," Christopher says, blinking. "Yeah. He's a teddy bear unless you get too close to someone he's protecting. Then he'll rip your head off."

"But that's not what happened tonight?"

It's interesting to watch Cooper at work. Stephanie and Christopher don't seem to have caught on that that's what Cooper is doing. To them, he appears to be a concerned big brother.

I, on the other hand, can tell he's piecing together the beginning of his own private investigation into what exactly went down on Varick Street.

"Oh no," Stephanie says, her eyes widening. In the glow from the fairy lights strung along the terrace walls, I can see that the vein in the middle of her forehead has calmed down. This is because Cooper has lulled her into thinking we're just four friends, sitting around a patio table, talking.

This is far from the truth, however.

"The police said it was probably teenagers goofing off," Stephanie says, "although when I was a teenager, we goofed off by throwing eggs at people's cars, not shooting at them with guns."

"But were the teenagers shooting at each other," Cooper asks, "or Bear? Or my brother?"

His gaze has drifted toward Jordan, who can be seen through the French doors looking on worriedly while the EMTs take Tania's vitals. I'll admit it's a fascinating sight, not just because the blood pressure cuff is so huge on Tania's tiny arm, but because Jordan is being so solicitous. This is apparently as foreign to Cooper as it is to me.

Stephanie looks shocked. "No one would have any reason to shoot Bear, much less Tania or your brother. Jordan and Tania are two of the most liked celebrities on Facebook. Jordan has 15 million friends, Tania over 20 million—"

"And yet," Cooper says, "they have a bodyguard."

"To keep away fans who get overly friendly, and overzealous paps."

Neither Cooper nor I need clarification. She means the paparazzi. The press wasn't such a big deal when I was in the business, but they're an ever-present hazard for Jordan and Tania, whose every move is followed voraciously by a pack of photographers bearing telephoto lenses. I know because I can't turn on the Internet without seeing some headline about where Jordan ate or what Tania was wearing.

Cooper lets it drop. "So, Chris, what's the name of your club?"

Christopher looks taken aback. "Well, Epiphany's not really *my* club . . ."

"Sorry, I thought you said it was."

"Christopher's one of a few investors," Stephanie says, quickly coming to the defense of her boyfriend. "That's how he and I met. One of my sorority sisters' brothers is also an investor, and I was there for her bachelorette party, and I met Chris, and one thing led to another, and—"

This appears to be too much information for Cooper. "Okay, then," he interrupts. "Why here?"

"Excuse me?" Christopher asks, looking confused.

"Why did you decide to film here instead of going back to Jordan and Tania's place after the shooting?"

"Oh, that's easy," Christopher says. "To avoid the paps."

"They heard about the shooting over the police scanners," Stephanie explains, "and it sent them into a feeding frenzy. They were all over us back at Epiphany. Anyway, afterward, Tania wasn't feeling well . . . understandably, since it was so hot and the police did hold us there for a while. The paps have Jordan and Tania's place staked out."

"I realized my parents' place, on the other hand, was close by," Christopher said, with a shrug. "And the paps don't know about it. So I offered the use of it. I knew Mom and Dad wouldn't mind." He gives me one of his boyish grins. "I have to admit, I forgot about you, Heather, and your over-protectiveness of the kids in this building. I didn't think you'd be here on a Sunday night."

I glare at him. "I wouldn't have to be overprotective of the kids in this building if *some* people weren't always trying to take advantage of them."

Stephanie's curiosity is aroused. She looks from Christopher to me. "What's she talking about?" she asks.

"Nothing," Christopher says quickly. "Water under the bridge."

"It wouldn't have occurred to you to call it quits for the day," Cooper says, steering the conversation back to the shooting. "After all, a violent crime was committed against one of your cast members."

Stephanie's eyes widen. *"Tania Trace's bodyguard was shot,"* she reminds us, in case we'd forgotten. "During the filming of a reality show *about* Tania Trace. It would be dishonest of us not to film the very natural emotional reaction of Tania and Jordan to the shooting, even though the wound turned out only to require a few stitches. It was a truly frightening experience, and our viewers are going to want to feel what it was like right along with Jordan and Tania. And we don't intend to let our viewers down. Not to mention we have only a limited amount of time in order to get the more, er, intimate footage between Tania and Jordan finished. Tania Trace Rock Camp starts in a matter of days, and—"

"Tania Trace *what?*" I interrupt.

"Tania Trace Rock Camp," Stephanie says. She blinks at me. "Oh my God, you haven't heard of it?"

I exchange a glance with Cooper after taking a sip from my water bottle. "We don't really keep up with Jordan's and Tania's professional activities," I say diplomatically.

"Tania Trace Rock Camp is an initiative started by Tania Trace," Stephanie says, like she's reading from a brochure, "to help empower young girls through music education. By providing them with opportunities to express themselves creatively through singing, songwriting, and performing, she's building up the self-esteem and musical awareness of a whole new generation of young women who might other-wise, because of the way women are portrayed through the media, as sexual objects for men's desire, develop negative self-images."

"Wow," I say, pleasantly surprised. This actually sounds really cool. I can't believe Tania thought it up.

Then I realize Tania probably didn't. A publicity team likely came up with the idea and approached her with it, or maybe it was commissioned by Cartwright Records, giving in to pressure from parents' groups upset with Tania's music videos, in which she's usually scantily clothed and on top of a pool table.

Even so, it's a great idea. Why didn't I think of doing something like this back when I had the money for it and people would actually have shown up?

"Where is the camp?" I ask.

"At the beautiful Fairview Resort in the Catskills," Stephanie says, still quoting from the brochure that appears to exist in her head. "We had over 200,000 applicants, but with Tania being pregnant, and the shooting schedule, not to mention the new record she's working on, Tania has only so much time and energy to give, so we could really only accept fifty."

Fifty? Out of 200,000? Well, I guess it's *something.*

"And we could only accept girls whose families were willing to sign the waivers allowing them to be on the show," Stephanie goes on.

Suddenly attending Tania Trace Rock Camp doesn't sound so great after all.

My cell phone vibrates. I check it and see that Sarah is finally calling back. Relieved to have an excuse not to listen to Stephanie Brewer go on about her difficulties as a TV producer anymore, I beg everyone's pardon, then get up from my chair to walk to the far side of the terrace so I can talk to Sarah in private.

"Hey, are you all right?" I ask her. "I was worried. I left like three messages."

"No, I'm not all right," she says crankily. "That's why I didn't pick up. What do you want?"

Whoa. I'm used to Sarah's moods, but this is snippy, even for her.

"Are you crying?" I ask. "Because your voice sounds—"

"Yes," Sarah says. "As a matter of fact, I am crying. Are you aware that someone called Protection to report an unconscious student and unauthorized party in the building?"

"Yes," I say. "I *am* aware of that, actually, and I have it covered. Why are you crying?"

"I don't see how you could have it covered when you aren't here," Sarah says, ignoring my question. "I understand you *were* here, but Simon says you left."

"Oh," I say. "You spoke with Simon?" I'm confused. "Is that why you're crying? He didn't try to blame you for the paintball war thing, did he? Because believe me, that was entirely—"

"I know Gavin and those stupid ballplayers cooked that up," Sarah says sourly. "We rounded up all the paint guns, and I'll make sure they get returned to the sports complex tomorrow. We couldn't locate anyone unconscious, though. Everyone seems to be accounted for. Simon left after giving each of the Pansies his card and telling them they can call him any time with their personal problems." A dry note has crept into Sarah's voice.

"Oh God," I say.

"Yes," Sarah says. "You know Simon's applied for the job of director of this building, right?"

"*What?*" I've already been hit with a paintball, found my staff drinking, and run into my ex-boyfriend and his new wife filming a reality show in the building where I work. I didn't think things could get worse. But guess what? "No way. He's got Wasser Hall, the crown jewel of residence halls. Why would he want to work *here?*"

"Uh," Sarah says, in a cynical tone, "because he thinks it'll look really good on his résumé to be the guy who pulled the dorm with the most deaths in it ever out from the depths of its misery. And it wouldn't hurt to be here to help the president and the basketball team through Pansygate either. He's an idiot, but he's no fool."

I say a word that I'm sure would be too dirty to air on Cartwright Records Television.

"Pretty much," Sarah says. "Dr. Jessup's reviewing his CV. Simon thinks he's a shoo-in because he's in-house. Anyway, do you have any idea why there's an ambulance parked outside but the attendants are nowhere to be found? Could they have gone into a neighboring building? The guard at the desk insists they came in here with some guy, but the guard's a temp and I don't think he knows what he's—"

"Sarah," I interrupt. "I don't want this to get around. You know how gossipy this department is. But I'm with the EMTs. They're in the president's apartment."

"Oh." Sarah's tone changes. "Is everyone all right?"

"So far," I say. "It's no one related to New York College."

"Really?" Sarah sounds less tearful. "It's not—?"

I know what she's about to ask—if it's Mrs. Allington.

"No," I say firmly. "Not even close. It has to do with Junior." That's our code name for Christopher.

"Oh God," Sarah says, sounding disgusted. "I don't want to know, do I?"

I look behind me. Through the French doors, I can see the

EMTs putting away their equipment. Tania is looking a bit less forlorn. She's even managing to smile a bit. Jordan is on his feet and shaking the female attendant's hand.

"No," I say to Sarah, turning around again. "You don't want to know. So why were you crying?"

"I don't feel like talking about it," Sarah says, sullen again. "It's personal."

I'm fairly certain I know what's troubling her. She's had another fight with Sebastian Blumenthal, the first real love of her life. Sebastian's head of the GSC, the Graduate Student Union, and teaches at New York College. I once strongly suspected him of murder, but I guess that's not unusual, given that he carries a man purse . . . not a messenger bag or a backpack, but an honest-to-goodness murse.

"That's all right," I say to Sarah. "Maybe we can talk about it tomor—"

"Great, bye," Sarah interrupts, and hangs up on me.

Wow. I can't keep track of all the ups and downs of Sarah's turbulent relationship, but I do know that tomorrow morning I'll be picking up chocolate croissants on my way in to work. They usually cheer her up.

I hang up too, then turn around and notice that Jordan has come out onto the terrace. He's joined Cooper and Christopher and Stephanie, who've stood up from the table. Tania is still sitting on the couch inside. She's pulled a large designer purse onto her lap and is digging around in it. The EMTs appear to have gone.

I go stand by Cooper's side and catch only the tail end of what Jordan is saying.

"—definitely dehydrated and most likely anemic."

"Well, that's no surprise," Stephanie says. "She's vegan."

Cooper says, without a hint of irony in his voice, "You know, Stephanie, I've heard it's possible these days to be vegan and not be anemic."

I hide a smile. Cooper eats cheeseburgers like they're about to be declared illegal, and he needs to get as many under his belt as possible before the legislation passes. The worst part of it is that he never gains an ounce—possibly from his enthusiastic exercise regime, which includes playing one-on-one basketball on the Third Street courts—and has the blood pressure of a polar bear. Some people have all the luck in the genetic lottery.

So it's amusing to see him coming to the defense of a vegetarian.

"I'm just saying." Stephanie had obviously been assuming, because Cooper's a guy, that she could score points with him by maligning vegans. Ha. Wrong. Cooper doesn't care what people do, so long as they don't hurt other people. "She's pregnant. She needs to be careful. Pregnant women need more iron than the rest of us, and there's a lot of iron in red meat."

"That's what the ambulance lady said." Jordan is looking worried. "She told us Tania should see her private physician tomorrow morning for blood work. But also that Tania should go home now and rest."

"Of course," Stephanie says, putting her hand on Jordan's shoulder and patting it. "Of course she should. You two go home and get some sleep. It's been a long night."

This is quite a turnaround from before, when Stephanie had been standing there practically forcing them to keep filming, even though Tania had fainted. I wonder what's changed.

"I'll set up an appointment with Tania's ob-gyn tomor-row morning. Don't you worry about a thing." She's already typing swiftly into her cell phone with one hand and at the same time snapping at the production assistant with the other. "Lauren. Lauren. Tell them to pull the car around. Jordan and Tania need to leave. Everyone, you can start loading up your stuff. We're going."

Lauren, standing at the far side of the terrace enjoying a cigarette with Marcos the boom guy, puts down her Red Bull and touches her headset, then begins speaking swiftly into it. The rest of the crew go inside and begin to pack away their equipment.

"So," Stephanie says to me and Cooper, "after we drop off Jordan and Tania, would you two like to join us for a drink back at Epiphany? I'd love to get to know you a little better. I think it would be *amazing* to have you do a little cameo on the show, Heather. The fact that you used to live with one Cartwright brother but now you—"

"Live with another?" I finish for her quickly, my gaze going to Jordan. "No, that's okay. My career in the entertainment business is finished, I'm afraid. Besides, it's a little late for drinks. I'm a regular working girl now and have to be back here at nine tomorrow morning, so, no."

Jordan is looking from me to Cooper. "You guys sure?" he asks. "It would be fun to have you on the show. Mom and Dad would love it."

"No thanks," Cooper says, like he's refusing seconds at dinner.

"Suit yourself," Jordan says. "But we should still do drinks sometime. Well, Tania can't drink, but, you know. Hey." He looks at Stephanie. "Speaking of Tania, that's not all."

"Uh-huh." Stephanie's gaze has gone back to her keypad, like the mere mention of Tania Trace forces her to start texting. "What else?"

Jordan's gaze strays toward Tania, back in the Allingtons' living room. She's found what it was she was looking for in her bag. Incredibly, it's a live dog—a Chihuahua—that Tania is holding up in the air, oblivious to everyone else in the room. The dog wriggles in ecstasy, probably from a combination of finally being released from the bag and seeing its mistress. Tania smiles fondly up at the dog, which promptly begins to lick her all over the face.

This is pretty normal behavior for a dog owner—Lucy and I regularly share the same plate. I can't help it if she jumps onto the couch and starts eating my food, and I've caught Cooper letting her do the exact same thing. I know the Dog Whisperer wouldn't approve, but what are we going to do, push her away? She came from the shelter, she was probably abused as a puppy.

Of course, it's a problem that lately the cat, Owen, has started to move in on the action as well.

I'm not at all surprised to see Tania letting her dog give her face a tongue bath, but Stephanie, who's also followed Jordan's gaze, looks away, revolted.

"What is it, Jordan?" she asks.

"It's about the camp," Jordan says. "The rock camp?"

"What about it?" Stephanie asks. I notice the vein in her head has begun to throb again.

"Tania says she doesn't want to go. Not without Bear."

"Well, she's going to have to go without Bear," Stephanie says, without looking up from her screen. "Because Bear is going to have to get his spleen removed thanks to the stray bullet that pierced it, and he's not going to be springing back from that any time soon. At least, not in time to go to rock camp with Tania."

"But," Jordan says.

"You know what your father's going to say, Jordan," Stephanie reminds him.

Jordan looks down at his shoes. "Oh," he says. "Okay. Yeah."

"But don't worry," Stephanie says. "We'll get her another bodyguard."

"Sure," Jordan says. He continues to stare at his shoes. They're some kind of trainers, huge and black with colorful neon swoops on the sides. "Of course."

Something is clearly bothering him. Whatever it is, he doesn't mention it out loud. He just stands there, staring down at the swoops on his shoes.

"Hey, buddy," Cooper says, noticing the same thing I am. "Everything all right?"

Jordan glances up, then smiles his sweet, dumb smile. "Yeah," he says. "Why wouldn't it be? I got my own TV show, dawg. It's all good." Then, as if really seeing the two of us for the first time, he asks, his eyes narrowing suspiciously, "Hey, are you two together or something?"

Christopher, to whom Cooper announced that we're engaged, glances at Jordan oddly, but before he can open his mouth to speak, Cooper says, "What would make you think that, Jordan?"

"I don't know," Jordan says, with a shrug. "You just look . . .

together. But I know my big brother Coop would never scam on my best girl." Jordan grins at Cooper, then raises his fist and gives him a mock punch in the shoulder.

There's an uncomfortable silence until finally Cooper asks Jordan the obvious question. "Isn't Tania your best girl? She's your wife."

"Well, yeah," Jordan says, lowering his fist. "But Heather was my first."

"Jordan, we were never married," I remind him, keeping the frustration from my voice with difficulty.

Sometimes it's hard to remember what I ever saw in Jordan. Except that he was cute and could be very sweet and affectionate when we were alone together, a lot like Tania's Chihuahua.

"And even if we were married," I say, "we're broken up now. So does that mean I can't go out with anyone else?"

Jordan looks confused. "No," he says. "You can go out with whoever you want to . . . except him." He points at Cooper. "Because that would be like incest."

Fortunately Lauren, the production assistant, pokes her head through the French doors and calls, tapping on her headset, "Car's ready downstairs."

"Oops," Jordan says. "Gotta go. Call me." He gives me a quick kiss on the top of the head, faux-punches Cooper in the shoulder again, then turns around to jog back into the Allingtons' apartment to collect his wife and her tiny dog.

When I glance at Stephanie and Christopher, I see both of them staring at Cooper and me, Stephanie with an expression that reminds me of Owen the cat when he is scheming a way to get more half-and-half out of one of us.

Cooper must have noticed Stephanie's expression too, since the next words out of his mouth are, "May I remind you that if either Jordan or Tania hears a single word about the two of us being engaged, I'll know it came from one of you, and I'll make certain that stories I'm pretty sure you want kept out of the press show up exactly where you least want them to. Understand?"

The smile vanishes from Stephanie's face. "What stories?"

"I understand," Christopher says quickly.

Stephanie glances at him, horrified. "He's talking about *you*? My God, I thought he meant some deep dark secret from the Cartwright family that could hurt the show. But he means *you*? What did *you* do?"

"Nothing," Christopher says, taking her arm and steering her away from us. "It was stupid."

"But—"

"Just drop it."

"So," I say to Cooper as they walk away, arguing in whispers. "That went well."

Cooper smiles, then glances at his watch. "I think the ball game is probably still on. If we walk fast, I can catch the last inning."

"By all means, then," I say. "Let us walk fast."

On our walk home—after making sure everyone involved with CRT is signed out of the building—I can't help dragging my feet a little, thinking back to the way Jordan kept staring down at his shoes. There was something he'd wanted to say, I'm sure of it. He'd either lacked the mental capacity or been too frightened to utter whatever it was out loud.

It's possible I'm projecting, though. We learned about projecting last week in my Psych 101 class. Projecting is when a person ascribes feelings or emotions that she herself is experiencing onto others as a psychological defense mechanism.

God knows I have reason to be frightened of the Allingtons' terrace, so I could be imagining the fear. Whatever it was Jordan had to say, it must not have been that important. Because if it was, wouldn't he have figured out how to say it?

Assuming this turns out to be my first mistake. Well, maybe my second. My first mistake was coming over to the building that night to begin with.

"You know," I say as Cooper and I are walking up the steps to the front door of what he now insists I call "our" brownstone, "for a guy who isn't that close with his little brother, you sure raced into the Allingtons' apartment pretty fast when you heard his voice. You practically ran Christopher Allington over."

Cooper is digging around in his pocket for his keys. "Yeah?" His tone is uninterested. "Well, Christopher Allington has a history of being a douchebag. I tend to use extra caution when dealing with known douchebags."

"That's probably wise," I say. "Is that why you were asking so many questions?"

"Heather, need I remind you that a man got shot?" He's found his key chain and hits the clicker on it that remotely deactivates the brownstone's alarm system. I hear the control panel inside the door beep, giving us the all clear. Only then does Cooper begin undoing the lock. "I might even stop by the hospital when Mr. Bear is feeling better and ask him a few questions. But that doesn't mean I'm getting involved in the mess that is my brother Jordan's life."

"What does it mean then?" I ask. "Because it sounds like you are getting involved. And you told me I have to stay out of the amateur sleuthing business."

"It means I'm allowed to get involved if I want to because I have a license to practice private investigation," he says. "Issued to me by the state of New York. Am I going to have to show it to you?"

"I think you are," I say gravely. "And possibly your wrist restraints too."

He grins as he kicks open the door. "Get inside and I will."

A Fine Line

He said he liked my lips
He said he liked my eyes
But I had to realize
I was big in the thighs

He said my mind was fine
My voice was sweet like wine
But I was the wrong size
And I'd have to realize

There's a fine fine line
Between good and great
A fine fine line
Between chance and fate

And to be with him,
I'd have to lose some weight
Because winners win
and losers don't wait

I said to him
As I sipped my wine
That I understood, and it was time
To say good-bye, 'cause my size is fine

There's a fine fine line
Between good and great
A fine fine line
Between chance and fate

A fine fine line
Between slide and skate
And winners may win
But losers don't wait

"A Fine Line"
Written by Heather Wells

A week and a half later, I'm staring at my reflection in the full-length mirrors of a local clothing store. Three full-length mirrors, to be exact, side by side, each telling me the same thing:

No, no, and definitely *not*.

"Oh," the saleswoman says, adjusting the shoulder strap of the floor-skimming, empire-waisted, pure white gown that I'm trying on. "It's you. It's just so you."

It's so *not* me.

"You look so beautiful." The saleswoman busies herself straightening out the folds of the gown I'd found crumpled in the sales rack, marked down to 75 percent off. That's the only reason I decided to try it on.

Well, that and the fact that it was the only one remotely close to my size. The last time I'd been shopping, I'd barely been able to squeeze into a 14. But I was surprised to see that when I held up this dress—a 12—to me, it looked as if it would fit.

It does.

Looks like the bridal gown designers have finally caught on to the vanity size thing like the rest of the fashion industry, though I'd like to think I've dropped a few pounds. I read somewhere that lovemaking burns two hundred calories an hour, a disappointingly low number compared to horseback riding (six hundred). But still impressive.

I *have* been eating a little less lately, not only because I've been too distracted by all the recent activity going on in my bedroom since Cooper and I started hooking up to go see what's in the fridge, but because the Fischer Hall cafeteria is closed for renovations too, which means I can no longer stroll fifty feet down the hall from my office to grab a free bagel and cream cheese (with bacon). I have to walk all the way across the park to the Pansy Café (the closest place that accepts New York College dining cards).

However, I went to the gyno last week for my annual, and I know I weigh exactly the same as last year, give or take a pound or two.

"You're having a beach wedding, right?" the saleswoman says, bringing my attention back to the situation at hand. "Then this is perfect, simply perfect."

I'd explained to her about Cooper's desire for an elopement. But Cooper's idea is that we're going to get married in October on the Cape, making this summery gown about as appropriate as a bikini in Anchorage. I don't even know what I'd been thinking, trying it on. I must have been seized by wedding madness, brought on by the fact that the store is slashing the prices of all its summer stock to make room for its fall clothes, even though it's still only July.

Maybe it would look better with one of those cute glittery cardigans they have on all the mannequins . . .

No. *No one* wears a cardigan with a wedding gown. Except Kate Middleton, but she only wore one with the dress she changed into for the reception. And there isn't going to be a reception, because so far we haven't told anyone about our wedding plans, except Christopher Allington and Stephanie Brewer the Sunday before last. But that hadn't exactly been an invitation.

So what am I doing, trying on wedding dresses? I know, but I don't want to think about it.

"Let me find you some accessories," the saleswoman says. It's like she's read my mind. "A cardi, in case it gets chilly. And how do you feel about headbands? Maybe one with a bow!"

Really, what can I say? When you spend your lunch hour in a store that specializes in preppy clothes that—you realize belatedly—really look good only on the stick-thin models they always show in the catalogs that are forever sliding through the mail slot of your house, you pretty much get what you deserve. Headbands? Sure. A bow? Why not?

Fortunately, my cell phone starts whooping Beyoncé's "Run the World."

"Oh," I say, glancing at the caller ID. "That's work. Looks like I gotta get back. Maybe another time."

The saleswoman looks disappointed. That's her commission off two hundred whole bucks down the drain. I feel kind of bad, except that she'd been trying to talk me into buying a dress in which I looked like a walking roll of toilet paper.

"Oh," the saleswoman says, smiling brightly. "Well, come back when you have more time. And bring a friend. Or your mom. It's a big decision to make on your own."

I try to keep my own smile in place. Most brides' mothers haven't stabbed their daughters in the back, the way mine did. It's not the saleswoman's fault.

"Sure," I say. "Thanks, I will."

But I won't be back. The company this woman works for obviously doesn't make dresses that look good on girls who are a size 12. Or possibly larger.

Safely back out onto the street, a little breathless from my narrow escape, I start down my favorite route back to the office. It's one that takes me past the window of a small antiques store on Fifth Avenue.

I'm not really a jewelry person, but there's a display of vintage jewelry in the window of this particular shop that really is breathtaking. And there's one particular ring in the display that I can't help staring at longingly every time I walk by.

As I call Sarah back I pause in front of the shop and see that the ring is still there, an oval sapphire with clusters of tiny diamonds on either side of it, set on a platinum band. It's sitting by itself on a dark green velvet pillow in one corner of the window.

"What's going on?" I ask Sarah when she picks up.

"Where are you?" she asks. "You've been gone forever. Are you looking at that ring again?"

"No," I say, startled, and turn away from the window. *How does she know?* "Of course not. Why would I be doing that?"

"Because you make me go by that store on our way to Barnes & Noble so you can stand and stare at that ring, even though it's completely out of our way. Why don't you just buy it? You do have a job, you know. Two of them, as a matter of fact. What do you work so much for, if not to buy yourself stuff?"

"Are you kidding?" I laugh so nervously I sound like a hyena. "It's an engagement ring."

"It doesn't have to be," Sarah says. "It can be whatever kind of ring you want it to be. You can be the boss of the ring."

"I can also admire something and not buy it," I say. "Especially if it's not practical and probably costs a fortune."

"How would you know? You won't even go inside to ask how much it is, even though I've told you a million times—"

"Because it doesn't matter," I say, cutting her off, "since I don't really want it. It's not my style. It's too fancy. And you never answered my question. What's going on?"

"Oh," Sarah says. "I got a call from Dr. Jessup's assistant over at Central. It looks like they did it."

I have no idea what she's talking about. "Did what?"

"They picked the new hall director for Fischer Hall. What else?"

"Holy crap!" I freeze in my tracks.

I'm standing on the corner of Fifth Avenue and Eighteenth Street. A *Sex and the City* double-decker tour bus is going by, taking summer tourists to see all the places where Carrie Bradshaw and the girls used to have Cosmos and cupcakes.

People glance at me, alternately concerned and annoyed. New Yorkers aren't as hardened as the media makes them out to be. If I were to fall down in a dead faint on the sidewalk right now because of Sarah's news, I'm positive several good Samaritans would stop to call 911 and maybe even prop up my head to make sure I had an open airway. But only because I'm wearing clean clothes and don't appear to be intoxicated. If I were drunk and covered in my own vomit, people would continue to step over me until the smell became too intolerable to bear. Then they might call the cops.

"Are you kidding me?" I yell into the phone. "Who? Who is it? Is it Simon? I swear to God, if it's Simon, I'm going to jump in front of this bus—"

"I don't know who it is," Sarah says. "Dr. Jessup's assistant called and said he's coming by right now with some people so he can make the introduction in person and tell us some news about the building—"

"*Now?*" I break into a jog. Big mistake. I'm not wearing a jogging bra. I don't even own a jogging bra. What am I thinking? I slow down. "Why didn't you tell me sooner? Are you sure he said 'make the introduction'? Because if he said that, it can't be Simon. We already know Simon. Why would he introduce us to Simon?"

"Maybe he means make the introduction as in, 'This is your new boss, Simon,'" Sarah says. "'You might know him as the former director of Wasser Hall, but now he's the director of Fischer Hall. Have a nice day, losers.'"

My heart feels as if it has sunk to my knees, where my boobs are, because I've been running in a bra not made for that kind of physical exertion.

"Oh God," I say, trying not to gag. "No. Anyone but Simon."

"Of course," Sarah says, "it could also be this woman I saw coming out from Dr. Jessup's office over at the Housing Office earlier today when I went to drop off the time sheets. Either way, we're dead."

"Why?" I ask, panicking. "Why are we dead if it's her? Did you look her up on the FBI's Most Wanted? Is she on there?"

"She just looked so . . . so . . ." Sarah seems unable to find the word she's looking for.

I start running again. I don't care how many tourists from the *Sex and the City* tour buses get photos of me holding my boobs up with one arm.

"Corporate? Stick up her butt?" I try to think of all the

kinds of women I'd least like to work with. "Wants to marry for money? Sociopath?"

"Perky," Sarah finishes.

"Oh," I say. I can't run anymore, and I've only reached Fifth and Fifteenth Street. A ribbon of sweat is trickling down my chest, always an attractive look when meeting your new boss for the first time. "Perky is good," I say between pants. "Perky is better than Simon, who's . . ." I can't even think of a word to describe Simon, my hatred for him is so blinding.

"Not this kind of perky," Sarah says. "She looked like a sorority girl. The bad kind. Like she majored in perk. The I-want-to-cram-my-fist-down-her-throat-she's-so-perky kind of perky."

"Sarah," I say. It doesn't seem possible, but her attitude is scarier than the idea of Simon becoming my boss. "She can't be *that* bad. What's wrong with you?"

Sarah's been in a horrible mood all week—more than a week, actually—and she hasn't explained why, at least not in a way that makes sense. She's tried to blame it on everything from the cafeteria in the building being closed so she has to walk all the way across the park to get her coffee at the Pansy Café, to the fact that I hired too many females to work in the office, which isn't even remotely true, because it's only the two of us and Brad, a resident whose father told him not to bother coming home for the summer when he found out Brad is gay, so Brad had nowhere to live, being a work-study student on a very limited income.

That's how Brad became another one of the misfit toys, when it was unanimously decided by myself *and* Sarah that

Brad would be offered a free room in Fischer Hall for the summer in exchange for working twenty hours a week in the office, covering our lunch shifts.

So when Sarah starts complaining over the phone as I'm standing there on Fifth Avenue, "Our ovulation cycles have synchronized. Everyone knows this happens when women spend too much time together. And this woman Dr. Jessup has hired is only going to make things worse. I almost wish he'd hired Simon," I nearly burst a blood vessel.

"Sarah," I snap, "Professor Lehman in my Psych 101 class says there's no such thing as menstrual synchrony. Its existence was debunked long ago—all the studies alleging to prove it later were shown to have faulty data and poor statistical analyses. Since you're a psychology major, I'm surprised you don't know that. Furthermore, there aren't only women working in the office, and you know it. There's Brad—"

"Gay," Sarah says. "Doesn't count."

"—and I'm on continuous-cycle birth control pills," I go on, ignoring her, "so I don't ovulate or have my period anymore."

"Well," Sarah says, sounding taken aback, "*that* can't be good for you."

"How would you know?" I ask, keeping my patience with an effort. "Are you my doctor? No. So you can't really make a judgment like that, can you?"

"Okay," Sarah says. "Sorry. I didn't know, all right?"

I take a deep breath, trying to remain calm. Sarah's right, she didn't know. It's not like we sit around the office discussing these things, like women do on those stupid commercials. "Well, I haven't ovulated in months, thanks to having gone on Exotique, the pill where you get your period only four times a year."

At my most recent checkup—the one last week—when my gynecologist asked how things were going in my romantic life and I mentioned I was secretly engaged (I guess it's starting not to be such a secret anymore), my doctor said, "Good for you, Heather! Though when you think you might be ready to start having children—which I hope at your age will be sooner rather later—we're probably going to have to have a talk. Evidence shows that for women like you it can sometimes be difficult to conceive."

"What do you mean, 'women like me'?" I asked, suspiciously. "Big girls?"

"No," my doctor said, shaking her head. "Actually, it can be harder for thinner women to conceive. Your BMI is in the overweight range but your blood pressure and cholesterol are both perfectly healthy. I meant women like you who suffer from chronic endometriosis."

"Endo-what-now?" I said.

"We discussed this last year, Heather," she reminded me with a sigh. "That's why I put you on the continuous-cycle contraceptive, and we agreed you'd start skipping your periods entirely. This reduces the tendency for your body to produce endometrial cysts. Remember those polyps I removed from your cervix?"

How could I forget? At least my dentist gives me nitrous oxide when I get a cleaning. My gynecologist had stuck a metal tube up my hoo-ha, and I didn't get so much as an ibuprofen.

"You said the polyps were normal," I pointed out to her.

"They *were* normal," my doctor said, "in that they were benign. What's abnormal is that they're *endometrial* polyps. Honestly, there's nothing to worry about yet, but after you go off the pill, if you have trouble conceiving, we'll probably need to go in for a look laparoscopically. That's all I'm saying."

I left her office feeling as if Jack, Emily, and Charlotte— the names I'd picked out long ago for my future children with Cooper—were little ghost kids who'd slipped away before I ever got the chance to introduce them to their dad.

The doctor said *if* I have trouble conceiving, not *when*. That doesn't mean I'm *going* to have trouble.

Still, I made the mistake of going online afterward to see how bad the odds are.

I should not have looked.

Now I suppose I've got to tell Cooper. Only how? When? *Is* there a right moment to tell your fiancé you have a strong chance of never being able to get pregnant, even with medical intervention?

It's more fun to hang out in preppy stores, trying on wedding dresses that look completely terrible, than face that kind of reality.

Maybe that's why I snapped when Sarah gave me her latest lame excuse for her bad mood.

"No," I say, scraping my fingers through my hair, "I'm the one who's sorry, Sarah. I know you didn't know. Back to this woman you saw at the Housing Office. She can't be *that* bad. Not worse than Simon. No one is worse than Simon—"

"I wouldn't be so sure," Sarah says. "Why else would Dr. Jessup say he has some news he can't wait to tell us and he wants to be sure to deliver it in person? Where *are* you anyway? I know we're closed, but that was the longest lunch break in the history of—"

"I'm coming," I say. "I'm just over on Fifth." I don't mention the cross street since it's so scandalously far. "I'll be right there." Then it hits me. "*News?* Besides the fact that he's hired someone as hall director? What kind of news?"

It can't be good news. When has Dr. Jessup ever stopped by anyone's building to give them *good* news?

I can't think of a single time. As a vice president—there is only one president at New York College, but there are several dozen vice presidents, all heads of nonacademic divisions of the college—Dr. Jessup is too busy to personally deliver good news. He has his assistant send it to us via e-mail.

Bad news, however, inevitably gets delivered by him via staff meeting—like the time we found out that, because of the hiring freeze and recession, there would be no merit raises. (Which didn't affect me. As a new employee, I'm not eligible for a merit raise until next year. But Simon took it very hard.)

"I would imagine the news probably has something to do with what happened last week," Sarah says. "*Remember?*" She's being purposefully vague. Brad must be in the office with her. The two of us have managed to keep the fact that Jordan Cartwright and Tania Trace were ever in Fischer Hall a secret (one I shared with her only out of necessity, since she caught me destroying the page from the Protection Services log on which Christopher signed them in).

So far the only mentions of the shooting outside of Epiphany have been on entertainment news shows, like Jordan and Tania's interview on *Access Hollywood* ("America's Favorite Musical Couple Talks About Their Brush with Death"), and in gossip magazines. (In one photograph captioned "Tania Trace Visits Beloved Bodyguard in Hospital," Tania is in a hospital room passing a large bouquet of "Get Well" balloons to an extremely large black man sitting up in bed. His gigantic hand makes hers look even tinier as he reaches out to accept the bouquet from her.)

"We didn't do anything wrong," I remind Sarah. "The paintball guns were bad, I'll admit, but they're owned by the college. No one got hurt. At least," I add after a second thought, "no students."

Cooper had reported back from his trip to Beth Israel Medical Center that Tania's bodyguard's injuries were a little more extensive than Stephanie led us to believe. Though Bear was expected to make a full recovery, not only had he had to have his spleen removed, but the bullet had gone straight through it and into his foot. He had weeks of physical therapy ahead of him.

Nevertheless, according to Cooper, it looked as if the shooting really had been completely random. The police found a shell casing they thought matched the bullet that struck Bear, but it was on the rooftop of an apartment building across the street from Epiphany that was littered with shell casings from dozens of other bullets as well . . . not to mention the remains of numerous firecrackers, discarded condoms, empty forty-ounce bottles of beer, and even a hibachi grill. This rooftop was obviously a popular hangout for kids, in addition to being accessible by residents of all the buildings across the street from Epiphany. (Access one roof and it was an easy leap to another.)

Other than from Cooper and *Access Hollywood*, I had heard nothing more about the incident. I saw neither Christopher nor Stephanie Brewer again in Fischer Hall, though I checked the sign-in logs for both of them every morning. There was no record of them having come back, though, and no mention in the press of anything related to Fischer Hall.

"I don't know," Sarah says. "Do you think Simon told about the beer? And the vodka?"

I grit my teeth. "Everyone was over twenty-one—"

"Well, whatever the deal is, it doesn't make a very good impression to be caught taking a two-hour lunch on your new boss's first day."

She's right about that. I need to get it together—

As if in answer to an unspoken prayer, I see a yellow streak out of the corner of my eye. At first I'm sure it can only be an illusion, a hallucination brought on by nerves. Then it slides into focus, and I realize my luck might actually be changing for the better: it's a New York City cab with the light on its roof glowing bright yellow, indicating that it's unoccupied. This is as rare a sight in this part of town as a hundred-dollar bill floating down from the heavens.

I leap upon it just as quickly. I don't shout "Taxi!" like they always show New Yorkers doing in movies and on TV shows, because that only alerts the unsuspecting people around you that there's a vacant cab nearby. Then the people closest to it will try to snag it before you can.

Instead, I make a run for it, yanking on the handle of its back passenger door as the light turns green and the cab begins to move.

"Sorry," I say to the driver as he jams on the brakes and looks around, startled to find a passenger climbing into his backseat. "I need to go to 55 Washington Square West. Can you take me there?"

The driver pauses in the conversation he's having on his hands-free cell phone long enough to say, "That's only eight blocks from here."

"I know," I say.

I try not to feel as if he's judging me. He probably isn't. He's probably thinking I'm a tourist who doesn't know how close she is to her destination.

"It's eight *long* blocks," I say. "And I'm super late. And it's *so* hot."

The driver smiles, hits the meter, and continues his cell-phone conversation in his native Farsi. I relax, feeling the cool air conditioning blast from the little vent at my feet. I actually might have died and gone to heaven. Maybe everything's going to be all right . . .

"My God!" I hear Sarah's voice shout from my hand. I've forgotten I'm still holding my phone. "You're still eight blocks away? They're going to be here *any minute!*"

"Stall them," I lift the phone to my face to instruct her. "Tell them I went to Disbursements. Tell them—"

"Oh," I hear Sarah say. "Hi, Dr. Jessup. You're here already?"

Then she hangs up on me.

I'm so dead.

Haters

Take a picture
Write it down
I don't give a ****

I know you think
You'll take me down
Well, boy, I wish you luck

I got haters
All around me
Up and in my face

You think you're gonna
Take me down
Get into my space

Well here's a tweet
A super text
An e-mail voice iCall

Take more than you
To bring me down
So write that on your wall

"Haters"
Performed by Tania Trace
Written by Weinberger/Trace
So Sue Me album
Cartwright Records
Eleven consecutive weeks
in the Top 10 Billboard Hot 100

I jump out of the cab as soon as it pulls up in front of Fischer Hall, throwing a ten-dollar bill into the front seat. The driver, still on his phone call, is once again startled, but I don't stop to wait for change, and he certainly doesn't stop to give it.

"Thanks!" he cries. "Have a great day!"

Too late.

I'm confused to see a fleet of delivery trucks outside the building. Moving men are unloading bubble-wrapped furniture, using the gray plastic carts reserved for Fischer Hall residents only.

This sight sets my already overtaxed heart beating unsteadily. When I see some of the men pushing the carts toward the Fischer Hall handicapped-accessible ramp, I begin to have palpitations.

"Excuse me," I go up to one of the men and say, "but who is this delivery for?"

He's as sweaty as I was a few minutes ago. He's been working hard for some time apparently and hasn't had a nice air-conditioned cab ride to cool off.

He looks down at his clipboard. "Heather Wells," he says, a bit impatiently, "Fischer Hall, 55 Washington Square West," and goes back to pushing his cart, which appears to be filled with an unassembled Ikea bedroom set.

"Wait a minute," I say, catching his arm, which is quite buff, if a bit moist with perspiration. "There must be some mistake. I didn't order any of these things." There are literally five trucks in front of me. "And this building is closed for renovations."

The man shrugs. "Well, this person here signed for it," he

says, pointing at the bottom of his clipboard. "So you're getting it whether you ordered it or not."

I look at the cursive scrawl he's pointing to.

Stephanie Brewer.

Now instead of palpitations, my heart feels as if it's exploding.

How could this be happening? And on the day my new boss is arriving?

I follow the men pushing the cart through the door to find Pete sitting at the security desk, on the interoffice phone. He puts his hand over the mouthpiece and asks, "Where have you been? Do you have any idea what's been going on here? Do you know who's in your office?"

"I think I can guess," I assure him sarcastically. A gray plastic cart piled high with accessories from Urban Outfitters rolls by. "Where are they taking all this stuff?" I ask him.

"Upstairs," he says, with a shrug.

"The penthouse?" I can't imagine what Eleanor Allington is going to want with a lava lamp.

"All I know is upstairs," he says. He seems supremely unconcerned. "Magda says hi." He indicates the phone. He and Magda, my best friend from Dining Services, have become a pretty hot item in recent months, but lately their flirting has to be carried out via telephone because Magda has been transferred over to the Pansy Café while the Fischer Hall cafeteria, where she normally works, is being renovated.

"Tell her hi back," I call vaguely over my shoulder as I begin wandering toward my office. I have to duck when I encounter Carl, the chief building engineer, striding down the hallway carrying an eight-foot ladder on his shoulder.

"Hey," he says cheerfully. "Look where you're going. What d'ya want, another body?"

"Not funny," I say to him. "What's going on here?"

"Don't know," he says. "Got a call from Facilities that I'm supposed to go up to the seventeenth floor to change all the lightbulbs in the vanity mirrors above the bathroom sinks to sixty-watt bulbs from the forty-watt energy-efficients that are in there. So that's what I'm doing."

I'm perplexed by this information. "We have sixty-watt regular lightbulbs?"

He snorts. "Been hoarding them for years. I saw this energy-saving bulb thing coming a decade ago. I knew it wouldn't go over well with you women. You like your lighting bright in the bathroom so you can see to put your makeup on."

I blink at this, not sure how to react.

"Oh," I say. "Well, good. I guess."

I walk away shaking my head. What is going on?

Then I round the corner into the hall director's office and find Stan Jessup standing there. Beside him is a young woman in jeans and a T-shirt who I've never seen before; Muffy Fowler, the head of the college's media relations department; Sarah; and Stephanie Brewer from Cartwright Records Television.

I freeze in the doorway, feeling all the sweat that dried up during the nice cool cab ride begin to prickle my skin again.

"W-what's happening?" I stammer, dumbfounded.

"Well, hey there," Muffy Fowler says in her southern accent. As usual, she's dressed to the nines, in white high-heeled pumps, a cream-colored linen pencil skirt, and a polka-dotted silk blouse. "So nice of you to join us. Can't believe you went for such a long lunch and didn't invite me. I thought we were friends."

I want to melt into a puddle on the floor.

"I didn't," I say. "I wasn't. I was at Disbursements."

"I'm just kidding," Muffy says, bursting into loud guffaws. "Would ya'll look at her face? Bless her heart. Heather, I think you've met Stephanie. She says you two had a little run-in the other night."

"I wouldn't call it a run-in," I say quickly, coming into the office.

"More like we had the pleasure of meeting," Stephanie says, reaching out to shake my hand. She looks a lot more pleasant than she did the last time I saw her. Her face is wreathed in smiles. She's wearing a light-gray business suit and clutching a designer tote that probably cost more than I make in a month. "So nice to see you again, Heather. I was just telling everyone how accommodating you were. Tania hasn't been able to stop raving about you."

I'm confused. "She what?"

"Heather," Dr. Jessup says, stepping forward. If I'm hot, he must be even more so, having surely walked all the way across the park from the Housing Office in that dark charcoal suit he's wearing, even though Sarah's set the office air conditioner on full blast. I can see a telltale sheen around the edges of his still-thick head of dark hair, peppered at the temples with gray. "We have some great news. So great I had to deliver it personally."

"Yeah," Sarah says from her desk over by the photocopier. She's wearing her everyday uniform of black T-shirt and overalls, but she's blown her usual mass of frizzy curls dry against the New York humidity and actually put on a bit of eyeliner. Sarah used to leave her face untouched by anything remotely resembling makeup, thinking it was a violation of feminist ethics to enhance what the Mother Goddess gave us, until I pointed out to her that if the Mother Goddess didn't want us to wear makeup, she would not have given some of us eyelashes so blond they are practically invisible, making us resemble white rabbits without our mascara on. "Wait until you hear this news, Heather. It couldn't be more great. It's truly great."

It's clear from Sarah's tone that she doesn't think the news is great at all. Unless you knew her as well as I do, you wouldn't pick up on the sarcasm.

"Fantastic," I say. "I'm so excited to hear this great news. Do I need to sit down?"

"Probably," Sarah says. "I would. Because this news is so great, you're going to want to be sitting down when you hear it or you might pass out from excitement."

I go around the side of my desk and sit down, glaring at her. She's pushing it a little far.

"Anyone else?" I ask, indicating the couch across from my desk, as well as the other chairs I rescued from the cafeteria before they began painting in there.

"Thanks," says the girl I don't recognize. "Don't mind if I do. My dogs are barking." She sits. I notice Sarah glaring at her. I don't know if it's because of the "my dogs are barking" remark (which admittedly was odd, but possibly as sarcastic as Sarah's "you might pass out from excitement"), or because they've had some kind of disagreement before I got here. They appear to be the same age and are dressed in a similarly slovenly style—though I realize I'm not one to talk—so I can't imagine what they could have found to disagree on, though the visitor's hair is definitely more neatly styled.

"Can I do it?" Muffy asks Dr. Jessup, bouncing on the toes of her pumps. "Puh-lease, Stan?"

He smiles at her graciously. "Be my guest."

I look up at Muffy. She and I are friends, if you can call it friendship to share a mutual desire not to see people get away with murder on the campus where we work and an attraction to the same guy (she's currently dating my ex-boyfriend and remedial math teacher, Tadd Tocco).

Fortunately, Tadd and Muffy make a much better couple than Tadd and I ever did, mostly owing to Tadd's commitment to veganism and my commitment to being in love with another man, namely Cooper Cartwright. Muffy told me at the last lunch we had together that she's pretty sure Tadd is going to propose (because she informed him that at their age, if there isn't forward momentum in a relationship after three months, it only makes sense to break up), but she's on the fence about accepting.

"On the one hand," she said over the healthy tuna salad wrap she purchased from the Pansy Café, "I'm not getting any younger, and since I definitely want kids, I might as well have them with Tadd. You know they'll be smart because his IQ is through the roof, and we'll save a lot on child care, since professors only work about three hours a week, so Tadd can stay home with them."

I'd been forced to admit this was true.

"On the other hand," Muffy said, "I'd always hoped to

marry a rich man so I could be the one to raise the kids. I'm not sure what the girls back home will think when they hear I'm still working."

"Who cares what anyone else thinks?" I asked with a shrug over my not-so-healthy Pansy Café burger and fries. "It's your life, not theirs. You love your job, don't you?"

"Yes," Muffy said firmly.

"Good," I said. "Just make sure you love Tadd too before you say yes when he asks you to marry him, or I don't think your plan has a very good chance at working out."

Now Muffy is looking at me with her perfectly made-up eyes glittering, bursting with eagerness to tell me whatever fabulous news it is she has to impart.

"Heather," she says, "I know how sad you were that your residence hall was closed for the summer, and ya'll were left with nothing to do but twiddle your thumbs. Now you can stop twiddling, because Fischer Hall's being officially reopened this weekend to host the first ever *Tania Trace Rock Camp!*"

I glance quickly from Muffy to Dr. Jessup to Stephanie, then to Sarah, then back again.

"Wait," I say intelligently. "What?"

"Yes," Sarah says unsmilingly. "Fifty fourteen-year-old girls here in the city for two weeks, living their dream of getting mentored by none other than Tania Trace. Isn't it *great?*"

"They're fourteen to sixteen years old, actually," Stephanie says. She's sunk down into a chair covered with blue vinyl—I watched Carl reupholster it myself, after mice ate through the original orange upholstery—and opened her tote. She pulls a brochure from it and hands it to me. I thumb through it as she talks. It's a wash of bright vibrant colors, like Tania herself when she isn't suffering from exhaustion. "You remember, Heather. I told you about it last week. Unfortunately, the Catskills location simply isn't going to work anymore."

"Why?" I ask. "It looks perfect." I point to a photo of a girl on horseback. "We don't have horses." I point to another photo. "Or an open-air amphitheater."

"We have plenty of performance spaces," Dr. Jessup says. "Our drama school is one of the best in the country. Our theaters aren't open-air, but it's my understanding that that is Ms. Trace's preference—"

"Tania wants everything moved indoors," Stephanie says crisply, plucking the brochure from my fingers.

I'm more confused than ever. "Then how is it camp?"

"It's still camp," Stephanie says. "It's just *inside* camp."

"What's 'inside camp'?" I ask, bewildered. "That doesn't even make sense."

"Of course it makes sense," Stephanie insists. "It's *college* camp. The girls are going to love it even more than they would have loved being at a resort in the Catskills. They'll be experiencing life on a college campus years before their peers. And not just any college campus, but New York College, one of the top ten most-applied-to colleges in the country. Not to mention, of course, they'll be spending every minute with Tania Trace. Or one of New York College's prestigious music instructors. Mostly with one of them. But for at least an hour a day, they'll be with Tania."

I sit where I am, stunned, while everyone else except Sarah beams at me.

"Told you so, didn't I, Heather?" Sarah asks me, leaning forward on her desk, her smile diabolical, but only I know her well enough to realize it. "Isn't it *great?*"

I ignore her.

"We're closed for renovations," I say to Dr. Jessup. I'm not arguing because Tania Trace is my ex's new wife and I don't want anything to do with this. I genuinely can't figure out how we're going to make it happen. "None of the rooms is even close to ready for occupancy. The paint crew's barely gotten through the top few floors. And most of those rooms haven't been fully maintenanced yet. I mean . . ." I can't believe I have to say this out loud, but I do it anyway. "What about the room to Narnia?"

Stephanie and the girl no one's introduced to me stare at me blankly, but I'm confident that Dr. Jessup and Muffy know exactly what I mean, because the room to Narnia, like Pansygate, was scandalous enough to have made the *New York Post*. After spring checkout, we found a room in which the four male suitemates had built "a door to Narnia"—a hole they'd cut into the back of a college-issued wardrobe that, when opened, led to an extra room of their suite in which they'd assembled a "love dungeon" complete with wall-to-wall mattresses, lava lamps, bongos, and posters of the actor who played Prince Caspian on every vertical surface.

What was even more annoying was that the suitemates' parents then had the nerve to refuse to pay the charges we billed them for the cost of repairing the hole in the wardrobe (and fumigation of the mattresses), even though I sent them photographic evidence of their sons' unusual extracurricular activities.

"No worries," Muffy says cheerfully. "We already received a list from Facilities of the rooms that need the least work—"

"Facilities?" Then I remember bumping into Carl in the hallway, with his ladder. "Of course," I murmur. "The lightbulbs."

"Exactly," Stephanie says. "Our girls are going to need good lighting to put their makeup on in the morning for the cameras."

"Cameras?" I fling a panicky look at Dr. Jessup, but it's Muffy who answers.

"New York College has been offered a tremendous opportunity, for which I'm told we have you to thank, Heather," she says.

I know what's coming, but I'm still hoping there's been some kind of mistake. "What opportunity?"

Stephanie's smile isn't reflected in her eyes.

"Tania felt like you handled the little crisis she had while she was here the other night so competently, she says the only place she can feel safe right now while filming *Jordan Loves Tania*—with Bear laid up in the hospital—is in Fischer Hall."

"This is going to do wonders to boost Fischer Hall's reputation when the show airs," Muffy says enthusiastically. "So long, Death Dorm! Hello, most-sought-after residence hall in the country! Everyone is going to want to live in the building where they hosted Tania Trace Rock Camp."

"But . . ." I look at Dr. Jessup in desperation. "But filming is not permitted in any New York College residence hall without proper authorization."

Dr. Jessup has his hands buried in the pockets of his suit trousers. He's rocking back and forth on his heels.

"What can I tell you, kid?" he says, his smile grim. "They got authorization, straight from the president's office."

I glance at Stephanie. Her own smile has gone catlike. "I told you President Allington is a big fan of Cartwright Records Television."

I frown. More like President Allington's son is a big fan of Stephanie and used his influence on his dad—who has no idea what's happening on his own campus because he's hiding in the Hamptons during Pansygate.

I look at the girl in the T-shirt and jeans on the couch. She's so cute and little, I assume she's with CRT, maybe another production assistant or Stephanie's personal assistant. Though I can't figure out why she's dressed like a student.

"Who are you?" I ask, trying to sound polite, but not sure I succeed. "A Tania Trace Rock Camp counselor?"

The girl raises her eyebrows, her mouth making a little round O of surprise.

"No, Heather." Dr. Jessup takes his hands out of his pockets. "This is the other piece of good news. I'd like you meet the new Fischer Hall residence director, Lisa Wu. Lisa, this is Heather Wells."

Triple A

Two in the morning
And my hopes were high
Till I saw you leave
With that other guy

Shoulda left then,
But she caught my eye
Whispered, "Come on, babe,
Let's go get high"

Shouldn't've listened,
Shoulda gone straight home
But I couldn't stand
Another night alone

Got what I deserved
For that misplaced desire
When I said I couldn't stay
She slashed all my tires

Now I'm standing in the cold
When's it gonna go my way?
You've got my heart
All I've got is Triple A

"Triple A"
Performed by Jordan Cartwright
Written by Jason/Benjamin
Goin' Solo album
Ten consecutive weeks in the
Top 10 Country Billboard Hot 100

"Hi, Heather," the girl says, jumping up from the couch with a huge grin, then leaning over my desk to pump my hand enthusiastically. "I've heard so much about you. I can't wait for us to start working together."

I stare in complete shock at the girl standing across from my desk.

"Uh," I say, putting my hand in hers and letting her shake it up and down. "Hi. Same here."

My gaze slides toward Sarah, checking to see if she's laughing. Maybe this is all a joke, part of the reality show. Possibly they're punking me?

Sarah's got her chin in her hands, watching me avidly for my reaction.

No, this isn't part of the show. This is real. This girl—who looks about ten years younger than I am—is my new boss.

"But," I say lamely, "what about Simon?"

"Simon?" Lisa glances uncertainly at Dr. Jessup. "Who's Simon?"

Dr. Jessup clears his throat. "We didn't feel Simon was the right fit for Fischer Hall."

Stephanie, who's pulled her cell phone from her tote bag and is texting, makes a face. "Do you mean that redheaded man? Oh God, no. He was *not* the right fit at all."

Wait. How does Stephanie know Simon? Was there a panel of judges auditioning my new boss, like *The X Factor* or something?

"We're going to have so much fun with this," Lisa is saying. "I can't wait! Fifty girls and a reality TV crew? This is going to be crazy." She sings the word "crazy" like it's part of a song lyric.

Meg Cabot

I'm glad someone's excited, because I'm sure not. Everything Sarah said over the phone about the woman she saw sitting in Dr. Jessup's office comes back to me. I can see what Sarah meant about Lisa Wu being so perky, Sarah wanted to cram her fist down her throat. Perky like a *reality television show host*.

It doesn't help that Lisa's wearing jeans and a T-shirt to her first day of work and that her dark hair has been swept back into a ponytail and that there is a scrunchie involved—who wears scrunchies anymore, except to wash her face? Plus, she has on flip-flops. Flip-flops. At work!

All right, this is the way my employees look, but they're in college. They sleep until noon whenever they can get away with it. They smoke weed (well, Gavin does, but he says he needs it medicinally for his ADHD) and build love dungeons in their rooms.

This is supposed to be my new boss. Yeah. Right.

"But you're a real residence hall director, right?" I ask, drawing my hand away from Lisa's like I'm afraid she might whip out a microphone and ask for a sound bite. "You didn't audition for the job through Cartwright Records Television?"

"Heather!" Muffy cries, shocked.

Stephanie bursts out laughing. So does Sarah, but for different reasons. Dr. Jessup looks amused, as does Lisa Wu.

"No," Lisa says, smiling. "I'm a real residence hall director. I have my master's degree and everything. I'll hang my diploma up in my new office as soon as they mail it. I'll admit this is my first professional position—"

I don't want to be rude by saying so out loud, but I can tell. Something in my expression must give it away, since

Dr. Jessup exclaims, "Jesus Christ, Wells, can't you see why I hired her?"

I glance at him, startled. "Um . . . no?"

"She seemed like she'd be a perfect fit with you!" he says. "You've been through such a hard time lately with bosses"—I notice how he tactfully avoids mentioning that all of my bosses have ended up dead, jailed for murder, and/ or promoted—"I thought the department should throw you a bone. Lisa Wu's *you* . . . well, except for the Asian part."

I look back at Lisa Wu, thinking that it's a shame about Dr. Jessup's early onset Alzheimer's.

Then I notice something. She *does* look a little like me, except younger and skinnier and Asian, of course.

I'm wearing jeans and a T-shirt. Well, mine isn't exactly a T-shirt, it's a nice fitted black shirt made of cotton material with ruching around the front to give a delicate smocking effect where I need it.

I've got on flip-flops (though mine are platforms with sequins). And my hair is in a ponytail (because it's so hot out). And I have, upon occasion, been accused of having too much energy . . . even of being perky, though I resent this.

Lisa must notice my scrutiny, since she smiles and says, a little sheepishly, "When Dr. Jessup called to say I got the job a little while ago, I was so excited. I said I happened to be in the city, and he said to come on over. I told him I wasn't exactly dressed properly, but he said it wouldn't matter. I was actually just over at Kleinfeld's, having my last fitting for my wedding gown—"

"You're getting *married*?" This is too weird.

"Yeah," Lisa says. "I never thought I'd go for the big wedding, but my parents are insisting, and so are Cory's. I found the cutest fit-n-flare, it was a sample on sale for only five hundred bucks." She reaches for a nearby tote bag. Unlike Stephanie's, it isn't designer. It's one that looks like she got it free for donating to PBS. Or probably her parents did. "I have a picture of it here in my wedding binder if you want to see it—"

She has a wedding binder? Maybe we don't have that much in common after all. I begin to think there might be things I could learn from Lisa Wu.

"If I could interrupt the girl talk," Stephanie says coldly, "scintillating as it is, could we get back to the subject at hand?"

I'd forgotten Stephanie was still in the room.

"Oh," I say, a little disappointed. *What's a wedding binder?* Whatever it is, I'm pretty sure there's someone out there who's tried to eat it. I would totally watch that. "Sure."

"Shooting is going to start this weekend, when the girls come to check in, so I need to see what rooms they're going to be put in." Stephanie has drawn her own binder from her tote bag. It doesn't look like it contains information about a wedding. "Some of them insist on bringing their mothers. This isn't going to suit the show at all. We can't have a bunch of stage moms running around, ruining things. So how can we get rid of these old biddies?"

"Legally," Muffy hurries to explain, tactfully, "no one under eighteen is allowed to reside in New York College's residence halls. So in order to facilitate the needs of your show, we were thinking we'd put in bunk beds—that's the furniture delivery you saw out front—and assign three to four girls per room, plus one mom as their legal chaperone."

"Well," Stephanie says baldly, "that sucks."

"Not really," I say. "We could use suites. That way we can put the girls in the back room and the moms in the outer rooms. Then the girls can't sneak out without waking the moms up."

"That sucks even more," Stephanie says.

"Good call, Heather," Muffy says, ignoring Stephanie. "That's the first thing I'd try to do if I were fourteen and staying in New York City for the summer. Get a fake ID and hit the bars."

"Actually," Stephanie says, pulling out her BlackBerry, "one of the things the network would like is if the girls *did* sneak out. That would add a lot more drama to the show."

"Really?" Lisa Wu says. "If an underage girl snuck out of this building and into a bar and something terrible happened to her in downtown New York City, it *would* add more drama to your show. But I don't think it would reflect very well on New York College, or on Tania Trace, and then ultimately on your network—do you, Stephanie?"

Oh my God. Lisa Wu just said out loud exactly what I was thinking in my head. Maybe Dr. Jessup was right after all.

"What?" Stephanie looks confused.

"I agree with Lisa," I say. "*Jordan Loves Tania* is supposed to be a husband-and-wife-themed reality show, not *Law and Order: Special Victims Unit*."

This Stephanie seems to understand. Her eyebrows rise. "It was only an idea," she says scathingly. "It's called brainstorming."

"Of course," Lisa says, smiling back at her. "You're in the

TV business. We're in the business of providing students with a safe and healthy community in which to live and develop while they achieve their academic goals. I'm sure we'll find a common meeting ground."

Impressed, I swing my gaze toward Dr. Jessup. Where did he find Lisa Wu? If our department had ten more like her and ten less like Simon Hague, we might actually stop being the laughingstock of higher education.

Dr. Jessup's too busy texting on his cell phone even to look my way.

"Ladies, shall we go check out those rooms?" he asks. "I hate to rush this, but Personnel would like me to bring Lisa over so they can get started on her paperwork—"

"Of course," I say. "But I have one question." I look at Stephanie. "Why does Tania feel so unsafe? I thought what happened to Bear was totally random. You *assured* us of that," I add, "over and over again, the other night."

"It was," Stephanie says quickly. "It was *completely* random. But you know how pop stars can be." She rolls her eyes. "Such divas."

There's a little bit of an uncomfortable silence. Maybe I'm only imagining it.

Or maybe everyone is thinking, the way I am, *Gee, Heather used to be a pop star. Was* she *a diva?*

Evidently Stephanie isn't thinking this, since she goes on: "Tania's convinced she needs to keep close to the city, where she plans on having the baby, and to the doctor who's delivering it, until it's born. And of course, since that's what Tania wants, Cartwright Records is only too happy to oblige. Even the Catskills is too far now for Tania. And she thinks having the camp moved to a nice, familiar, *containable* location like the New York College campus, as opposed to the woods—let's face it, Tania is *not* a country girl—will be more comfortable for her."

I'm not sure how any of this makes sense, especially considering that Bear was shot in the city not more than twenty blocks from the New York College campus.

"Tania's barely in her second trimester," I say. "It seems a little extreme for her to be sticking so close to her doctor. When she visited her ob-gyn, like the EMTs told her to, she didn't get a health scare or anything?"

Maybe I'm projecting again, because of my own health scare. Not that I got a scare. I have nothing to be *scared* about. Not even anything to be concerned about. Just—

"No," Stephanie says, glancing at Dr. Jessup and Muffy with a laugh. Is it my imagination, or does her laugh sound nervous? "She's in perfect health, except for being a little anemic, which you already know about. Do you think we'd let her go on filming if she wasn't?"

Yes, I want to say. Instead, I say only, "Of course not. I want to make sure there's nothing . . . well, nothing you aren't telling us."

"What on earth would I not be telling you?" Stephanie asks.

"I don't know," I say, truthfully. "But I do know that my staff has been through a lot this year, and the last thing they need is any more"—I realize I have to choose my next words carefully—"drama. So if there *is* something going on with Tania that you're not telling us, I wish you'd do so now."

"Drama?" Stephanie's smile is brittle. "You don't need to worry, Heather. Because I can assure you, what we'll be filming here in your building won't be a *drama*. It will be pure, unscripted reality."

The problem, of course, is that I know Jordan too well to find any comfort in that assurance. His reality has never been anything *but* drama. And it's hard to shake the feeling— especially given what I know about her—that Tania's isn't any different.

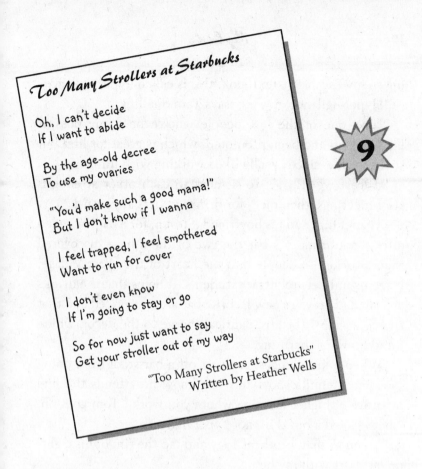

Too Many Strollers at Starbucks

Oh, I can't decide
If I want to abide

By the age-old decree
To use my ovaries

"You'd make such a good mama!"
But I don't know if I wanna

I feel trapped, I feel smothered
Want to run for cover

I don't even know
If I'm going to stay or go

So for now just want to say
Get your stroller out of my way

"Too Many Strollers at Starbucks"
Written by Heather Wells

It's getting harder and harder to find a bar to hang out in after work. All the good ones have either closed, owing to the soaring rents in downtown Manhattan, or been taken over by students, although of course this isn't as big an issue in the summertime.

I don't have a problem frequenting places popular with people younger than I am, but lately I have a hard time drinking comfortably around New York College students. According to my Psych 101 textbook, this is called hypervigilance.

"Hypervigilance, my ass," says Tom Snelling.

Tom's one of the few people who've been my boss at Fischer Hall and been promoted, which is great for him but sucks for me, since I really liked working with him.

At least we still get to sit next to each other at endless staff meetings, then meet for drinks in bars afterward.

I've met him and his boyfriend, Steven, for a badly needed after-work drink in a bar the two of them have discovered that is tucked so deeply into the heart of the West Village, it seems unlikely to attract students. It helps that the drinks at Tom and Steven's new favorite bar are overpriced and that there's a slightly bizarre nautical theme to the decor, which I find quirkily charming.

"When a kid plunges face-first off a bar stool from doing too many tequila shots and you know he attends the fine institute of higher learning where you work," Tom goes on, "that's called a buzzkill, not hypervigilance."

"Amen to that, brother," I say and tap the rim of his eight-dollar draft with my own.

We're sitting at a booth—built to resemble a ship's galley—in the front window of the bar. Outside, people are hurrying home from the office, their heads bowed over their cell phones as they make their own after-work plans, some nearly crashing into one another or the many trees that line the still sunlit street in their eagerness to send off their texts. There are dogs of every variety at the ends of leashes, ceaselessly lifting their legs against the trunks of the trees, though little signs beg their masters to curb them.

I'd feel guilty about not having rushed home to walk my

own dog, but ever since Cooper installed a pet door, I know Lucy can get out into the brownstone's backyard if she needs to. Not as good as a walk, but according to a text I received prior to leaving my own office, Cooper took her out earlier, before he had to attend some mysterious meeting.

This isn't unusual. Cooper rarely talks about his work. As a private investigator, he's very sensitive to the *private* part of his clients' investigative needs. I've always admired this about him, even though as the person who sorts, organizes, files, and mails his clients' bills, I'm aware of a lot of what he does. I think he doesn't like talking about it because many of his cases are bitter divorce disputes in which he has been hired to acquire photographic proof of the soon-to-be ex-spouse's marital infidelities, and he's afraid my delicate feminine sensibilities will be offended.

We all have our little secrets. It's nice to know there are people who'll keep them.

"Although it's a lot more than a buzzkill when it's a fourteen-year-old girl," I continue to complain to Tom and Steven, "and she's been set loose on the city while attending Tania Trace Rock Camp, which is in the building where you work and, P.S., is being filmed by a reality show television crew for the new television network your boyfriend's parents own."

"Christ," says Tom. "There's no word for that."

"Well, that's what I'm going to be dealing with for the next two weeks."

"Steven and I will pray for you," Tom says, and like the altar boy he used to be before he came out of the closet (his mother now says she always knew he was gay and that she doesn't care so long as he and Steven adopt one of those adorable Chinese babies like that gay couple did on that funny TV show), he makes the sign of the cross over me with his beer glass.

"So how did your staff take the news?" Steven wants to know. "Are they looking at it as their God-given chance to bang Tania Trace? Because that's all I'm hearing from my boys." Steven is the New York College basketball coach. "They think because they live in the building, they may actually have a chance at her."

"I highly doubt they're going to be able to get anywhere near her," I say. "She's got bodyguards. Or she will have, once they hire someone to replace the one who got shot. And they do realize she's married and pregnant, right? Not that married pregnant ladies can't still be incredibly sexy, but to a teenage boy—"

Steven rolls his eyes. "Please. She's female. To some of those guys, that's all that matters. They'd bang a tree if it was female."

I bite my lip nervously. "Well, they better not be planning on banging the campers," I say. "They're underage."

"I'll remind them," Steven says. "But I highly doubt they'll be interested in some sixteen-year-old from Kansas when Tania Trace is around, pregnant or not. What about your staff?"

"I wouldn't know," I say. "Their schedules are so insane, I hardly ever see them." Unless, of course, I've given them money for pizza. "I sent them a mass text. Of the replies I got, three were smiley-face emoticons, four were nothing but exclamation points, and one, from Gavin—of course—

was a long diatribe against the evils of reality television as opposed to the scripted drama and how auteurs like himself are going to suffer because of it. Like I can do something to change the nature of the show."

It had become more and more apparent to me as the day wore on and I got to know more people involved with the shooting of *Jordan Loves Tania* that no one was going to listen to my opinion about anything.

As I gave Stephanie Brewer and another of the show's producers—how many producers did one show need anyway?—a tour of the building, I began to realize how little of "reality television" is actually "reality." Stephanie and the other producer, a tall, lanky guy named Jared Greenberg, were already determining what would be shot where (very little outside the rooms where the girls would live, they decided once they saw Fischer Hall's common areas, which were "all wrong").

"*God-awful*" was how Jared described the cafeteria when I took them in there.

Once a ballroom, the caf still had what *I* considered to be a certain elegance, with a large chandelier (admittedly not so elegantly lit by fluorescent bulbs) hanging from a skylit rotunda in the center of its twenty-foot ceiling, a rotunda that, okay, yes, had lost some of its Belle Epoque luster, not just from the weather over the decades but from a body landing on it in the past year.

"It's being renovated," I explained defensively as I saw them taking in the white sheets of plastic covering all the piled-up tables and chairs and heard Stephanie's scream at the audible scurrying that occurred when I flicked on the lights.

Tom and Steven have a good laugh over this story—the fancy TV producers screaming over a few little mice.

But as we sit in the nice, nearly empty bar with our overpriced beers, the late afternoon sun pouring in through the plate-glass windows, I can't help wondering a little sadly if *we* are the oddballs, not the producers. Doesn't everyone find mice a little scary? What does it say about us that we do not?

I guess it says that some of us have encountered much scarier things than mice—things I didn't mention to the crew of *Jordan Loves Tania* as they tried to figure out if they could use the Fischer Hall cafeteria for their show.

"If we bring in our own tables and chairs—maybe some really funky ones from that design place we used for *Rock the Kasbah*, remember, Steph?—and shoot only in this corner," Jared Greenberg said, "I think we could make it work."

Stephanie shuddered. "I wouldn't eat here if you paid me."

"Well, you won't have to." Jared's tone was withering. "The girls will. We'll order in, and charge it to the network, of course."

I was a little insulted. It's true that New York College uses the same food-service company as the New York State prison system, but it also services many of the hotel chains and theme parks in this country.

And Julio, the head of Housekeeping, had done a very good job of getting the remains off the outside of the skylight. I'd never known before starting this job—and there was no reason to tell the crew of *Jordan Loves Tania*—but it isn't the responsibility of rescue services to clean the bodily fluids of a corpse from the sidewalk, floor, window, or roof that it lands on. The coroner takes only the body. Anything else that's leaked out is the responsibility of building management.

That's something I'd learned assistant-directing Fischer Hall. It's why I've resolved that if I ever have to kill myself (because I've found out I have a painful life-threatening disease for which there is no cure, or the apes have suddenly acquired superintelligence and are about to take over the planet and enslave humankind), I'll make sure to do it in a bathtub or shower or somewhere else that promotes easy cleanup. Otherwise, it will be up to my landlord or some poor maid or janitor (or, God forbid, my family members) to *literally* have to clean up my shit. That isn't fair (or the way I want to be remembered).

My cell phone vibrates. I pick it up.

"Oh, wait, hold on, here's another text from my staff now," I say. "Brad thinks this is his big chance to, and I quote, 'Tap Jordan Cartwright.' "

"I'd tap that too," Tom admits with a gusty sigh. Then, when Steven elbows him, he remembers himself, sucks in his breath, and looks guiltily at me. "Oh God, Heather. Sorry. I forgot."

I shrug. "It's okay. I like to think it's because I'm so down to earth and normal now, everyone forgets that I too was once part of the Cartwright family freak show. I take it as a compliment." My cell hums again. "Oh good. Cooper's on his way over," I say after reading the text that appears on the screen. "Whatever that meeting was that he had, it appears to have agitated him. He's neglected to use any capital letters or punctuation."

"It would seem," Tom says, with a glance at Steven, "that you're still part of the Cartwright family freak show."

I'm distracted, texting Cooper back. "What do you mean? Because of this Tania Trace thing?"

"Because you're so obviously with Cooper now, you dumb slut," Tom says. "Dumb slut" is a term of endearment to Tom, the way Magda, in the cafeteria, calls the students her movie stars. "Did you think we were never going to notice? You can try to pretend you two are just friends, but—"

"Your eyes do kind of light up when you mention him," Steven says, "and it's obvious from the way he looks at you that he's in love with you."

"Is it?" I ask, delighted in spite of the fact that we were trying to keep our relationship a secret and I already know Cooper is in love with me since he's said so himself, multiple times.

"Not to mention you two have been attached at the hip all summer," Tom complains. "When we asked you to come see the latest Reese Witherspoon rom-com with us and you dragged the poor man along—"

"He likes comedies," I say in Cooper's defense. *Golden Girls* is one of his favorite TV shows . . . although in some ways I think he watches it more as cheap therapy than as a comedy.

"I get why you're keeping it on the down low," Tom says, as if I hadn't spoken. "It'd be awkward in any circumstances, dating your ex's big brother, but it's got to be especially bad in this case, given the Cartwright family freak-show factor. Still, you're all grown-ups. I expect everyone should be able to handle it."

"I don't know about that," I say, thinking back to the way

Jordan had reacted at the Allingtons' when a relationship between his brother and me had been suggested. Not good.

I still haven't been able to shake the image of Tania the last time I saw her, huddled on President Allington's couch, looking so lost and alone . . . all except for her dog, which she'd been clutching as if it were the only creature in the world she could trust. Shouldn't that have been *Jordan?* Something seems a little off in that relationship.

Well, I'm sure when the baby comes, Jordan and Tania will be so caught up in their blissful happiness, they won't even notice anything else going on around them. Cooper and I will be able to run off and get married, and it will all be water under the bridge . . . until, of course, everyone starts asking when *we're* going to have kids.

"Have you told Cooper the news yet?" Steve asks.

"About my endometriosis?" I widen my eyes at him. "God no." How did Steven even know about that? I haven't told a soul.

Then I realize, even before Tom reacts, that of course Steven wasn't referring to that. "I mean—"

"I think Steve meant about Cooper's brother's show being shot at your place of work," Tom says, his eyebrows raised. "But if you'd prefer to give us an update on the status of your vagina, by all means, go ahead."

Steven puts his beer glass down with a thump, causing its contents to slosh over the sides. "*Really?*" he says to his boyfriend.

Tom looks innocent. "She brought it up, not me," he says. "So, Heather, is there something you want to tell us about your vagina?"

"I think you mean her uterus," Steven says.

"*No*," I say firmly, feeling my cheeks begin to heat up. "There's nothing I want to tell you about my uterus. I'm sorry, I was thinking about something else. I've had some things on my mind lately . . ." I shake my head. "Never mind. I clearly need more female friends."

"It must be difficult," Steven sympathizes, "with Magda transferred to the Pansy, and Patty gone."

My best friend Patty is married to a well-known musician, Frank Robillard. Though we speak and e-mail often, I don't want to burden her with my problems, which seem petty compared to hers, given that she's traveling on a multination world tour with her husband, their small child, the baby they have on the way, and her husband's band, a bunch of musicians who not only act like children but often need supervision. I mainly forward Patty videos of funny things I've seen on the Internet so she can have a gentle laugh at the end of a long day.

"I'm fine," I say. "Don't worry about me. I'm going to be swimming in estrogen in a couple of days, once Lisa moves in, not to mention the girls from Tania's camp—"

Lisa Wu had said her family, who live in Staten Island, would be helping her and her fiancé, Cory, who works for an investment company, move in over the weekend. The residence hall director position, unlike my own, is live-in, so that the director can be on hand for any emergency that occurs after hours. The director's apartment in Fischer Hall is a stunning corner suite on the sixteenth floor, with views of the Hudson River, the West Village, and SoHo. Not knowing when it would next be occupied or by whom after the loss of our last director, the building facilities staff has worked at keeping it move-in ready at all times. Julio and his nephew Manuel restored the parquet floor until it shone a rich mahogany brown, and Carl, the building engineer, painted the walls in the living room a feminine powder blue and the bedroom, kitchen, and bath a soft eggshell white.

Their efforts had paid off: the second Lisa stepped into the apartment she gasped with delight.

"Cory's going to shit his pants," she said, to my surprise and, by the look on his face, Dr. Jessup's.

"Are you sure Cory's a guy?" Tom asks when I relate this story at the bar. "Maybe it's a lesbian wedding. That would be awesome. We need more lesbians on staff. Too bad Sarah's not a—"

"Tom," Steven says in a warning tone.

"I'm just saying," Tom says. "She could do so much better than Sebastian."

Steven nods in agreement. It takes a lot to get him to say anything bad about anyone. "He's a bit of a—"

"*Dick?*" Cooper slides into our booth.

"*Cooper.*" I'm shocked. I hadn't noticed him walk in, which is unusual. Normally when he enters any room, my gaze is drawn to him first thing. I don't think it's because I'm in love with him. He simply exudes something. Not masculinity exactly, because he isn't a bodybuilder or anything like that, and he isn't always the tallest or fittest man in the room. My Psych 101 professor would probably call it pheromones.

But since it's actually part of Cooper's job to be unobtrusive when he needs to be, he can sneak up on people, which is what he's done now, startling all three of us.

"Dick," he says again, and points to the name on the drink menu in front of us. His dark eyebrows are raised skeptically. "Really? A gay bar named Dick? Couldn't they have thought of something a little more subtle?"

Tom has collapsed into giggles across the table, but Steven is clutching the menu and pointing at the tiny line beneath the word "Dick."

"*Moby*-Dick," Steven says. "As in Herman Melville's greatest novel. That's why there are spear guns and fishing nets on the walls. This is a Herman Melville tribute bar."

Cooper isn't having any of it.

"Sure it is," he says. He glances at the bored-looking waiter who's wandered toward our table. "I'll take a—Christ, look at these prices. Whatever you have on draft. And a shot of Glenfiddich." Cooper turns to me. "You'll never guess who I spent my afternoon with."

I'm startled. He's actually going to share something about his work?

"The fact that you just ordered a shot tells me a little something," I say. "You're not much of a drinker, except under certain conditions. Were you with your family?"

His frown is all the answer I need.

"But," I say in surprise, "you said you had a meeting—"

"I did," he says. "I *did* have a meeting. The woman who made the appointment said it was with a Mr. Grant, and gave an address I didn't realize until I got there was the new office for Cartwright Records Television. Obviously I was suspicious at that point, but it wasn't until I walked in and saw Grant Cartwright standing behind the desk that I knew what was going on."

I wince, picturing it. "That must have been . . . unpleasant."

"It was." He looks across the table at Tom and Steven. "Hi," he says, as if seeing them for the first time, though they'd already had the conversation about the name of the place. "How you guys doing?"

"Better than you, evidently," Tom says.

"Grant Cartwright," Steven says, apparently attempting to clarify. "CEO of Cartwright Records, and . . . your father?"

"Correct," Cooper says, the word almost a growl.

"What did he want?" I ask curiously. Cooper dislikes his family so much and speaks to them so rarely, I'm not surprised his father had to stoop to subterfuge to get him to have a conversation with him.

"To offer me a job," Cooper says.

I *am* surprised to hear this. The last time Grant Cartwright offered Cooper a job, it was to sing in Easy Street. The offer had gone so poorly that the rift that started then had continued to this day.

"What kind of job?" I ask him. I have a sinking feeling, however, that I know.

Cooper's drinks arrive, and the way he downs most of the whiskey, then half the beer, as Tom and Steven and I watch, confirms my suspicions. Cooper's family is the one thing that never fails to discombobulate him. Well, that and a few other things, but those are private, between him and me, and I'm pretty sure he enjoys them.

"Feel better?" Tom asks Cooper when he slams down the shot glass.

"Not really," Cooper says, and signals the waiter for another shot.

"A full-time job?" I ask him. "Like with his company? Or a private inquiry?"

"Oh," he says. "It'll be full-time all right."

I swallow. "Does it have anything to do with Tania Trace Rock Camp being moved into Fischer Hall?" I ask, dreading the answer but at the same time almost certain I know what it is.

"As a matter of fact," Cooper says, "it does. My dad wants me to be Tania's new bodyguard."

I laugh. I don't know why. It's so absurd. Not the idea of Cooper being someone's bodyguard—I'm positive he'd be superb in that capacity. Just the idea of him being *Tania Trace's* bodyguard, because Tania Trace is married to my ex-boyfriend, whom she stole from me. And now I'm engaged to that boyfriend's brother.

I look at Tom and Steven, and they begin to laugh too. We're all laughing at the idea of Cooper being Tania Trace's bodyguard.

But when I glance at Cooper, I see that he's frowning. He doesn't seem to think the idea is funny at all.

"Wait," I say, the laughter dying in my throat. "You didn't say yes, did you?"

"Actually," Cooper says as his second whiskey arrives, "I did."

Thank You

I gave you my heart
Thought you were all there could be
Instead you left me for her,
Said she was better than me

But I thank you now
For setting me free
I said thank you now
For choosing her over me

'Cause the man I have now
Is the best I've ever known
The love I have now is
The kind you'll never know

You were awful in bed
Just thought you should know
So thanks for dumping me
'Cause otherwise I'd never have known

So I thank you now
For setting me free
I said thank you now
So please stop Facebooking me

"Thank You"
Written by Heather Wells

A few hours later, Cooper rolls away from me to lie panting on his back in my bed, beneath the watchful—yet to my mind, comforting—gazes of the dolls of many nations.

"Feel better?" I ask him. After getting home from the bar, I offered to give him some deep tissue massage therapy. I felt it was the least I could do to help him get over his stressful day.

"I've never had a massage quite like that," he says.

"I don't have any professional training in the art of massage," I admit.

"I don't mind," he says. "But I'm a little worried about what they must be thinking of us." He nods at the dolls.

Miss Mexico is the fanciest, in her hot-pink flamenco dress and elaborate pointy hair comb. Miss Ireland is the one for whom I feel worst. She's made of cloth, and her legs, beneath her red skirt covered in green four-leaf clovers, are made out of black pipe cleaners. My mom apparently grabbed the first doll she saw on her way to the plane. I always treat Miss Ireland with extra care, fearful Miss Mexico's fanciness might have given her a complex over the years.

"Oh," I say, "they're extremely nonjudgmental."

"That's good," he says and rolls over to reach for the water glass on the nightstand next to his side of the bed—after a workout like the one I've given him, hydrating is both necessary and advisable—only to find Owen, the orange tabby cat, perched there, watching him.

"Jesus Christ," he says, startled, as Owen blinks at him. "We might as well get cameras in here and put on our own reality show."

"I told you we could go to your place," I say, holding out my index finger so Owen will move from the nightstand to the bed. An outstretched index finger is, as any cat person knows, irresistible to most cats, as they cannot help but move toward one to rub their face against it. Owen is no exception, and Cooper is able to reach the water glass as Owen leaps from the nightstand to the bed. "Then we wouldn't have an audience."

"No," Cooper says after swallowing down half the contents of the glass. "I like your place better."

He doesn't need to explain. His place—one floor of the brownstone below mine—is bigger, but it's also been Cooperized, with curtains that don't close all the way (particularly in the bedroom), books and papers piled on nearly every surface, and at least five pairs of shoes left in the middle of the floor in every room because, as he explains, "that way I know I can find them." I personally don't understand why anyone needs to have seven bottles of nearly empty conditioner in the shower, and clearly Cooper doesn't either since he spends nearly all his time on my floor, leaving it only to use his admittedly fantastic kitchen, his office, and his bedroom to change clothes. Even the animals prefer my place, except when we're in the kitchen downstairs. My floor only has a kitchenette.

One thing for which I've been campaigning is a housekeeper, especially since Magda has a cousin who runs a cleaning service. Although Cooper is horrified at the idea—he grew up on the Cartwright compound, split between Westchester and a huge penthouse apartment in Manhattan, with a full-time staff of nannies, maids, cooks, and chauffeurs, and so as an adult is determined to do his own dishes and laundry—it's a battle I'm equally determined to win. There's no reason two busy working people—one of whom is also in school—shouldn't pool their money to pay a third person who is in the business of cleaning homes to come to theirs to do so. It's practically unpatriotic, as a matter of fact, for them not to do so, especially in this economy. We're depriving someone of badly needed work.

I've *almost* got Cooper believing in this argument.

"So," I say to him, now that we're both feeling more relaxed and the cat has made a neat little ball of himself between us. Lucy, in her own doggie bed on the floor, is snoring softly. "I know you didn't want to talk about it in front of Tom and Steven. But don't you think in this particular case client-detective privilege should extend to me?"

Except for telling us that he'd taken the assignment his father had offered, Cooper had refused to elaborate further on what had happened in the offices of Cartwright Records Television. At the bar, he'd just ordered another beer, then wolfed down a plate of fish and chips, fried oysters, and half the contents of the basket of mozzarella sticks I'd ordered for the table. (Though mozzarella sticks are basically my favorite thing, I didn't object too much. I had a pizza Margherita with which to console myself.)

"In this particular case, the client is going to be my sister-in-law," I go on, "and working in my building. So I really think I should be let in on what's going on."

"Why do you think I took the case?" Cooper asks, lifting an arm so I can snuggle closer.

I'm perplexed. "Your dad offered you a million dollars?" I offer hopefully. With that kind of money, we could get weekly housekeeping, and also all the brownstone's walls painted, get new window treatments, the windows cleaned—they need it badly—and re-do all the bathrooms, not to mention maybe put in a hot tub in the backyard.

"Not quite that much," he says with a chuckle. "Although I did give my father a quote that's triple my normal rate, and he didn't even blink an eye. If I'm going to have to be spending all my time with Tania, I'm going to need to be amply compensated for it."

"Yes," I say, running a finger along his arm, all the way down to the complicated watch I've never seen him remove. "How much time exactly *are* you going to have to be spending with Tania?"

"Every minute she's at Fischer Hall," he says. "Once they've got her tucked into her Maybach and headed back up to Park Avenue, I'm off duty. That's the deal I made with my dad. I'm only interested in protecting Tania during the hours her presence might be putting your life in jeopardy—though I didn't tell him so, of course. They'll have to find alternative security the rest of the time."

"Wait." I lift my head from his shoulder and stare into his face. "*What?* How is Tania's presence putting my life in jeopardy? Or anyone's? I thought that bullet that hit her bodyguard was random—"

His smile is grim. "If everyone still believes that shot was random, why the sudden move to film the show at New York College? Do you have any idea how much it must be costing CRT to move location from that resort, which they had to have paid millions to secure?"

Now I'm sitting up, holding my—admittedly way too expensive, but I did get them significantly marked down at T.J.Maxx—dark purple Calvin Klein sheets to my chest. Cooper's chest is protected by a fine mat of dark hair. I'm not that wild about hairless chests—Jordan used to wax his in order to appear nonthreatening to his fans, primarily tween girls.

"They're furnishing all the rooms," I say, "and paying to have the cafeteria restaffed and set up over the next couple of days. That can't be cheap."

"Granted, the college is probably letting them have the space for nothing," Cooper says. "The promotion for the school alone will be worth it—"

"*If* the show casts the school in a positive light," I murmur, thinking about the horrible things Stephanie Brewer suggested, about how we could let the girls sneak out, chaperoneless, into the city to create "drama."

"It does make one wonder," Cooper says. He shrugs, seemingly done with the subject, and reaches for the remote. "Oh well. What sadly morbid glimpses into the lives of the less fortunate have you got recorded for us tonight?"

He might be done with the subject, but I most definitely am not.

"Hold on," I say. I can't help remembering that look I'd seen on Jordan's face in the Allingtons' penthouse. There'd been something he'd wanted to say, something he might have been too frightened to say. "What's Tania so afraid of? Did you ask? Has she had any actual threats?"

He sighs and lowers the remote. "My dad swears up and down that she hasn't and that she's fine . . . maybe a little shaken up from what happened in front of Christopher's club. Because we handled the crisis she had while she was at Fischer Hall last week so competently—"

I can't help snorting. "Stephanie Brewer fed me almost the exact same line," I say.

"Well," Cooper says, "it could be true, you know. With her

longtime bodyguard—Bear's worked for her for two years—down for now, Tania might truly want people around her who she thinks she can trust, especially when she's in such a delicate state."

"Delicate state? The girl is having a baby. People have been having babies for thousands of years, often in the middle of fields with no painkillers, while running from woolly mammoths."

Cooper raises an eyebrow at me. "Are you all right?" he asks.

"Yes," I say. "Of course I'm all right."

I realize I need to cool it a little. Tania may have stolen one Cartwright brother away from me, and now, by getting herself pregnant by him, is using that "delicate state" as an excuse to hire a second Cartwright brother to "protect" her—or at least her father-in-law is.

But that doesn't mean she's going to steal Cooper away from me, first, because Cooper is in love with me, and second, because she's married now and having a child. And third, because if she lays so much as a finger on Cooper, I will break it off. Unlike when I found her messing around with Jordan, I will actually fight for Cooper, as the love I have for Cooper is a dazzling supernova, whereas the love I had for Jordan was a wet sparkler no one could light on a soggy Fourth of July.

"Pass me that water glass, will you?" I say to Cooper. I figure I could probably use some hydration too. Cooper is no slouch in the therapeutic massage department either, and Patty has a theory that 50 percent of life's ills can be solved simply by stopping and drinking a glass of water.

"Look," I say after I've downed the remains of the glass's contents. Better. "You do realize it's actually kind of unlikely that at Tania's level of fame she wouldn't have any stalkers. How many Facebook fans did Stephanie say she has, like twenty million or something? I'm sorry, but even back in my day, before social networking was at its current height and at my much, much lower level of success, I had a few wackos who wanted me to be their teen bride."

Cooper raises both eyebrows. "I thought I got that restraining order against me lifted. How'd you find out about it?"

I'm in no mood to joke. "I know if this has occurred to me, it's occurred to you. Why is everyone so adamant that there isn't anyone in the world who'd want to hurt Tania? It's obvious CRT takes her security seriously."

Cooper looks uncomfortable. "As I'm sure you remember from your days onstage, fans can express as much admiration as they want—even propose marriage—but it's not considered stalking or even a threat until they say something that suggests violent intent. I talked to Bear and to my father, and as far as either of them knows, Tania's received no threats of a violent nature. All her fans are of the overly ardent kind."

"No one at Cartwright Records would be likely to admit it if she *had* been getting serious threats," I say, "because if she had and New York College got wind of it, they wouldn't let her come film her show on campus. They wouldn't want to risk the possible lawsuits if any students were endangered . . ." My voice trails off, and I look at him, wide-eyed. "Unless," I say, "they decided to let them film in a building that's empty for the summer. A building that Christopher Allington tipped them off has a reputation that couldn't possibly get any worse, regardless of what happens."

Cooper looks at me steadily with those calm gray-blue eyes of his. "That's one theory," he says, in a voice that is suspiciously neutral, "I suppose."

"My God." My heart feels as if it's turned to gelato in my chest. "That's it, isn't it? *That's* why you took the job. You don't think that was a random shooting at all. That's why you went and talked to Bear. You think there *is* a serious threat, and CRT is hiding it, but going ahead with filming anyway, because they're in too deep financially to get out of it now. Cartwright Records isn't doing very well, is it?"

"I already told you," Cooper says, taking the empty water glass from my suddenly limp fingers and setting it back on the nightstand. "That isn't why I took the job. The fact that they moved the filming of *Jordan Loves Tania* to your place of work means that, whatever is going on with my brother's wife, I have an obligation to make sure my own bride-to-be remains in one piece. And that's what I plan on doing. You do have something of a reputation, Heather, for attracting people with homicidal tendencies."

His tone is light, but I've known him long enough to tell he's deadly serious.

"What about Tania?" I ask him. "Why would anyone want to kill *her*?" Besides myself, I can't think of anyone who'd hate Tania Trace enough to murder her. Even *I* don't hate her that much—at least not anymore—and I have more reason than anyone.

"We don't know for certain that someone does," he reminds me.

"Your dad doesn't approve of what you do for a living, and

yet he went to all the trouble of setting up a fake meeting so he could hire you—"

"Because Tania specifically asked for me, remember? Anyway, we'll find out soon enough whether or not it's true."

My heart freezes up again, remembering what happened to Tania's last bodyguard. "Oh God, Cooper," I say. "Promise me you won't do anything brave. Don't throw yourself in the path of any bullets for her. I realize she's carrying your unborn niece, but—"

He looks at me like I'm crazy.

"I'm a detective, Heather," he says, "not Secret Service. I meant I'll find out soon enough when I begin using my investigative skills. I'm going to *ask* Tania if there's someone who might have reason to want her dead."

"Oh," I say, biting my lip. "Of course. Do you think she'll tell you?"

"Tania's never struck me as the sharpest knife in the drawer," he says, "but my dad said that she basically demanded that the show be transferred to your building or she'd quit, which tells me something about her."

I snort. "Yeah," I say, thinking of the cafeteria's dismal appearance, "that she secretly enjoys slumming it."

"No," Cooper says, reaching out to stroke a strand of my hair. "It tells me that, despite the fact that she married my brother, she's got the good sense to know when she's found someone she can trust."

I shake my head, refusing to believe it. "You mean *me*? Oh no, you've got it all wrong. It must have been you. *You're* the one she asked to be her bodyguard. She and I have barely exchanged two words since—"

"I don't think Tania has a lot of people in her life she feels close to. Did you see the way she was kissing that dog?"

I nod, remembering the image with a pang. I'm not surprised Cooper noticed it as well.

"I guess a part of me felt a little sorry for her," I confess. "And I've never actually thought she was dumb. People like to think pretty girls who run around in short skirts carrying tiny dogs can't be intelligent, but unless they've inherited their money, they usually don't get to where they are on looks alone. Tania's incredibly talented. She's got the same octave range as an opera singer, for instance."

"Excuse me?"

I frown at him. "How could you grow up in the Cartwright Records household and not know what that means?"

"You know I purposefully blocked out all music-related discussions growing up. I had to, or I'd have ended up prancing around on stage in a pair of leather pants like Jordan."

I smile at him. "Simply put, the span from the lowest to the highest notes Tania's voice can produce without straining is about three octaves—that's really rare. All that stuff about Mariah Carey and Céline Dion hitting five octaves is crap. I mean, they can hit the notes, but not without straining. They have about the same range as Tania. Even though the songs Tania chooses to sing aren't the best, she's got a really great voice. I don't know how she has the lung capacity to do it with that tiny body, especially since she was never classically trained, but she has a vocal range that's practically operatic, way broader than mine ever was, even when I was taking regular voice lessons and at the top of my form. Not many people realize this, but to hit the notes that she can, as consistently as she does, in a live performance, night after night, she actually has to be really, really talented and really, really dedicated to her craft."

Cooper reaches out and pulls me down against him, disturbing Owen, who gives us a dirty look and stalks to the far end of the bed where he won't be jostled.

"I don't know," Cooper says as my hair tumbles across his chest. "I heard you belting out something this morning in the bathroom and you sounded really, really talented to me."

"That was ABBA," I say with a sniff. "Everyone sounds good singing ABBA, especially in the bathroom. Why do you think they're so popular?"

He lifts the sheet to peer beneath it. "You look at the top of your form to me," he says. "As a licensed investigator, I suppose I better check to make sure."

Before I could stop him, he did. Though truthfully, I didn't try that hard.

Welcome to Check-In Day at Your New York College Residence Hall!

To help make the check-in process a little easier, follow these three simple steps:

Stop

Stop your car where directed by the New York College campus protection officer. He or she will direct you to an area where it is safe to—

Drop

Unload your belongings. Remember, this area may not be a legal parking space. Please do not leave your vehicle unattended, as it may be ticketed and/or towed. Note: Never leave personal items unattended on the sidewalk, as they may be stolen.

Sign

Proceed to the front desk, then sign your registration card to receive the key to your new room at New York College!

— Stop — Drop — Sign —

What could be easier?

Check-in day for Tania Trace Rock Camp doesn't start like one during which you might expect to witness a homicide, even if you work in a place referred to by many as Death Dorm. Besides, I'd been so busy during the few days preceding it, I completely forgot there might be someone—besides me—who wanted Tania dead.

This proves to be a fatal mistake.

But I don't know this when I step outside into the backyard to check the temperature after waking up. Instead, I find that it's one of those rare perfect summer days when people can lie out and work on their tans without sweating (which is why my tan is mostly the result of tinted moisturizer—I hate sweating). There isn't a cloud in the sky, and the humidity is low. When I go back inside, I find I'm able to blow my hair out straight, and it stays that way for once.

I haven't seen much of Cooper over the past few days, not only because whatever he's been doing to prep for guarding Tania is taking up so much of his time, but also because I've been having to stay later and later at Fischer Hall every night. Miraculously, I've accomplished practically everything on my pre-check-in to-do list:

Made sure we have enough keys for each resident? (You would not believe the number of students who move out and forget to give back their key.) Check.

Gone over every detail about the assigned rooms, from the toilets (do they flush without flooding the room below?) to the window guards. (Does every window have one? Often residents remove the window guards so they can open the windows wider than the regulation two inches in order to stick their heads through the gap to smoke. In my experience, this only ends with bodies falling out of windows and hitting the skylight in the cafeteria.) Check.

Met with the housekeepers, building engineers, and resident assistants (thank goodness I hired one for every two basketball players—I've put them in charge of making cute name tags to stick on the front of each camper's door) to make sure everything is ready and nothing could possibly go wrong, including confiscating the not-so-secret stash of cigars that belongs to Carl, the chief engineer? (I'll return them to him by the end of the day.) Check.

Spoken with every single mail attendant, member of the paint crew, and security guard to ensure that, despite the presence of major celebrities in our midst, regular daily tasks like sorting and forwarding the mail and painting the rooms will continue as usual and every single visitor to the building, no matter how famous, will be required to leave photo ID and be signed in at the security desk? Check, check, and *check*.

Sure, I'm exhausted, because I've had to do all of this on my own, since Lisa Wu was still moving in and Sarah was continuing to work through whatever it is she's working through and was too grumpy to be helpful. One of the tasks on my to-do list was to find out what was wrong with Sarah. Sadly, I wasn't able to put a check next to this item.

"Sarah," I said to her the day before check-in, "do you want to take a break and go get a cup of coffee? Brad can cover the office while we're gone. I think we need to talk about . . . well . . . whatever it is that's been bugging you."

I suspected—but could not prove—that what was bugging Sarah was Sarah's boyfriend. For most of the summer, I hadn't been able to get Sebastian to leave the office, and technically he didn't even work there. He hung around all the time because he was so in love with Sarah.

Lately, however, the office has been a Sebastian-free zone. I've noticed a distinct lack of phone calls to Sebastian on Sarah's part, and whenever her cell phone rings, she viciously sends the call to voice mail. All is clearly not well in Sarah-and-Sebastian land.

When I asked if she wanted to talk about it, however, Sarah looked up from the supply request she was filling out on the computer and said angrily, "Not unless you want to tell me what's been bugging *you*."

I blinked back at her, surprised. "Nothing's bugging me. Well, aside from the fact that we have fifty teenage girls checking in here tomorrow and we're nowhere close to ready—"

"Really?" Sarah interrupted. "You don't have *anything* to tell me? Nothing at all going on in your life that might have been distracting you? So much so that you forgot to bring me back a Shack Attack from Shake Shack after your doctor's appointment last Monday even though you said you would because your doctor's office is right around the Madison Park Shake Shack and you can never resist a visit to Shake Shack? But evidently *something* stopped you from going, didn't it, or at least from remembering my Shack Attack. And you never even said you were sorry."

I stared at her, openmouthed. I'd been so stunned after my doctor's appointment, I hadn't even noticed the Shake Shack, which *was* odd, because the line snaked almost all the way through the park.

"Sarah," I said, "I'm so sorry. Your shake completely slipped my mind—"

"It's no big deal," Sarah said, with the kind of hostile shrug that indicated it was a very big deal indeed. "I realize I'm just someone you work with, not a friend with whom you might share confidences. And a Shack Attack is a frozen custard, not a shake, FYI."

"Sarah," I said, "of *course* you're my friend—"

"But not one with whom you share personal news," she said with a sniff. "Like you do with Muffy Fowler."

"Muffy Fowler?" What was she talking about? "I haven't shared any personal news with Muffy."

I hadn't even shared with Cooper the personal news I'd learned from that doctor's appointment. Not that it was anything to worry about.

"Oh really?" Sarah asked. "Then how come I overheard her and that Brewer woman talking about how you and Cooper are engaged? If you and I are such good friends, why am I the last to know you're getting married? You've never even told me you're officially going out. Although only a blind person wouldn't have noticed."

Stephanie. I should have known she wouldn't keep her mouth shut.

"Sarah," I said, "I'm sorry. Cooper and I are going out. But we've been trying to keep it on the down-low because it's complicated with his family, as you can probably imagine. I can assure you, we aren't engaged." I waved my hand at her. "See? No ring. It's true we've talked about marriage, but there's no date set." None of this was technically a lie. "And I'm surprised at you, listening to office gossip. Aren't you the one who once told me that gossip is a social weapon that's used more often to hurt than to help?"

Though I said all this with what I considered a teasing, humorous tone, Sarah only grew sulkier.

"Yes. But—"

"So what's really going on with you?" I asked. "Is it Sebastian? Because I've noticed he hasn't been around here much lately—"

Sarah ripped the supply request form from the printer and said, "I'm going to Central Supply to get more markers and construction paper. Thanks to all the floor decorations the RAs made, we're almost out," and barreled from the office, almost colliding with Lisa Wu, who was on her way *into* the office. Sarah didn't stop to apologize.

"What's with her?" Lisa asked as Sarah fled past, stifling a sob.

"She won't say. How are you?" I asked. I was kind of relieved for the interruption. "Almost moved in?"

"Getting there." Lisa, dressed in flip-flops, shorts, and one of her seemingly endless supply of T-shirts, was holding a tray of enormous iced coffee drinks in one hand and a leash in the other. At the end of the leash was a small brown and white dog. "I wanted to stop by and introduce you to the other man in my life, since this one'll probably be spending a lot of time with us in the office. This is Tricky. I call him Tricky because he knows a lot of tricks. Tricky, bang."

Tricky, a Jack Russell terrier, promptly fell over onto the office floor, pretending to be dead.

Charmed, I said, "He's adorable. I have a dog too. Her name is Lucy. But she doesn't know any—"

"Freeze," a voice called from the hallway. Startled, Lisa's dog leapt back to his feet.

It was only Jared Greenberg, *Jordan Loves Tania*'s "field producer." With him was the camera guy I remembered from the night of the Tania Incident, along with Marcos, the sound guy. The camera appeared to be on, since I could see a red light blinking on the side of it and the camera operator had the lens up to his face.

"Can you make him do that again?" Jared asked Lisa excitedly, pointing at Tricky.

"Uh," she said, looking panicky. I would too if I was sweaty from moving stuff all day and had on no makeup and cutoffs, and some big-time TV producer was trying to film me. "Not right now. I only came down to get these drinks for my parents—they're upstairs in my apartment, helping me unpack. Hafta be ready for tomorrow, right? Oh, there's the elevator, gotta go, bye."

She fled, scrambling with her dog to catch the elevator, the doors of which had opened with a ding.

Jared looked at me and said, a little mournfully, "We're not monsters, you know. We don't bite."

I shrugged. "It's nothing personal. None of us signed up to be on a TV show, that's all."

"You think any of *us* wants to be here?" Jared lowered himself into the visitor's chair next to my desk. I know the seat looks inviting, but I really wish people wouldn't sit there unless asked. How am I supposed to get any of my homework from Psych 101 (or actual work-work) done if someone is always sitting next to my desk, wanting to chat? "I went to this school, you know. I graduated from the film department. All of us did." He nodded at Marcos, who'd lowered the boom and whipped out his cell phone, and at the camera operator, who'd started zooming in on the candy jar on my desk, which I keep stocked with condoms instead of candy. I guessed he was filming it for practice. I was pretty sure they weren't going to use footage of a jar of condoms for *Jordan Loves Tania*. "Except Stephanie, of course. I suppose she told you about her MBA from Harvard."

I nodded. I wasn't sure what I'd done to encourage this idea Jared had that we were buddies. Maybe Cooper was right about my inspiring trust in people. Maybe I should consider a psych minor.

"*I* want to make documentaries," Jared said, stabbing his thumb at his own chest. "Important documentaries about people who are wrongfully convicted of crimes they did not commit. I want my films to help people, make a difference, you know? Maybe get someone's conviction overturned." I knew exactly what kind of films he was talking about. I'd seen them on HBO. "Can I get a single studio to fund *that* idea? No. But Stephanie got Cartwright Television to fund her piece of crap, no problem. You know what they're calling *Jordan Loves Tania*?"

I shook my head. "No . . ."

"A docu-reality series. Can you believe that?"

"Is that not what it is?" I asked.

"Wait until you see the final product," Jared said ominously.

"Why?" I asked.

"I'm guessing you're going to be amazed," he said, "at how little actual reality is in it."

Before I had a chance to ask what he meant, the camera guy lowered his lens.

"Let's go, Jare," he said. "I'm hungry. You promised you'd get the network to reimburse us for Ray's."

Jared sighed. "See?" he said, smiling. "See what I have to deal with?" He said good-bye, then left.

I suppose, given all that, I should have been expecting what occurs the morning the girls from Tania Trace Rock Camp check in. Instead, I'm blindsided.

It's hard to believe anything bad can happen on such a glorious summer day, especially when, on my way to work, my phone rings and I answer it to hear Cooper say: "I can't find my pants."

"And a good morning to you too, honey," I sing.

"I'm serious," he says. "Did you put them somewhere?"

"Where would I have put your pants?" I ask, all wide-eyed innocence.

"Like in the laundry basket or something?"

"Cooper," I say, with a laugh. "I value this relationship. I'm not doing your laundry anymore. I know how you are about your clothes. That time I *accidentally*—because despite what you seem to think, it *was* an accident—shrunk your Knicks T-shirt? I thought you were going to have an embolism. I told you, we need a skilled professional whom we *pay* to handle our household chores. And I know the perfect person, Magda's cousin, the one who—"

Cooper interrupts. "I was wearing them yesterday. They were right by the bed when I took them off last night."

"I remember," I say with a meaningful leer, which of course he can't see, since he's back home, pantless.

A man going through the garbage cans at the bottom of a nearby stoop does see my leer, however, and shouts an obscenity at me, somewhat spoiling the mood.

"Cooper, you're a private investigator," I say, turning the corner onto Washington Square West, leaving the homeless man and his desire for me to do something unspeakable to his private parts behind. "Shouldn't you be able to find your own pants?"

"Not when someone in my own home is deliberately hiding them from me," Cooper points out. I can't believe he's caught on to me. "Did someone just shout what I think they did at you?"

"I don't know what you're talking about," I reply. "And why would I do something as childish as hide your pants?"

"I don't know," Cooper says. "You're a complicated woman. But you're right. I didn't mean to accuse you. The thing is, I really need those pants today. I can't think where they could have disappeared to."

"You have plenty of other pants," I say. "Why do you have to wear the cargo pants? What about those nice flat-front khakis I got you? Or those jeans you had on the other day. You looked very sexy in those." I'm leering again. I can't help it.

"I *need* my cargo pants, Heather," Cooper says. "For work. I like to keep things in the pockets."

I don't understand this.

"Jeans have pockets too," I remind him, noticing there are quite a few cars parked outside Fischer Hall, which is un-usual for so early on a Saturday morning, especially since parking on Washington Square West is illegal.

"Not enough of them," Cooper says. "And they aren't deep enough."

"Deep enough for what? Next thing I know," I say lightly, "you're going to start wearing a fanny pack."

Cooper doesn't say anything.

In addition to the cars, I notice there is a larger than usual number of people milling around in front of Fischer Hall. They aren't students, because they're the wrong age and dressed much too nicely. I've gotten used to seeing groups of tourists being led around the Village by guides wearing funny hats and holding signs, but these people don't seem like tourists. There's no real cohesion to the group. Some of them are leaning against their cars, and others are standing together in small clusters, eyeing the front door to Fischer Hall suspiciously—almost with hostility.

Also, there's an unusually high number of thin young women, all very colorfully dressed, doing stretches and cart-wheels along the sidewalk. Tourists wouldn't do this, and neither would students. Maybe, I think with a spurt of excitement, there's going to be a flash mob.

Then, as I get closer, I realize the thin young women in the brightly colored clothes aren't young women at all, but girls, and the people leaning against the cars, fanning themselves impatiently in the heat that is starting to grow a little uncomfortable, are all women—most likely the girls' mothers—all waiting to check in for Tania Trace Rock Camp.

Except I'd been assured by Cartwright Records Television that check-in wasn't going to start until ten o'clock sharp, giving me, arriving at nine, an hour to make any necessary last-minute adjustments.

"*Shit,*" I say.

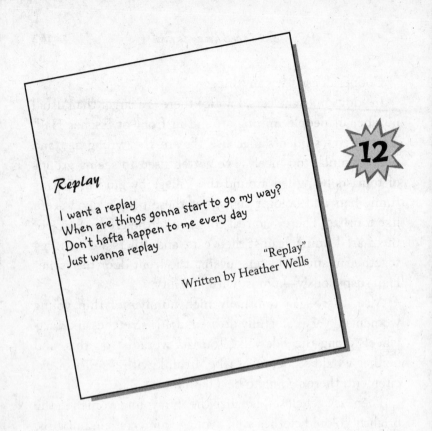

12

Replay

I want a replay
When are things gonna start to go my way?
Don't hafta happen to me every day
Just wanna replay

"Replay"
Written by Heather Wells

"What's wrong?" Cooper asks over the phone.

"All the campers are here an hour early."

I've noticed a couple of familiar-looking people leaning against the redbrick building, on one side of the front
door—namely Pete, in his New York College security guard
uniform, and Magda, dressed in her pink food service uniform. They're both holding cups of coffee. Magda, for some
reason, is holding two.

"Early bird gets the part, I guess," Cooper says.

"That's not a show business term," I say. "That doesn't even make any sense. They already got the parts." Then I realize Cooper never replied to my previous statement. "Wait a minute," I say into the phone. "You don't *own* a fanny pack, do you?"

"I have to go meet Tania now." Cooper's voice sounds funny. "She's coming later this afternoon to give the welcome speech. Give my regards to Broadway."

He hangs up. So do I, but not before squinting curiously down at the phone. Men are so weird.

"I think Cooper just admitted to me that he sometimes wears a fanny pack," I say as I walk up to Magda and Pete.

"Of course he does," Pete says. "Where else is he gonna keep his gun in the summertime?"

"Cooper doesn't own a gun," I say as Magda passes me a tall plastic refillable mug in New York College colors. "Thanks. What are *you* doing here? Not that I'm not overjoyed to see you, but—"

"You didn't hear?" Magda reaches up to pat her hair, which she's teased to stand nearly six inches from her head. Her nails have each been painted with a tiny letter. When I peer at them, I see they spell out H-O-L-L-Y-W-O-O-D! "The producer man came into the café last week to buy a latte, and he said he liked my style so much, he had to have me on the show."

"Of course he did," I say, sipping from the mug. My favorite, a café mocha. Delicious.

"He said they're reopening the cafeteria," Magda goes on. "Have you seen it? They fixed it up to look so byootiful!" Magda's voice, with its heavy Spanish accent, is so distinctive that several of the young girls stop doing their gymnastics and their mothers glance up from their cell phones, all looking curiously in our direction. Coming from the heart of the Midwest or wherever, it's possible they've never heard—or seen—anyone quite like Magda, except maybe on TV.

"Excuse me," one of the mothers says, hurrying toward us. She has on more necklaces than Mr. T used to wear back on those *A-Team* reruns, and enough makeup to make Magda look like she's going au naturel. "Are you someone in charge?"

Startled, I look around for Stephanie or Jared, but it's clear she's speaking to me. "Me? No, I just work here."

The woman doesn't seem to believe me. "You look so familiar," she says. "Weren't you at the Nashville callbacks?"

"I'm sorry," I say. "I have no idea what you're talking about."

"Lady, like I told you before," Pete says in a tired voice, "when the people with *Jordan Loves Tania* are ready for you, they'll come out and say so. In the meantime, you can't come in. You'll just have to wait like all the others—"

"I don't think you understand. We've been waiting here for an hour already," the woman says, annoyed. "My Cassidy is very special. The producer said so when she auditioned. And now she is starting to sweat." She points a perfectly manicured nail at a young girl dressed in a lime green tank top and black leggings who does indeed look a little sweaty, but probably because a minute before she was demonstrating how to do a handstand to some of the other girls, who were admiring her perfect form. "How is Cassidy going to look her best on camera when she is sweating?"

"I don't know," Pete says. "Maybe if you'd come when you were supposed to, which is at ten—"

"There are some coffee shops in the area where you could take your daughter to get her a soda or something to cool off while you wait," I hurry to offer, thinking Pete is being a little gruff. These people are from out of town, after all. They don't know about New Yorkers and their notorious brusqueness. "The Washington Square Diner is right around the corner—"

"Oh, everyone would like that," the woman steams, "wouldn't they, for my Cassidy to get addicted to soda and get so chubby that she looks like a blimp at the Rock Off? Well, it's *not going to happen.*"

I widen my eyes. I'm finding this lady as familiar as she seems to find me, but I can't quite put my finger on why that is.

"Tell me this," she says. "Are professional hair and makeup stylists going to be provided for the girls? Because I don't see a trailer parked anywhere nearby. Are they in a room inside?"

I'm so confused by this question, I can't speak. Fortunately, Magda takes over.

"No, ma'am," she says. "I already asked this, and they said only Tania Trace gets professional hair and makeup, because she's the star. The rest of us have to provide our own."

The woman looks so outraged, I half expect, when she reaches into her enormous designer tote, for her to pull out a weapon. Instead, she's simply diving for her cell phone. "We'll just see what Cassidy's agent has to say about this," she says and stalks away on her spindly high heels, the phone to her ear. "Girls," she calls to the other mothers, "you will never believe this."

I glance at Pete, my eyebrows raised. "And I thought the parents of the undergrads were bad," I say.

"You see?" he asks, calmly taking a sip of his coffee. "You see why I get paid the big bucks? This is what I've been putting up with all morning. That's Mrs. Upton, by the way, also known as Cassidy's mom."

I feel a sense of horror come over me. I did all of the Tania Trace Rock Camp room assignments myself, by hand, so I recognize the name instantly. "Oh God," I say. "Mrs. Upton's one of the chaperones. I assigned her and Cassidy to the room to Narnia."

"Nice one," Pete says with a big smile. "Better hope the deodorizers Manuel put in there work. I don't think she's the type to appreciate eau de ganja."

"This check-in is a disaster already," I say, dropping my face into my hand. "Why are they making them wait? Why aren't they letting them in?"

"Bunch of yukkity-yuks in there," Pete says, nodding toward the door behind us. "Everyone from the president on down wants to stop by and say hi and congrats while they're setting up. So back to the fanny pack. That's where a lot of off-duty cops keep their guns when they carry. That or in the pocket of their cargo pants."

This distracts me completely from my worries about Mrs. Upton and what she might say upon opening the door to room 1621. "Are you serious? Because I hid a pair of cargo pants Cooper's been insisting on wearing a lot lately—"

Pete looks disgusted. "What's wrong with you? You don't hide a man's pants. What's so bad about cargo pants anyway?"

"Everything," Magda says, her heavily made-up eyes rolling toward the sky.

"Seriously," I say. "They're *all* wrong in every way unless you're a forest ranger. And you're crazy. Cooper doesn't own a gun. He told me."

"Sure," Pete says calmly. "Of course he told you that, because he lives with you and you're a woman, the kind of woman who might get upset to learn that there's a gun in the house."

When I start to protest that this isn't true, he gives me a sarcastic look and I shut up. It's sort of true that I might get upset to learn that Cooper carries a gun, but only because he lied to me about it. And because he might shoot himself with it. Or get shot, drawing it on someone else.

"He's working as Tania Trace's bodyguard right now," Pete points out. "And didn't I hear on the news that her last bodyguard got shot?"

Until that very moment, I'd forgotten all about Bear, and about Cooper's suspicion that his shooting might not have been so random after all, given the network's willingness to move Tania Trace's rock camp at such great expense.

"Okay," I say, "but—"

"Shoulder holsters work only under jackets," Pete goes on. He's waxing poetic about where he likes to keep his gun when he's off-duty. New York College protection officers aren't allowed to carry guns (at least, not officially), only Tasers. "Ankle holsters make you chafe. You can carry a Glock on your belt, but then everybody's gonna see it, unless you wear a jacket or keep your shirt untucked. You ladies have it easy, with your purses. You can hide anything in there."

I'm starting to regret that I ever said anything.

That's when the front door to Fischer Hall bursts open and Gavin runs through it, calling, "Heather! Heather, come quick!"

So Sue Me

All those times you said
I'd never make it
All those times you said
I should quit

All those times you said
I'm nothing without you
The sad part is
I believed it too

Then you left and
What do you know
I made it on
My very own

So go ahead and sue me
You heard me
Go ahead and sue me

Now that I've made it
You say it's you I owe
Well, you owe me too
For the heart you stole

If I've got one regret
It's all the time I spent
All the tears I wept
Thinking you were worth the bet

Go ahead, go all the way
Take me to court
It'll make my day
So sue me

Go ahead and sue me

"So Sue Me"
Performed and written by Tania Trace
So Sue Me album
Cartwright Records
Nine consecutive weeks as the
Number 1 Hit Billboard Hot 100

I don't know how he realized I was there. Maybe it's that kind of sixth sense animals have when they know their mothers are nearby.

Wait . . . that's mother bears, and it's what they use to find their missing cubs. Probably Gavin saw me through the window.

In any case, I shove my coffee mug back at Magda and race into Fischer Hall after Gavin, expecting to find the place on fire at the very least.

Instead, I discover Davinia, one of the RAs, in tears, with Sarah, Lisa Wu, and Gavin's girlfriend, Jamie, clustered around her. My entire staff, it seems, has gathered in the lobby, as has the crew of *Jordan Loves Tania*, minus the stars. Stephanie Brewer is standing in front of the desk, giving instructions of some urgency to her crew, who are for some reason *behind* the desk, where they have no business being. This is where we keep all the mail and deliveries for the residents.

Or possibly the message isn't urgent. Maybe she's shouting at the top of her lungs because Manuel, the head housekeeper, has decided to go over the lobby floors one last time with his industrial electric buffer. The noise is incredible . . . so loud that Dr. Jessup, who has shown up on a Saturday, has his hands over his ears as he stands beside Muffy Fowler, President Allington and Christopher Allington, and, of all people, Simon Hague.

These must be the yukkity-yuks that Pete was talking about. I suppose it makes sense. Why *wouldn't* Simon Hague stroll over from his residence hall to mine on a Saturday morning to watch the check-in for Tania Trace Rock Camp? It's not like he has a life.

"Well, hey, Heather," Muffy yells in order to be heard above the buffer. "Nice of you to stop on by."

I narrow my eyes at her. I can tell she thinks the entire situation is funny, but it's so not. President Allington—dressed, as usual, in the New York College colors of blue and gold, in this case a blue-and-gold velour warm-up suit over a white tank top—is leaning negligently against the security monitors at the guard's desk, eating fruit salad from a paper plate. There is no guard to tell him not to, because Pete is outside, keeping Mrs. Upton and the other moms from rushing over to Pitchforks "R" Us and instigating a rebellion.

The entire building, it appears, has hopped aboard the train to Crazy Town.

I hesitate, uncertain where to head first: To the front desk, to demand an explanation for why Stephanie's crew is standing where they shouldn't be? To my department head, to let him know that none of this is my fault? To the president, to tell him not to spill fruit salad on our very expensive security equipment? To Davinia, a student in need, to find out what's wrong? Or to Manuel, to tell him to turn that damned thing off, for the love of God?

I head toward Davinia, making a slashing motion beneath my chin at Manuel, who's looked up as I've entered, waving cheerfully, as is his custom.

When he sees me make the slashing motion, he appears startled. He clearly hasn't noticed all the activity around him, having been too absorbed in his work . . . which, considering it's Manuel, who takes extreme pride in keeping Fischer Hall's brass fixtures and marble floors immaculate, isn't surprising. He removes his earplugs, then turns off the floor polisher. The noise level in the lobby doesn't decrease by much.

"Heather," he rushes over to say to me, looking stricken. "I'm so sorry! I want the lobby to look nice for the movie, and for all those ladies who keep trying to come in."

"It's okay, Manuel," I say. "I appreciate it. The lobby looks great."

It actually looks so much cleaner than my own apartment, I consider hiring Manuel on the spot as my housekeeper. I know, however, that not only would this idea deeply insult him—he doesn't do laundry—but he belongs to one of the most powerful unions in New York City and makes approximately three times what I do. Cooper and I could never afford him.

I hurry over to the sobbing girl. "Davinia," I say. "What's wrong?"

"N-nothing," Davinia says, wiping her tears with the back of her hands.

"It's *not* nothing," Simon Hague assures me with malevolent delight, shoveling some fruit salad into his mouth. He has a paper plate too, same as the president. I look around and notice that the doors to the cafeteria are open. The cafeteria is open again, and everyone is helping themselves. Nice.

Sarah sends a dark look in Simon's direction. "Thanks," she says to him. "But we can handle it." To me, she hisses, "That bitch Stephanie—"

"Everything's all right," Lisa says, glancing nervously in Dr. Jessup's direction. Fortunately, he's deeply absorbed in the plate of fruit salad with which he's returning from the cafeteria. He's also snagged a few strips of bacon, I notice, and a bagel. "Ms. Brewer hurt Davinia's feelings by saying the hallway decorations for the sixteenth floor aren't any good—"

"She tore down all the mermaid door tags Davinia stayed up until one o'clock in the morning hand-drawing," Sarah interrupts, practically foaming at the mouth she's so angry. "Just ripped them down and threw them in the trash."

I glance questioningly at the resident assistant. Davinia's a tall art major who got a fantastic internship at the Met but was going to have to turn it down and go back to India because her parents couldn't afford rent for her for the summer . . . at least not until the Queen of the Island of Misfit Toys, also known as Heather Wells, came along and made it all better.

"The door tags were supposed to be a tribute to *The Little Mermaid*," Davinia whispers. "Ariel's my favorite Disney princess. And *Little Mermaid* is a musical, so it still fits in with singing camp. But Ms. Brewer said the sixteenth floor's color scheme should be black and purple, something with more of an edge."

I have no idea what she's talking about. I also can't believe this is what they're all so freaked out about.

"Black and purple? Like a bruise?" I ask.

"No, not a bruise," Stephanie says, so loudly that I jump. I have no idea she's snuck up behind me. "Catwoman, or in this case, Tania's face superimposed over Catwoman's body, with a bubble coming out of her mouth saying, 'You're purrfect,' and the girls' names. And the Catwoman figure is going to be holding a whip. Lauren, find out how long the art department is going to be on those door tags."

Lauren, the ever-faithful production assistant, lifts her phone to shoot off a text message.

"Check-in is today," I remind Stephanie, feeling panic beginning to swell in my chest. "In *one hour*, actually. The campers and their moms are all waiting outside. They're really angry we're not letting them in now—"

"That's not my problem," Stephanie says in an infuriatingly calm voice. "No one told them to get here early. We do things on our schedule, not theirs."

I glare at Stephanie. It's way too early in the morning—and way too humiliating—to be having this discussion in front of my new boss. And *her* boss. And *his* boss, and *his* son, who is clearly so bored by all of this, he's taken out his cell phone and is texting someone. Maybe even Stephanie, since she lifts her phone and starts laughing at something. Seriously?

"Does it really matter what the door tags look like?" I whisper, trying to get Stephanie's attention. I tilt my head at Davinia, who is looking crushed that her mermaids have been replaced by dominatrixes in cat suits. "She worked super hard on them."

"Uh, yeah, it does matter," Stephanie says, not looking up from her phone. "The color scheme didn't work. She had some sort of aquatic theme going, and the sixteenth floor is supposed to be hard rock. Bridget and Cassidy are going to be on that floor, with that Mallory girl. Right?"

I have no idea she's even addressing me and not her phone until Simon Hague, who of course has been paying keen attention to the conversation, says, his mouth full of honeydew, "Uh, I think she's talking to you, Heather."

"Oh." I spring into action, but only because all of my supervisors are watching. "You need their room assignments? Let me see."

I hurry to the front desk, where the binder containing the room assignments is kept. None of the front desks at New York College has a computer, allegedly due to budgetary constraints, but actually due to the fact that the front desks are manned by student workers and the president's office fears the computers will be used to look up porn or stolen.

"Hey," I say to Gavin. He's sitting in the tall swivel padded chair behind the front desk, where he has access to the room assignments, the lockbox containing keys to every room in the building, the intercom system (the only way students can be contacted in their rooms to be told a visitor has arrived, unless they've given that visitor their cell-phone number), and the student mailboxes. "Give me the roster."

He slaps a black binder into my hand.

"Why'd you let them back there?" I whisper to him, nodding at Jared and the film crew, who are crowded behind him, sitting on the edge of the air-conditioning unit, the windowsill, and the table where mail is usually sorted, having an earnest conversation about the merits of zombie films over slasher pics. "You know no one's allowed back there but you guys."

"Dude in the suit told me to," Gavin whispers back, nodding at Dr. Jessup. I wonder briefly how the vice president would feel to hear that he's been referred as the "dude in the suit." Dr. Jessup tries hard to keep up with what he thinks is the Millennial generation's lingo. I once heard him refer to a movie he'd seen directed by Woody Allen as "baller." "They want to film the reactions of the girls as they check in. Their screams of excitement and joy or whatever as they get the keys to their rooms in fabulous New York City."

He's trying to sound sarcastic, but I can see that he's put on a pair of clean khakis—long ones, not shorts—and a white button-down shirt that someone—I'm guessing his girlfriend, Jamie—has taken the trouble to iron. His hair is wet around the edges, indicating that he showered before coming down for work. Normally he rolls out of bed and comes to the desk eating a bowl of Fruit Loops in his pajamas. The distinctly pungent odor of Axe body spray lies heavy in the air.

What is going on? Gavin—who, out of all my student employees, tries hardest to act like he doesn't care—is actually trying to look good for a goofy docu-reality series being filmed for the Cartwright Records Television network? I'm struck by a sudden urge to cry at how cute this is. Maybe my continuous-cycle birth control pills aren't entirely suppressing my hormones after all.

"Why are *you* back there?" I ask, narrowing my eyes at Brad, since he's leaning on the edge of the intercom system next to Gavin. I need to distract myself before I begin weeping in front of both of them.

Brad looks startled, which is his normal expression.

"It's check-in," he says. "I thought we all had to be here."

At least Brad hasn't showered *or* dressed up. But then, Brad doesn't need to. With a body like a Dolce & Gabbana cologne model from his strict workout routine—his fallback plan, if his physical therapy major doesn't pan out—he'd look good wearing a paper bag. This has nothing to do with why Sarah and I hired him, of course.

"Yeah," I say, flipping open the binder. It's divided into sections, first alphabetically by resident, then by floor. "Well, thanks for coming." I wrinkle my nose. "What's that smell?" I don't mean the body spray. This is, if possible, stronger and more cloying.

"Oh," Gavin says. "That'd be the flowers. They're for Tania. Her fans know this is where her rock camp is being held and Tweeted about it. They've been coming in and leaving 'em all morning, hoping they're going to see her," Gavin goes on. "But Pete's been making them drop them off and get out, telling them they can't hang around."

I look where he's pointed and realize that lining the windowsill behind the *Jordan Loves Tania* film crew are enough bouquets of roses to make a florist jealous. Some of them have balloons attached.

I groan. This is the last thing we need.

"They've been leaving other stuff too," Brad says excitedly, holding up a pink box. "Look! Ice-cream cake." His tone turns reverential. "It's *Carvel*."

"Ew," I say, wrinkling my nose. "You are *not* eating that."

"Of course not," Brad says, looking hurt. "It's for Ms. Trace. Besides, I would never put all that processed sugar and flour into my body."

"I would," Gavin declares. "I'm just waiting for Jamie to bring me a spoon from the caf. She's been too busy dealing with Davinia's meltdown—"

"*No*," I say firmly. "What is wrong with you? Didn't your mother tell you not to accept candy from strangers? Throw that away right now before it melts and makes everything all sticky."

"No one's throwing anything away," Jared says, in a warning voice, suddenly paying attention to our conversation. "After Tania's seen everything that's been dropped off to her by her fans, we'll gather it all up and take it over to one of the hospitals and donate it to the children's wing. That's what she likes us to do."

"Wait," I say, noticing for the first time how he's occupying his time while waiting for filming to begin, besides his horror film discussion. "What are you doing?"

"Well, we obviously don't donate the *perishable* items," Jared says with his mouth full. "We eat those ourselves. Want one?" He tilts a pink-and-white polka-dotted bakery box toward me. "They're good. From Pattycakes, that vegan bakery over on Bleecker Street."

"Oh, Pattycakes?" Muffy Fowler suddenly throws herself into the conversation, leaning against the desk beside me. "How sweet. You know Tania and Jordan used Pattycakes to make their wedding cake."

"That's why no one but Jared will eat those nasty things,"

Marcos, the sound guy, says with a snort. He's got his hand in a bag of vegan pita chips that has a note—"For Tania, Divalicious"—taped to it. "Who wants a cupcake made with no eggs, dairy, or processed sugar?"

"I'll have you know," Jared says, taking another bite from the heavily frosted cupcake in his hand, "that these cupcakes won *Cupcake Wars* on Food Network."

"They won *Cupcake Wars?*" Now Stephanie is interested. "Give me one."

"Oh, I'd like to try one too, please," Simon says, bellying up to the desk.

I can't tell if it's Stephanie that Simon is interested in or the cupcakes—they do look good, piled high with vanilla frosting and finished with a purple candied flower on top. But either way, I don't like how this is going, especially given the fact that no one seems to remember there are fifty campers and their mothers waiting on the sidewalk outside and I'm working on a Saturday, hours for which I'm not paid overtime or compensated with time off.

"Can we at least," I say, "start check-in, since we're all here?"

"God no," Stephanie says. "Let everyone finish breakfast in peace. The minute we let them in, they'll start making demands. I'm surprised at you, Heather. I'd think you'd know a little something about pushy stage moms."

I smile humorlessly back at her. Ha ha.

Gavin swivels on the desk chair to complain, as Jared passes Stephanie a cupcake, "How come *they* get to eat the stuff people have dropped off for Tania, and you won't let us have any?"

"Because," I mutter—even more irritated when Christopher Allington saunters over to Stephanie and murmurs, "Gimme a bite, babe"—"in this building we have a policy. We don't take—or *eat*—things that don't belong to us."

"And Heather was right when she said that you don't know where those came from," Lisa points out. But I don't miss the envious glow in her eye as she watches Stephanie take a bite.

"We know exactly where these came from," Stephanie says, chewing. "Tania's fans. Let's not forget, they're the ones"—she makes a slight face—"paying our salaries."

Christopher walks over to the nearest trash can and spits out what was in his mouth, but Simon tries to be more discreet.

"I think it's quite good," he says, chewing. "A bit dry maybe." I notice, however, that he leaves the rest of his on the paper plate holding his fruit salad.

Muffy looks disappointed. "Oh, now that's a darn shame," she says. "And I heard so many good things about them too."

President Allington has been holding his hand out across the desk. Now he withdraws it.

"No thanks," he says. "Trying to keep my girlish figure. No sense wasting calories on something that doesn't taste as good as it looks."

I notice some of the basketball players have gathered in the lobby as well. Nothing would keep them away from a chance at grabbing some free food and perhaps a glimpse of Tania Trace, and they glance at one another with barely suppressed smirks on their faces.

"Honestly, Jared, he's right," Stephanie says, oblivious to

what's going on behind her. "How can you sit there and eat those? They taste like cardboard."

"I don't know," Jared says. He seems to have lost some of his previous enthusiasm and is dabbing at his nose with his sleeve. "I was hungry. I skipped breakfast."

"Well, go get a bagel in the cafeteria," Stephanie says irritably. "So what rooms are Cassidy and those other girls in?" she asks me.

"Sixteen twenty-one," I reply without checking the roster.

Lisa smiles at me, impressed, but the truth is, I've known all along. I've been stalling for time in order to get a sense of what's going on behind the desk. I have all the room assignments memorized, given that I did them myself. I can't use the computer system—for which Muffy Fowler told me the college spent a "scandalous" amount of money—to do Fischer Hall's room assignments because it makes too many mistakes, assigning people who've requested a room on a "low floor, south-facing window," to a room on a high floor with windows that face north. It's easier for me simply to do the assignments by hand.

"There was a note telling me to put Bridget, Cassidy, and Mallory in the same room," I explain to Stephanie. "So I did, with Cassidy's mom in the outer room as chaperone. But now that I've met Mrs. Upton, I think she might not be too—"

"Brilliant," Stephanie says, not waiting for me to finish. "Those three girls got the highest TVQ ratings from the test audiences who viewed their audition tapes. If we could get a smackdown going on between them for the Rock Off, it'd be terrific."

My eyebrows go up, and I hear Lisa ask, "*What?*" in alarm.

"Not a real smackdown," Lauren the PA assures us. She hasn't been in the television business long enough to have become as jaded as her boss. "She means a vocal smackdown. The Rock Off is the talent show we're going to have the final night of camp to see who the most gifted performer is. The winner gets fifty thousand dollars and a recording deal with Cartwright Records."

"Those three girls all sang the same song when they auditioned for the show," Stephanie says. I notice that she says "the show" and not "camp." "It was 'So Sue Me.'"

"Oh, I love that song," says Jamie, and the other female RAs, Tina and Jean and even Davinia, all nod enthusiastically.

I don't blame them. "So Sue Me" *does* have a different feel than any of Tania's previous songs, and not just because it perfectly showcases her powerful voice, or because it's the title track to her newest album and her first real Mariah-style power ballad. Although singers—especially popular ones like Tania—are often given cowriter credit for the songs they sing, it's not always because they've actually written the song. Songwriters are guaranteed residuals by the label, but musicians and performers are not.

Every word of "So Sue Me," on which Tania has a cowriter credit, sounds like it means something personal to her, however, and is coming from a place deep within her soul. Since every time I hear her singing it I get chills, I can almost believe she wrote it herself.

And so must everyone else, since it's been the number-one song in the country—and Europe—for weeks.

"*That's* why we want the floor to have a rock 'n' roll feel," Lauren explains, more to Davinia than to me. "Mallory and Bridget will probably go edgy for their songs for the Rock Off. We can't be sure about Cassidy, with that mother—"

"We'll get her agent to have her go pop," Stephanie says firmly. "She'll sing 'So Sue Me,' blow away all the competition, Tania will cry, Cassidy will win, and the sponsors will *love* it."

I'm starting to understand what Jared meant in my office when he said I'd be amazed at how little actual reality ends up in their "docu-reality" series.

"Speaking of Cassidy," I say, "when I met Mrs. Upton outside just now, I—"

"Later, okay?" Stephanie says. "Lauren, what did Art say?"

"Done," Lauren says, checking her phone. "Can we print them out in your office, Lisa?"

"Uh," Lisa says uncertainly. "Sure, I guess—"

"Fantastic," Stephanie says and glances at Davinia. "It wasn't that yours weren't right, sweetie. They weren't right for the *show*."

"I don't feel so good," Jared says from behind the desk.

Gavin spins to face him on the tall front-desk chair. "Dude. You got a nosebleed."

This is the understatement of the summer—possibly of the year. Blood is flowing in two steady streams from Jared's nostrils, dripping down onto his faded gray New York College T-shirt.

I'm immediately alarmed, especially when Jared says sarcastically, "You think I don't know that?" and raises his arm.

He's apparently been dabbing his nose for a little while, since the sleeve of his blue hoodie has turned black. "It won't stop. And I think I'm going to throw up. If someone could just call my doctor—here, he's in my important contacts . . ." He fumbles in his pocket for his iPhone, then drops it. "Shoot."

My mind darts to one of the many episodes of *Freaky Eaters* I've seen . . . and also one of the mandatory staff meetings I was forced to attend in the past few months.

"Gavin," I say, throwing open the door to the front desk, "call 911. Brad, get the first aid kit. There's a bottle of hydrogen peroxide in it—"

Gavin reaches for the phone. "Don't let him hurl back here," he says as he dials. "Take him to the bathroom."

"What is it?" Stephanie's eyes are wide. "What's wrong with him?"

"I think it's warfarin," I say, grabbing a roll of toilet paper— toilet paper is one of the few things residents at Fischer Hall get for free—from beneath the desk and shoving it against Jared's nostrils. "It's an anticoagulant. It's the active ingredient in a lot of rat poisons."

"Oh my God," Lisa cries, following me. She snatches the bottle of hydrogen peroxide from Brad and rips off the top, shoving it toward Jared's face. "How much should he drink?"

I'm trying to remember. "I don't know. Just make him throw up."

"Uh," Dr. Jessup says, approaching the desk, Simon and Muffy close behind him. "Maybe this isn't—"

"Aw, jeez," Jared is saying, pushing Lisa away. "Don't worry. It's not poison. It's just a—"

"Don't stand up!" Lisa and I cry at the exact same time as Jared attempts to climb to his feet.

It's too late. His legs crumple beneath him as his eyes roll back into his head, and neither Lisa nor I is strong enough to support his weight as he collapses.

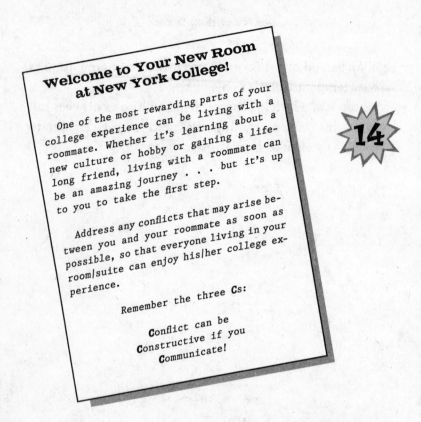

14

Muffy Fowler decides—and Dr. Jessup agrees—that it's not a good idea for the moms to see the show's field producer being carted out of Fischer Hall covered in blood and on a stretcher. Nor does she think it's a good idea for them to see Detective Canavan and the other law-enforcement officers from the Sixth Precinct who show up to question Gavin and anyone else who might have had contact with the individual who dropped off the cupcakes (though until there is a toxicology report proving they actually did contain a poisonous substance, we're urged by Detective Canavan "not to make any assumptions").

It also seems wise to keep the campers and their moms from witnessing the breakdown that Simon Hague has in the middle of the lobby, shortly after Jared's collapse.

"*I* ate one!" he shrieks. "*I* swallowed a bite of one of those cupcakes too! Dear God in heaven, I don't want to die!"

That's when Lisa and I force him—and Stephanie too—to swallow some hydrogen peroxide and vomit into various trash cans (so we can preserve the evidence).

Then we send the RAs outside to invite all the campers into the cafeteria to enjoy breakfast and "bond" with one another. It seems to work. Not only do none of the moms notice the unconscious man being smuggled out of the building through a side exit into the waiting ambulance—or the staff members who leap into a taxi to follow it (Muffy feels that representatives from New York College should go along to the hospital to support Jared and Stephanie, and of course Simon)—but they seem unfazed by the announcement that filming has been postponed until tomorrow because of a "technical delay." It helps that Magda does such a terrific job of telling them how "byootiful" they all look, like true movie stars, making sure they get all the fruit salad and nonfat yogurt they can eat.

The rest of the staff do their own jobs amazingly as well, exactly the way they've been trained . . . well, except for the president, who leaves, muttering, "Glad I didn't eat one of those things."

I'm sitting at my desk, waiting to give my statement to

Detective Canavan and staring at a red spot on the sleeve of my white blouse—a spot, I realize, that is probably never going to come out, no matter how much stain remover I use, because it's Jared Greenberg's blood.

Otherwise check-in has gone on as planned, just a couple of hours later than scheduled. All of the girls (and their mothers) seem happy with their rooms—which, given how much money CRT has spent on the decor, they should be. There are flat-screen TVs bigger than my desk in each room, as well as bucketloads of swag donated from Sephora and Bed, Bath & Beyond. Davinia reported having been able to hear the squeals of delight all the way down the hall in her own room.

My phone rings, but it's my cell, not my office phone.

"I just heard," Cooper says when I pick up. "Are you all right?"

"I'm fine," I lie. My fingers still haven't stopped shaking, despite the two—nondiet—sodas and Reuben sandwich I've downed to cushion the shock. "*I'm* not the one who swallowed a vegan cupcake dusted with rat poison."

"Thank God," he says. "My dad says they're doing everything they can for the guy, but that it's not looking good. Stephanie Brewer seems to be in the clear, though, and so does the guy from the other residence hall—"

I've forgotten all about Simon.

"Too bad," I say before I can stop myself. "If anyone deserves to die like a rat—"

Then I clamp my mouth shut guiltily. I can't wish that kind of death on anyone, not even Simon . . . especially when Sarah, sitting at her desk nearby, looks up in surprise from the hushed conversation she's having on her cell phone. I feel ashamed of myself. I'm supposed to be a role model.

"Heather, there's no proof it was poison," Cooper says. "The guy could have had a heart attack, for all you know."

"Cooper." I lower my voice, conscious of Sarah's gaze on me and the fact that Detective Canavan is in Lisa's office with another officer, interviewing Gavin and Brad. Her office is separated from the outer office—where my desk is located—by only a half wall and a metal grate. Muffy's given us all strict instructions that if a single word of what's happened gets out, we're going to lose our jobs. Even though I know Cooper isn't going to run to the *Post* with what I'm telling him, I don't want to get caught gossiping. "A heart attack? Are you kidding me? Blood was gushing out of the guy's nose like a fountain. Just seconds before he was eating cupcakes some fan dropped off at the building for Tania."

"That doesn't mean—"

"Cooper, they taught us at a staff meeting not long ago what symptoms to look for in human poison ingestion. Nosebleeds and nausea were two of them. Jared was suffering from both before he passed out. Warfarin, the active ingredient in older rat poisons, is both odorless and tasteless. I saw an episode of *Freaky Eaters* about a woman who loved eating it, only in small amounts. It was killing her too, just much more slowly."

"Who the hell," Cooper asks, "eats rat poison on purpose?"

"I don't know," I say. "There was one guy on there who ate his own car. 'When a hobby becomes an obsession,'" I inform him, quoting from one of my other favorite shows, "'it's called an addiction. That's when you need an *intervention*.'"

Cooper is silent for a moment. Then he says, "I'm cancel-
ing our cable subscription. You watch way, way too much
television."

"Said the man who carries a gun in a fanny pack. You're
hardly one to talk."

"I do not—what are you—" he sputters. *"Who told you
that?"*

"Whatever, Cooper," I say, glancing at Sarah. She's spun
her desk chair to face the wall and is speaking in hushed,
angry whispers into her phone. I assume she's talking to
Sebastian. After the near-death experience we've both wit-
nessed, it makes sense that we'd reach out to loved ones. It
also makes sense that we might lash out at them. Tensions
are running high. "I know all about it, okay? I know why you
were so hot and bothered about finding your cargo pants. I
know you lied to me about owning a gun. And that's fine,
because guess what? I have secrets too."

"What secrets?" Cooper demands. "And I didn't lie to you
exactly. I omitted telling you the truth about something I
knew was only going to—"

"Excuse us." Two figures appear in the doorway to the
office. It's Mrs. Upton and her daughter Cassidy. I have to
restrain a groan. Really? *Now?*

"I have to go," I say to Cooper. "I will speak to you at a
later time about that subject of which we were discussing." I
hang up and smile at the Uptons with as much graciousness
as I can muster. "Hello, ladies. Is there something I can do
for you?"

"I certainly hope so," Mrs. Upton says, steering her daughter by the shoulders into the office first, then plunking her

onto the couch across from my desk. Cassidy's expression is mulish, and when her mother releases her shoulders, she collapses onto the couch as if there isn't a solid bone in her body.

Her mother settles herself into the chair next to my desk. I'm willing to overlook it this time, because I'm so terrified of Mrs. Upton, but I didn't ask her to sit down.

"The young woman at the front desk told me you were the person to whom I should speak about this," Mrs. Upton says with a gracious smile, evidently not remembering our encounter from earlier in the morning. Jamie, I know, is working the desk while Gavin and Brad are in with the police. "I'd like to see what I can do about having our room changed."

I look from Cassidy to Mrs. Upton and back again. Cassidy's expression is still mulish. Her elfin face is tilted at the ceiling, her lower lip jutting out, her long blond hair splayed out across the blue couch.

"I see," I say. "May I ask what's wrong with your current room?" Besides the fact that it used to be a creepy tribute to Prince Caspian. "Because I know that Cartwright Records went to a great deal of trouble to furnish it—"

"Oh, it's not the furnishings," Mrs. Upton says pleasantly. "They're very nice. It's just that Cassidy has never had to share a room before, and now she's sharing one with not just one but two other girls, as well as me, and I'm afraid that isn't going—"

"You're in a separate room," I point out. I know it's rude to interrupt, but after the day I've had, I can't help it.

"Yes," Mrs. Upton says, her voice not quite as pleasant as before. "But the girls have to walk through mine in order to enter and exit the suite."

"Right," I say. "Because they're fifteen years old, and you agreed to be their chaperone. New York College doesn't allow residents under the age of eighteen—"

"Well, that's plain silly," Mrs. Upton says, beginning to swing her Louboutined foot. "My Cassidy is very mature for her age. She knows perfectly well how to handle herself—"

"What are those?" Cassidy asks, pointing at the condoms in the candy jar on my desk.

Mrs. Upton looks in the direction that Cassidy is pointing and turns a shade of pink that contrasts nicely with the many yellow gold necklaces she's wearing.

"Put your finger down, Cass," she says, glancing quickly away. "You know better than to point."

"But what *are* they?" Cassidy asks. "I've never seen candy like that." There's a slyness to her perfect little smile that tells me she knows *exactly* what they are and is toying with us—she's a teenager after all, surely she's watched MTV— but her mother evidently doesn't notice.

"That's because they aren't candy," Mrs. Upton explains in disapproving tones. "They're something that doesn't have any place being in a candy jar on a lady's desk."

"Then why does this lady have them on hers?" Cassidy asks, cocking her head at me the way Owen cocks his head at the wall when he hears mice scratching inside.

Over at her own desk, Sarah hangs up her cell phone and says loudly, "They're condoms, as you know very well, Cassidy. Condoms, not candy. Now you know where to get them, since you're so mature."

Mrs. Upton inhales sharply. "Ex-*cuse* me?"

"I'm sorry, Mrs. Upton," I lean forward to say, swiftly lifting the jar and setting it onto the floor, out of the girl's line of sight. "I'm afraid I can't give you a room change. You signed on to be a chaperone, and if I move you, Mallory and Bridget won't have an adult of legal age to look after them. I can, of course, move Cassidy if she wants—"

"That'd be fine," Cassidy says eagerly.

"No," Mrs. Upton says. "Cassidy, don't be silly, you can't live away from me."

"Why?" Cassidy demands bluntly. "That's what I want."

I'm not sure what to do. Maybe Cassidy really does need this room change, to get away from her overbearing mother. Most teenage girls don't attend summer camp with their mothers sleeping in the next room. I feel a little sorry for Cassidy, despite her seeming like such a conniving little weasel.

"If I move you, you'll still have roommates," I warn her, reaching for my roster. "And an adult chaperone in the next room, just like you do now." I can make the change, but I'm pretty sure Stephanie will have an embolism if I do. But the Rock Off will no doubt turn out the same, if Cassidy is as talented as everyone says . . .

"Fine," Cassidy says. "I'll live with anyone except my *mom*."

I raise my eyebrows at this burst of teenage snarkiness, my compassion switching instantly to Mrs. Upton.

"Cassidy," Mrs. Upton says, climbing to her feet, "now you're being rude. You know you don't mean that. Come on, we've bothered Miss . . ." She looks at me questioningly.

"*Ms.* Wells," I say, with the emphasis on the "Ms."

". . . Miss Wells enough for one day. Let's go."

"Yes, I *do* mean that," Cassidy protests. "It's not fair. Mallory and Bridget don't have to live with *their* mom—"

"Well, their mothers don't care like I do," Mrs. Upton says. "They didn't sign up to do this." She reaches down to grasp Cassidy by the arm, pulling her on the word "this."

Although the gesture is abrupt, I can see that the woman has no intention of hurting Cassidy. She's just grown frustrated with her daughter's sulky behavior.

Still, Cassidy reacts as if her mother has stabbed her.

"Ow!" she cries, leaping to her feet and cradling her arm. Mrs. Upton recoils in alarm. "Did you see?" Cassidy asks Sarah and me, large tears glistening in her baby blues. Her acting skills are phenomenal. "Did you see what she did to me?"

"Zip it up, drama queen," Sarah snarks from her desk. "People are trying to have a meeting in there." She points at the door to Lisa's office. "And yes, we both saw it. Your mother barely touched you."

"But"—Cassidy swings her teary-eyed gaze at me—"but you saw it. She *hit* me."

Mrs. Upton gasps. "Cassidy! I did nothing of the sort. What's wrong with you?"

"I'll tell you what's wrong with her," Sarah says. "Classic narcissistic personality disorder, brought on by a mother who's constantly reinforced her conviction that she's the most gifted and talented child who ever lived—"

"Sarah." I close my roster. Cassidy is getting a room change over my dead body . . . er, poor choice of words. What I mean is, I'm not moving her to make her some other chaperone's problem. "I've got this. You know something,

Cassidy?" I look the girl straight in the eye. "You're lucky you have a mom who cares about you so much. Some of us aren't as fortunate. Now . . . go to your room."

The tears in Cassidy's blue eyes dry up instantly.

"We'll see what Tania has to say about all this," she says coldly. "Won't we?"

"Oh, we certainly will," I reply, just as coldly. Is this girl kidding me? Who does she think she is?

"Come on, Cass," Mrs. Upton says, grabbing her daughter's hand and pulling her out into the hallway. "Let's go upstairs and see what Mallory and Bridget are doing."

"I hate them," I hear Cassidy whine.

"Don't forget, part of your Tania Trace Rock Camp experience," I call after them, "is getting to know new people and new cultures at New York College in New York City." This is the line we're supposed to say to students and parents who come into our office complaining about their roommates, usually because they're of a race, religion, or sexual orientation not their own. "Keep an open mind and open heart!"

"Exactly," Cassidy's mother says. I hear her bang on the button for the elevators. "Did you hear what the lady said? We don't *hate* anyone . . ."

"I hate you," Cassidy assures her, making sure her voice is loud enough for me to hear. "And I hate that fat lady in there."

Before I have a chance to properly digest this, the door to Lisa's office is thrown open and Detective Canavan from the Sixth Precinct steps out of it. He's spent so much time in Fischer Hall over the past year due to all the deaths in the building, I'm not surprised that he feels as if he works here. But that doesn't give him the right to yell.

"What the hell," he asks, his gray mustache bristling, "is going on out here? It sounds like an episode of that damned show my daughter is always watching, the one about Bruce Jenner's daughters."

It takes me a second to realize he's talking about the Kardashians.

"They're his stepdaughters," I say. "And it was only girl talk."

"Huh," the detective says, but looks as if he doesn't believe it. He plucks an unlit cigar from the pocket of his khaki trousers and jams it into one side of his mouth. "So what's this I hear about you being engaged?"

I glare at Sarah, but she only shakes her head vigorously and mouths, *It wasn't me.* "I'm not engaged." I hold up my left hand. "See? No ring."

"That doesn't mean anything," Detective Canavan says. "I heard you're eloping. Don't give me that dopey look. I been in this business thirty years. Anyway, mazel tov."

"I'm not eloping," I say, feeling my face heating up.

"Sure you're not," Detective Canavan says. "Don't forget to register somewhere. My wife'll send you and Cartwright a nice Crock-Pot. You two." He turns and gestures into the inner office. "Come on."

Gavin and Brad come slinking out of the residence hall director's office. They both have their heads sunk between their shoulders, looking like kids who've been caught shoplifting.

"What's wrong with you guys?" I ask, relieved to have the detective's attention off me.

"Apparently my powers of observation leave something to

be desired," Gavin says, shooting an indignant glance in Detective Canavan's direction.

"Worst witness I ever had," the detective agrees, glowering at Gavin in disapproval. "And then he tells me he wants to direct. Films, no less. Scorsese, he ain't."

"It was really crowded when I opened the desk this morning," Gavin says to me. "People were pushing roses and boxes at me right and left. How am I supposed to remember who left what?"

"If it was the ice cream cake," Brad chimes in, "I could tell you. That I remember, 'cause I really wanted a piece. Not that I'd have one, because all that sugar is really bad for your body."

"I think it was a guy," Gavin says.

"A guy," Detective Canavan says. "Do you hear this kid? He thinks it was 'a guy.' A real Francis Ford Coppola he's going to be when he graduates. Tell her what 'the guy' looked like."

Gavin looks down at me uncomfortably.

"Um," he says. "I don't know. I think he was wearing a baseball cap. And a hoodie. I couldn't really see because there was a big crowd. I just took everything they handed to me and put it on the table."

Back in Lisa's office, the police officer taking notes can't stifle his laughter.

"Don't call us," Detective Canavan says to Gavin and Brad, making a pistol out of his index finger, then shooting. "We'll call you."

Dejected, Gavin and Brad slink from the office. When they're gone, I say scoldingly, "You didn't have to be so hard on them. We have the security footage from the lobby and the cameras in front of the building. Didn't you get anything from those?"

Detective Canavan shakes his head. "Oh yes," he says. "A grainy image of a large crowd of Tania Trace fans, one of whom was male and wearing a baseball cap and a hoodie. He was carrying a white plastic bag that appeared to contain a box. My guess is that it was a box of Pattycakes cupcakes. Highly observant, that lad of yours."

My phone rings . . . my office phone this time. I see a number on the caller ID that I don't recognize. I pick up and say, "Hello, Fischer Hall, this is Heather, how may I help you?"

"Oh, hi, Heather, it's Lisa." Lisa's voice sounds strained. "Stan—Dr. Jessup—asked me to give you a heads-up. We're still at the hospital."

"Oh," I say. "Great. How are things going?"

"Well, there's good news and bad news," Lisa says, still sounding upset, but as if she's trying to hide it. "The good news is, the hospital has figured out what's wrong. You were right, there was rat poison in those cupcakes."

"Oh," I say. I'm not sure how this is good news. "Okay."

"Fortunately, neither Stephanie nor Simon ate enough of them to be affected."

Oh. That's how.

"The bad news," Lisa goes on, "is that Jared Greenberg did. He passed away a little over an hour ago."

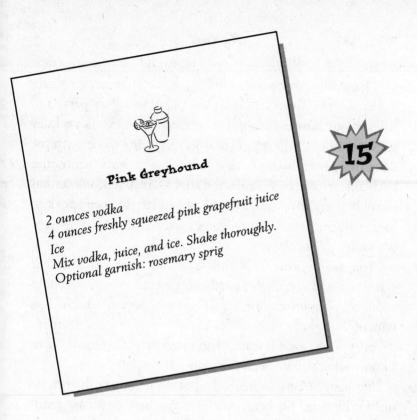

Pink Greyhound

2 ounces vodka
4 ounces freshly squeezed pink grapefruit juice
Ice
Mix vodka, juice, and ice. Shake thoroughly.
Optional garnish: rosemary sprig

15

All I want to do when I get home that night is make myself a stiff drink, strip off my clothes—which smell faintly of vomit, and on which I've found even more spots of Jared Greenberg's blood—get into a hot bubble bath, and soak my troubles away.

Instead, I find myself squeezed into a dress that I hardly ever wear, a pair of Spanx, and a pair of too-tight high heels, heading uptown in the back of a black Town Car sent to fetch me by Cartwright Records Television.

It isn't by choice.

"Please," Cooper begs.

I notice the Town Car with the tinted windows parked in front of our brownstone as I'm returning from walking Lucy after work, but I don't realize it has anything to do with me until Cooper calls to say that he's at his parents' penthouse with a near-catatonic Tania and that Detective Canavan has just left there, frustrated. Tania would barely even speak to him. Cooper wants me to come uptown to help him deal with her . . . and the rest of his family.

"You seem pretty optimistic about what my answer's going to be," I say. "You already sent a car."

I hear Cooper making a slight hissing sound. I know he's wincing.

"Sorry," he says. "It wasn't supposed to be there yet. Look, I know what you've been through—"

"Do you?" I ask. "When's the last time you got thrown up on? Or bled on? Or been called fat by a bratty teenage girl?"

I know the last one shouldn't bother me so much given that a man has lost his life—and it *doesn't* bother me that much—but it hasn't done much to enhance my mood.

"One of them called you fat?" Cooper sounds amused. "Did you tell her that your boyfriend thinks you're perfect just the way you are and also that your boyfriend owns a gun and a permit to carry it in New York City?"

I don't find this amusing.

"No. What I should have told her," I say, "is that she isn't going to get very far in life if she doesn't learn not to insult people who don't give her exactly what she wants."

"Interesting," Cooper says. "She reminds me of someone. Who could it be? Oh, right. My *dad*."

I swallow. Grant Cartwright was so furious when his eldest son declined to enter the family music business that he cut Cooper off, refusing even to pay for college. Cooper wouldn't back down, however, working round the clock in order to pay for school himself, so impressing his grandfather Arthur that he paid off Cooper's tuition bills, then left him the brownstone when he died . . . which only further enraged Grant Cartwright.

I too had earned Cooper's father's scorn for trying to think for myself. Tired of the bubble-gum stuff the label was churning out for me to sing, I convinced Grant Cartwright to listen to some songs I'd written myself. This turned out to be a big mistake. Next thing I knew, Tania Trace was opening for Jordan instead of me . . . in more ways than one.

"Look, Heather," Cooper says, "I get that you don't want to be here tonight. *I* don't want to be here tonight. But this is the first family dinner I've been to in ten years. I can't handle it without you."

"I know," I say with a sigh. I peel back the curtain and look down at the car. The driver is leaning against the passenger-side door, chatting with someone on his cell phone. "And I'll be there, Coop. But just so you know, hanging out with your dad wasn't real high on my list of things I was hoping to do tonight. Getting into my PJs, ordering a pizza from Tre Giovanni's, and watching *Tabitha Takes Over* in bed with you was more what I had in mind—"

"Forget Tabitha," Cooper says, sounding relieved. "I'll let *you* take over. You can hire as many people as you want to clean the house. Federal Emergency Management Agency, Mary Poppins, the National Guard, whoever you want."

"Really?" My mood brightens.

"Really. Just get over here." He lowers his voice. Apparently someone has just entered the room. "Fair warning, though, Jordan's here, too."

"I figured." Hanging out with my ex and his new wife is even lower on my list of things I was hoping to do tonight than hanging out with Grant Cartwright. "How's Tania doing?"

"Well, remember when we saw her that night at the Allingtons' apartment," Cooper says, "and all she'd do was sit there and kiss that damned dog—whose name is Baby, by the way?"

"Yeah," I say.

"Picture her the same way, but times a thousand."

"That's not good."

"No," Cooper says. "And now my *sisters* have shown up—"

"Your sisters?" I haven't seen Cooper and Jordan's twin sisters—the result of a late-in-life "surprise" pregnancy from which Mrs. Cartwright never quite seemed to recover—since they were shipped off to boarding school, at their father's request. They have to have graduated from college by now.

"Yes," he says. His voice dips sarcastically. "Nicole has volunteered to be a source of comfort to Tania, who's blaming herself for what happened to Jared, although of course she's claiming she doesn't have a single fan who'd ever want to hurt a hair on her head. Jessica has already volunteered to murder Nicole. Between the three of them, I might swallow some rat poison myself."

"See you in forty-five minutes," I say and hang up.

The Town Car drops me in front of a building on Park Avenue that I remember only too well from the many uncomfortable dinners I attended there back when I used to date Jordan. Even the doorman is the same.

"Hello, Ms. Wells," he says, smiling at me with what looks like genuine pleasure. "How are you? It's very good to see you again."

"It's good to see you too, Eddie," I say. Suddenly I feel nervous. The lobby is a thousand times fancier than I remember it being. Everything has been tastefully updated, from Eddie's dark-green uniform to the multiple gilt-frame mirrors showing me my own reflection. The only thing that looks out of place is me.

That's because I'm so much older and wiser now than I was the last time I was in it, I tell myself. My blowout is long gone, but my long blond hair looks shiny and healthy, and though the dress I'm wearing might have been picked up at a deep discount, it fits perfectly, emphasizing all the right things and hiding what I don't care to advertise. If my feet are already throbbing because I'm so unaccustomed to wearing the high heels into which I've stuffed them, at least no one but me will be able to tell.

Still . . . what am I doing here? Why did I agree to come? Sure, Cooper said he needed me, but he has a gun. He could whip it out and tell his family to leave him alone.

"Mrs. Cartwright called down to say she's expecting you," Eddie informs me, smiling as he guides me toward an open elevator and presses the button for the penthouse. "She said you can go straight up."

"Thanks," I say, feeling queasy. The elevator doors close before I can turn around and run for my life . . . not that I'd have made it far in my heels.

When the doors slide open again—far sooner than I'd have liked—it's onto a stunning vista. The Cartwrights' building lobby isn't the only thing that's been remodeled: the penthouse has been redone too. Now, instead of stepping into a stuffy foyer, the elevator doors open directly into Cooper's parents' living room, most of the walls of which have been torn down and replaced with floor-to-ceiling glass doors to the terrace, so the first thing you see when you step off the elevator is the fiery glow of the sun sinking down into the west.

What isn't glass is white pillars, stainless steel, and concrete. The place looks like something out of *Architectural Digest*, and knowing Grant Cartwright, I'd guess that the penthouse has probably been featured in it.

I step onto the highly polished ebony floor. "Hello?"

"Heather?" I'm startled when a petite, rail-thin young woman—with vanity sizing, she's probably a two—and stick-straight dark-brown hair steps out from behind a white pillar and eyes me, her manner guarded but not unfriendly. "Oh my God, it *is* you. It's me, Jessica."

Then, to my surprise, she pulls me into her arms and hugs me. It's like being held by a very skinny cat . . . if cats wore a lot of smoky eyeliner and silver wrist bangles and smelled like cigarette smoke.

"It's so good to see you," she says into my hair. "It's been *ages*. You look great."

"Thanks," I say, my voice a little hoarse since her head is jammed into my throat. "So do you."

The last time I saw Cooper's little sister Jessica, she was in pigtails and on the way out the door to her pony-riding lesson. She had braces, a lisp, and attitude that was worse, in many ways, than Cassidy Upton's.

"Cooper told me everything," she says when she finally lets go of me.

"He did?" I have no idea what's she talking about. Cooper's not close with either of his sisters, since his dad threw him out when he was so young, and the age gap between them is more than fifteen years.

"Well," she says, motioning to me to follow her and leading me into an open kitchen, all stainless steel appliances and granite countertops, "I more or less bribed it out of him. I'm working this summer as an intern for Marc Jacobs, and I told him I could get you all the clothes and accessories you want for, like, free. But he wouldn't've told me if he didn't want me to know, because it's not like you can get Cooper to tell you something he doesn't want you to know. You know?"

It's only then that I realize that Jessica is half in the bag. She's not falling-down drunk, but she's barefoot—a look that doesn't go badly with her silver bangles and the flowy black blouse and pants she has on. But she's definitely not sober.

"Do you want a drink?" she asks. "Everyone else is having martinis before dinner out on the terrace, but I freaking hate martinis. I'm having pink greyhounds. I'll make you one, if you want. It's a brunch drink, but who the hell cares

what time it is when someone's trying to kill you, right?"
She giggles, then holds a finger—the nail painted black, of
course—to her lips. "Oops, sorry, I mean Tania. I don't mean
to steal her thunder. Nicole's the one who thinks someone's
trying to kill us all. But you know how Nicole is." Jessica
rolls her eyes as she pours a generous amount of vodka into
two highball glasses filled with ice.

"Watch out," I say as she spills half of what she's pouring
onto the counter.

"Oops," Jessica says again and giggles some more. "Anyway,
I'm super glad about you and Coop. Jordan's such an ass. I
always thought you could do way better."

I realize Cooper really *did* tell Jessica everything.

"Gee," I say as Jessica pours freshly squeezed pink grapefruit juice from a pitcher into the glasses. "Thanks."

"No, seriously. I know Jordan's my brother and all"—she
plops a sprig of rosemary as a surprise garnish into each
glass, then begins to stir the contents of each violently with
a long silver spoon that was probably passed down to her
family from some Puritan who was on the *Mayflower* and
never envisioned his family heirloom being used as a cock-
tail stirrer—"but he's such an ass kisser. He does whatever
Dad says. Here." She passes me one of the glasses. "Cheers
to being with the right guy. *L'chaim.* Oh yeah, Nicole is con-
verting to Judaism to piss off my dad."

"*L'chaim.*" I clink the rim of my glass to hers. Pink greyhounds taste like heaven, if heaven can be something con-
cocted by barefoot girls wearing a lot of dark eyeliner.
"Wow," I say.

"I know, they're good, right?" Jessica beams. "Let's get shit-faced."

"You're here." Cooper appears in the kitchen holding a tray of empty glasses.

As usual, I feel a twinge in my solar plexus at how handsome he looks, especially since he's wearing jeans and not the cargo pants he couldn't find because I hid them behind the dryer. There's no sign of a fanny pack. He's wearing a gray short-sleeved linen shirt that makes his eyes look even more blue than gray, two colors between which they're always shifting. The shirt is untucked, though, which gives me a qualm as I remember what Pete said.

"I'm here," I murmur. Our gazes meet, and I want to throw down my drink and run across the kitchen and leap into his arms, despite the fact that he's probably packing. But something in his glance says, *Don't.*

At first I think it's because he doesn't want me feeling for bulges where his gun might be. A second later I realize it's because his mother is right behind him.

"Cooper, why have you stopped in the middle of the kitchen, how am I supposed to get by—*oh.*"

Patricia Cartwright looks startled to see me standing in her kitchen, even though her doorman said she'd told him to send me up. Dressed all in tones of beige and holding an empty martini glass, she's either been taking very good care of herself or has an excellent plastic surgeon, because she looks *younger* than the last time I saw her.

Then again, her husband's company—and my manager— made millions of dollars off the songs I recorded for them.

Cooper's mother can afford the most expensive skin care products in the world, even ones made out of baby-whale placenta.

"Heather," she cries, floating toward me with a tiny smile on her face . . . tiny because I'm not sure the rest of her face can move, thanks to all the Botox she's had. "How wonderful that you could come. I'm so sorry it had to be under such terrible circumstances. Was it *awful?*"

Mrs. Cartwright throws her arms around me exactly the way Jessica did, only the mother is, if anything, even bonier. If hugging Jessica was like hugging a skinny cat, hugging Mrs. Cartwright is like hugging the skeleton of a cat.

I look over her shoulder at Cooper and watch as he shudders comically for my benefit. Jessica, standing beside me, notices her brother's antics and lets out a horse laugh.

"It was pretty awful," I say, trying to cover for Jessica's laugh as Mrs. Cartwright releases me.

"I can believe it," Cooper's mother says, her blue eyes—so like Cooper's and yet so unlike them—narrowing with disapproval at Jessica. Apparently she didn't miss the laugh. "The poor man was right here in this house only last week, filming footage of Tania and Jordan for their show and trying to get me to invest privately in some horrible documentary he was doing about a death row inmate. And now *he's* the one who's dead." Patricia places a hand over her heart, and I can't help noticing the large emerald on her left finger. " 'Each man's death diminishes me, for I am involved in mankind. Therefore, ask not to know for whom the bell tolls. It tolls for thee.' " She lowers her hand and says solemnly, "F. Scott Fitzgerald. Such a wonderful writer."

"John Donne, actually," Cooper says, setting down the tray he's been holding. "Born approximately four centuries before Fitzgerald, but who's counting? Why don't I get you a glass of water, Mother? Or some coffee?"

"Don't be silly," Mrs. Cartwright says. "We'll be serving dinner shortly. We should open the wine. Heather, I hope you won't mind, we had to order in from the Palm. After such awful news, no one felt like cooking, much less going out. Palm doesn't normally deliver, of course, but the owner does it as a special favor for Grant, because he knows how much Grant loves their steaks and they're close, personal friends."

"And," Jessica says, rattling the ice in her glass, "since we were *supposed* to be in the Hamptons, Mom gave the staff the week off—"

Patricia Cartwright holds her empty martini glass imperiously at her outspoken daughter, not even glancing in Jessica's direction. Jessica, getting the message, takes the glass and walks over to the bar at the end of the kitchen counter to mix her mother's drink.

"Heather," Mrs. Cartwright says, reaching up to stroke a loose strand of hair away from my face. "It's been so long. Too long. I'm so sorry about what happened between you and Jordan. I won't speak to any of that unpleasantness except to say that it was such a blow to me personally. I really did feel as if I'd lost a daughter."

I notice that Cooper is making himself a drink in the background, putting ice in a low glass and reaching for the vodka bottle his sister used to make our pink greyhounds. He doesn't bother with the grapefruit juice.

"Thanks so much, Mrs. Cartwright," I say.

"You know, Mother," Jessica says as she fills a silver martini shaker with ice, "you may not have lost Heather as a daughter after all. Maybe your other son might—"

The next thing I know, Cooper has his sister in a headlock.

"While Jessica and I are refreshing everyone's drinks, Mother," he says casually, as if it's not unusual for him to walk around with Jessica's head trapped in the crook of his elbow, "why don't you and Heather go out onto the deck and join Dad and the others?"

"Ergh," Jessica says, struggling to set herself free. I notice she can't be in that much distress, however, since she's holding the martini mixer carefully aloft and hasn't spilled a drop.

"Yes, of course," Patricia Cartwright says. She takes my arm and begins to lead me toward the floor-to-ceiling glass doors to the penthouse terrace. "I'm sure you're anxious to see the rest of the apartment. You haven't been here since we renovated. We used Dominique Fabré, do you know him? He's a simply fabulous architect. We had quite a lot of trouble getting the plan through the board, of course. Oh my, how soft your skin is. What products do you use, if you don't mind my asking?"

"The tears of homesick college students," I reply gravely.

Mrs. Cartwright looks up at me sharply—in my heels, I'm quite a bit taller than she is.

"Oh, you're joking," she says. "I see. Yes, you were always clever, I remember now. I often wondered what you saw in Jordan, because though I love him dearly, I'm well aware he isn't my brightest child. That would be Cooper, though he's always been his father's biggest disappointment. So talented, so bright, he could have done anything, but he decides to become a private detective." She gives a rueful laugh. "You should hear what our friends say when we try to explain. What kind of person becomes a private detective?"

It's an idle question, tossed off casually as she pulls open one of the glass doors and we step out onto the roof deck. I'm sure she doesn't expect an answer, but I give her one anyway.

"Someone who wants to use his gifts to help people who are in trouble. In a different era, I think they were called knights in shining armor."

Mrs. Cartright glances at me in surprise. "Yes," she says, her tone no longer casual. "He certainly rescued you, from what I hear."

"I don't know what you mean," I say, flushing. "I just do his client billing."

"Of course," she says, her smile catlike. "His billing. Why not? Well, come along and say hello to everyone."

The Cartwrights' roof deck is a great deal longer and wider than the Allingtons' terrace. A helicopter could easily land on the putting green that Grant Cartwright has had planted at one end, and the pool, while not Olympic size, could fit enough Victoria's Secret models to make even a celebrity nightclub promoter happy.

The members of the Cartwright family, including Tania, are sitting on luxuriously cushioned lounge chairs ranged around an outdoor firepit, the gas flames set low because it's so warm outside. I can see that Mr. Cartwright is texting busily away, completely ignoring the beautiful sunset before him, but Jordan is giving it his full attention. Tania is curled on a lounge chair not far from Jordan's, looking even smaller than when I saw her last time, "Baby" in her lap. Even from where I stand, her skin tone looks off. Her eyes are hidden behind dark sunglasses.

On the opposite side of the firepit, a girl I recognize as Nicole—a decade older than when I'd last seen her—is strumming on a guitar. She resembles her twin in only the most basic ways. Her long hair is the same chocolate brown, but she's twisted it into twin braids. She isn't wearing the slightest bit of makeup, and instead of silver bangles, she has on beaded leather twists. She's about fifty pounds heavier than Jessica, and instead of all black, she's wearing a white vintage dress dotted with cheerful red cherries. On her feet is a pair of red flats, and thick-framed black glasses are balanced on her nose.

"Oh God," I hear Patricia murmur when the notes from the guitar drift toward us. "Not again."

"Why?" I ask. I cock my head, straining to catch more of the sound. The wind on the thirtieth floor is warm, but not gentle. I'm keeping a careful hold on the hem of my skirt. "She sounds great."

"Oh, Jesus Christ," I hear Jessica snarl as she comes up behind us. She's holding her pink greyhound in one hand and her mother's drink in the other. "Mom, I thought you said you were going to make her stop."

"What do you want me to do, " Mrs. Cartwright asks, "gag her?"

"You will if you want to keep me from jumping," Jessica says and barrels past me. "Nic," she shouts angrily as she strides toward the firepit, "give it a rest already. Daddy's not going to buy your stupid songs."

I follow Jessica, having to be extra careful with my drink since the path to the firepit is made of real grass and my high heels are sinking into the soil.

"Here," a masculine voice at my elbow says. "Allow me."

It's Cooper. He's carrying a tray of assorted drinks in one hand. With the other, he takes my arm, helping me maneuver the tricky pathway to the firepit.

"So what's this secret that you were talking about on the phone earlier?" he asks in a low voice. "Does it have anything to do with what you're wearing under that dress?"

His smile is playful. Unfortunately, my secret is anything but.

"We'll talk about it later," I say. "At the same time we talk about where you keep your gun when it's in the house."

"Heather," he begins, but I cut him off.

"Not now," I say. "Let's figure out who's trying to kill Tania first. Then we can deal with our own problems."

As I get closer to the firepit, I pick up on some of the lyrics Nicole is singing. Her voice is pleasing, with a lovely lightness to it.

Unfortunately, the same can't be said for the words to her song.

"'My blood,'" Nicole is singing soulfully as she gazes into the sunset, "'my blood, I tasted my menstrual blood. And yes, it tasted good, just like I knew it would . . .'"

Jessica utters an ear-burning expletive, then says, "Mom, I swear to God if you don't make her stop, I'll do it. I'll jump."

"Welcome back to the family," Cooper whispers and drops a quick kiss on my cheek before he drifts away to serve drinks.

The Palm's Special
Vegan Salad Made
Exclusively for Tania Trace

16

Serves 4
Ingredients for Tania Salad
½ pound string beans, cleaned and cut into
one-inch pieces, cooked until crisp-tender,
about 4 minutes
1–2 large beefsteak tomatoes, seeded and
chopped into one-inch cubes
1 sweet onion, such as Vidalia, chopped into
half-inch pieces

Method for Tania Salad
Pour salad dressing ingredients together in a
jar and shake to combine.
Taste for seasoning.
Combine string beans, tomatoes, and onions.
Toss with dressing.
Serve on chilled salad plate.

Dinner is served outdoors on a table carved out of rock—most likely stolen from Stonehenge—under the stars, which begin to shine shortly after the sun goes down. Two waiters and a busboy from the Palm show up with an extraordinarily large number of insulated bags containing the steaks, lobsters, fries, mashed potatoes, and cheesecakes that Grant Cartwright ordered. They come out onto the deck and begin setting the table as if this is something they do every other night. For all I know, maybe they do.

For Tania there's a special vegetarian salad that the owner named in her honor—a variation of a salad already on the menu—after Tania famously ordered it (shrimp and bacon omitted) at every Palm steakhouse in the country during her last national tour, making it one of the most popular items on the menu.

But after the waiters go to all the trouble of specially dressing and plating it, then presenting it to her with a very charming flourish, all Tania does—after thanking them sweetly—is pick at it. Even her dog, which she keeps on her lap the entire time, doesn't appear interested in eating it. (I wouldn't have been either, unless it still had the shrimp and bacon on it. Lucy frequently attempts to eat out of Owen's litter box, so I'm pretty sure *she'd* have eaten it, even without the shrimp and bacon.)

Most of the people at the dinner table do their best to politely steer the conversation away from the horrible occurrence at my place of work. Even Grant Cartwright, the person responsible for my current state of poverty (not counting my mother and her boyfriend, Ricardo), pretends to be superinterested in where I've been since the last time I saw him.

"I had no idea you had such a good head for numbers, Heather," he says. "You always struck me as more the creative type."

"People can be both, Dad," Nicole chimes in. "For instance, I write songs, but I'm also doing Teach for America, because I really want to give back—"

"Can someone please pass the wiiiiiine," Jessica says loudly.

"Jessica," her mother says, with a disapproving glance. "Don't."

"So you do the payroll for the whole building?" Mr. Cartwright asks me, ignoring his daughters. "And Cooper's billing as well?"

"Not the whole building," I say. "Just the student work-study staff. And Cooper's bookkeeping turned out to be a breeze once I got a system in place." I politely refrain from telling Cooper's parents that his former system was no system. I found receipts dating from a half-decade ago tucked away in his underwear drawer. That, of course, was a recent discovery, as I have not been privy to the contents of his underwear until lately.

"She's turned my whole business around," Cooper says, and there's a hint of pride in his voice.

"It helps that we found an accountant who isn't currently incarcerated," I say, not wanting to take all the credit.

"I owed him a favor," Cooper explains. "You don't have to work in an office to be a good accountant."

"I totally agree," I say. "And Cooper does have a very . . . diverse set of friends. But it's easier to call an accountant who isn't locked in a five-by-nine cell for most hours of the day."

"Heather's always had a good head for business," Jordan says as he sucks on a lobster claw. "That's why I never understood people who made dumb blonde jokes. I was like, 'You haven't met my girlfriend.'" He winces, having apparently received a kick from one of his sisters under the table. He glances nervously over at Tania. "I mean ex-girlfriend. But Tania's real smart about that stuff too."

Tania doesn't seem to be paying the least bit of attention.

She's playing with her salad, separating the green beans from the tomatoes and onions, until her plate begins to resemble a small Italian flag.

"Well, I think it's lovely Heather was able to join us tonight," Mrs. Cartwright says. She's on her third—or maybe fourth—glass of wine. Grant Cartwright has a full-size refrigerator in his kitchen devoted exclusively to wine and set at multiple temperatures—one compartment for the reds, the other for the whites. "If I were Heather, I'd have told this whole family to go to hell. It's so nice when exes can remain friends, instead of being at one another's throats."

Tania drops her fork.

"Just leave it," Jordan says, laying a hand across his wife's to keep her from ducking beneath the table to retrieve the utensil, which she seems about to do. "Are you all right, hon?"

"I'm still not feeling very well." Tania slides her hand free of his and wraps her fingers around the water bottle she's been sucking all evening. "If it's all right, I'm going to go inside and lie down."

"Of course it's all right," Grant Cartwright says, actually appearing genuinely concerned about someone besides himself for once in his life. It's easy to see where his sons inherited their good looks, since Grant has the same lean height, square jawline, and piercing gray-blue eyes. The only real difference is that his hair has gone completely white, and of course, I've yet to see real evidence of his possessing a soul, just like I sometimes suspect Jordan lacks a fully functioning brain. "Nicole, why don't you take her to your room—"

Nicole nearly knocks over her chair in her eagerness to help.

"Of course," she says. "Come on, Tania. I'll play you the new song I've been working on. It's called 'My Twin, My Oppressor'—"

"Are you *kidding* me with this shit?" Jessica demands, slamming her wineglass down so hard I'm surprised it doesn't shatter.

"Oh, I'm sorry," Nicole says, not sounding sorry at all. "I didn't think you'd want me to show Tania to *your* room, because it reeks of cigarette smoke and that isn't good for the unborn."

Mrs. Cartwright, at the other end of the table, looks toward Jessica in surprise. "You're *smoking* now?"

"The doctor prescribed it," Jessica insists. "As a way to control my irritable bowel syndrome—"

"Oh right," Nicole says, with a sarcastic laugh. "It has nothing to do with you wanting to suppress your appetite, working all day with size zero models—"

"At least I'm actually getting *paid* at my job," Jessica snaps, "instead of mooching off Mom and Dad like you've done every summer every year since, oh, your entire life—"

Nicole narrows her eyes and sits back down, ready for battle. "Excuse me, Miss I-Work-in-an-Industry-That-Encourages-Women-to-Starve, but as soon as my Teach for America training institute is over, I'll actually be doing something important with my life. What will *you* be doing? Oh, right: going to work for Daddy. *I'll be teaching children to read.*"

Yowza. It's hard to keep score, but I think I have to give the point to Nicole for this one, although in our psych class we learned that the three basic human needs are food (including water), shelter, and clothing. Reading was nowhere on the list until scientists started experimenting with monkeys, depriving them of their mothers as tiny babies and raising them in isolation cages without any contact whatsoever with other monkeys or humans, noting that the baby monkeys became completely antisocial, tried to claw the scientists' eyes out, flung their own poo at them, then died.

Only then did the scientists decide to add love, socialization, sanitation, education, and health care to the list of basic needs, without which all creatures will eventually go mental and die (not to mention fling their own poo).

I've decided to stick with criminal justice as a major, as psychology seems a bit harsh.

It takes me a minute to realize that Tania is gone, having slipped away unnoticed during the girls' argument. I only spy her as she reaches the glass doors to the penthouse and goes inside, Baby at her heels. I throw a questioning glance at Cooper, and he nods.

I wipe my mouth with my napkin and lay it beside my near-empty plate—my serving of rib eye was too large even for me to finish, and I'm a girl who appreciates a well-prepared steak. But I managed to polish off all my mashed potatoes.

"Excuse me," I murmur and stand up, not missing the look of gratitude Cooper sends me across the table. He knows where I'm headed and is thankful. Tania needs looking after. No one else notices I've gotten up.

"Jess," I hear his brother Jordan say in a sympathetic voice as I head away from the table, "I get the appetite suppressant thing, I really do. But smoking cigarettes is so bad for you. Get Dr. Shipley to write you a script for an ADD med instead. That's what I do when I need to lose a few before an appearance. Those things work like magic. And the side benefit is that the pills really help me focus, like, on my choreography and stuff."

"Perhaps because you actually have ADD," Cooper suggests, but Jordan only laughs and punches him in the arm.

"In our day," Grant Cartwright says, "they called those pills 'speed.'"

"Right," his wife agrees. "Remember that time we took all that speed, then went for the drive on Martha's Vineyard, darling?"

"No," Grant Cartwright says. "That was the time we had all the margaritas."

"Oh, right," Patricia Cartwright says. "People didn't seem to frown on drinking and driving as much then as they do now. Although that farmer was upset about his fence."

"You people are disgusting," Nicole says.

Jessica seems to agree with her sister for once. "Seriously."

Their voices fade into the background as I follow the pathway—now subtly lit by halogen bulbs hidden in plantings—into the penthouse. There's no sign of Tania when I get inside, but I hear the sound of a television and the tinkling of a dog's collar . . . Baby is scratching himself. I go toward it until I find myself in a media room, all dark-wood paneling and black leather couches, and spy Tania sunk into the middle of one, bathed in the light of a flat-screen TV. She has a faux-fur chinchilla throw pulled up over her bare legs to ward off the chilly air conditioning, and Baby is on her lap, energetically scratching his ears. Both of them look up at me as I appear in the doorway.

"Oh hi," I say hesitantly. Neither dog nor mistress seems particularly glad to see me. "I was just . . ."

Trying to find the bathroom? On my way out and I took a wrong turn?

You know what? Screw that. A producer this girl has been working with daily died today, practically in my arms. I deserve some answers, and it's time to see if she has any.

"I was wondering if I could join you," I say and come into the room, closing the door behind me. "I can only take so much Cartwright family togetherness." I cross the room, looping around the large glass coffee table on which rests a decorative basket of rattan balls (dear decorators of the world: what's up with the rattan balls?), heading directly for the couch on which she's sitting. "Scoot over."

She remains exactly where she is, wide-eyed and confused.

"There's lots of room over there," she says, pointing with the remote control she's clutching at the couch opposite hers.

"Yes," I agree, "but you've got all the blankets."

I lift the faux chinchilla and sit down beside her, careful not to touch her, slipping off my shoes—what a relief!—and tucking my legs beneath me, imitating her posture. We learned in our psych class that study after study has shown that subtly imitating another person's body movements heightens one's chances of a successful interpersonal involvement. Baby certainly appears to find the situation acceptable, since he quickly settles into the small faux-fur gulley that has formed between us.

"So," I say. "The Cartwrights seem to really like you. That's nice. They're kind of nuts, but I think most families are. Certainly all the ones down at New York College, where I work, are. I don't think there's any such thing as a normal family. What does normal even mean anyway?"

Tania doesn't reply. She keeps her gaze on the TV. She's switching channels like no one's business, seeming to be having trouble finding anything to watch, although the Cartwrights have satellite and Tania's already reached the 900s. But she's turned the sound down, which is a good sign.

"It's nice," I say, trying again, "that when you have your baby, she'll have so many people to care about her, even if their sanity might be slightly questionable. I've heard you can restrict how many people can be in the room when you give birth, so you might want to consider that. Otherwise, I could see Nicole wanting to be there through the whole thing so she can gather material for a song about tasting the placenta—"

Tania finally cracks a smile.

"No," she says, dragging her gaze away from the television screen. "She wouldn't."

"I'm serious," I say. "She might. It's hard to find words to rhyme with 'placenta,' but I bet Nicole will manage. 'It was the color magenta. It tasted like polenta.'"

"Stop," Tania says, laughing. Picking up a nearby throw pillow, she tosses it lightly at me, causing Baby to let out a tiny bark.

I pick up the pillow and pretend to conk Tania over the head with it, then say, while Tania is still laughing and Baby is running around the faux chinchilla in excited circles, "So. Do you want to tell me who hates you enough to try to poison you? Because I think you know."

Tania's laughter abruptly dies. She sinks back against the leather cushions and stares up at the TV screen, but it doesn't seem to me as if she's really seeing it.

"I don't," she says. She's wearing a filmy, multicolored dress, her shoulders bare, her hair loosely curling all over. When she shakes her head, the curls tremble. "I don't know."

"Don't lie to me, Tania," I say. I'm no longer mirroring her posture, which is slumped in defeat. I'm sitting up straight. "You can lie to everybody else, but you can't lie to me. You *owe* me. You actually owe me double, because Jared died in my building." This is a slight exaggeration, because Jared died hours after he collapsed in front of me, in the hospital, but I'm pretty sure Tania doesn't know this. "And if it wasn't for you, *I'd* be the one married to Jordan."

I'm piling lie on top of lie, but I tell myself it's for the greater good, which is getting to the truth. If I hadn't caught Tania with Jordan, he and I would have broken up anyway, because I'd have wised up on my own and realized what a terrible couple we made . . . and how much of a better fit I'd be with his older brother, Cooper, if only I could get him to glance my way. (I can't believe it took as long as it did to get him to.)

Tania doesn't need to know this, however.

Finally, she glances at me.

"I thought you were over Jordan," she says, looking slightly suspicious. "I thought you were with Cooper now."

I'm so stunned, I nearly kick Baby off the blanket and across the room, like he's a little Chihuahua football.

"How did you know *that?*" I demand, my voice rising to a squeak.

"Stephanie told me," Tania says.

Who *didn't* Stephanie tell?

"Does Jordan know?" I ask. I assume not, or Jordan wouldn't have been so chummy with Cooper at the dinner table . . . unless that was all an act to lull Cooper into a false sense of security so Jordan can push Cooper off the deck later. But I don't think Jordan is capable of that kind of duplicity, and Cooper is armed anyway.

"No," Tania says, shaking her head. The curls tremble. "Jordan doesn't know. Stephanie said not to tell him. She says . . . she says you guys are getting married."

"Well," I say. I'm going to punch Stephanie in the face next time I see her. I don't care that she spent the day getting her stomach pumped full of charcoal because she ate rat poison. "There's no date set or anything, but it's something Cooper and I have talked about. Stephanie's right, it would be great if you wouldn't tell Jordan yet. It's a little . . . awkward."

"I understand," Tania says, and she looks down at her fingers. On the third finger of her left hand is a diamond that's approximately the size of Dayton, Ohio, or possibly even Paris, France. "Jordan can be a little . . . babyish about some things."

"Yes," I say, surprised by the maturity both of the admission and of her tone. "He can be sometimes."

"I'm sorry I did that to you," Tania says, speaking to her

diamond ring. "What you caught me doing that day with Jordan. I knew you were still with him, but I . . . I *needed* to."

You *needed* to give my live-in boyfriend a blow job? I want to ask.

Instead I say, "I understand," even though I don't.

"Have you ever been married before, Heather?" Tania asks, still looking at her ring.

"No," I say, unable to restrain a smile. Tania doesn't mean to be funny, I know, but I can't help laughing a little. It suddenly strikes me as amusing that she's about to give *me* some marital advice, even though I'm so much older than she is. She's closer to Jessica and Nicole's age than Jordan's.

"Well," she says with a gusty sigh, "I have. That's why all this is happening."

"Wait," I say, my smile disappearing as I realize Tania was asking if I've been married before because *she* has. But that's impossible, because the girl is barely old enough to drink legally . . . plus a few years. "*What?*"

"That's why all this is happening," she repeats. "You're right, I *do* owe you the truth. And you know what? I feel better about it now that I've told you." She smiles and picks up her dog, giving him a little squeeze. "Wow, you're easy to talk to. I knew you'd understand. No wonder you're so good at your job. I bet those students tell you stuff all the time. Secret stuff they've never told anyone before, like what I just told you. I've never told that to anyone before, not even my stylist. Or Jordan."

I've thrown off the chinchilla rug, put both feet on the floor, and am staring her straight in the face. Only she won't look at me, because her face is buried in Baby's fur.

"Tania," I say. "What *exactly* are you talking about? What secret? What is happening?"

"Everything," she says with a shrug of her elfin shoulders as she hugs Baby so tightly that he begins to struggle. She doesn't let him go, she doesn't look up, and her voice is muffled as she hides her face in shame. "Why I had to steal Jordan away from you. Why Bear got shot. And why Jared died today."

"Why?" I ask, even though I think I finally know.

When she looks up at last, her cheeks are wet with tears.

"Because of my ex-husband," she says. "He says he's going to kill me."

Baby Mama Drama

Baby mama
That's what he calls me

Don't want no drama
So I don't say a thing

But I ain't his mama
And this ain't his baby

So there's gonna be trauma
If I don't nip this thing

"Baby Mama"
Performed by Tania Trace
Written by Larson/Trace
Cartwright Records
So Sue Me album

17

"So what'd she say?" Cooper asks as soon as he climbs back into the Cadillac Escalade in which we're being driven home. He's just come from escorting Tania and Jordan up to their apartment, which is in a building a few blocks downtown and west, on Fifth Avenue, from Grant Cartwright's. I elected to stay in the car, too disturbed by the story Tania told me back at Cooper's parents' place to do more than utter a polite good night.

"I'll tell you when we get home," I say, my gaze on the driver.

"Are you sure?" Cooper asks, looking surprised.

"Oh yes," I say. "I'm sure."

Cooper, after giving me a questioning glance, leans forward to give the driver our address, and I sink back against the hand-stitched leather seats, staring unseeingly out the tinted window.

"Just making sure Dad gets his money's worth," Cooper had joked when Jordan—and the building's doorman—insisted it wasn't necessary for him to accompany Tania all the way to the door and then *inside* the apartment she shares with Jordan.

"Our security in this building is very good, sir," the doorman said to Cooper. "We have a night watchman posted at the door to the garage downstairs and monitors on all the exits and stairwells."

"And our lock's a Medeco," Jordan pointed out proudly.

"I think you should let him," I'd said from inside the Escalade.

Cooper, Jordan, and the doorman had all leaned into the open car door to look at me oddly. Tania kept her face buried in her Chihuahua's sparkly jacket, looking at no one at all.

"Excuse me, miss?" the doorman had said.

"I think they should let this man escort them to their apartment," I'd said. "I'll wait down here in the car for them. It will just take a minute. I don't know if you heard, but there was a murder today. A stalker of Ms. Trace sent her a box of cupcakes tainted with rat poison, and someone ate one and died. Whatever your building's normal security precautions are for her, quadruple them. And do not eat or

even open anything addressed to her. I'm sure the police
have been by—"

The doorman was a young guy. "Actually," he said, swallowing hard, "I just started my shift. I haven't even had a
chance to read the log notes—"

"That's what I'm here for," Cooper said and draped his
linen sport coat over Tania's shoulders as he walked her
into the building, the doorman and Jordan following closely
behind. "Cooper Cartwright Security Services. Can't get
rid of me until I've briefed all your staff and checked under
your bed for intruders. Only then do I call it quits for the
evening."

The funny part—if you can call it funny—is that I haven't
yet had a chance to tell Cooper the terrifying tale Tania
had dropped on me like a hydrogen bomb an hour earlier.
It had been almost a relief when Nicole had come bursting
into the media room, demanding that Tania and I watch a
DVD of her performance in the talent competition at her
all-women's college the year before, in which she'd come in
third (in the single-vocalist division).

"Moooom," Jessica had shrieked, coming close on her
twin's heels, "she's making people watch it again!"

I enjoyed the video—in which Nicole performed the
Eagles' "Witchy Woman" on guitar—since it gave me a
chance to try to process Tania's confidences. Eventually the
whole family drifted in from the deck, Cooper ending up
sitting on the arm of the leather couch beside me.

"Are you all right?" he'd leaned in to whisper at one
point, pretending to be reaching for one of the whiskeys

his father had poured for everyone but Tania. "You look . . . freaked out."

Who wouldn't have been? Tania's story had bordered on the . . . I didn't even know what.

"Fine," I'd whispered back. But I was relieved when Cooper suggested we all head home a few minutes later, noting that Tania seemed tired.

"Are you sure?" Jordan had asked, seeming reluctant for the evening to end. "We could stop by my place and have a Drambuie. Well, *we* three could." He gave his sisters a dark look. "*They're* not invited. And Tania usually likes chamomile tea before bed these days."

The girl known for raunchy hits like "Bitch Slap" and "Candy Man" hadn't tried to deny it. Instead, she and I exchanged glances. She'd made me swear to tell no one—*no one*—what she'd told me. It was a matter, she'd said, of life and death. Her baby's life and her death.

I believed her, now more than ever. In the few minutes Cooper was upstairs in Tania and Jordan's apartment, leaving me alone in the car with my thoughts and the Cartwrights' driver, I heard the words "New York College" from the radio the driver was listening to softly in the front seat.

"Can you turn that up, please?" I asked and then regretted it immediately when he did so.

"No word yet from police as to whether the poisoning was accidental," said the familiar voice of the announcer. It was a twenty-four-hour news radio station, the one Sarah insisted we listen to endlessly in the office for news of the Israeli-Palestinian conflict. Not that I didn't feel badly about the Israeli-Palestinian conflict. I just preferred listening to music while I worked. "According to a statement issued by Grant Cartwright, president and CEO of Cartwright Records Television, the producer had been working on a new reality show starring Jordan Cartwright, the lead singer of the now-defunct boy band Easy Street, and his new wife, Tania Trace, whose song 'So Sue Me' is the nation's number-one single. The show is being filmed at Fischer Hall, a New York College dormitory known for having been the site of numerous violent deaths this year, some involving New York College students. It's currently housing fifty teenage girls, nonstudents, all attending a rock camp hosted by Trace. No word on whether or not the camp—or filming of the reality show—will be suspended in light of the death."

I dropped my face into my hands, Tania's words echoing in my head. "I met my husband in high school. We were in choir together. I was a soprano. He was a tenor. But I could sing any part, so sometimes if Mr. Hall needed me to, I'd sing alto. I didn't care, as long as I was singing. Singing is the only thing that's ever made me truly happy."

I'd sat looking at Tania in the glow of the television screen—the only light in the windowless room. She'd seemed so fragile and vulnerable.

"Maybe," she'd added, glancing down at the barely perceptible bulge of her belly, "having a baby will make me happy. I've heard people say they never knew true joy until they looked down into the eyes of their newborn, but I don't think those people know what it feels like to sing. When I sing . . . it's like nothing can touch me. You know?"

This statement didn't surprise me. Given her meteoric rise to fame, it made sense. Successful people are generally happiest when they're doing what they love.

What *did* surprise me was the odd statement about why she loved singing so much. That I couldn't relate to. Like nothing could touch her? What did that even mean? Who— or what—was trying to touch her?

And where had this ex-husband come from? I'd never heard about Tania having an ex-husband, let alone one from as far back as high school. How could Tania Trace have an ex-husband? How had Cartwright Records managed to keep *this* off her Wikipedia page, let alone "Page Six"? She and Jordan had just had a million-dollar wedding—in St. Patrick's Cathedral no less! The Catholic Church is generally pretty thorough about checking up on this stuff.

"We were good," Tania said, rubbing Baby's ears. "We were the smallest school from the poorest district in our county, but we got invited to State. You know when you're singing onstage in a group, and all the voices blend together perfectly, and you hear that ringing sound, like a bell, inside your head?"

That's when I realized she was talking about her choir, not how well she and her high school boyfriend had gotten along as a couple.

"Uh . . . sure, I guess," I said, lowering my gaze. I didn't want her to see the tears that formed in my eyes. It sounded silly, but I was familiar with the sound she was talking about. I hadn't realized until precisely that moment how much I missed it. "So that's what happened when you performed? You guys got that ringing sound together?"

"Yes," she said, smiling as if relieved that I understood. "We . . . blended, you know? The whole auditorium would fall silent after one of our performances, sitting there, listening to the last echo of our voices fading away . . . only then would they stand up and start clapping. What's that called, Heather?" she asked me, with a naïveté that reminded me a little of Jordan.

"A standing ovation?" I asked.

"No, not that. When voices blend together like that?"

Generosity, I wanted to tell her. When no single vocalist tries to outperform any of the others onstage, because they're all working for the good of the group. It's called good showmanship and generosity, and it's extremely rare. It tends to happen only in professional choirs and, I was fairly certain, in whatever choir Tania Trace happened to be in, because everyone else in it sensed what a fantastic talent she had and was hoping some of it might rub off on them.

If one wanted to be cynical about it, one could surmise that maybe they'd hoped that, if they stayed on her good side, Tania would think kindly of them when she was famous one day, as surely they'd known she would be, and treat them kindly in return. That's what show business was all about.

"I don't know," I'd said instead, wanting to steer the conversation back to her boyfriend . . . and now ex-husband, stalker, and would-be killer. "Tania, I don't think that had anything to do with him or the rest of the choir. I think that was you. Because obviously you're the one who went on to have such a fantastic career. Did you ever think of that?"

She shook her head so vehemently that the curls went

flying everywhere. "No," she said. "We came in first. First in the whole state. That was because of him, because he was *so* talented and *so* driven, and made me believe I could be someone special. He was the one who said we should get married and move to New York City, and that I should try auditioning for Broadway shows."

Of course he had. There'd been no generosity involved. The guy had wanted to use her as his ticket to fame, the way Mrs. Upton was using Cassidy, the way my mom and Ricardo (and let's face it, my dad) had used me.

"What about your parents?" I asked. "Didn't they think you should maybe slow it down some, take some college classes or whatever first?"

"I'm not like you, Heather," Tania said, smiling a little ruefully, like I'd said something sweetly funny. "I didn't have parents who did things like save up for college."

As it happened, neither did I, but I didn't see the point in mentioning this.

"My dad left when I was a baby," Tania went on. "My mom was real supportive when I told her I was moving to New York, because she was having a hard enough time feeding my three little brothers on what she was making at the restaurant. Plus"—the color began to rise in Tania's face—"she'd remarried, and with my new stepdad, well, it was getting kind of crowded in the house . . ."

I could only imagine how "crowded" it was getting in the house and how positively Tania's mother must have viewed Tania's decision to move to New York, especially when it came to getting her away from the new stepdad. You don't

become one of *People* magazine's fifty most beautiful overnight. Tania must have been as much of a knockout back
then as she was now.

"So you got married and moved here," I said.

"Yeah," Tania said, looking at one of her bare feet, peeking out from beneath the faux-fur chinchilla. She had a gorgeous pedicure to match her dark, glossy purple manicure.
The manicurist must have bungled the finish on her smallest
toe, since Tania found a rough spot and began to pick at it.
"And even though I know we should have been happy as
newlyweds, it was much harder than I thought it was going
to be, at first. The only apartment we could afford was this
tiny one-room studio in Queens on the second floor above
this bar, so not only was it noisy, but it was filled with cockroaches. When you turned the light on, they'd all skitter
away to hide under the refrigerator." I noticed she was tug-
ging harder at the nail polish. "But Gary said as soon as I got
a job, we'd move to a better place. And we did, after I got
signed as one of the backup singers on *Williamsburg Live*,
do you remember that show? Probably not, it got canceled
after one season. Then we got a better place, in Chinatown.
It was still only one room, but at least it didn't have roaches.
And then we got an even *better* apartment after I got hired
as a backup singer for Easy Street when they went on that
European tour. And then I got the contract with Cartwright
Records—"

"And what was Gary doing while you were working at all
these jobs?" I asked, thinking how common her story was,
repeated day in, day out, at least in New York City. Poor girl

meets poor boy. Poor girl marries poor boy, and they move to the big city to pursue their big dream. There, poor girl meets rich boy, becomes a big star, and dumps poor boy. Poor boy tries to murder girl in revenge.

"Well," she said, biting her lip, "that was the thing. Gary was my manager—"

"*What?*" This was a different twist on the story.

"Gary was my manager," Tania repeated. "So he worked real hard with me on my vocal training and spent a lot of time on the phone with people, trying to get me auditions and stuff. The thing was, I don't think he really had that many connections, or as many as he said he did, coming from Florida. I started getting the feeling he was mostly annoying people—"

I bet he was, some high school kid who'd hitched himself to a star like Tania's. I bet he'd annoyed a *lot* of people. It was amazing no one had tried to murder *him*.

"So . . ."—Tania picked harder at her toe—"I started going out to auditions on my own, jobs I heard about through other girls. I didn't want to make Gary mad. I did it because I loved him, and I wanted to prove what we had was special. I thought things would get better when I got some work. He was so stressed out because I wasn't really making a lot of money for us," Tania said. "It was my fault, really. He'd get so stressed, he'd say things he didn't mean."

"What kinds of things?" I asked, keeping my voice neutral with an effort. I wanted to go back out onto the deck, find Cooper, and tell him to go after this Gary guy with everything he had—including, and most especially, his gun.

But I knew I had to get the whole story first. Besides, no

one knew better than I did that violence doesn't solve anything. Most of the time.

"Oh," Tania said with a shrug, still picking at her toe, "stupid things, like I was never going to make it because I wasn't talented enough and maybe I should quit."

The lyrics from her hit song "So Sue Me," the one that was so different from her others, popped into my head.

All those times you said
I'd never make it
All those times you said
I should quit

"But that didn't make any sense, because if I quit, then we'd have *no* money," Tania said. I noticed her eyes were filled with tears. "And then when I *did* get work," she went on, "he'd get so mad, because of course the jobs were never through *his* contacts. I'd have to pretend they were, you know, make things up, like that someone he'd called had hired me instead of someone I knew. Otherwise, the things he'd say . . . they were even worse."

"Like what?" I asked carefully.

All those times you said
I'm nothing without you
The sad part is
I believed it too

"I don't know," she said, her shoulders hunched defensively. "Just . . . things."

Then I left and
What do you know
I made it on
My very own

"Tania," I said, still keeping my voice neutral, "did Gary
hit you?"

"Oh," Tania said, in dismay. "Oh no. Not again."

I looked down and saw that blood was welling from her
toe. She'd peeled off the nail polish and in doing so had
ripped part of the nail. Her face crumpled.

"I don't want to get blood on their furry thing," she said,
tears flowing down her face.

"Don't worry," I said, though my heart had begun to race.
She'd ripped part of her own toenail off, right in front of
me, when I'd asked if Gary ever hit her. "Here, I have a
Band-Aid."

My fingers shaking, I reached for my purse. I had tucked a
handful of adhesive bandages into it before leaving home in
anticipation of the blisters I was going to get from my high
heels . . . although truthfully, I nearly always had a Band-
Aid or two with me. It was another symptom of the hypervigilance from which I suffered, working in Death Dorm.
Though how a Band-Aid would have helped Jared today, I
don't know. I didn't know how it was going to help Tania,
either. I knew only I had to try.

I peeled the packaging off the Band-Aid and wrapped it
gently around Tania's toe, which she was holding out toward
me like an injured child. In many ways, I felt she *was* an

injured child . . . an injured child who was carrying a child
inside of her in more ways than one.

"There," I said when I was through. "Does that feel better?"

"Yes, thank you. I'm so stupid," she murmured through
her tears. "I'm sorry. I'm so sorry for what happened to Jared.
It was all my fault. I shouldn't have stopped paying Gary, I
should have believed him when he said he was going to hurt
someone if I didn't—"

"You were paying him?" I interrupted. "He's been *black-
mailing* you?"

"Not blackmail," Tania said quickly. "Alimony. Well, sort
of alimony. I owe him that much—"

More lyrics from her song pop into my head:

Go ahead, go all the way
Take me to court
It'll make my day
So sue me

No wonder she sang "So Sue Me" with so much feeling.
She'd not only written it herself, she'd *lived* it.

Frankly, I didn't think she owed him a damned thing, but
apparently a New York divorce court disagreed.

"—but mostly I'm sorry for what I did to you, Heather,
with Jordan," she went on. "I knew it was wrong. I knew
Jordan was with you, but it was like I couldn't control myself.
Maybe it was because I knew I had to get away from Gary
somehow, and I couldn't do it on my own, and I knew . . . I
don't know. It was like a part of me knew you'd always be

okay?" Tears dripped off her pointed chin. "I don't mean that how it sounds, and I know it's not a good excuse, but that's why I did what I did. I'm not like you, I'm not strong. I'm so sorry—"

"Shhh," I said to her. "It's okay." She was starting to sob hysterically. Nothing she said made any sense.

The thing that was getting through to me, though, was that she kept apologizing . . . for picking at her toe until it bled, for not making enough money for Gary, and now for seeking love, one of the basic human needs, from someone else. There was something so wrong with her, so broken, and yet she was one of the most successful women in the music industry . . . at least for the moment. I couldn't help wonder what her fans—what *anyone*—would think if they knew the truth about Tania Trace.

No wonder she was so desperate to hide it.

"Listen, all of that's in the past," I said, desperate to get her to stop crying. "I forgive you. And I'm sure the Cartwrights don't care about the stupid furry thing."

"Are you sure?" she asked. Baby had clambered onto her chest and was licking her tears, but Tania paid no attention. "That makes me feel so much better. Plus . . . well, I really do love Jordan. As soon as we started singing together, I knew. Our voices blend. I don't know if you've ever heard his song 'Triple A,' but I sing backup on it. I heard that ringing sound in my head right away, as soon as we started singing, just like I used to with my old choir."

"You mean with Gary," I said.

"Gary?" She looked confused. "Gary and I never performed together."

"But," I said, now unsure of anything I'd heard, "you told me that your choir got a first in State . . . that he led you there."

"Of course," she said. "Because Mr. Hall was the conductor. He was the greatest teacher I ever had."

"Wait a minute," I said. A horrible feeling had begun to creep over me, sort of like one of the cockroaches Tania had mentioned, only instead of skittering under the refrigerator, it was skittering down my spine. "Tania, was Gary your *high school choir teacher?*"

She nodded. "Yes," she said. "Did I not mention that?"

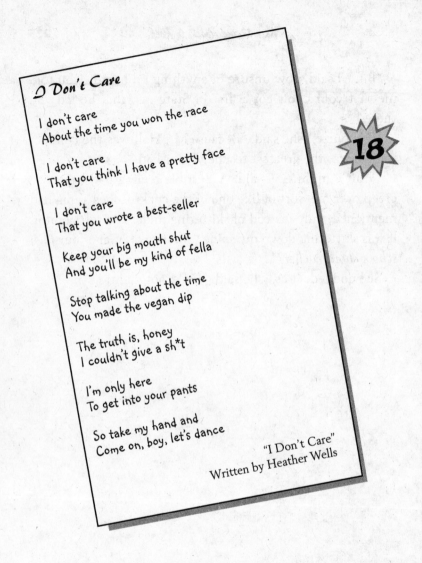

♪ I Don't Care

I don't care
About the time you won the race

I don't care
That you think I have a pretty face

I don't care
That you wrote a best-seller

Keep your big mouth shut
And you'll be my kind of fella

Stop talking about the time
You made the vegan dip

The truth is, honey
I couldn't give a sh*t

I'm only here
To get into your pants

So take my hand and
Come on, boy, let's dance

"I Don't Care"
Written by Heather Wells

No sooner has Cooper locked the front door behind us—even before I've had a chance to tell him what Tania told me—than he announces, "I have *got* to take this thing off. Don't freak out. But it's been killing me all night."

Then he reaches around and pulls his gun from the holster clipped to his belt at the small of his back, where it's been hidden beneath his shirt the whole evening.

I don't freak out. I don't so much as raise an eyebrow.

Instead, I say, "Don't you freak out either, but I have got to take *this* thing off too. It may not be a deadly weapon, but it's killing me just the same." Then I peel off my Spanx, right there in the foyer, after first kicking off my high heels.

Cooper does raise an eyebrow. "Does this mean what I think it does?" he asks, casting a hopeful look at the floor.

"Ew," I say. "No." Why do guys always want to do it on the floor? What's so wrong with a nice cozy bed? "Sex is the last thing I've got on my mind right now, Cooper. I need a drink—a *real* drink—and probably about five movies in which Tyler Perry dressed as Madea goes to jail in order to get over what I just had to hear at your parents' place."

He winces. "That bad, huh?"

"The *worst,*" I say, heading up the stairs, Spanx and shoes in hand. "Not to mention the fact that you've been lying to me about owning a gun all along. Oh, and did I mention I happened to witness a *murder* earlier this afternoon?"

"Yes," he says, "I did lie to you, and yes, a man died today. And yes, you did have to hear my sister sing about tasting her own menstrual blood, all of which were, indeed, tragic events. But I think both Jared and my sister would want us to go on enjoying making sweet love toge—"

I throw one of my shoes at him from the top of the stairs.

"Put that gun away," I yell. "You'll be lucky if I ever make sweet love with you again. 'No, I don't own a gun.'" I stride toward my bedroom, imitating him. "'I don't need a gun, I'm a brown belt in karate.'"

"Black belt," I hear him call from the basement, where I'm not surprised to learn he stores the gun safe. It explains why I never noticed it. I try never to go into the basement. Why would I? It's where Cooper keeps all his sporting equipment, such as his golf clubs, ten-speed, basketballs, racquetballs, and also, apparently, his gun collection. Plus, it's where all the spiders are.

When I come back downstairs, having changed into my "relaxing clothes"—oversize sweats and a large T-shirt left over from the Sugar Rush tour—I have to deal with Lucy, who seems to be able to sense how unnerved I am . . . or maybe it's the steak I consumed at the Cartwrights' . . . or possibly it's the lingering scent of Tania's dog, Baby. In any case, she's all over me, wanting to crawl into my lap the way Baby had, but Lucy isn't a Chihuahua, so this isn't practical. I have to give her a rawhide bone, with which she quickly disappears through her dog door. Lucy always buries her toys . . . for what purpose I'll have to take a course in doggie psychology to learn.

"Here," Cooper says, placing a scotch on the rocks in front of my chair at the kitchen table. "It's not a pink greyhound, but at least it's not Drambuie, and it's the best I can do on short notice. Don't hate me."

"I don't hate you," I say, sitting down and lifting the drink. "I hate secrets. They always come out, and then they ruin everything."

"Well," he says, "you know mine now. Tell me yours."

The fumes from the whiskey make me feel a little sick. I realize what I want is milk and cookies, because everything I've heard tonight makes me long to revert back to my childhood—the one I never actually got to have. I put down the glass.

"My secret seems stupid now," I say, "compared to Tania's. She's got the secret that ended up getting Jared Greenberg killed."

"I'm sure your secret isn't stupid," Cooper says, sitting down across from me. "But tell me what Tania said."

And so, beneath the large, greenhouse-like windows facing the back of Fischer Hall, in which I can see a few lights blazing, I tell him everything Tania told me, even though she'd made me promise never to repeat a single word . . .

If there's anything I've learned over the past year, it's that some promises are better off broken. The one I made to Tania is one of them.

"How could Tania Trace have married her high school choir teacher," Cooper asks in disbelief when I'm through, "and that story isn't plastered all over the Internet?"

"Well, maybe for one thing," I say, dunking an Oreo into the glass of two-percent milk in front of me, "because she was paying him ten grand a month to keep his mouth shut about it."

"*Ten grand a month?*" Cooper nearly spits out the sip of coffee he's just taken. Cooper's got his laptop in front of him. Midway through my tale, he went to his office to get it so he could double-check facts relating to the story as I related them. "Sorry," he says, dabbing at the screen with a napkin. "Didn't mean to be sexist. I've got male clients who pay four to five times that much in alimony to their ex-wives. But *ten grand* a month to her high school choir teacher?"

"She can afford it," I say with a shrug. "She's got the

number-one hit single in the country . . . and unlike me
when I was in her shoes, she actually wrote the song. She'll
be earning residuals on it forever. But what judge in his—or
her—right mind would award alimony in *any* amount to a
creep like Gary Hall?"

"No judge would *want* to," Cooper says, "if they knew the
whole story. But if Tania filed for a no-fault divorce, they'd
have to. In New York State, unlike Florida and California,
you still have the choice—no-fault or with cause. That's how
I make the bulk of my living—clients who choose to divorce
with grounds and need evidence of their spouse's adultery,
or cruel and inhuman treatment, in order to make their case.
Clearly, Tania chose not to go that route in court. It sounds
like she's still in pretty deep denial about her marriage."

"She's in pretty deep denial about *everything*," I say bit-
terly. "She really thought if she paid the creep, he'd keep
quiet about the whole thing. And for a long time it worked.
Until he found out she was marrying Jordan and having his
baby. Then—like any enterprising sleazeball—he decided to
up the ante and said he wanted *twenty* thousand a month
or he'd go to the press. And that's when Tania finally got
a spine and said no. She even started writing those kiss-off
anthems—"

"Kiss-off anthems?" Cooper looks confused.

"Like 'So Sue Me,'" I explain, peeling open an Oreo and
scraping the filling out with my finger. "Apparently that's
exactly what she told Gary to do . . . sue her if he wanted
more money. He got mad and said she owed him because
he was her manager when she was first starting out and he
made her what she is today, blah blah blah."

"Jesus," Cooper says. "I am really starting to dislike this guy."

"Welcome to the club," I say. "He must not think he has much of a case, though, because instead of going to court, he's been e-mailing her—if she doesn't pay what she owes him, she'll get what she deserves, that kind of thing."

"He's good," Cooper says with grudging admiration. "There's no explicit threat of violence there, so nothing she can take to the police to get a cease and desist or a restraining order—and that would be *if* she wanted to risk letting any of this become public information, which of course she doesn't. How old is this guy?"

"*Only* forty," I say. "That's how Tania put it. At least he was *only forty* when they started going out. But she says Gary—I mean, Mr. Hall—and she never 'messed around' until she was eighteen. That's the age of consent in Florida, where she's from. She says he was real careful about that."

"Oh," Cooper says with a snort, beginning to type on his laptop's keyboard. "I'm sure he was. *Real* careful. He sounds like a pro."

I'd been fairly certain at that point in my conversation with Tania that I was going to vomit all the steak and mashed potatoes I'd eaten. But somehow I'd managed to keep them down.

"I know a twenty-two-year age difference can work," I say to Cooper, laying aside the cookie part of my Oreo after eating the filling. "There've been some very happy, long-lasting marriages in which the age gap has been even more vast. I think Mr. Rochester was that much older than Jane Eyre, or close to it, and that book is considered one of the greatest romances of all time."

"Sure," Cooper says. "And there've been some teacher-student relationships that have worked too. But I'm not aware of any in which murder and blackmail have been factored into the mix. Anyway, according to Wikipedia, Tania's twenty-four now, making our pal Gary forty-six." He taps some more on his laptop. "So we're looking for guys named Gary Hall—although I highly doubt that's his real name—who were born approximately forty-six years ago and have lived in Florida. I take it she doesn't know his social security number, current address, anything like that?"

"God no," I say. "She said she's been having her accountant wire ten thousand dollars into a bank account in his name every month. Her accountant is under the impression—because Tania said she told him as much—that the money is for her ailing grandfather. Since Tania's also supporting her mother and brothers"—the marriage to the new step-dad had not worked out—"this arrangement has never been questioned by anyone."

"Of course not," Cooper says, still typing. "And because Tania is supporting her, the mother has never sold the story about the injudicious first marriage to the press either, even though she could probably make a pretty bundle off it. She's a real little UN, our Tania, supporting so many in need."

I think back to the conversation I'd had with Tania in her in-laws' media room. I'd urged her—no, *begged* her—to go to the police with me, right there, right then, with everything she knew about her ex. She'd refused.

"You don't understand," she'd said. "I *went* to the police. I did, Heather, I swear, the first time he . . . the first time. It took everything I had, but I showed them what he did to me. There were bruises and everything. And do you know what they said? They said I could file a report, and they'd arrest him, but most likely all it would do is make him madder, and he'd be out of jail in a few days—maybe even a few hours—and then he'd come home and hit me harder, even if I got an order of protection against him. What I needed to do, they said, was find a safe place to go that he didn't know about and go stay there, and then if I still wanted to file the report, they'd arrest him. But I didn't have anywhere like that to go—"

"That's why there are women's shelters, Tania," I'd explained to her. "They're for women who are being battered. Didn't the police tell you about them?"

She made a face. "Oh yeah, of course. But I wasn't going to go to one of *them*. I wasn't being battered. Gary just hit me sometimes when he was super-stressed."

Wow, was all I could think.

"So I never filed," she said. "Mr. Hall—I mean, Gary—he says if I tell . . ." Her voice had trailed off.

"What?" I could hardly believe what I was hearing. "What, Tania? What's the worst that he can do to you? He's already murdered Jared, and he tried to kill Bear. Or are you going to sit there and tell me that shooting was totally random, the way you've been telling everyone else?"

Tears had filled Tania's huge Bambi eyes.

"Not me," she said, with a sob. "I don't care about me. There's nothing he can do to me that he hasn't already done. I just . . . I don't want him to hurt the baby. I can't let anything happen to her."

So that's what had done it. Tania didn't care what happened to her—she seemed to think she deserved physical pain, enough to inflict it on herself. But her maternal instinct had already kicked in and would not allow her to let anyone injure her unborn baby.

"All right," I'd said to her. "But what if he goes after Jordan next? Don't you think Jordan has a right to know? Jordan loves you. Jordan will understand."

She'd shaken her head vehemently.

"You don't understand," she whispered. "*He has photos.* He says he'll send them to Jordan."

Oh no, I thought to myself. Could this get any worse?

"Tania," I said, "lots of female performers have had embarrassing photos of themselves published on the Internet. Madonna. Scarlett Johansson. Katy Perry on Twitter that time she wasn't wearing any makeup. I don't think Jordan is going to care, and your career can certainly survive it." A good publicist, I thought, could spin this whole thing into gold in a heartbeat. All Tania would have to do was appear on an Oprah special, provide some pictures of herself as a child in her undoubtedly run-down home, and Gary Hall was going to come off as the monster he was. "A couple of sexy photos—even a sex tape—aren't going to hurt your marriage or your career."

"Not *those* kinds of photos," Tania said, looking shocked. "I'd never do *that*. I'm not *stupid*. I always knew I was going to be famous, and I'd never let some guy—not even my husband—take nasty photos of me. No, he said he's going to publish the *wedding* photos"—for the first time all evening I saw a hint of the girl from the "So Sue Me" video, the fierce diva holding the whip who wasn't going to take any guff from any man—"and that is *not* going to happen. *No police. No one.* Just you."

"Okay," I'd said, backing off. "We'll handle it privately."

Of course I was lying.

"You said he e-mails her his blackmail demands," Cooper says. "He's probably smart enough to write to her only from computers in Internet cafés, but did she give you copies of any of the e-mails? Because they could help us track him down if he's living off the grid."

"Off the grid?" I ask. "You mean like in the Everglades or something?"

Cooper grins. "No. Guys like him don't usually have credit cards," he explains, "because they don't want to leave a paper trail, anything that might identify them or connect them to a certain place they might have been, either because they're paranoid or, as in the case of our Mr. Hall, because they're a criminal. They carry out all their transactions in cash, and they definitely don't pay taxes. This makes it even more difficult to track their whereabouts. It's possible he only carries an ATM card connected to the bank in which Tania makes her deposits, so he can withdraw cash whenever he needs it."

I shake my head. "She didn't give me copies of his e-mails, but I can try to get some from her."

"Okay," Cooper says. "He's smart, but I doubt he's smart enough to forge the IP address in his e-mail headers."

"What kind of website is that?" I ask, squinting at Cooper's

234

screen. I'm pretty sure I need glasses for looking at computer screens, but I'm trying to fight the inevitable. "One that's only available to detectives?"

"And anyone else who pays fifteen dollars a month," Cooper says. "You shouldn't shop so freely online, by the way. Do you have any idea how many times I've had to take down your social security number? And your loyal fans have tracked down this address and put it on Google Earth. I've had to take that down a few times too."

"Aw," I say, leaning over to kiss his whisker-scruffed cheek. "My hero."

"Yes, well," he says, looking embarrassed. "I wouldn't want any rat-poison-tainted cupcakes delivered here."

"I think I can resist the urge to eat food that shows up on our front stoop," I say. "And what makes you think Gary Hall isn't his real name?"

"Because I just found two hundred Gary Halls," he says. "All in their mid to late forties, all of whom seem to have lived in Florida at some time or other. I'll never be able to figure out which one is the Gary Hall we want. Seems a little convenient to me."

"Can't you find out from their marriage certificate?" I ask. "Or their divorce certificate? Those are matters of public record."

"Sure," Cooper says. "But we won't be able to get our hands on either of those until the courthouse opens Monday morning."

I point to the computer. "Can't you look them up online, like they do on *CSI*?"

He lets out a cynical laugh. "Oh, you sweet, naive girl. Some information is still available only in paper format, and then only to immediate family members. If you aren't a family member, you have to physically present yourself at the county clerk's office, usually with a small bribe, in order to obtain it. And the county clerk will still give it to you only if you're as suave and debonair as I am, with a bold yet insouciant twinkle in your eye. Otherwise, they're always on break."

"I can't believe you called yourself debonair," I say. "Bold yes, and definitely insouciant, but debonair? And I've never noticed you were particularly suave either."

"Suave enough to get you, baby," he says with a wink.

I reach for another Oreo, ignoring him. "Can't you track him down through the high school's website?"

"You mean this one?" he says, pointing his laptop screen at me. I blink at the blue-and-white background.

"Does that say Lake Istokpoga High School? How do you even pronounce that?"

"It's Seminole Indian for 'many men died here.' A group of them were swallowed by whirlpools trying to cross the lake." Cooper has swung the laptop around and is reading from the high school's web page. "Lake Istokpoga is only four feet deep in most places. Boaters need to be careful not to get stuck in bogs. Interesting that they mention this but not that the town is the birthplace of Tania Trace."

"Maybe it isn't something they want to advertise," I say. Lucy has come back inside, her bone apparently buried to her satisfaction. She trots over to lean against my chair for praise, and I stroke her soft coat. "Especially considering the high school choir teacher ran off with her."

"Still," Cooper says, clicking through the school's website, "you'd think someone might have mentioned it. But it's not a very detailed site."

"Tania said it's not the largest school district—"

"Or . . ." Cooper says in an *Aha!* tone, turning the computer screen toward me, "maybe no one there is aware of who Tatiana Malcuzynski grew up to be."

I stare at the photo he's discovered of the first high school choir in the district ever to place in the Florida state finals. Grinning at me cherubically from the second row of sopranos is Tania Trace . . . but unless I'd been looking for her, I wouldn't have realized it. She's six years younger, thirty pounds heavier, and a few inches shorter than the Tania with whom I've spent most of my evening, her hair a fluffy black aurora around her face and her teeth in braces.

"Okay," I say. "So she's basically unrecognizable."

"What about him?" Cooper taps the screen, and I get my first look at a photo of Gary Hall.

Brown-haired and brown-eyed, neither attractive nor unattractive, not the kind of man who'd ever stand out in a crowd, he looks exactly like . . .

A forty-year-old high school choir teacher.

"Mr. Hall," I breathe.

"The game," Cooper says, "is on."

"Are you going to shoot him?" I ask.

"I am going to do what I've been hired to do," Cooper says, closing his laptop. "Protect my client."

"So," I say, "you're going to shoot him."

"If he is threatening my client and happens to wander into range," he says, "then probably, yes. Do you have a problem with that?"

I keep my hand on Lucy's head. "Not so long as you don't miss," I say.

New York College Checkout Information

Checking out of your New York College residence hall?

Follow these five easy steps!

Remove all personal items and garbage from your room. (Remember, a fine will be assessed for students who leave their room in an unacceptable condition.)

Schedule a room assessment with your RA.

Return all keys to the front desk. (Any unreturned keys will result in a key or lock-change charge.)

Sign and date your checkout card.

Have a great summer!

19

Other than my bed, there aren't a lot of places I can stand being on a Sunday morning, but Fischer Hall is one of them. That's because no one there gets up before noon on weekends—unless they have to, for check-in or checkout. I usually have the place all to myself.

And this morning I need that kind of peace and quiet so I can concentrate. I have a lot of work to do.

I pull open the front door and say hi to the security guard, a woman named Wynona who often works nights, a shift that can sometimes get a bit rough if drunks wander in from the park (or happen to be some of our own residents). But Wynona is no-nonsense enough—and large enough—to handle just about anyone, drunk or sober.

Wynona nods at me over the large coffee she's holding in both hands, but doesn't speak. I don't blame her. It's been a long night for me too. I have a similar cup in my own hands, even though I know they've probably stocked the cafeteria with breakfast for the girls and their chaperones. I couldn't wait. I nod back.

Jamie is slumped behind the front desk, still in her pajamas. She's thumbing sleepily through leftover magazines since the post office will allow us to forward only first-class mail.

"Hey," Jamie says in surprise when she looks up and sees me. "What are *you* doing here?"

"Don't even ask," I say. "How did things go last night after I left?"

Jamie shrugs. "Not bad, I guess. Wynona could probably tell you more."

I glance questioningly at Wynona, but she only shakes her head and says, "Mmm-mmm-mmm," over her coffee, her signal that she's not ready to speak about it. I turn back to Jamie.

"Four service requests and one incident report," Jamie says, pulling the administrative forms from the residence hall director's in-box. "Looks like there was a leaky sink in 1718. The engineer on duty fixed it. The rest of the stuff was kids asking to get the guards taken off their windows so they could open them wider than two inches to take a picture of the fountain in the park. Like that will happen. Oh," she adds—and it's an "Oh" that's accompanied by a face crinkled with concern—"one thing . . ."

I do not like the sound of that.

"What," I say flatly.

"Well, it looks like a group of girls from one of the suites ditched their chaperone after she fell asleep and snuck downstairs—"

"*What?*" I demand, taking the incident report from her and scanning it. As I do, my heart begins to thump. The form, which is in triplicate, has been filled out in blue ink by Rajiv—he was the resident assistant who'd been alerted to the situation—is extremely detailed, and goes on for some pages. The girls are named. The first name I see is Cassidy Upton.

"Why?" I ask. "Where did they think they were going to go? Didn't we relieve them of their IDs last night?" This was a plan Lisa and I had hatched. In order to keep the girls from sneaking out of the building at night, we were requiring them to surrender their New York College–issued photo IDs to the resident assistant on duty every evening. That way, if they did sneak out, they'd have to notify the RA in order to get back into the building.

"Yeah," Jamie says. "Well, it didn't matter, because the girls didn't leave the building. They ran into some of the basketball players in the lobby—"

I drop my head onto the desk with a groan. "Don't even tell me."

"I'm afraid so," Jamie says.

"Please say"—I lift my head to beg Jamie— "that they

made popcorn, watched a *Glee* marathon in the lounge, and went to bed. In separate rooms."

"I can't," Jamie says. "Because they didn't. You know Magnus, the really tall one? Well, he bought them some beer from that deli around the corner. Then they all went downstairs to the game room to drink and play foosball and pool."

I continue to scan Rajiv's cramped handwriting, anxious to find out what happened next. "This is not appropriate Tania Trace Rock Camp for Girls behavior," I mutter under my breath.

"No, I'd say not," Jamie says, looking vaguely amused. "Wynona was watching them the whole time, of course, on the security monitors."

I glance over at Wynona, who looks up from her coffee and says mildly, "You should have seen those girls' faces when I went down there and asked what in the hell they thought they were doing."

I want to walk over and throw my arms around Wynona's neck. But I realize that would be inappropriate.

"Were they surprised?" I ask her instead.

"I don't know what kind of place they think we're running here," Wynona says. "One of them was actually standing on the pool table, doing a kind of stripper dance for the boys. 'Does this look like a Hooters?' I asked her. And those boys. They know better than that. I asked them, 'Aren't you in enough trouble already? Do you really want the president of this college finding out you're buying beer for girls who are in the ninth grade?'"

"Then what happened?" I ask.

"Well, of course, the boys claimed the girls told them that they were twenty-one. But what twenty-one-year-old wears Hello Kitty underwear? I said to the girl on the pool table, 'Baby, put your clothes back on. You know I got that entire stripper dance you just did on my security camera? I'm of half a mind right now to give that tape to your mama. And if you were my child, I would slap you from here to Newark.'"

"Let me guess," I say, not even having to glance down at the incident report form to check the name. "That was Cassidy Upton?"

"How would I know?" Wynona demands. "They all look the same to me, with those skinny bodies and all the makeup. I called for Rajiv, took away the beer, and sent for the coach."

My eyes nearly pop out of my head.

"You called Steven—I mean, Coach Andrews?"

"You best believe I did. He posted his private cell number right here"—she points to a slip of paper taped to the guard's desk—"with a note that says, 'Call if boys get out of hand.' So I called, because I knew he'd want me to. He came over, got those boys down from their rooms, took them outside, and when they came back—probably two hours later—I have never seen anyone look as dog-tired. He made them run around the square fifty times."

Whoa. I had tried to run around the square once and had been pretty sure my uterus was going to fall out.

"What I want to know is," Wynona asks after taking a sip of her coffee, "what's going to happen to those girls? What those boys did was wrong, but those girls weren't exactly innocent flowers either, if you ask me."

I nod. She's right about that. Rajiv had noted in his report that, after he escorted the girls back upstairs, a fight broke out. Mallory St. Clare had called Cassidy Upton "a stuck-up bitch." Cassidy responded by calling Mallory "a dirty whore who needs to take a shower in order not to be so dirty."

All three girls, of course—along with the basketball players, despite Steven's punishment—would be having a mandatory meeting with Lisa after such antics. The question was whether Lisa would tell Mrs. Upton what had gone on. As the girls were minors, it seemed likely.

But what about Tania? She was the one—along with Cartwright Records Television—who was supposed to be responsible for keeping these girls busy during their stay at her camp.

"Perfect," I say. "This is just perfect." Stephanie will be thrilled that her plan to turn three talented vocalists into backstabbing little divas is turning out so nicely.

"There are also," Jamie says, "these." She hands me ten registration cards. They're the cards residents sign upon checking in, noting that they've received their key. All ten have keys taped to them and signatures under the checkout line.

"They checked out?" I ask, bewildered, even though it's obvious.

"Yeah," Jamie says. "Last night. I guess Tania Trace Rock Camp didn't sound like so much fun after hearing that a guy got murdered by one of Tania's own fans, right here in the building."

I can feel my mouth pressing into a thin line. "That isn't exactly how it happened—"

"Well," Jamie says, "that's how they're reporting it on the news. A few of the girls' parents heard about it and freaked.

Some of the moms checked out with their daughters. One dad drove all the way from Delaware to pick up his daughter. The roommate went with them. The others checked into hotels. I'll guess they'll be flying home today. Lisa dealt with it. I'm sure you'll hear all about it."

I'm sure I will.

"Thanks, Jamie," I say.

"I'm sorry, Heather," she says, looking as if she means it. "I guess none of this is going the way we'd hoped. Oh, and none of us is quite sure what to do about the stuff in the package room."

"What stuff in the package room?" I ask, perplexed.

She hands me the key. I walk over to the door, unlock it, and can barely believe the sight that meets my eyes. The entire room is filled with deliveries. Not just roses, but every conceivable kind of flower, including lilies and carnations and huge sunbursts of gerbera daisies, bunches of balloons, teddy bears, candles, fruit baskets, store-bought cards, and handmade cards, some three feet tall. Most of them are addressed to Tania, but some are addressed to Jared, or "In Memory of . . ."

"People started stopping by with this stuff last night, and it's been coming ever since," Jamie says. "I'm not sure why. Tania's not the one who died. But I think they figured out that the cupcakes were for her and that someone wanted to hurt her. Some of them have been crying so much they could hardly talk. We didn't really know what to do with it all, so Gavin started locking everything into the package room. We're going to run out of space in a little while, though."

My eyes inexplicably fill with tears, looking at all the teddy bears holding signs that say, GOD BLESS YOU! and the handmade cards—some of them in Spanish—that say, WE WILL ALWAYS LOVE YOU. Tania may have her problems, but there's something about her with which people really seem to connect. I can't help thinking that if people knew the truth about the hardships she's had to overcome—the *real* hardships, the ones she's too ashamed to speak of and has struggled so long to hide—they'd love her even more.

"Thanks, Jamie," I say, closing the door and handing the key back to her. "I'll talk to the network and see if they can send someone down to collect it all. Keep accepting whatever people bring—unless it's food, of course. Tell people you're not allowed to accept any food. And if a creepy-looking middle-aged man comes by—"

She looks at me blankly. "A middle-aged man? What exactly does 'creepy-looking' mean? Because some of the girls' dads have been by, and they're a little creepy-looking—"

I realize I've jumped the gun a little. Cooper had left a message for Detective Canavan the night before, asking him to call us back as soon as he could, even though I'd argued that this would betray Tania's trust.

"She told me to tell *no one*," I'd said to him. "And I've already told you, and now you're going to tell the police—"

"The man is a murderer, Heather," Cooper said. "Tania's going to need to stop worrying so much about the public relations angle of this thing and get real. It's all going to come out, one way or another."

"It isn't the bad PR she's worried about," I'd said. "It's that he's going to hurt her baby."

"Well, his chances of doing that are going to be a lot slimmer once he's locked up in Rikers," Cooper said.

It was hard to argue with that line of reasoning. When Detective Canavan called back early this morning, I was the one who picked up the phone. He'd listened to everything I'd had to say about Tania's former husband—I didn't sugarcoat it—interrupting only to say the occasional swear word. When I'd finished, he'd said, in his most sarcastic tone, "Well, this is great, Wells. This is just fantastic. We got a homicidal maniac on the loose, and you tell me I have to keep it to myself because of your ex-boyfriend's new wife's *feelings*? I got news for you. This ain't a Lifetime special, and I ain't John Stamos."

I refrained from mentioning that it was hardly likely that Lifetime would cast someone as young as John Stamos to play him. Possibly Tom Selleck.

"We're only keeping you in the loop as a courtesy," I said, "because you're a friend."

Cooper winced when I said this. At the time I hadn't realized why . . . until the detective blew up.

"I'm not your friend!" he shouted into the phone. "I'm an officer of the law! You just told me a witness—your good friend Tania Trace—lied under questioning, not once but twice. As a citizen of this city, she had a duty to reveal what she knew."

"She's scared," I said. "She went to the police before for help, and they didn't offer her any. Isn't there a statute or something for that? Like the burning bed defense?" I'd actually seen a movie about this on Lifetime.

"Burning bed, my ass," Detective Canavan growled. "I *wish* she'd burn this guy in his bed. That'd save me a whole lot of paperwork. You know what I was doing all night? Questioning hippie vegetarian cupcake bakers, trying to figure out if anyone at that Pattycakes place might remember having sold a dozen gluten-free jimmy jobs with vanilla soy gummy whatevers to anyone who mentioned Tania Trace, or if any of them put the poison in the cakes personally. But guess what? Lab results actually came back in a timely fashion for a change, and it turns out those things weren't vegan or vegetarian or whatever the hell they were supposed to be at all. They didn't even come from Pattycakes. Guy only used a Pattycakes box. He made the damned cupcakes himself out of a mix, which, if you ask me, is how the hell you're supposed to make a cake in the first place. Quite the artist he was too, with the icing. Bought the little violets, though. He didn't make those."

"This is good to know," Cooper said, looking excited. "It means Gary Hall is definitely staying someplace in the city, a place with a full kitchen, so that narrows down the number of hotels it could be. He could even have a lease, which we could trace—"

"Goddammit, Cartwright," Detective Canavan yelled. "Take me off speakerphone! You know how much I hate that."

Cooper picked up the phone, and the two men started talking. That's when I decided it was time to go to work, so I could do what I'm about to go into my office to do now.

"You know what," I say to Jamie. "I'll type up a Persona Non Grata—"

"Wait," Jamie says. "A PNG? So they know who did it? They figured it out? Because Gavin still feels really bad he couldn't describe the guy all that well—"

"We're not completely sure," I say carefully. "But we think

we have a lead. And tell Gavin not to worry. The guy's not really all that memorable."

Unless, of course, you happen to have married him. Then you may not only remember him, you may never be able to get rid of him.

Jamie heaves a shudder. "I bet *I'd* remember him," she says.

I'm hoping that, with my efforts, Jamie never has a chance to test her theory.

Persona Non Grata

This individual is RESTRICTED from entering Fischer Hall, or any event or activity taking place in or sponsored by Fischer Hall. If this individual attempts to enter Fischer Hall, or any event or activity taking place in or sponsored by Fischer, he is to be escorted immediately from the premises, and NYPD is to be contacted. If he resists, use of Tasers is strongly encouraged.

Name: Gary Hall
ID/SS#: Unknown
Age: 46
Height: Unknown
Weight: Unknown
Hair: Brown
Eyes: Brown
Race: Caucasian
Other distinguishing characteristics: Unknown
Photo (if available): See attached
Reason for PNG: Stalking. Assault with a deadly weapon. Murder.

I look down at my handiwork after I've pulled it from the office printer. Is it too much, I wonder? Gary hasn't, after all, been *convicted* of murder. Maybe I should have written "*suspected* of assault with a deadly weapon and murder."

On the other hand, we're down to forty campers. Gary Hall's managed to kill one crew member and rid us of ten campers in a twenty-four-hour period.

Screw it, I decide. I'm hanging this memo at the front desk, and the security desk as well. The photo—blown up from the one printed off the website of Tania's high school—isn't very clear, but it's all I've got. I'll make enough copies to distribute one to each of the RAs, the desk attendants, and the mail forwarders, and even to the basketball team. No reason everyone shouldn't be put on alert.

Maybe not the campers, though. Don't want to start a panic.

Except in the people who need it. Time to place a wake-up call. I sit down at my desk and take out my cell phone.

"Hello?" The voice on the other end of the phone sounds only half awake.

"Hi, Jordan," I say more cheerfully than I actually feel. "May I please speak to Tania?"

"Tania?" I can picture Jordan in his enormous circular bed—why circular? He'd never been able to offer an adequate explanation—with its gray silk sheets. "She's asleep. Heather, is that you? Why are you calling here so early? It's like . . ."—there's a pause as he looks for a clock—" . . . ten."

"I know," I say. "And I'm sorry. But Tania and I made plans to have a girls' day out, and I just wanted to let her know that—"

"Heather?" Tania picks up on the other line. She sounds wide awake, but I'm certain Jordan wasn't lying. She's always reminded me a little of a cat, so I'm not surprised she's capable of becoming wide awake at a split second's notice. "What's wrong?"

"Nothing's wrong," I say. "I was calling about that plan we made to go shopping today at that new store in SoHo, Gary Hall—"

"You guys are going shopping?" Jordan says, his voice doubly amplified because he hasn't hung up the phone on his side of the bed and is also lying beside Tania, who is on the extension a few feet away from him. "How come you didn't tell me?"

"Jordan," Tania says. "Hang up the phone."

"But I want to go to Gary Hall. It sounds cool."

"Jordan," Tania says again, her tone deadly. "Hang up the phone."

There's a click, and then Tania says, her voice a little breathless, as if she's been moving rapidly—probably to shut herself into their master bathroom—"What do you want, Heather?"

"I just thought you'd want to know," I say, "that ten of your campers moved out last night. Ten girls lost the opportunity to become empowered through music, like it says on the Tania Trace Rock Camp brochure, all because you're too frightened of Gary to stand up to him."

"I *did* stand up to him," Tania hisses. There's an echo-y quality to her voice. She's definitely in a bathroom. "And it got someone killed. It's all they were talking about on the news last night after we got home. *And* there was a message from Jordan's dad saying that they might have to cancel filming. So I can understand why all the parents are upset. Maybe it's best that we—"

"Tania," I say. "Did you know that I walked into Fischer Hall this morning to find it filled with flowers and cards and balloons from your fans? So many of them, we don't even have the space to put them all. And they aren't from Gary. They're from your *real* fans. The fans who love you and want nothing from you but for you to go on performing and helping them forget their own problems with your beautiful voice."

God, I think to myself. *I'm good at this*. Maybe I should change my major and become a publicist instead of an international crime-solver . . .

"Yeah?" Tania says, sounding tired. "Well, for me to do that I have to figure out a way to handle my own problems. Listen, Heather, I've decided. I'm just going to send him the money. I'm going to pay him what he wants and maybe he'll stop. Maybe he'll finally go away."

"No, Tania," I say to her. "That's the *worst* thing you could do. Before he was asking for ten thousand a month. Now it's twenty. What amount is going to be enough? A hundred thousand? *Two* hundred? When is he going to stop?"

"That's fine," Tania says, sounding like she's about to cry. "Two hundred thousand is fine. Two million. What do I care? I have the money. I have nothing *but* money. What I don't have is peace of mind that when I walk out my door he's not going to be there with a gun, trying to shoot me—"

"Why would he try to shoot you, Tania?" I ask her. "You're his only source of income."

"He tried to poison me, didn't he?" she asks.

"Tania, he knew you were never going to eat those cupcakes. Come on. You're a professional. Have you ever once eaten a gift of food a fan has left you at a concert or venue? He knows you. He's probably the one who warned you against doing that."

Tania sniffles. "Which means he did it on purpose to hurt someone else. And that's even worse."

"Of course it is," I say. "It's why you were right to stop paying him all along. It's why you've got to keep doing what you said in the song . . . stand up to him, make it on your own. You've got to be an example to these girls, because I'm telling you, Tania, they need you. You've got to show them that by expressing themselves creatively through singing, songwriting, and performing, they can be whoever they want to be . . . not someone who takes off her clothes on top of a pool table for beer, not someone who can be bought and sold, not some sexual object for a man's desire, but a strong, tough businesswoman and artist."

Tania sniffles again. "That's a really great speech, Heather," she says. "But he almost killed Bear. And he *did* kill poor Jared. I'm not going to risk him killing one of those girls, or Jordan, or the baby, or Cooper, or *you*. And that's what he'll be mad enough to do if I don't—"

"*Good*," I say. "Let's *make* him that mad."

There's an astonished pause before Tania says, "What?"

"You heard me," I say. "Let's make him mad. Good and mad. Let's kick *his* ass for a change."

"I already told you, that's exactly what the police said *not* to do when I—"

"Tania," I say. "When you talked to the police before, was Bear around?"

"No," she admits tearfully.

"What about Cooper? Was Cooper around?"

"No," she says. "But—"

"Was *I* around? How about Jordan? Or his dad? Or Jessica or Nicole? Were any of the people who love you and are around you now, around you back then?"

"No. But—"

"No. Things are different now. We're going to help you, but you have to let us. I think you want to. That's why you asked for the rock camp to be moved out of the Catskills and into my building. Am I right about that?"

I hear her voice break.

"Ye-e-es," she says uncertainly. "But I only did it because you've caught so many bad people, and I thought if there was anyone who could catch Gary, it would be you. But I was wrong. I didn't think anyone else was going to get hurt—"

"I know," I say. I've never thought of myself as someone who catches "bad people," even though I've done it before. It's strange to hear that this is how I'm perceived by a stunningly gorgeous—if completely messed-up—rock diva. "But if we're going to fix this thing, you have to be honest with me. You've got to trust me and you've got to help. Okay? Do you think you can do that?"

She sniffles some more, but finally says, "All right. I'll try. Help how?"

"You say Gary's been e-mailing you. Can you forward me copies of his e-mails to you?"

"What are you going to do with them?" Tania asks suspiciously.

"Tania," I say in a warning tone. "Just do it." I give her my e-mail address.

"Okay. Is that all?" Tania asks, sounding as if she feels a little sick to her stomach.

"That's it for now," I say. "Just remember. You are a role model to all these girls. You cannot hide, and you cannot give in to Gary's demands." Then I add, as an afterthought, remembering Detective Canavan's comment about Lifetime movies, "But don't do anything dumb either, like go meet him alone on some dark street corner."

"Why would I do that?" Tania asks. "I hate him. Heather, did you tell him?"

Confused, I ask, "Tell who what?"

"Cooper," Tania says. "You did, didn't you?"

I hear a key being slid into the office door's lock. Rather than propping it open, as I always do on weekdays, I'd closed it behind me.

"Uh, Tania," I say, "I gotta go. Someone is coming."

"You told him," Tania says in a resigned voice. "It's all right. I knew you would. So long as he doesn't tell Jordan, I don't mind."

"I think *you* should tell Jordan," I say. "He's going to find out anyway. And I promise, he'll understand. Bye for now." I hang up just as Lisa comes in, her dog Tricky at her side.

"Oh," she says, looking surprised but not displeased to see me at my desk. "Hi! What are you doing here?"

"Yesterday was such a disaster," I say, indicating the key cards and service requests on my desk. "I thought I'd come in and try to catch up."

Lisa rolls her eyes. "Oh my God," she says. "I know. Me too. Did you hear about the ten checkouts? And the girls from 1621, with the basketball players?"

"Yes," I say, picking up the incident report and reading from it. "I also heard that you're a dirty whore who needs to take a shower in order not to be so dirty."

"Well," Lisa says, laughing, "what I heard is that *you're* a stuck-up bitch."

We both begin laughing. Once we start it's hard to stop. It's probably because we're a little giddy from all the stress. But it feels good.

"Oh God," I say after we've calmed down a little. "Has anyone heard from Stephanie?"

"I haven't," Lisa says. "She didn't look so good when she left the hospital yesterday."

"Well," I say, "I can't imagine why she would. I'm guessing she's going to be out of commission for a few days."

"Which leaves us with a dorm full of adolescent girls with nothing to do," Lisa says, "and a male Division III college basketball team that we physically cannot watch all the time. This is a recipe for disaster. Did you ever get an itinerary for the camp activities?"

"No," I say. "Did you?"

"Why would Stephanie share it with me?" Lisa leans back against the couch onto which she's sunk. "I'm just a lowly dorm administrator."

"Residence hall," I correct her somberly.

"Right," she says and looks thoughtful. "We better think up some activities for these girls, and fast. *Outside* the building, so they don't happen to run into Magnus and his crew while they're painting the lower floors. How about one of those *Sex and the City* tours? Everybody would like that, even the moms."

"That's good," I say. "But how about first we take all the flowers and stuffed animals that people have been dropping off for Tania and deliver them to the Children's Hospital of New York? Jared told me before he died that that's what Tania likes for people to do with the gifts her fans bring her. And we could make sure that the cards get sent to his family."

Lisa's eyes look as if they've suddenly filled with tears. "Oh," she says. "Oh, I think that would be a great programming activity for all the girls. But it would be especially meaningful for the girls in 1621, who don't seem to have their priorities very straight."

"Exactly," I say. "You know what else would be fun to do with them? Take them to famous rock-and-roll landmarks in New York City."

Lisa claps her hands. "Like that place where John Lennon got shot. Or the hotel where that Sid guy murdered Nancy!"

"Or," I say calmly, "places not associated with murder, to get their minds off what happened here. Maybe a more positive, female-centric tour."

"*Are* there any places having to do with female rock-and-rollers that don't involve drug overdoses or murder?"

"Yes," I say, giving her a horrified look. "Of course. Just a block away from this building, there's the Washington Square Hotel, where Joan Baez lived. She sings about her stay there in her song 'Diamonds and Rust.' Not very flatteringly—she refers to it as a 'crummy hotel,' which it probably was back then. But she mentions it."

"Joan *who?*" Lisa asks, looking bewildered.

"Never mind," I say, my heart breaking a little. How could she not know who Joan Baez is? It's weird working with a boss who's younger than I am. Not that Joan and I are exactly contemporaries, but at least I've *heard* of her. "There's Webster Hall, where everyone from Tina Turner to the Ting Tings has performed. And the Limelight, where Gloria Estefan and Britney Spears and Whitney Houston all performed before it got shut down. And . . ." I say, leaning forward, starting to feel excited, " . . . there's John Varvatos. He's a fashion designer who has a menswear store at 315 Bowery, where CBGB used to be, but he uses the underground night-club scene as his inspiration, so we could take them there, and they could feel what it was like when Deborah Harry was bringing the house down with Blondie and 'Heart of Glass' . . . sort of. And Madonna lived in the Chelsea Hotel, so we could emphasize that part of it, not the death part. Janis Joplin, Joni Mitchell, Patti Smith, you name it, there are so many great rock-and-rollers who stayed there—"

"I have no idea who Patti Smith is," Lisa says, scratching Tricky on the head as he leaps up onto the couch beside her. "But I'm sure he's great. This *all* sounds great."

"What's great?" Sarah says, stomping into the office in her Doc Martens. Her dark hair is flying every which way, and one of the straps to her overall shorts is undone. This comes off as less sexily mussed than harried and upset.

"Heather's going to take the campers on a rock-and-roll tour of New York," Lisa says brightly. "After we take all of Tania's gifts from her fans to the Children's Hospital."

"Wait a minute," I say, leaning back in my chair. "I didn't say *I* was going to do it. I said *we* should do it—"

"But you know so much about it," Lisa says. "Who else could do it? I don't know who half those people are you just named, and I've never heard of the Limelight or—what was that other place? John Varvargoes?"

"That guy?" Sarah looks at me incredulously. "That guy made Sebastian's murse." Then she bursts into tears.

"Oh my God," Lisa says, glancing at me in surprise, then back at Sarah. "What's wrong, Sarah?"

"Nothing," she says, plopping down behind her desk, tears running freely down her face. "I'm fine. Just ignore me. In case you haven't noticed, Sebastian and I have been having problems."

Finally, I think to myself. *She admits it.* I reach for the box of tissues I keep on my desk, then roll my chair toward her to pass it to her.

"What kinds of problems?" I ask, thinking about how delighted this will make Tom and Steven. Not delighted that Sarah is unhappy, of course, but delighted that she and Sebastian are breaking up, because they can't stand him.

"Well," Sarah says, taking a handful of tissues and pressing them to her face, "if you must know, they're problems about the future of our relationship. I feel ridiculous discussing this with you two, because you're so happy, both engaged—"

Lisa glances at me sharply. "You're engaged?"

I shrug. "Nothing official. We've just discussed it."

"—and I can't even get a guy who carries a murse to commit," Sarah wails.

"Well," I say, scooting my office chair closer to Sarah's desk, "if Sebastian can't see how great you are, you're better off without him."

"No, I'm not," Sarah wails. "I love him, even though he's a rat bastard who didn't have the courtesy to tell me to my face that he's moving to Israel." Sarah pulls out her phone and shows me the screen. "He *texted* me. Can you believe that? He's leaving for *a year and a half* to join the Israeli Defense Forces. He feels like it's his duty, as a Jewish American. Why can't he just go live on a kibbutz for a summer, like I did?"

Then Sarah is off, going on about how Sebastian will get himself killed, and how she's never heard anything so stupid . . . although, on the other hand, Sebastian probably will develop excellent muscle definition. But what is the point, since some hot Israeli girl who looks like Natalie Portman is just going to steal his heart away (Sarah says)?

Lisa appears stunned. She's never before been subject to one of Sarah's impassioned speeches. Fortunately, this one is cut off (just as Sarah is getting to the part about how if Sebastian thinks she's going to wait for him, he's crazy) by a knock.

"Excuse me." We all turn to see Mrs. Upton standing in the doorway, her hands on her daughter Cassidy's shoulders. Mrs. Upton is wearing white jeans and a subdued but very expensive-looking top. Cassidy is wearing cutoffs, Uggs, and an obstinate expression.

"I'm so sorry to interrupt," Mrs. Upton says. "But I received this letter under the door"—she flashes a note on Fischer Hall Director's Office stationery—"requesting a meeting with me, and I was wondering if this would be a good time."

"This is a great time," Lisa says, springing up from the couch and heading into her office. Tricky darts after her. "Won't you both come in?"

"Good," Mrs. Upton says, giving me a smile that doesn't go all the way up to her eyes, then flashing Sarah a *What's wrong with you?* look as she and her daughter follow Lisa into her office. "I'm afraid there's been a terrible misunderstanding, so thank you for giving us this opportunity to clear it up."

"Oh," I hear Lisa say as she closes the door, "there's no misunderstanding, Mrs. Upton—"

After this, their voices are muted, but it's still possible to hear every word they're saying through the long grate above my desk and Sarah's. Even Sarah is intrigued enough that she stops crying and leans over to listen.

"What?" Mrs. Upton exclaims, sounding startled after something Lisa murmurs. "Cassidy most certainly did *not*. Cassidy already told me everything, and it was that horrible girl Mallory. She was the one who—"

"Mrs. Upton," Lisa interrupts calmly, "we have security cameras in the game room. Would you like me to play the tape on which your daughter is clearly shown—"

"No, I would not."

After that, things become more muted. I grow tired of having to listen so hard and say gently to Sarah, "So, are you going to be all right?"

Sarah looks down at her lap. "I guess so. This is my first breakup. First breakups are supposed to be hard, aren't they?"

I think about my first breakup. It had been with Jordan. Now that I'm with Cooper, my love for Jordan seems like a silly schoolgirl crush, gotten over in a day. If Cooper and I were to break up—which I can't imagine would ever happen, unless he died—it would take years to get over, maybe a lifetime.

"Breakups are hard," I say. "But they get a little bit easier every day, until one day you meet someone who makes you forget all about that other person, and you realize that breakup was the best thing that ever happened to you."

"Really?" Sarah looks at me with red-rimmed eyes. "I'm finding that nearly impossible to believe right now."

"Truly," I assure her. "Although rocky road ice cream also helps a lot."

Sarah sighs. "I guess I better go see if they've got any in the caf."

"Here," I say, handing her my dining card. "It's on me."

She hesitates as if she's not going to take it, then changes her mind. "I'm sorry I've been so horrible lately," she says as she gets up. "I guess you know why now. I knew Sebastian was thinking about doing this, but I never imagined he'd go through with it. I guess I thought if he loved me enough, that love would be stronger than his urge to go . . . but it wasn't."

"He could love you and still feel like he needs to do this anyway, Sarah," I say gently. "That doesn't mean his love for you isn't strong. It means it's just a different kind of love than the love he has for . . . well, this thing he has to do."

"Yeah," Sarah says, looking down at my dining card. "Well, it doesn't matter. Like I said, I'm not waiting around for him."

"I didn't say you should. But I didn't hear you say he broke up with you. He just texted you that he's going. *You're* the one breaking up with him over it. And if you love him, that seems kind of unfair. Maybe you guys need to talk some more about it—and not in texts."

Sarah turns my dining card over in her hands a few times.

"Okay," she says finally. "I guess I owe him that much at least." Then she glances at me. "When did you get so smart about this stuff?"

"Well, I *am* taking Psych 101," I say modestly.

Sarah shakes her head. "No," she says. "That doesn't explain it. That course is just an overview," and then she leaves.

The door to Lisa's office opens and Mrs. Upton comes out, Cassidy dragging the heels of her Uggs behind her.

"I sincerely hope," Mrs. Upton is saying, "that you'll be having those boys down here, Ms. Wu, because they were as instrumental as the girls in all of this, if not more so, because they're older—"

"I'm aware of that, Mrs. Upton," Lisa says. "And while they've already been disciplined by their athletic coach, you can be certain they'll be receiving an administrative sanction from this office as well."

"What about Mallory?" Cassidy finally opens her mouth to demand. "She was drinking too. Isn't anything going to happen to *her*?"

"Mallory will be hearing from me as well," Lisa says. "Bridget too."

A self-satisfied smirk spreads across Cassidy's face . . . at least until her mother takes her arm and says, "Come on, Cass. Let's go get breakfast. We have a lot of talking to do, young lady."

As soon as they're gone, Lisa collapses back onto the couch in my office with a groan. Tricky leaps onto her stomach, and Lisa lets out another groan. "Tricks, get off," she says and shoves him to the side, where he sits, looking dejected.

"I'm *never* having kids," Lisa declares.

"Really?" I ask, interested.

"Did you listen to that woman back there?" Lisa throws me an incredulous look. "She is convinced her precious Cassidy could *never* have done what we caught her dead to rights on tape doing. And that Cassidy—holy moly, I wanted to punch that kid in the mouth. If she wasn't smirking, she was simpering. Don't get me wrong, some kids are great. But enough is *enough*, man. Between us, Cory and I have eight brothers and sisters, and now we're going on *nineteen* nieces and nephews. I've been changing diapers nonstop since I was ten. If I have to empty one more Diaper Genie, I'm going to puke."

I look at her in astonishment. I wasn't expecting this kind of revelation from her.

"So why bother getting married?" I ask. "Why not just live together?"

"Well, I still want *presents*," she says, looking at me like I'm an idiot. "Like I said, we're from big families, and both Cory and I were in the Greek system in college. I've been a bridesmaid *eight* times. It's time for a little payback. And they better fork over the loot. I want a top-of-the-line blender so I can have you up after work for margaritas."

"Cool," I say, smiling. "Invitation accepted."

"I'll show you my registry online sometime. Since you're getting married, you need to learn the ropes."

"I-I'm not," I stammer. "I mean, we're not planning on a big wedding. We're eloping, actually."

"It doesn't matter," Lisa says with a shrug. "People will still want to buy you stuff, so you better register or they'll get you crappy shit you don't want. What's that?" She points at something on my desk.

"This?" I hand her the PNG form. "Just something I made up this morning."

She reads it quickly. "God. Is this the guy? The guy from yesterday?"

"Yeah," I say. "I was thinking . . . should I change it from 'murder' to 'suspected murder'?"

Lisa studies the PNG for a while. Then she hands it back to me and says, "How about simply 'harassment'? The thing is, they haven't proved he murdered or assaulted anyone yet, and we don't want to leave the college open to any lawsuits if he should happen to see this. That's the kind of world we're living in. We say he murdered someone, and he didn't, and he can sue us. It's harder to define harassment . . . a guy whipped out his junk to show it to me on the subway the other day. I suppose he thought it was a compliment."

As a native New Yorker, Lisa must find this kind of thing pretty run-of-the-mill . . . as, apparently, are guys who stalk and kill people, like on my PNG. So run-of-the-mill, you have to be careful not to insult *them*.

"Actually," she goes on, "this is a good story to tell the campers when we go on the subway to the hospital this afternoon. Many of them not only may never have taken public transportation in a large city, they may never have encountered a flasher before. I want to make sure they know what to do."

"What did you do?" I ask her. "When the guy whipped out his junk?"

"Oh," she says with a shrug, passing the PNG back to me,

"I took a video of him with my cell phone. He got off at the next stop and ran away. I posted the video on YouTube and Facebook. I hope his mom sees it. I'm sure she'd be very proud to know how her boy turned out."

"That is exactly," I say, "the kind of story the girls who go to Tania Trace Rock Camp need to hear."

Hebrew Fever

Joshua and Jericho
Moses and the deep red sea
Why does my name only echo?
Why does he never think of me?

I've got Hebrew fever
But he sees only her
I've got Hebrew fever
Why won't he leave her?

I've known but one Israelite
My heart for him's like Isaac's rock
But no late ram, no saving light
To him I'm nothing but a lost sock

I've got Hebrew fever
But he only sees her
I've got Hebrew fever
Why won't he leave her?

From Tel Aviv to Haifa
From Elat to Jerusalem
They dance and sing the hora
As if there was no one but them*

I've got Hebrew fever
But he only sees her
I've got Hebrew fever
Why won't he leave her?

*Alternate line: I am filled with dirty phlegm

This song written, produced, and created by
Sarah Rosenberg, New York College
Department of Housing.

"So when you sit down to write a song," says Tania, sitting perched on a high stool at the far end of the second-floor library, well away from the windows, "what you want to do is tell a story—"

A hand goes up. Tania points at the hand. "Yes? Your name?"

"Emmanuella," the owner of the hand says. "Yeah, so—"

Stephanie, standing beside Tania, out of the way of the cameras, makes an urgent *Stand up! Stand up, you fool!* motion with her arms at Emmanuella. Emmanuella, a plump, bright-eyed girl with blue-framed glasses, finally gets the message and stands up. A collective sigh of relief is heard from the film crew.

"So my question is, how do you know what to write *about?*" Emmanuella asks. "I get that a song has to tell a story, but how do you know *which* story to tell? I have so many ideas in my head—stuff happens to me every day, and I think, *Oh, that might make a good song,* but then I write it down and it just seems dumb."

Cassidy, whom I happen to be sitting close to—she's on a couch next to her best frenemy Mallory; I'm on the floor, out of camera range—leans over to say, "*She's* dumb," to Mallory. Mallory giggles.

"Shhh," Sarah hisses at the two of them. Sarah, who's sitting beside me, has written down every word Tania has said during the songwriting section of the rock camp, having decided that this might be a therapeutic way to work through her grief over her breakup with Sebastian, which is ongoing.

I try not to take it personally that Sarah has been sitting next to me for nearly a year and never once asked me a question about songwriting, even though I've written way more songs than Tania ever has. I've never actually sold one, though, so point taken.

"Try writing something about which you feel passionate," Tania says, in answer to Emmanuella's question. "My best songs all come from my heart. They tell stories about times when I felt real emotion about something . . . or I guess, some*one*—"

Tania casts down her long—fake—eyelashes shyly, and all the girls titter excitedly. They think she's talking about Jordan. The effect *is* pretty cute, like Tania is embarrassed to have been caught thinking about her crush, which just happens to be on her adorable rock-star husband . . .

But of course, I know she's talking about someone else, and it isn't Jordan.

Jordan has made a few appearances in Fischer Hall, though, ever since Tania—to my utter surprise—decided to take the speech I gave her to heart, got out of bed, and started showing up at her own rock camp. Every time either of them has set foot in the building, a frisson has seemed to come over the place. Far from people being upset with Tania for what's happened, however, the frisson isn't from fear. It's excitement. People—even people who hate both her and Jordan's music, like Sarah—have come to adore the two of them. They're so attractive that when they're together, they radiate an almost otherworldly glow.

Even now, sitting by herself in her brown leather pants—so inappropriate for summer—and six-inch heels, white-sequined tank top, and smoky eye shadow, Tania looks like something ethereal.

The girls seated at the base of her stool can't stop gazing at her. Neither can Sarah.

Tell story about time when you felt most emotional, I see Sarah scribble in her notebook. *Like time when Sebastian went to Israel and tore your heart out.*

Cassidy also notices that Sarah is taking notes and leans over to whisper something to Mallory, and the two of them giggle again. I kick the leg of their couch, and they both turn to scowl at me. I scowl back.

"Pay attention," I whisper.

Cassidy gives me the finger. I look for her mother, but she's nowhere to be seen. Most of the chaperones consider "class" time to be "me" time—as opposed to "performance" time, when they're always present to cheer on their little darlings, or "meal" time, when the cameras are almost always on. They run off to shop, work out at the Winer Sports Complex, get their hair and nails done, or—as in the case of at least a couple of the moms—drink as many Cosmos as they can at the bar in the lounge of the Washington Square Hotel down the street.

"Write about the person you love the most," Tania goes on, strumming the guitar that Lauren the PA has suddenly handed her. "Write about the person you hate."

I notice that when Tania says the words "person you hate," Cassidy begins to scan the room for someone. Who does she hate this week, I wonder? Last week it was Mallory, but now the two of them are best friends forever . . .

Ah. Bridget. Cassidy's gaze falls on the pretty dark-haired girl, curled by herself in one of the charmingly Victorian chairs purchased by CRT for the filming. Bridget is gazing dreamily out the casement windows, paying no attention to what's going on around her. Cassidy, noticing this, elbows Mallory and nods toward their roommate. Mallory rolls her eyes, and Cassidy smirks.

Hmmm. So this week, *both* Cassidy and Mallory are ganging up on Bridget. I wonder if this has anything to do with the hot-pink silk scarf Bridget has taken to wearing, Bollywood style, around her neck.

"She's doing it to pop on camera," I'd overheard Mallory complaining to some of the other girls as they stood outside my office the other day, waiting for the elevator to arrive. "Especially in HD."

"No. I know why she's doing it," Cassidy said authoritatively. "She's got so many zits, she thinks a scarf will draw attention away from her face. But I'm sorry, it isn't working. And she doesn't have enough talent to draw attention away from that pizza face either. If she thinks she has a chance in hell of winning the Rock Off, she's sadly deluded."

The other girls agreed.

I've come to the conclusion that, aside from Nazis, the Taliban, and possibly the honey badger, there is no one on the planet more merciless than a teenage girl once she's decided she dislikes you.

"Write about what would happen if you lost the person you loved most in the entire world," Tania goes on, strumming on the guitar. I hadn't known she could play, but she does, quite competently. "Write about what would happen if the person you hate more than anyone else in the world"— Tania's expression grows faraway—"suddenly started threatening that he was going to kill the person you love more than anything else in the entire world. How would that make you feel?"

Uh-oh. I glance over at Cooper, who is standing discreetly out of camera range. He meets my gaze, raising his dark eyebrows. *This* has taken an unexpected turn.

"Would you lie awake every night, thinking of how empty and alone you'd feel without that person? How meaningless life would be without him or her?" Tania is strumming the guitar strings with unnecessary force. "What would you do? Would you kill yourself? But maybe you can't, because you've got a dog, and that dog needs you—"

"Okay, cut," Stephanie yells, looking a little red-faced. "Great." She pulls off the headset she was wearing. "Sorry, everyone. Tania, that was fantastic, can we just go back to writing about what you love and concentrate more on the part about . . ." She drops her voice and turns her back on the rest of us, speaking to Tania so softly that we can no longer hear what she's saying.

The girls, growing restless from the hour they've already spent filming this workshop, stretch, then begin to whine for a break. They don't seem to have been affected by Tania's trip to the dark side, or even to have paid much attention to it.

"Wow," a masculine voice says from beside me, "if this is what it's like to work on a professional film production, I might have to rethink my chosen career path."

I turn to find Gavin leaning against the wall.

"How'd you get in here?" I demand.

"I saved you from dying once last year, remember?" Gavin nods at Cooper. "He told me that gives me a free pass for life, as far as he's concerned."

I try to repress a smile but fail. "Cooper said that?"

"Yeah," Gavin says. "But I have to watch myself, or he'll knock me around. What's so wrong with me being here, anyway? I don't exactly fit this Gary Hall's description, do I?"

I frown. "No," I say. "You don't."

Though Tania hadn't liked it one bit, going to Detective Canavan had turned out to be the right thing to do . . . not, of course, that the police were having any better luck finding Gary Hall than Cooper was. Aside from locating a more recent photo of him on file with the New York State Department of Motor Vehicles from when Gary had gone to get a new driver's license—in which he seemed to have put on a good deal of weight, dyed his hair red, donned a pair of thick-framed black glasses that made him look, if anything, even more unhinged, and added a goatee, also dyed red, in some sort of misguided effort to look younger—there appeared to be no sign of the guy whatsoever.

"How is that possible?" I'd asked Cooper when days passed and the police still had no leads, despite their having plastered the photo everywhere.

"Easy, actually," he explained. "There are over eight million people in this city. All he has to do is shave off the goatee, dye his hair back to its original color, ditch the glasses, not use a credit card to pay for anything, and no one'll ever find him."

"But what about ATMs?" I asked. "You said—"

"The last time this guy made a withdrawal," Cooper said, "was nine weeks ago. Guess how much is left in that account?"

"I don't know," I said. "You said he probably doesn't pay taxes, so I'm assuming a lot—"

"Zero," Cooper said. "He withdrew it all. The guy is carrying a ton of cash on him . . . either that or he's opened another account under another name, probably an alias, that we can't locate."

"But on TV—"

"If you say, 'But on TV . . .' one more time," Cooper said, "I will refuse to discuss this further with you. Real life isn't like TV. On TV the police have computers with facial recognition software that can hook up to security cameras in banks and scan photos of people, then match those photos up with a national database of known criminals. In real life, not only do most police stations *not* have this kind of technology, but even if they did, all the criminals would have to do is *slightly* alter their looks or even keep their faces in profile the whole time, and the whole thing would go kaplooey."

"So . . ." I was stumped. "What about the IP address from his e-mail?"

"Nothing," Cooper said. "He used a bunch of Internet cafés here in the city, just as I suspected. You know, I couldn't find the divorce record between those two on file anywhere."

"What?" I asked. "Didn't you use your insouciance with the court clerks?"

"Every ounce I possess," he said. "Plus multiple fifty-dollar bills and Tania's real name *and* her stage name. But I came up with bupkus. I'm starting to wonder if they even—"

"'If they even' what?" I asked when he fell silent.

"Nothing," he said. "Never mind. It doesn't matter."

"No, really," I said. "You can tell me. If they even what?"

But he only shook his head. "Tania has enough to worry about."

She certainly did. After our trip to the Children's Hospital of New York went so well—despite Cassidy and Mallory sulking all the way through it—word got out almost immediately that Tania Trace Rock Camp was going to "Rock On" (in the words of the *Post*) despite yet another tragedy in "Death Dorm." I won't say that that's why I planned the whole thing, but it might have been in the back of my mind.

Stephanie Brewer got wind of our field trip—and of the tour we took to New York City's greatest female-centric rock-and-roll sights afterward—and finally decided to get out of bed and convince the network executives (namely, Grant Cartwright) not to cancel *Jordan Loves Tania* preemptively.

I was never quite certain how she managed this, but once Gary Hall's driver's license photo got plastered all over the local papers and newscasts—which of course meant Cartwright Records had to make up a story about his being "an overly zealous longtime fan" of Tania's, a story which was immediately picked up by every gossip website and media outlet known to man—the whole thing had avalanched well out of Tania's control anyway. I don't think anyone, with the exception of Cooper, Detective Canavan, and of course

Tania herself, knew the truth about her relationship to Gary. But the media was hungry for more information.

As a result, we couldn't walk outside the doors to Fischer Hall without running into paparazzi asking if we felt we were taking our lives into our own hands by living and working there.

"We're taking it in stride," I'd overhear the girls from the camp say from time to time. (They'd received extensive media coaching from Cartwright Records Television publicists, and of course there'd been some hasty salary negotiations to convince them and their chaperones to stay despite the fact that a psychotic killer was stalking their camp's hostess. Three more girls had bowed out anyway, despite the new incentives.)

"It's actually good training," I'd overheard Cassidy say to a reporter from *Entertainment Tonight*, "for when I'm famous and have my own stalker."

Not to be outdone, Mallory elbowed Cassidy out of the way and said, "Tania's a really good role model of how you can't let something like this keep you from living your life. I really admire her." This sound bite was quoted in numerous newspapers and used over and over again online, to Cassidy's fury.

"Not in my cafeteria," I caught Magda saying to a CNN reporter. "The food we serve is always fresh and byootiful, and we never have any rats, ever!"

"Uh, Magda," I'd whispered to her as we walked into the building together, "you know we actually do get rats sometimes, right?"

"Yes, of course," she said. "But we put traps out for them, not poison."

This really was the truth, so even if enterprising journalists had bothered to look into it, they couldn't have corrected her. But of course none did. They were more interested in writing sensational pieces about how everyday items in your home might contain poison, such as those supposedly healthy vitamins you bought at the drugstore.

Tania may have seemed to others as if she were taking it all in stride—well, except for today's filming—but those of us who knew her well could see that she was slowly crumbling under the pressure. Every day she appeared thinner and more fragile. Cooper reported that she barely ate—his sister Nicole had accused her of being "pregnorexic"—and Jordan said she couldn't sleep.

Of course, neither Nicole nor Jordan knew the truth about Gary Hall. But the more Tania fretted that it was going to come out, the less likely it seemed it was going to. No one had yet made the connection between the New York Gary Hall, with the thick glasses and red hair and goatee, and the Florida Gary Hall, with the clip-on tie and conductor's baton. The only way anyone might ever catch on was if Gary Hall himself spilled the beans.

And to do that, he'd have to come out of hiding, like one of those cockroaches Tania said used to live under the refrigerator in the first apartment she shared with him.

As soon as that happened, there were 36,000 NYPD officers—not to mention my boyfriend and me—waiting to squash him.

In the Fischer Hall library, Tania says "Okay," with a nod as Stephanie backs away from her. "I got it."

"Great," Stephanie says. "All right, everybody," she says to the girls, "I know it's hot in here and you're tired, but I really like the energy we've got going right now. We'll break for lunch right after this."

All the girls groan . . . except for Sarah, who looks eager to get back to her note-taking.

"Come on," says Chuck, the assistant camera operator, in an attempt to jolly them along. "Lunch. It's fajita day. Who can resist a delicious fajita?"

The girls titter because Chuck has made the word "fajita" sound vaguely lascivious. Sarah looks confused. "It's just meat and vegetables in a tortilla," she says.

"I actually came up here for a reason," Gavin says to me as Marcos gets the boom back in place, "besides wanting to watch the collapse of the American entertainment industry. Lisa wants to see you down in the office."

"Why?" I ask, straightening up.

"I don't know," Gavin says, with a shrug. "She saw me walking by in the hall and told me to come find you. She says it's important."

I nod and leave the room quietly, just as Tania is saying, "Write about what you wish would happen to you, your hopes and dreams, what you wish you'd done differently, what you wish you could change but how, if those things hadn't happened to you, you might not be the strong person you are today—"

Hopes and dreams, I see Sarah scribble as I'm leaving.

That's it, Stephanie, I think as I softly close the door to the library behind me. *Keep her mind off the dark stuff.* Can't have Tania breaking down now, when the Rock Off is just a week away and she's so close to the finish line.

The funny thing is that I had no idea how close we *all* were to the finish line as I was thinking this. Particularly me.

New York College
Housing and Residence Life
Incident Report Form

Reported by: Davinia Patel

Date: July 31

Building: Fischer Hall

Position: Resident assistant

Persons involved in incident (other than reporter):

Name: Cassidy Upton

Residence: Fischer Hall, Room 1621

Name: Mallory St. Clare

Residence: Fischer Hall, Room 1621

Name: Bridget Cameron

Residence: Fischer Hall, Room 1621

Information about the incident:

Incident date: July 31

Location, nature, and description of incident:

Cassidy and Mallory came to my door at approximately nine in the morning and asked if they could speak to me in private about their roommate, Bridget.

Action taken:

I spoke to them, then said I would take their concerns to the building manager.

Recommendation for further action:

TBA

Residence hall director comments, follow-up, and current status:

TBA

For Central Housing Office use only:

Check as many as apply:

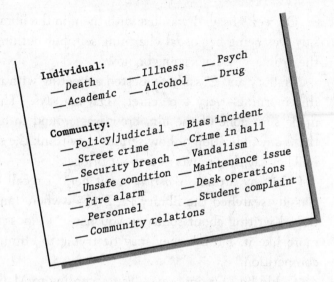

Individual:
__ Death __ Illness __ Psych
__ Academic __ Alcohol __ Drug

Community:
__ Policy/judicial __ Bias incident
__ Street crime __ Crime in hall
__ Security breach __ Vandalism
__ Unsafe condition __ Maintenance issue
__ Fire alarm __ Desk operations
__ Personnel __ Student complaint
__ Community relations

Lisa is at her desk and Davinia, the resident assistant from the sixteenth floor, is sitting in a chair beside her when I walk into our office. Neither of them looks too happy.

"Hey," Lisa says to me gloomily.

"Hey," I say back. "Gavin said you needed to see me?"

"Yeah," Lisa says. "Davinia thinks we've got a problem."

I sit down at my desk, then spin my chair around so I can look at them both through Lisa's open office door. "We had a guy die of cupcake poisoning last week, and *TMZ* is hiding in the bushes this week," I say. "What could possibly be worse?"

"Well, this isn't necessarily worse," Lisa says. "But it has to do with the girls in 1621." She lifts an incident report that's sitting on her desk. "Need I say more?"

"Oh jeez," I say. "I was just with them in the library. Cassidy was being her usual charming self, but nothing out of the ordinary. What's going on now?"

"Mallory and Cassidy requested a meeting with me early this morning—very top secret," Davinia says. "They even made sure none of the film crew was around to film it, if that's any indication of how serious they think the situation is. They say they're worried about Bridget."

I knit my brows. "*Worried* about her?" I recall the way Cassidy searched the library for Bridget when Tania mentioned writing about someone you hate. "Jealous of her is more like it. I think they may be trying to eliminate the competition."

"Could be," Davinia says. "But according to Mallory and Cassidy, Bridget's got a boyfriend—"

"Wait." I don't believe a word of it. "She's sneaking out? I can't believe, after last time, that any of those girls would dare—"

"That's what I asked," Davinia says. "They say she's not sneaking out at night. She sees him during the day whenever there's time off from filming and the other girls are practicing their solos for the Rock Off and the chaperones are busy—"

"—doing other things," I finish for her, knowing all about happy hour at the Washington Square Hotel. "Who's the guy? Not Magnus," I say, suddenly feeling my heart begin to race. "Please not one of the basketball players—"

"He *is* attending summer classes here at New York College," Davinia says. "But he doesn't live in this building. Mallory says he lives in Wasser Hall, across the park. She and

Cassidy only found out because Bridget has been texting someone nonstop for the past week and wouldn't tell them who, so one day when they were all supposed to be going into rehearsal they followed her—"

"Weasels," I say, not in the least surprised.

"—and they saw her go to Wasser Hall and get signed in by him. Obviously, later on, they confronted her—off camera, thank God—and Bridget begged them not to tell, because apparently the boy is Orthodox Jewish and not allowed to date outside the faith, so if their relationship gets shown on camera and his family ever sees the show, he'll be disowned."

"Oh please," Lisa says with disgust. "Is she kidding?"

I tap my front teeth, thinking. "This could actually be true," I say. "One of the reasons Wasser Hall is so popular is because some of the suites on the lower floors have kitchens, so residents who keep kosher can cook in them, *and* they don't have to use the elevator to get to them on the Sabbath. The dining hall is also big enough to serve both kosher and non-kosher meal plans. So if he *is* Orthodox, it'd make sense for him to live in Wasser Hall."

"How does Bridget say they met?" Lisa asks, looking at Davinia.

Davinia shrugs. "How does anyone hook up with anyone around here? In the park, of course. That's why the girls came to me. They say they feel like they're being 'disloyal' to Tania by keeping this huge secret, but this show is supposed to be about 'reality,' and the 'reality' is, Bridget isn't being real."

I roll my eyes. "Oh right. *That's* why they want to tell, out of fear that the integrity of *Jordan Loves Tania* is being compromised. Not because they're huge drama queens and want to get more airtime on the show for themselves."

"But she's definitely not sneaking out at night?" Lisa asks.

Davinia shakes her head. "The girls say no, because we confiscate all their IDs. She'd never be able to get back in without getting caught. She visits him at his place and only during the day."

I look at Lisa. "I don't know. What do you think we should do about it?"

"That's what I'm wondering," Lisa says, her expression concerned. "We're responsible for her while she's here, and so is Cartwright Records Television. But there's no law in New York that says a fifteen-year-old girl can't have a boyfriend, so long as he's younger than eighteen."

"On the other hand, if he's a legal adult and the two of them are engaged in sexual relations and we knowingly let it go on, we can be held liable," I say with a sigh, and spin around in my chair to reach for the campus directory. "Do you know the guy's name, Davinia?"

"No," she says. "What do you mean, we can be held liable?"

"It's statutory rape," Lisa explains. "The age of legal consent in New York is seventeen."

"But we don't know that Bridget—"

"We don't know that she's not," I say. "Hi," I say when someone on the other end of the number I've dialed on my office phone finally picks up. "Is this Wasser Hall? It is? Well, when you pick up, you should say that. You should say, 'Hello, Wasser Hall,' or something like that. Anyway, this is Heather the assistant hall director from over at Fischer Hall. Could you please put me through to Simon?

Simon Hague, the residence hall director. *Simon Hague*, the guy who hired you."

I hold the receiver away from me and say to Lisa and Davinia, "Oh my God, it sounds like a zoo over there. And *we're* the ones with a reality show being filmed here. Yes," I say into the phone. "I would be happy to hold."

"Should we tell Ms. Brewer what's going on?" Davinia asks, looking worried.

I frown. "That's exactly what Cassidy and Mallory want us to do. Then, when Bridget goes back to the room in tears and Cassidy and Mallory are all, 'What's wrong?' Stephanie can get the entire confrontation on film."

Lisa nods. "I agree with Heather. Let's keep this to ourselves for now. I'll call Bridget down for a one-on-one with me in order to let her know that we know and to make sure she's doing okay emotionally and—"

"Hello?" I say when someone on the other end of the line picks up. "I called to speak to Simon, please. He's not? Well, is anyone in the residence hall director's office? Anyone at all? How about the assistant residence hall director? Is there anyone there at all who can tell me . . . How about . . . Oh? Oh, really. Oh, okay, I see. That's very interesting. You know what, that's okay. I'll just come over and do it myself. Okay, bye."

I hang up.

"Simon's not in the office today," I say, climbing to my feet. "He's still in the Hamptons."

Lisa stares at me. "What? It's *Tuesday*."

"Yeah," I say, trying not to allow the glee I'm feeling inside show on my face. "He has a summer rental where he's been spending every Thursday through Tuesday, except when he's on weekend duty, which is only every fourth weekend. He's sharing the rental with his assistant resident hall director, Paula. She's in the Hamptons with him now."

Lisa's jaw drops. Davinia looks confused. "Then who's running the office?"

"That's a very good question, Davinia," I say. "I'll be sure to let you know when I get back. Right now I have to go check the Wasser Hall security desk's sign-in logs to find out the name of this guy Bridget's being signed in by. I'll see you guys later."

23

By the time I get across Washington Square Park and into the air-conditioned lobby of Wasser Hall, I'm sweating beneath my bra, which somewhat ruins the good mood I'd been in after discovering Simon's dirty little secret. It's another beautiful summer day, which means that the park is crowded with the kind of people who have the leisure time to stroll around a park when the weather is fine: workers on their lunch hour, dog walkers, nannies pushing baby strollers, students taking a break between classes to study outdoors, tourists snapping photos, and of course the type of people who make their living off tourists—buskers beating on drums or playing guitar for spare change, grifters pretending to have lost their keys and to need five dollars (five dollars only) to get a locksmith, and the drug dealers who discreetly offer their wares all over the park, most of them undercover police officers.

"Not today," I growl at one of them when he heads in my direction.

He backs off immediately with a murmured "Sorry, ma'am," causing me to wonder when I went from a "miss" to a "ma'am."

Once I reach the security desk in the front of Wasser Hall's gleaming modern lobby, it takes me three seconds to figure out the name of Bridget Cameron's boyfriend. That's because I find her New York College ID. It's in the protection officer's ID box.

"You have *got* to be kidding me," I say, straightening up. "She's here *right now?*"

Filming of *Jordan Loves Tania* must have broken for lunch. Bridget had to have hightailed it across the park pretty quickly to have gotten to Wasser Hall before me. But she *is* quite a bit younger than I am, young enough to be my daughter . . . *if* I had been a teen mom and did not have chronic endometriosis.

"Yeah," Pete says from behind the desk. "I guess so. Wynona, did you see this girl sign in?"

Pete, in his quest to earn more overtime, happens to be covering the lunch shift at Wasser Hall. With Fischer Hall closed—only the Tania Trace campers are allowed to eat in its cafeteria—Wasser has been getting slammed at mealtimes, and they've needed to double up on the Protection Services staff to make sure everyone entering the building uses the correct sets of doors . . . one set goes downstairs, to the cafeteria, through which there is no access to the rest of the building. The other set goes into the main residence hall.

"No," Wynona says irritably. She's earning overtime covering the Wasser Hall lunch shift as well. "I can't be watching every single person who comes in here, only the ones on my side of the desk. You have to be watching yours. Hey!" she yells at a student carrying an enormous backpack. "Where do you think you're going?"

The student, looking terrified, says, "Lunch?"

"Other doors," Wynona says, and points. The student turns around, his face flushing crimson, and heads toward the appropriate doors. "You're okay," Wynona says to him more kindly as he passes by. "Just remember next time."

"There's your answer," Pete says to me. "Wynona did not see this girl get signed in. Must have been Eduardo, he was on before we got here. Why, is there a problem?"

"Yeah, there's a problem," I say. "This girl is fifteen. She's here for Tania Trace Rock Camp."

Pete makes a hissing noise. "Ay-yi-yi," he says. "Mommy's mad."

"I'm not her mother," I say to Pete, yanking Bridget's ID card. "And I'm not mad. I'm just saying. Let me see who signed her in."

Pete slides the log toward me, looking defensive. "I'm supposed to be keeping an eye out for every kid from Fischer Hall who gets invited over here to eat lunch? It's *lunch*, for chrissakes. How much trouble could a kid be getting into at lunch?"

"If she was only going to lunch, she wouldn't need to be signed in. Obviously, the guy took her to his room. If it was your daughter Nancy and she was at one of those sleepaway camps you're working all this overtime to pay for, wouldn't you want someone to be looking out for *her*?"

"Nancy," Pete says, "wouldn't go to Tania Trace Rock Camp, because she's going to be a pediatrician. I wouldn't pay to let her go to anything so—"

"Watch it," I growl at him. "And these girls aren't paying for this camp, they auditioned and got in. In fact, they're getting paid to attend. So anyway—" I push back the hair that's fallen into my face during this exchange and run my finger along the list of names in front of me. "Bill Bigelow? That can't be right. He's supposed to be an Orthodox Jew. Also, Bill Bigelow . . ."

I let my voice trail off. Why does that name seem so familiar to me?

Pete turns the sign-in log toward himself. "'Bigelow' doesn't sound very Jewish to me either. Wait. Did that sound racist?"

"Dude." A group of students walks up to the security desk. "I need the logbook. I gotta sign these guys in."

"In a minute," Pete says to them. He shows Wynona the logbook. "Wyn, have you ever seen this guy? Does he wear a yarmulke?"

"How would I know?" Wynona asks, glancing at the name. "The minimum stay in this place in the summertime is only two weeks, and they'll rent a room out to anyone who pays in advance. I can't remember every face, let alone the name that goes with it."

"Dude," the student who asked for the logbook says, "can I please sign in my guests? We've got to shoot a film for my intensive screenwriting class."

"Do I look like a dude to you?" Wynona asks, her voice rising. "And there's no filming in the residence halls."

"But if I don't finish this project by Friday," the student whines, "I won't graduate."

"You should've thought about that before now," Wynona says. "You're not bringing that equipment in here. It's a fire hazard."

Bill Bigelow. Bill Bigelow. Bill Bigelow.

"Whoa, dude," the resident's friend says. "What a bitch."

"Who are you calling a bitch?" Wynona demands, rising from behind her desk.

The resident's friend grows pale. "No one."

To Pete, I say, "I need access to the student ID system from a computer. I have to look up this guy, find out how old he is, and also see if he's a full-time student or just living here for the summer."

Pete shakes his head. "Sorry, Heather," he says. "The only

computer around here is in the director's office, and that's closed. It's always closed this time of day."

"It's always closed, period," Wynona says. She's settled back down into her seat, having chased the film student away. "Wish I had that job. I wouldn't mind having to work two days a week and still getting paid for five."

I need to think fast. Bridget is in Bill Bigelow's room now, right this very moment, maybe, *probably*, having sex.

This is none of my business, of course. I'm not her mother, as I pointed out to Pete. For all I know, Bill Bigelow could be her age and living in a New York College residence hall for the summer because he, like her, is a talented prodigy, taking classes in computer science or violin. Maybe they're up there playing chess. Maybe—

Oh, screw it.

I pull out my cell phone and am about to punch in Lisa's number when two large, familiar figures saunter into the Wasser Hall lobby, one of them wearing a warm-up suit and the other dressed in linen trousers and a polo shirt, both looking as if they own the place. Relief surges through me as I rush across the lobby.

"Hey, you guys," I say, "can either one of you access the student system with your phone?"

"Well," Tom says, looking affronted, "nice to see you too, Heather. And how is *your* day going?"

"This is serious," I say to him. "I need to look up a student, but the residence hall office is closed, and my phone is a zillion years old." I hold up my mobile to prove it.

"Is that an *antenna?*" Steven asks in horror.

"Oh, you sad little thing," Tom says, taking his phone

from the pocket of his linen trousers and pressing the screen. "Who am I looking up and why? And are you joining us for lunch? I hear it's beef macaroni and cheese, your fave."

"Bill Bigelow," I say. "And maybe. One of the Tania Trace campers is signed in to his room, and I need to make sure he's on the up-and-up. If he's not, I have to go up there and drag her back to Fischer Hall."

Tom gasps delightedly. "Before he's besmirched her honor? Oh, can we help? Steven *lives* to defend the honor of young maidens, don't you, Steven?"

Steven looks annoyed. "That was just that one time," he says. "I'm really sorry about that, Heather, I hope it hasn't happened again—"

Tom gasps again, this time at something he's seen on his phone. "Wait, how old is the girl?" he asks.

"She's fifteen," I say. "Why? Did you find Bill Bigelow?"

"I sure did," Tom says, looking, if anything, even more delighted. "It says here he's *not* a full-time student at New York College, but he's signed up for seven weeks of summer housing in Wasser Hall while taking an intensive course in musical theater. A musical theater intensive! I think I just wet my pants a little."

"Musical theater?" My hypervigilance has kicked into high gear. "*Bill Bigelow?*"

"I know," Tom says. "Right? That's what I thought. And he likes girls? But it happens, I guess. Look at Hugh Jackman."

"No," I say. "That's not what I mean." I remember now where I've heard the name. "*Billy Bigelow.* That's a character from the musical *Carousel.*"

Tom gasps. "That's right! My mom used to sing that song

Billy Bigelow sings to my sister and me every night before bed, the one about little girls, pink and white as peaches and cream."

"I don't want to say this, but someone has to." Steven shakes his head. "It's no wonder you're gay."

My heart has begun to pound. "You guys, this isn't good. How old does it say he is?"

"Oh." Tom looks down at his phone. "Um . . . twenty-nine."

I whirl around and head back to the security desk.

"Wait." Tom trots after me. "What are you going to do?"

"I'm going up there," I say, taking the sign-in log from Pete and rechecking the number of the room Bridget is in. "I'm going to room . . . 401A, and I'm seeing who this Bill person is for myself. Then I'm telling Bridget—and Bill, *if* that's who he really is—that this whole thing ends now."

"Oh," Tom says. "Beef macaroni and cheese can wait."

24

Only once we step into the Wasser Hall elevator and the doors close do I begin to have reservations.

This is crazy. *I'm* crazy. It's not him. Gary Hall could *not* be living in a New York College residence hall, not even Wasser Hall, where the residence hall director takes extended long weekends in the Hamptons, and the lobby is so packed due to the crowds at mealtimes that it would be quite easy to slip in and out without being noticed.

It's not *im*possible. Simply highly unlikely.

What would be the point, though? *Why* would he take such a crazy risk? And why befriend a Tania Trace camper?

We've been learning about the different personality disorders in Psych 101. It's hard to read about them and not apply them to people you know. Schizoid, narcissistic, obsessive-compulsive, borderline, depressive. What would Gary be?

Antisocial. Complete disregard for the law and the rights of others. But also an obsessive compulsion to get Tania's attention, even if it's by hurting her or the people she knows.

I'm dying to test my diagnosis by seeing if Tom and Steven agree with it, but a kid with bright blue hair has gotten onto the elevator with us, so I can't.

The kid's not the only one who's joined us. Wynona insisted on our taking Pete.

"Oh please," she'd said, rolling her eyes when Pete asked if she could handle the lunch crowd without him. "Go on. You know you've been wanting to use that Taser since the day they handed them out."

So Pete's come along, his right hand resting lightly on the grip of his Taser. This isn't as reassuring as one might think. I keep my gaze on the poster on the back of the Wasser Hall elevator urging residents to come to the "Wasser Hall Family Franks 'n' Fun Night." I'm seized by an almost overwhelming urge to write "*FU*" on it.

Sadly I can't, because of the blue-haired kid, and the fact that I don't have a pen on me, and of course this would be super-immature.

The elevator doors open at the third floor, and the blue-haired kid steps off. As soon as the doors close again, I say, "I hate this building."

"It does seem smug," Tom agrees. "For a building."

"Who says frankfurters?" I ask, pointing at the sign. "Everyone knows they're called hot dogs. Simon just called them that for the alliteration."

"Simon's a dick," Tom says.

"Simmer down, you two," Steven says.

"You guys," I say, "I think Bill Bigelow is—"

The music hits us as soon as the doors open on Four. It's almost shockingly loud, and I've worked in a residence hall long enough to know from loud music. I recognize it at once:

Tania Trace's new hit single, "So Sue Me."

My heart begins to beat a little faster. I wonder if I should call Cooper, then remind myself that there's nothing he can do. His job is to protect his client.

"Wow," Tom says as we step into the hallway. "Somebody likes their Tania Trace, huh?"

That, I think to myself, may be the problem.

Even though Wasser Hall is so much newer than Fischer Hall—made of concrete cinder blocks and drywall, whereas Fischer Hall is made of wood and bricks and, I sometimes think, Manuel's floor wax—the walls are much thinner. The pulsating bass seems to be coming right at us.

Then I turn and see that it *is* coming right at us. Room 401 is right next door to the elevators, and it's from this room that the music is emanating. Surprisingly, the door is ajar. This often happens in residence halls. To foster a feeling of community—but more often because they're too lazy to carry their keys—students will leave their doors open, thinking that no one on their floor would ever steal from them because they're too close of a family unit.

This kind of false thinking is, of course, how their laptops, cell phones, and expensive leather jackets get stolen all the time by guests other residents have signed in.

In the case of 401, the open door turns out to be to a suite. Bill Bigelow's room, 401A, shares a common room containing a kitchen, bathroom, and small living area with rooms 401B and 401C. It's the door to this living area that is open. The pounding music is coming from 401A, Bill's room, the door to which is closed.

I step into the common room. It's depressingly bare, the college-issued furniture—a vinyl-covered couch and chairs—having seen better days. There are no posters on the walls, but there are Chinese food delivery bags stuffed into the single trash can, as well as a significant number of bottles of Mike's Hard Lemonade.

"Well," Tom says snobbishly, "it's clear no one in this suite cares very much about recycling, do they?"

The doors to 401B and C are both wide open, the rooms unoccupied, their single beds stripped, their walls, like the walls of the common room, bare. No one has lived in them in a while.

"Looks like old Bill Bigelow's got a single," Tom says. He doesn't bother to whisper. There's no way anyone could hear us over that music. "This would be a nice setup for an undergrad. You get your own room and only have to share a bathroom and kitchen with two other guys."

Steven is of a different opinion. "But that view?" He points out the windows of the unoccupied rooms, then shudders. "The poor girl. She'd have been better off losing it in a car with the captain of the football team back in her hometown than with this."

Tom smiles at him. "You big romantic fool."

The view *is* depressing. The gravel-strewn rooftop, immense water tower, and air ducts of the building next door to Wasser Hall are so close that, if the windows opened, residents could go out onto the roof and sunbathe.

"Let's do this," Pete says. He looks angry, perhaps thinking about his own daughters after Steven's remark.

"Allow me," I say and stride up to 401A to pound on the door with my fist.

"Residence hall director," I yell in order to be heard over the music, which seems to have been set on repeat. Tania is daring us, once again, to sue her. "Mr. Bigelow? We know you're in there. Please open the door."

There is no response. I pound again, harder this time.

"Bridget? It's me, Heather Wells, from Fischer Hall. You aren't in trouble." She is in *so* much trouble. "Please open up."

Bridget does know me, albeit only a little, from when I gave the rock-and-roll tour. She'd even asked a question. She'd wanted to know if we could go to that store where Madonna bought the jacket in the movie *Desperately Seeking Susan*. My answer, sadly, had been no. That store, Love Saves the Day, had shut down due to the landlord's having raised the rent so outrageously. It is now home to a noodle shop.

"Bridget?" I try the knob. The door is locked.

If Simon or the assistant hall director had been at work,

we'd have had one of them escort us up here with the master key and unlock the door so we could go in. If I'd had any luck finding someone at the front desk who knew what they were doing, I'd have asked them for the key to 401A. But the only person in Wasser Hall who had access to the key cabinet, I was informed, was "on a break."

"Should I go back downstairs and ask the desk to call the building engineer?" I ask Pete worriedly. "Surely he'll have a master key, or at the very least a drill to take out the core—"

Pete puts his hands on my shoulders and moves me gently out of the way.

"Allow me," he says. And then, in a voice that is much deeper than the one he usually uses, he bellows, "This is New York College Campus Protection Officer Rivera speaking. You have until the count of three to open this door or I and my fellow officers will knock it down. One. Two—"

There is a sound of breaking glass. Not like a single drinking glass breaking because someone has dropped it, but like a windowpane shattering because something—or someone— has been flung through it.

"Oh my God," I cry, my hands flying to my face. What have we done?

Tom has rushed into 401C and is looking out the window. "He used the desk chair to—Jesus, he's climbing onto the roof! Oh my God, if it weren't for these stupid window guards—"

"That's it," Pete says, backing up. He looks at Steven. "You ever done this before?"

Steven sighs. "Unfortunately," he says, with a shrug. "Let's go."

Pete and Steven hit the door to 401A with their shoulders. Because Wasser Hall was so shoddily constructed, the door splinters easily beneath their combined weight, causing both men to stagger. Through the now-open doorway, I see a trim, blond-haired man, dressed all in black, darting across the roof of the building next door to Wasser Hall. He disappears behind the water tower.

"Got him," Steven says and dashes through the room, then hoists himself up over the air-conditioning unit and out the window. "You guys call 911!"

"Be careful!" Tom calls after him. "He could be armed!" He looks at Bridget, who is sitting cross-legged in the middle of the bed, regarding us with a frightened expression on her face. "Is he armed?"

Bridget shakes her head. "No," she says, wide-eyed.

"I got my Taser," Pete says, scrambling up after Steven. "If Coach catches him, I can subdue him." Glass crunches beneath Pete's thick-soled shoes. He seems to be having some problems getting through the window. "Look out," Tom says, helping him get around the remaining shards of glass.

Meanwhile, I try to take in what I'm seeing. Bill Bigelow's room has been decorated to resemble the inside of a maharajah's tent. From the fluorescent light fixture and ceiling he's hung so many rich, colorful silk scarves and strands of imitation gold coins and crystals that it's almost impossible to see the room's original paint color. The bed is covered in jewel-toned silk sheets and pillows, and the dresser and desk have also been draped in scarves. Even Bridget herself, sitting so quietly on the bed in her white cami-top, blue denim shorts, and flip-flops, has a silk scarf wrapped loosely around her neck, half hidden beneath her long dark hair.

Ah. Now I get why she's been wearing the scarf. Not to pop on camera or, as Cassidy so cruelly suggested, to draw attention away from her blemished skin, but because it was given to her as a gift by someone special.

I sit down on the bed beside her. The coverlet, of imitation silk, feels slick beneath my fingers.

"Bridget," I say carefully. "You remember me, don't you? Heather, from Fischer Hall. Are you all right?"

"*Me?*" The girl tears her gaze away from the window. Her tone is mildly surprised, as if there might be some other Bridget in the room I could be referring to. "*I'm* fine."

The thumping beat of "So Sue Me" pulses from a set of stereo speakers on the desk nearby, but she doesn't appear to be bothered by it, or by the fact that a man has thrown the desk chair through a window and then climbed out after it, and that two other men have leapt through it in pursuit of him.

Tom walks over to the MP3 player in its dock and switches off the music. A blessed silence descends over the room, except for the distant sound of shouting from the rooftop outside, and then Tom's voice as he pulls out his phone and says, "Yes, I need the police and an ambulance at Wasser Hall at New York College right away. That's 14 College Place between Broadway and—"

Bridget, appearing worried, asks, "He's not calling the police about Mr. Bigelow, is he? Because he didn't do anything wrong. He was only helping me. I know it was wrong, but—"

I send Tom a warning look. He nods, getting the message, and leaves the room, the cell phone still pressed to his ear.

"Well," I say to Bridget, "Mr. Bigelow"—did she really just call him this?—"broke a window. That's destruction of college property, and that's very serious. He also didn't answer the door when we knocked, and that's a violation of New York College residence hall rules and regulations."

Bridget, still appearing fearful—but for Mr. Bigelow, not herself—nods. "Oh," she says. "Okay. I-I guess. I know what we were doing was wrong, but we didn't mean to hurt anyone."

"Of course you didn't," I say, reaching up to push some of Bridget's dark hair from her eyes so I can check her pupils. I think she must be in shock. There don't appear to be any cuts or bruises on her face, arms, or legs, or anywhere else that I can see. She appears pale, but otherwise in good health. She's begun to tremble, though.

"If all Mr. Bigelow was doing was helping you, like you said," I ask, "why didn't you open the door when we knocked? And why did he run away?"

"Well," Bridget says, wrapping her arms around herself and curling into the same ball in which I'd seen her sitting earlier in the library, "I guess we *were* violating the rules—"

My heart is thumping harder than ever. "What rules?" I ask.

"He was coaching me," Bridget says. Now her large dark eyes fill with tears. She doesn't appear to be in pain, however. They seem to be tears of shame. "Okay? Please don't tell. Do you promise? I'll die if Cassidy and Mallory find out. They'll tell Stephanie, and then I'll get disqualified."

"Disqualified?" The voices from the rooftop are getting closer. Through the broken window, I see Steven and Pete returning . . . unfortunately, Bill Bigelow is not with them.

Pete is limping, Steven's arm around his waist. "Disqualified from what?"

"Mr. Bigelow knows a lot about communicating emotion through musical performance—he's an expert in it," Bridget goes on, as if she hasn't heard my question. She's speaking very quickly, like she's had a lot of caffeine. "He used to teach it professionally. And he said he could teach me some tricks that would help me beat Cassidy and all those other girls in the Rock Off."

Tom's come back, waving something through the splintered remains of the door that he wants me to see. "No," he's saying to the 911 operator, "I won't hold. I don't think you really understand—"

What he's waving is a cupcake pan that he's apparently found in the kitchen.

It doesn't prove anything, but I feel the blood in my veins freeze all the same.

"So," I say, trying to stay focused on Bridget, "Mr. Bigelow was your teacher?"

She nods, seeming relieved that I've finally caught on. "Yes," she says. "Yes. He's really, really good."

"Then why," I say, feeling a little sick to my stomach, "did you tell your roommates that he was your boyfriend?"

Color swiftly suffuses her cheeks, turning them the shade of her scarf, and she glances down and away, at the bare knees she's hugging to her chest.

"Because I didn't want them to know what we were really doing together," she says, still speaking so quickly that her words run over themselves, like water from an overflowing hydrant. "They'd think it was cheating. But it wasn't, really.

Mr. Bigelow says it's important to do whatever you have to in order to get a competitive edge. I mean, Cassidy, she has an agent. I don't. We don't have agents in my town. So Mr. Bigelow said he was going to be my agent, and my private coach and manager—"

I don't know what compels me to reach up and gently unwind the hot-pink scarf from her neck as she's speaking. But when I do, both Tom and I see them at the same time. I know because I hear the gasp that comes from Tom's direction—the gasp that he, like me, tries quickly to stifle.

Forming a perfect circle all around Bridget's throat—as if she were wearing a necklace of amethyst stones—are bruises. They're in the exact shape and size of a man's fingers.

We must not do a very good job of hiding our horror, since Bridget seems to realize right away what we've seen. She reaches for the scarf lying limply in my hands and says matter-of-factly as she wraps the silk material back around her neck, her voice a distant, horrifying echo of Tania's that night in the Cartwrights' media room, "Oh, never mind about those. They're my fault. Sometimes Mr. Bigelow gets stressed when I don't hit the notes right. Please don't blame him. I need to work harder, he says."

25

Spice of Life

Girl, you are so sweet
I love you desperately
But that doesn't mean
I wanna date exclusively

I'm a man who needs variety
It's the spice of life, ya see?
Girl, you know we'll always be
Together for eternity

Babe, you know I'd never say good-bye
You'll always be my favorite ride
But I need freedom in my life
From that fact, we just can't hide

I'm a man who needs variety
It's the spice of life, ya see?
Girl, you know we'll always be
Together for eternity

Girl, you must believe
I'll be here for you any day of the week
But that doesn't mean
I want to date exclusively

I'm a man who needs variety
It's the spice of life, ya see?
Girl, you know we'll always be
Together for eternity

"Spice of Life"
Performed by Easy Street
Written by Larson/Sohn
Girl, U So Fine album
Cartwright Records
One week in the Top 10
Billboard Hot 100

"Don't worry," Cooper says. "Canavan said there was blood on the cardboard boxes in the Dumpster that Steven said he saw him jump into. That means he's injured. With the new description of him that's gone out everywhere, Hall won't be able to get far."

"Don't *worry?*" I echo in disbelief. I'm standing on the window seat in Cooper's bedroom, attempting to adjust his curtains so that when the sun comes up in the morning it won't blind us, but I'm not having much luck. "The guy turns out to have been living in Wasser Hall this whole time. He registered for a summer class and managed to convince everyone he was twenty-nine simply by losing fifty pounds and dying his hair blond. He brainwashed a fifteen-year-old girl from my building into thinking that choking her with his bare hands is an appropriate teaching method. And you're telling me not to worry?"

"Okay," Cooper says, with a glance at the ceiling. "Keep worrying. But maybe not so loudly."

"Sorry," I say, lowering my voice. "I forgot for a minute that we're running a safe house for the victims of Gary Hall."

"Just his main victim." Cooper is sitting on his bed, the sheets of which I still need to change because I can't remember how long it's been since either of us have slept in it, but the amount of dog hair accumulated there indicates it's become Lucy's favorite place to nap. "And I thought you said you didn't mind."

"Of course I don't mind." I climb down from the window seat. The curtains appear to be a lost cause. "I just think she should be in the hospital with Bridget, not *here*. We're not

qualified to give Tania the mental health care she obviously
needs, Cooper."

"I'm aware of that." He looks down at the ice at the bottom
of the glass of whiskey he's been nursing all night. One glass
only. He told me he wants to stay alert. For what, I'm not
allowing myself to think. "But this is the only place I could
get her to go, she was so terrified when she heard what happened. What else was I supposed to do?"

I sink down onto the bed beside him. I don't blame
Cooper. None of it's his fault.

I place the blame squarely on Christopher Allington's
shoulders. *He's* the jerk who heard the news about Gary
Hall's being discovered in Wasser Hall—he was in his father's office, no doubt asking for a loan—then rushed over to
Fischer Hall to "make sure Stephanie was all right."

Tania overheard the two of them talking about what had
happened—how I had gone with the wounded protection
officer and the "girl from Tania Trace Rock Camp" to Belle-
vue Hospital—and promptly went into hysterics.

Cooper, in an attempt to get her away from the startled
gazes of the campers and their mothers before they could
figure out what was going on, asked Tania where he could
take her.

"That's the part I still don't understand," I say. "What
made her want to come *here*? She's never been here before.
How did she even think of it?"

Cooper looks uncomfortable. "I may have suggested it as
an option." Seeing my expression, he says, "Look, I was desperate. I suggested her place, my parents' place, even her and
Jordan's place in the Hamptons . . . every place I could think

of, and she kept saying no, no. No place I suggested was 'safe' enough. She kept saying Gary was going to find her. And she was crying . . . I've never seen anybody cry that much. I didn't know how to handle it. All I could think was that if *you'd* been there, you'd have known what to do. And all I wanted to do was come here . . . home. I have a bad feeling I may have said something to that effect, and she latched on to it . . . next thing I know, she was saying something about this being the last place he'd ever look for her. It made her stop crying anyway, enough to get her out the door and into the car. I didn't think much more about it after that, I was so relieved." He looks at the ceiling. "I didn't think she was going to *move in.*"

I sigh. "It sort of makes sense, I guess," I say. "I could see her feeling unsafe in her and Jordan's apartment, and even at your parents', though it's highly unlikely Gary would ever be able to get in. Still, I think she'd be harder to find—and more anonymous—checked into a hotel. We don't have a doorman or even a super—"

"That's true," Cooper says. "On the other hand, here it's only us. There's no one to leak her presence to the press, no unsuspecting busboy who can be bribed to let some guy in 'just to slip something under her door.' No maid service, no room service, no one knocking to ask if she wants turn-down service. Once the deadlock on the front door is bolted and we switch on the alarm, there's no way anyone can get in or out without us knowing about it. Considering the level of anxiety she's been living with, being here must be something of a relief."

"And," I point out, "you have your gun."

"And," he agrees, "I have my gun. And don't forget, there's you, with your sunny disposition and that welcoming smile you gave her when you first came through the door and saw her—"

I lift a pillow and bop him on the head with it.

"Still," I say, as he laughs, "if she's expecting the Waldorf, she's going to be sadly disappointed. No one's going to be putting a mint on her pillow. I ate all the Oreos the other night."

"I think all she wants—" Cooper begins to say, but he's interrupted by a knock on the door. Literally, someone says, "Knock, knock."

Cooper looks at me curiously, then calls, "Come in."

Jordan, in black silk pajamas and a robe, leans in and says, "Oh, hey. Sorry to disturb you guys. Where do you keep your herbal tea? Tania wants some. I was trying to find some myself in that little kitchenette upstairs so as not to be a pain, but this big orange cat started following me around, and I think he wants me to feed him or something—"

"You know what," I say, getting up off the bed, "why don't I make some tea for Tania and take it upstairs to her?"

"Are you sure?" Jordan looks worried. "We really don't want to be any bother. We feel bad enough, putting Heather out of her apartment the way we have."

"It isn't a bother at all," Cooper says. "Is it, Heather?"

I narrow my eyes at him.

"Oh no," I say. "Cooper was happy to surrender his room to me. He likes sleeping *on the couch*."

Upstairs I find Tania huddled in the middle of my bed,

piled beneath so many down comforters that only her head is peeping out. In her hand is the remote to my television. She's bathed in the rosy glow of my bedside lamp and the bright colors of *Freaky Eaters*.

"You really like this show, don't you?" Tania asks as I come in holding a steaming mug of tea. "You have nine episodes of it recorded, both new ones and repeats."

"Well," I say, "you certainly know your way around a digital video recorder, don't you?"

"You watch a lot of *Intervention* too," Tania remarks. "I think that show is sad."

"Not really," I say, setting the mug down on the nightstand. "The people on it usually beat their addictions and go on to live productive lives." Although considering what Jared told me about how docu-reality series manipulate the truth—and what I've seen Stephanie doing around Fischer Hall—I'm beginning to wonder if there is any honesty at all reflected in the shows I like to watch. "Here's some chamomile tea. Jordan said you wanted some. How are you feeling?"

"Much better," Tania says. "I like it here. It's snug, like my grandma's house."

I'm sure Tania means this as a compliment, but I'm not 100 percent positive I want my home being compared to someone's grandma's house.

"And look," she says, pointing to the floor, "our dogs are in love."

I glance down and see that her dog, Baby, is curled up in Lucy's bed, fast asleep. Lucy is sitting a few feet away, looking distressed. She blinks from her bed to me as if to say, *Help!* I'm not certain how Tania can interpret this as two dogs being in love.

"Yeah," I say. "Sweet. So, is there anything else you need?"

Tania reaches for the tea I've brought her, then looks at the built-ins above our heads. "What's going on with all those dolls?"

Crap.

"Oh," I say. "Well, that's my collection of dolls from many nations. My mom got me one from each country I toured in."

"Aw," Tania says, taking a sip of the tea and looking positively delighted. "That's so cute."

"Not really," I say. "I should have taken the time to visit the sights in the countries, not let my mom grab a doll from the airport in each one. When will I ever be able to afford to go to South Africa again? Or Brazil? Or Japan? Never. But, you know." I shrug. "I love them. They're sort of talismans, or whatever."

"You're lucky," Tania says. "My mom never gave me anything like that. She worked really hard, but she didn't have money to spend on presents. That's really special, to have a doll collection, or anything you can pass on to your own daughter."

I glance back at the dolls. "Yeah," I say thoughtfully. It seems as if neither Tania nor I lucked out in the mom department. Hers was working too hard to notice what was happening to her, and mine was working *me* too hard to care what was happening to me. "I guess it is . . . if you have a daughter of your own."

"The pink one is especially beautiful," Tania says admiringly.

"That's Miss Mexico," I say.

"She's so elegant. I love her dress. And her fan."

"Here," I say, and reach up to take Miss Mexico down from the shelf. "You can have her."

Tania gasps. "Oh no. I couldn't!"

"Yes," I say. "You can. You can give it to your daughter. Miss Mexico can be the first in her collection."

Tania puts down her mug and takes Miss Mexico gingerly in her hands, as if she's afraid the doll will fall apart at her touch. But she won't. Miss Mexico is beautiful, but tough underneath—a lot like Tania.

"Thank you," Tania says. "She's so gorgeous. I . . . I don't deserve her. That thing today . . . that girl's mom must hate me," Tania says.

I don't ask what girl she means.

"No one hates you," I say. "You didn't do anything to Bridget. *Gary* did. And Bridget is going to be all right. Her family is driving up to get her, and I'm sure Cartwright Records Television is going to give her a nice scholarship to wherever she wants to go to college." I was betting New York College was going to offer her one too, but I had my doubts she'd want to attend. "She's going to need a lot of counseling . . . which, if you don't mind my saying, Tania, is something you could probably—"

"It *is* my fault," Tania interrupts firmly. "If I had told people sooner—"

"It's only one person's fault," I say. "And that's Gary's." And Simon Hague's. But I suppose a residence hall director can't personally meet *every* person who checks into his building. Still, I couldn't wait to hear what the fallout was going to be when it's discovered that Simon has been taking extra-long weekends in the Hamptons with his assistant.

"Will you tell the girl," Tania asks in a tiny voice, "that I'm so, so sorry about what happened to her? And the security guard too?"

"No," I say. "You're going to tell them yourself."

She stares at me. Then her face crumples, and she's crying. "I know I have to," she says, "but I don't think I can. I don't think I can leave this room."

"You can stay here for a while," I say. "But eventually you're going to have to leave."

"But not right away," she says, holding Miss Mexico close—which can't be comfortable, considering her pointy Spanish comb and fan.

"No," I say. "Not right away."

I leave Tania not long afterward, since either the chamomile or the stress of the day appears to have knocked her out. She falls asleep clutching Miss Mexico to her, like a little girl with a new birthday present.

I turn off the television and walk out of my room, holding the mug of tea. The last thing I expect is to bump into Jordan on my way downstairs to the main kitchen—I've forgotten he's in the house—but I do.

"Sorry," he says when I nearly throw the mug in his face, I'm so startled. "I was coming up to see how she's doing."

"She's asleep," I say. "Don't sneak up on people like that!"

"Sorry," he says again. "Here, I can take that back to the kitchen."

"No, I can do it."

"Really," he says. "I want to help."

Except that he won't help. He'll just make a mess. Jordan doesn't know where the trash is, nor has he ever rinsed out a mug in his life. He leaves every dish he's ever touched for the maid or room service to clean up. He is so annoying. How did we date—let alone live together—for so many years?

"Fine, you can help," I say with ill grace.

He follows me like a puppy back to the kitchen, then sits down at the table and does nothing as I put the tea bag in the trash and rinse out the mug.

"Where's Cooper?" I ask, hyperconscious of his gaze on me.

"He's taking a shower," Jordan says. "Can I ask you something?"

Oh great. I knew this was coming, but had been hoping to avoid it.

"Not right now," I say, drying my hands on a dish towel. "I . . . I have to take the dog for a walk."

"But it's eleven o'clock at night," Jordan says, looking shocked.

"I can't help it," I say. "When Lucy's got to go, she's got to go." This is a complete fabrication. When Lucy has to go, she goes through the doggie door to the backyard. But I need some excuse to get away from Jordan.

"Baby just goes on a wee-wee pad," he says, in a tone that suggests this in some way makes Tania's dog superior to mine.

"Well," I say, "good for Baby."

"I don't think you should walk the dog at this time of night when there is a deranged psychopath on the loose who might be watching the house and wants to kill my wife."

"My not walking my dog when I normally do so at this

time of night might tip the deranged psychopath off that your wife is here," I counter.

Jordan considers this. "Can I still ask you one thing before you go?"

I realize I can't avoid him forever, especially when we're both living in the same house, and I have no intention of going outside with Gary Hall—injured as he might be—on the loose in the neighborhood. I pull out a kitchen chair and sink into it. "What is it, Jordan?"

"Is this guy who's after Tania really her husband?"

Little Girl Rap

My little girl
Any boy pursues her
Ever tries to woo her
I will knock him dead
Boy, don't mess with me

When she comes
Won't be with no bums
Or end up in the slums
She'll only ever come
Home to me

She got to be dressed
Only in the best
Never need to guess
Who her dad might be

Don't know how I'm gonna make it
Beg, borrow, steal, or fake it
But I swear I'm gonna make her
Proud of me

"Little Girl Rap"
Performed by Jordan Cartwright
Written by Jordan Cartwright,
with thanks to Rodgers and Hammerstein
Goin' Solo album

26

"What makes you ask that, Jordan?"

I'm trying to keep my outward demeanor calm so that Jordan doesn't suspect that inside I'm cursing to myself. How has he found out? Was he eavesdropping? But I could have sworn that Tania and I never once used the word "husband" or even "marriage." How had Jordan guessed?

"A long time ago—well, maybe not that long—he sent me a letter," Jordan says, pulling a folded piece of paper from the pocket of his robe. "I got it a few days before Tania and I were married."

I take the paper from him. "Okay," I say. "Go on."

"Anyway, I didn't think much of it. I get so much mail—not to brag or anything. I'm just stating a fact. My assistant, she only passes on what she thinks is important. Then I put it in one of three files—the Dad File, the Friends File, or the Crazy File. If it seems like it's something that might come back to bite me on the ass, I send it to Dad to take care of. If it's a girl who sends me a picture of her with her"—he glances at me—"well, then I usually forward it to all my friends. You know. Everything else goes in the Crazy File, which means I ignore it. Most crazy people are harmless, right? All they want is to let off a little steam, let their freak flag fly. And if I'm the target of their freak, well, okay, whatever. That's cool. Long as they don't hurt anyone."

I unfold the letter. "Keep going."

Cooper, wearing shorts and a T-shirt, a damp towel around his neck, appears in the kitchen. "What's going on?" he asks curiously, seeing us sitting together.

"Jordan says he got a letter from Gary Hall a few days before he and Tania were married," I say, numbly scanning the page in front of me. "If you don't . . ." and "a million dollars . . ." and "I will . . ." jump out at me.

"You did?" His hand on the door handle of the refrigerator, Cooper is about to go for what he's been calling lately one of his "midnight snacks," a ridiculously large, insanely good sandwich that involves a great deal of mustard, mayonnaise, pickles, cheese, and lunch meat. Normally nothing can tear him away from one. Me either.

Until now.

"Yeah," Jordan says. "I thought it was a joke. If Tania was married, people would know about it, right? TMZ and Dad and stuff. So it couldn't be true. It seemed crazy. So I put it in the Crazy File and ignored it." He gives Cooper a worried smile. "Guess maybe I should have sent it to Dad, huh, bro?"

Cooper drops his hand away from the refrigerator door handle.

"What does the letter say?" he asks carefully.

I gaze at the neatly typewritten script.

"It says that unless Jordan pays Gary Hall a million dollars, Gary will go public with the information that he and Tania were once married," I say, feeling a strange tightness in my throat, "and that they never divorced. He'll also cause Tania 'a world of hurt.'"

"Oh God," Jordan says, burying his head in his hands. "Oh God, oh God. I knew I should have told you guys about this that night Bear got shot, when we saw you at those people's apartment. I *knew* it. Then Jared never would have died, right? And this little girl today would never have been hurt. This is all my fault for not paying him. Oh *God*."

Cooper walks over to the kitchen table, pulls out a chair, and sits down in it. "*When* did you get this letter?" he asks, taking the towel from around his neck.

"About a week before Tania and I got married," Jordan says. "I'm telling you, I thought this guy was just another crazy fan! Tania's never been married." He laughs, but nervously. "She'd have told me, right? How could she not have told me?"

"My guess? Because she's never been divorced," Cooper says.

"Cooper—" I look worriedly at Jordan.

"He's a grown man, Heather," Cooper says. "Even if he doesn't look like one in that bathrobe."

"It's a genuine samurai warrior—" Jordan begins to explain.

"Shut up," Cooper says. "I couldn't find any record of Tania being divorced from this guy, but she's been paying him ten grand a month. If I had to guess? It's not alimony. She's been paying straight-up blackmail to this guy for him to keep his mouth shut so *you* wouldn't find out she's still married to him. That's how much she loves you."

I glare at Cooper, wondering what's happened to his code of ethics. It's not like him to betray the privacy of a client.

On the other hand, this isn't just any client. Tania is family.

"I'm not surprised either," Cooper says. "What else was she supposed to do? It wasn't like she could turn to you, her loving husband, for support. You'd simply put it in the Crazy File."

"Cooper," I say again. I don't approve of the way Jordan's handled the situation, but I can't help feeling a little sorry for him. He's led a privileged life, allowing his parents to do everything for him, and has never had to deal with anything like this before. "Come on. He didn't know."

"Didn't know that someone threatened to cause his pregnant wife 'a world of hurt'?" Cooper snaps, his eyes flashing.

"Yes, he did, Heather. And if someone did that to you, I would not put it in my Crazy File. I would *go* crazy on that person."

"What are you guys talking about?" Jordan asks, looking from one to the other of us. His expression is queasy. "Are you two—?"

"Hate to give you all the bad news in one night, *bro*," Cooper says, leaning over to clap a hand to his brother's shoulder. "But the answer is yes."

Jordan lets out an expletive, then stares unseeingly at Owen, who has strolled into the kitchen and is stretching luxuriously in the middle of the floor. "So you two are together. And I'm . . . what? A polygamist? Like that guy on TV?"

"The correct term, when it's a woman with more than one husband, is polyandrist, not polygamist," Cooper says. "And no, you're not. Tania is. You're just an idiot."

Jordan's face disappears into his hands once more—only this time it stays there. I see his shoulders begin to shake. He's weeping.

I send Cooper a look of disbelief. *Really? You had to make your brother cry?*

Cooper shakes his head at me and leans back in his chair, his arms folded, refusing to utter a single word of sympathy.

"It isn't entirely your fault, Jordan," I get up and say, going to Jordan's side and laying my hands on his shoulders. "Nor is it Tania's. Gary Hall has been terrorizing her. She was probably too traumatized to file for a divorce."

This only seems to make him weep harder. Cooper, unimpressed, reaches down to stroke Owen under the chin.

"And I think she might not entirely trust authority figures," I add desperately, "and she might not have been in the best state of mind when the two of you decided to get married to make the right judgment calls. There was a lot of pressure on you both—"

Jordan finally lifts his head.

"Cooper's right," he says. "I *am* an idiot."

"Finally," Cooper says with a nod. "The first step is admitting it. The second step is deciding what you're going to do about it."

Jordan wipes his face with the wide sleeve of his robe. "A samurai," he says after some consideration, "would find this guy and kill him."

Cooper suppresses a smile. "You're headed in the right direction," he says. "But 'Turn him over to the authorities' is the correct answer."

"Jordan?"

The voice is sweetly soft and comes from the kitchen doorway. We all turn toward it, startled. None of us heard Tania approach, and no wonder, considering she's in her bare feet, wearing only one of my many Sugar Rush T-shirts. Though both Baby and Lucy followed her, we even failed to hear the click of the dogs' claws on the hardwood floors.

"Tania," Jordan says, standing up. His jaw has gone slack. "I . . . I . . . ." He appears at a loss for words.

Tania's gaze darts toward me, her eyes filling with tears. "You *told* him?" she cries, so hurt you'd have thought I'd stabbed her in the heart.

I shake my head. "No," I say. "I swear, Tania, he figured it out all on his—"

"Christ, Jordan," Cooper says angrily. "Tell her the truth."

"Tania." Jordan staggers out from behind the table, the sleeves of his samurai robe falling over his hands as he holds them out in supplication to his wife. "Baby. It's all my fault. He wrote to me too—"

Tania's voice breaks. "He *did?*"

Jordan nods. "He did, baby. But I didn't do the right thing. I know that now. I should have been there for you. You never should have had to go through this alone."

"I thought you'd hate me," Tania says with a sob.

"Tania," Jordan says with a sob of his own, "how could you ever think such a thing? You're my angel."

Tania takes two staggering steps forward and ends up being enveloped in Jordan's arms, disappearing into the multicolored silks of his robe. Jordan buries his face in her tousled curls, and the two of them stand together weeping beneath the kitchen greenhouse windows, the lights of Fischer Hall twinkling in the distance. The Hallmark moment is only somewhat ruined when Baby finds Lucy's dog bowl and begins to crunch noisily on its contents.

"It's all right, girl," I say, scratching Lucy's ears. "You've been a very good hostess."

She seems placated by this.

"Well, we're going to bed," Cooper announces after some moments pass and Jordan and Tania show no sign of breaking their embrace.

"All right," Jordan says, his voice muffled in Tania's hair. "See you in the morning."

Cooper looks at me, his expression comically perplexed. "Okay," he says. "Don't try to open any of the windows or go out—even onto any of the balconies—without waking one of us up first to enter the alarm code, because if you do, it will automatically make a sound that will wake the entire neighborhood, plus notify the alarm company *and* the NYPD that there is an intruder, and they'll be here in two to three minutes. But before they get here, I will already have shot you."

"All right," Jordan says, still speaking into Tania's hair.

"We won't try to go out," Tania says, her own voice muffled against Jordan's chest and the folds of his samurai robe. "We're going to stay in Heather's room with Miss Mexico."

Cooper looks at me questioningly. I shake my head. "Don't ask," I say.

27

For Immediate Release

Tania Trace Rock Camp
and Cartwright Records Television
present the first-ever
ROCK OFF

Thirty-six of the most talented teen girls in America will compete Saturday night at the Tania Trace Rock Camp for the title of Girl Rockrrr of the Year. The camp—which has been held for the past two weeks at New York College—helps to provide young women with opportunities they might not otherwise have had through music education.

"The purpose of this camp was to empower young women through songwriting and performing," says Tania Trace, winner of four Grammy Awards and a mother-to-be. "Instead, these girls have empowered me with their strength and courage in the face of adversity."

The winner of the Rock Off will receive $50,000 and a recording deal with Cartwright Records.

I'm staring at my reflection in the dressing room mirror. I look nothing like my usual self. That's because I've been covered from head to toe—that is, on all the parts of my skin that are showing outside the neckline, sleeves, and sparkly hem of the dress I'm wearing—in airbrush foundation, my blond hair has been piled onto the top of my head with about a million bobby pins, my lips have been slathered in tawny lipstick, and false eyelashes have been stuck onto my lids.

"I look like a freak," I say.

"You look beautiful," Tania says as the stylist sticks one last bobby pin into my hair. "Like Miss Mexico."

"Oh, I worked that pageant this year," the stylist says. "I thought Miss Mexico was a brunette."

"She's not talking about the pageant," I say.

The dressing rooms beneath New York College's Winer Auditorium for the Performing Arts are state of the art, but purposefully designed to look like the old-fashioned ones they always show in movies, where the star is sitting in front of a mirror, framed by dozens of shiny round lightbulbs. For their performance in the Rock Off, the campers are being allowed to use the dressing rooms, but they still have to do their own hair and makeup, as well as provide their own wardrobe . . . except, of course, those girls like Cassidy whose mothers were savvy enough—or rich enough—to hire someone to be their daughter's own professional stylist. This has already caused enough drama among the campers to give Stephanie hours of footage.

The judges of the Rock Off, however, get hair and wardrobe provided by Cartwright Records Television. That's why I'm sitting in a vintage Givenchy gown, having bobby pins stuck into my updo. Tania's personal hair and makeup people are working me over because somehow I got strong-armed into being one of the Rock Off's celebrity judges.

I'm still not certain how it happened. Up until the last minute, I was telling Tania that she really needed to find someone else.

And yet, here I am, coated in Nude Beige Number 105 so my skin tone will look even in high definition.

"You're not going to regret it," Tania says from the makeup chair beside me. She has a large plastic smock covering the gown she's wearing for the evening, which is black, slit up the side, covered in sequins, and made by Oscar de la Renta. "We're going to have so much fun! It's not like we have to worry about what to say either. Everything is going to be on the teleprompter. So don't worry. Just read your lines."

I smile nervously at her reflection in the mirror. It's not the event that has me worried. I enjoy performing, even if it's sitting in a judge's seat, saying a bunch of lines written by someone else (so long as the lines aren't *too* dopey).

We spent the day in rehearsals, running through what marks to hit when we walk out on the stage. As the evening's official hostess and emcee, Tania has to walk out first, then introduce Jordan and me, before we each go to our judge's seats. I tried to point out that there were plenty of better—or at least more current—celebrities they could have asked to judge instead of me, but Tania was still feeling insecure from what happened earlier in the week and said she needed "family only" around her.

Cooper, of course, will be in the auditorium the whole time, along with a half-dozen NYPD officers and almost every campus protection officer the college employs, including the department head, who stopped by the dressing room a little while ago to assure "Miss Trace" that her personal security was foremost in his and every single one of his officers' minds.

"*Nothing,*" he'd said, his crinkled blue eyes becoming moist, "is more heartbreaking to me than what happened to that young lady in Wasser Hall. *Nothing.* I hope you will accept my deepest apologies and sincerest promise that that man will get nowhere near you tonight."

Tania had been very gracious in assuring him that the incident wasn't his fault. And it wasn't . . . at least not personally. But the president's office had a lot of questions about how a suspected murderer was able to walk in and out of so many New York College buildings for the past several weeks without being recognized, let alone able to register for housing and classes using false identification in the first place.

"Although with that kind of customer volume," Cooper had pointed out, "it's bound to happen once in a while. Do you have any idea of the percentage of people who check into hotels under fake names?"

What had happened to Bridget was appalling, but, as I had predicted, the college was offering her a full scholarship, and Cartwright Records had topped it by offering to pay full tuition and room and board at any American college she wished to attend.

Muffy Fowler had been philosophical when I'd congratulated her at lunch earlier in the week for managing to keep the story about what happened to Bridget out of the press.

"No one wants to write about an underage girl who was mentally tortured by a psychotic stalker that the police can't seem to catch," she said, shrugging over her habitual tuna-salad wrap. "And they can't mention her name anyway, since she's a minor. I had no trouble at all getting that one squelched. They were *thrilled* to write instead about how that stalker managed to secure student housing and participate in our summer session for weeks and none of us noticed. I don't know how we'll ever live this one down." She bit into her sandwich. "On the bright side, though, at least no one's talking about Pansygate anymore. And in the meantime, I'm going to play up the Rock Off angle as much as possible. That's the only positive development that I can see."

Muffy was right. The fact that Tania as well as all the girls and their mothers were so determined to put on the camp Rock Off despite the fact that Gary Hall was still at large in the tristate area (if he hadn't yet found his way to Canada) had touched and even charmed the media, and the network had been inundated with requests for press passes to the event. Every major network was sending a reporter, and as a result, with all the girls' families attending and many of the college's donors insisting on coming too, every seat in the auditorium was full.

This was probably the reason why most of the girls—especially the extremely PR-savvy Cassidy and her mother—were so determined to go on with the show in the first place . . . and also the reason why I was so ready to be rid of them. In the corridor outside the dressing rooms earlier in the evening, I'd overheard Mallory say, "Hey, you guys, I forgot to tell you. I got a text from Bridget today. She says to tell everyone to break a leg."

"*Awww*," said several of the other girls. But not, of course, Cassidy.

"Knowing her, she means it," she'd huffed. "She probably wants me to break a leg for real."

"Oh, Cass, get over yourself," Emmanuella had said. "You're just jealous because you know if Bridget were here tonight, she could beat you, vocal nodules or not."

"Yeah," said Mallory. "It's lucky for you she got those and had to be put on complete vocal rest, or you'd have to beat me *and* her."

This brought laughter from all the girls . . . except Cassidy.

"Bridget did *not* get vocal nodules," Cassidy said, her voice rising. "She stole that idea from Adele, and you know it, Mallory. You know she was seeing a guy over in Wasser Hall, probably that same guy—"

"Cut." Stephanie's voice had sounded sharp. "Girls, re-member what we talked about? The legal department has said that any mention of that man will result in *all* your scenes being eliminated from the show. Is that what you want, Cassidy?"

"No, ma'am," Cassidy said, but there was still resentment in her voice.

"Fine," Stephanie said. "Why don't we go back to how you got a text from Bridget today, Mallory, and all you girls say something supportive about her. Cassidy, you can say some-thing bitchy, just don't mention a man."

Cassidy then muttered something about reality shows "not being very real" that got her sent down the hall by Stephanie "to cool off."

A little while later, when I went to the ladies' room, I'd found Stephanie standing over a sink, staring at her own reflection, circles under her eyes. Stephanie no longer wore cute suits and Louboutins to work. Instead, she wore jeans and Uggs and a pained expression.

"How's it going?" I asked her, even though I knew the answer.

"I'm never having children," she answered bleakly.

I hesitated before closing my stall door. "Yours wouldn't necessarily turn out like Cassidy," I pointed out.

"No," she said. "But what if they did?"

There was no reply I could make to that. So, in an attempt to cheer her up, I said, "Tomorrow it'll be over."

"*Thank God*," Stephanie said with a groan and turned on the faucet to plunge her face into the cool water.

That's the thought I keep clinging to . . . that it's the last night of Tania Trace Rock Camp, and tomorrow all the girls are going to check out and go home. Which means that Stephanie and the film crew will leave too. Which means that maybe my life will start to go back to normal.

Except that Tania and Jordan are still living in my house. And Gary Hall is still at large.

"Five minutes." Lauren the PA ducks into the dressing room. She has her headset on. "Five minutes to curtain, ladies. You going to be ready?"

"No," says Ashley, one of Tania's stylists. She's still flat-ironing Tania's hair. "Why do we have to be on time if they aren't shooting live?"

"Because we've got all the girls' families out there," Lauren says. "They came in to see their daughters perform. And we're already running twenty minutes late. The natives are getting restless. There are little brothers and sisters out there who are starting not to look so adorable for the camera. Do the best you can, okay?"

Ashley sends Lauren a look over the top of Tania's head, so Tania can't see it. I've seen the look before. It means, *Get off my back*, only less polite.

"Where's Jordan?" Tania asks Lauren.

"I don't know," Lauren says after hesitating for only a fraction of a second. "I thought he was in here with you."

"We sprayed him, put him in his tux, and sent him on his way about ten minutes ago," Anna, one of the other stylists, says.

"Well, then he's either in the bathroom or saying hi to his family," Lauren says. "I heard they all just came in." She touches her headset. "Let me check—"

"It's okay." Tania whips her crystal-covered phone out from beneath her smock and begins to thumb a text. Baby, on her lap, appears undisturbed. "This is the first time he's ever been ready before me. He's usually always last."

I look back at my reflection. My scalp is itching beneath my towering updo. I wish I had a pen or a chopstick or something I could use to poke in there to scratch it.

I hear a low whistle from the doorway and turn my head to see Cooper standing there. He's wearing a tux, to blend in with the other male judges . . . namely Jordan.

"*Ay, caramba*," he says, his gaze on my reflection.

"There's that insouciant wit I love so much," I say. "You don't look so bad yourself, big guy."

He spins around. "Big Ted's House of Tuxedos."

Tania looks dismayed. "I told your dad to make sure they

sent you an Armani. I never heard of a designer named Big Ted."

"He's joking," I tell her. "It's Armani."

"What's taking you guys so long?" Cooper asks. "You both look great. And the audience is getting a little cranky. They booed my soft-shoe routine. I don't know how much longer I can keep them entertained."

"You don't have to entertain them," Tania says, still looking dismayed. "We're doing that part."

"He's kidding," I say to Tania.

"Oh," she says, and smiles a little shyly. "I get it."

"Done," Ashley says and pats Tania's last curl into place. Her hair looks exactly the same as it always does. I'm perplexed as to why a flatiron was used to make dozens of spiral curls, but there are some mysteries to which I guess I'll never know the answer.

"Thank you," Tania says politely and lifts Baby from her lap as the hairstylist pulls off her smock. I see that, besides her matching black-sequined clutch, she's also been keeping Miss Mexico underneath it.

Cooper notices the doll at the same time and raises a questioning eyebrow, but knows better now than to ask.

"Where's Jordan?" he asks.

"He went to say hi to your mom and sisters," Tania says. She's reading a text from her cell phone. "He says Nicole is upset because she wants to sing one of her songs. I'm not changing the rules, though, just for her." Tania tosses some of her ringlets. "The only people who can perform tonight are the girls from camp. And me, of course."

"Of course," Cooper says gravely and holds his elbow out

to her. Tonight he's her escort because he's also her body-guard. "Shall we?"

"Thank you," Tania says, handing Baby and her clutch off to me. She hangs on to Miss Mexico. "We shall."

Cooper and Tania start down the long white corridor to the stage door. It's lined by Tania Trace campers—their chaperones are out in the audience, eagerly awaiting their performances—dressed in their Rockrrr Girl chic, either thigh-high boots and face paint—like Mallory—or crystal-studded evening gowns, like Cassidy. As we pass by, the girls murmur, admiringly, "You look so nice, Ms. Trace," and, "Oh my God, so pretty." A couple of them take pictures with their cell-phone cameras.

"Break a leg, girls," Tania calls back to them when she gets to the stage door. She throws them a kiss. "Remember, I couldn't be prouder of you!"

Emmanuella makes a heart shape out of her fingers and holds it up. "We love you, Tania!" she shouts.

Lauren, speaking into her headset, says, "Ready? He's on his way? Great." She looks at us. "Jordan'll meet you in the wings, okay? It's showtime." Then she pulls open the heavy stage doors.

28

Welcome to the First Annual
Tania Trace Rock Camp
Rock Off

Please turn off all mobile devices
so that everyone may enjoy the show

It's dark—as it always is—backstage. It takes a moment for my eyes to adjust enough to the sudden dimness to see that we're standing in a small space beside numerous levers and pulleys that operate the thick velvet curtains, which are already open to reveal a scrim that bears the projected message: WELCOME TO THE FIRST ANNUAL TANIA TRACE ROCK CAMP ROCK OFF! Behind the scrim is stacked scenery from the various shows that the drama classes are working on . . . chunks of chain-link fence and ancient couches and streetlamps made of plywood. The audience can't see these, however. Only we can, because we're standing to stage right of the scrim.

A few feet away and down a narrow flight of stairs is a door marked EXIT. That's the door the crew uses to get backstage quickly from the main auditorium, which is quite large for a private college.

In the center of the stage is the podium where Tania has to stand when she makes her introductions. It's lit with some flattering rose-colored gels, and the clear teleprompter screens from which we're to read are already set up. A professional crew from Cartwright Records Television is running the light and sound board. Grant Cartwright isn't leaving anything, even the words we're to speak, to chance tonight.

"Ooooh," Tania says when she peeks out at the packed house from behind the thick blue velvet curtains. "That's as many people as I got in that one place in Quebec. Cute."

I realize then that, to Tania, filling a thousand-seat auditorium is "cute." To any other performer, it would be "amazing."

I can't resist stepping up behind her and taking a peek as well, even though my mother always warned me when I did this, "If you can see them, they can see you." There are camera operators roving the aisles. These belong to networks other than CRT.

For the first time, I'm starting to feel nervous. Thank God I'm not singing. I always thought I had a good singing

voice—definitely better than a lot of so-called pop stars—
until I heard Tania's.

"Oh look," Tania says. "There's that boy from your building. The tall one who always gets so dressed up around me.
He looks like he's wearing his father's suit. How funny."

"Gavin?" I look where she's pointing, shocked not just by
hearing this odd description of him, but also by learning that
he's in the audience. "How did *he* get in?"

"I made sure that all the staff of Fischer Hall got invita-
tions," Tania says casually. "You have to do things like that
when you're in my position, you know. Image."

When she says the word "image," she waves her hand like
a royal—with no movement of the wrist—to show that she
means "image" as in *You have to look out for your image*.

I raise my eyebrows, impressed. I knew Tania was as PR
savvy, in her own way, as Cassidy. But I wasn't aware until
she moved in with us of how kind she was. One of the first
things she'd done after she and Jordan took over the top floor
of the brownstone was to hire a cleaning service—Magda's
cousin's—not because she felt guilty about the added burden
that their presence might put on us, but because she heard
Cooper mention that I'd been meaning to hire them. I'd
come home from work Friday afternoon and *boom*, the house
was immaculate—the windows clean, even the curtains in
Cooper's bedroom repaired, Tania grinning from ear to ear
at my stupefied expression.

"They're going to come every Friday," she said. "Tuesdays
too. They have to. It's the only way they'll be able to keep
up, they say. This place is huge, and you two are filthy."

"Oh," she says now, pointing to someone else in the audience. "There's that girl from your office, the one who wrote that song—"

I see that she's pointing at Sarah. Surprisingly, Sarah's sitting with Sebastian. Even more surprisingly, the two of them are conversing with each other in a cordial fashion. Perhaps there's hope for them yet. Sitting beside them is Lisa with a clean-cut young man, her fiancé, Cory. They both look excited and happy.

"And there are those nice men who helped you save Bridget," Tania says. "What are their names?"

"Tom," I say, unable to pick them out from the crowd, since the lights are going down and there seem to be so many men in suits. "And Steven."

"Yes," she says. "I like them. And the one who hurt his foot—"

"Pete?"

"Yes. He should be out there somewhere too. I invited him, and his daughters and girlfriend, that nice lady with the hair. But not that ugly and stupid man. I made sure he wasn't invited."

Cooper is standing nearby cradling Baby, since the dog's claws were catching on the sequins of my dress.

"I believe she's referring to Simon Hague," he says wryly.

Tania makes a face and straightens up. There's no use peeking anymore, since now that the auditorium lights have dimmed, we can no longer see the audience.

"Oh yes," she says. "I made sure he wasn't on the list."

I suppress my smile of delight at hearing Simon referred

to as "that ugly and stupid man." Hard as we've tried, Tom and I still haven't been able to find out what sort of disciplinary action—if any—has been taken against Simon for his long weekends in the Hamptons, which we're fairly sure weren't departmentally sanctioned. But the fact that he's been denied entry to the Rock Off—which even the student-run newspaper will be covering—could turn out to be punishment enough.

Lauren opens the door from the hallway to the dressing rooms. "Where's Jordan?" she demands when she sees he isn't with us.

"What do you mean?" Cooper asks. I see his dark eyebrows constrict in the slice of white fluorescent light thrown from behind Lauren. "He hasn't shown up yet?"

"No," Lauren says. I know she's trying to hide the concern in her voice. "And Stephanie says he's not responding to her—"

From behind her, there's a piercing scream. It's the scream of a young girl. It's followed immediately by a second scream, then a third. One of them distinctly shrieks the name, "*Cassidy!*"

Lauren jerks her head from the open doorway, looking behind her. "*Shit*—" she says, ripping off her headset and diving back into the hallway. The stage door swings abruptly closed, plunging us once more into darkness.

I can still hear the girls screaming, however. The sound is simply more muted. I know it can't be heard by the audience, especially as they murmur restlessly, waiting for the show to begin.

"Stay here," Cooper says, thrusting Tania's dog at me, then pulling his gun from the holster beneath his tuxedo jacket. "Do you understand?" I can't see him so well in the gloom, but I know his gaze is raking my face. "*Do not follow me through this door*, no matter what you hear."

I nod mutely as Cooper pulls open the stage door—releasing, as he does, another round of horrified screams—then disappears through it. A second later, Tania and I are alone in the darkness, me clutching Baby to my chest, her holding Miss Mexico.

"W-what do you think is going on back there?" she asks, her gaze glued to the door to the dressing rooms.

"Probably nothing," I lie. Baby's skin is so thin, her ribs so fragile, that I can feel her heart thumping against mine, like a tiny bird's. She smells faintly of Tania's perfume. "They probably saw a spider or something."

"Yeah," Tania says. There are ghostly pink shadows across her face from the gels on the podium onstage. They've cast her eyes into sunken hollows. "You're right. Where do you think Jordan is?"

"He's probably still talking to his mom," I say. "Why don't you try to call him? He wouldn't answer any of Stephanie's texts, but I'm sure he'll answer yours." Anything to keep her mind off what's happening outside that door. I'm certain it isn't a spider.

"That's a good idea." Tania kneels to lift her clutch, which I've somehow dropped to the ground. "I'll—"

The other stage door—the one that leads to the auditorium—opens, and we hear the sound of dress shoes—a man's—skipping lightly up the steps.

"Oh, there he is," Tania says, laughing in relief. She straightens up as a tall masculine figure comes toward us through the darkness. "Jordan, we were worried. What took you so long?"

It all happens so fast. One second, that's all it takes. In the blink of an eye, I realize the person striding toward us isn't Jordan. It's a man I don't recognize, a stranger I've never seen before.

A second later, my mind reeling, I realize I *have* seen him before, only in another context . . . a photo on a website. But then he had brown hair and was clean-shaven. The next time, it was on a driver's license photo, but his hair was red and he had on glasses and wore a goatee . . . and then, most recently, he was blond . . .

Now the hair is brown again. His button-down shirt is neat and clean under a boringly ordinary coat and tie, the coat and tie of . . . a suburban choir teacher or a dad. He could be driving the kids to soccer practice or taking the babysitter home. You wouldn't notice the bandage on his hand if you weren't looking for it. You probably wouldn't notice the revolver he's holding in that same hand either, if you weren't looking for it.

But I am. And I do.

"I . . . I don't understand," Tania says, looking from the revolver to his face. Her expression is bewildered. "How . . . how did you get in here?"

I don't blame her for feeling confused. I feel confused too. A minute ago, I'd been sure it was Jordan coming toward us from the darkness. I'd *expected* it to be Jordan.

Except it's not Jordan at all, but Gary Hall, dressed as

himself, his *true* self, a forty-six-year-old abusive husband . . . who, it turns out, can look like anyone at all.

"Hello, Tatiana," he says, smiling. "Do you like this outfit?" He reaches up to straighten the brown knit tie with one hand, keeping the muzzle of the gun pointed straight at us with the other. "I do too. It's comfortable. I'm Mallory St. Clare's dad tonight. You know Mallory, don't you? Of course you do. She's one of your little protégés. Of course, the truth is, according to Bridget, that Mallory's dad left the family when she was ten, but tonight he's making a surprise return. I called ahead and made sure his name got put on the list. The student at the box office was so sympathetic. Most people are when it comes to single dads and their teenage daughters. They want everything to work out."

Tania doesn't say anything. I don't blame her. I feel as if an earthquake is going on, only inside of me instead of beneath my feet. The ground is shifting, shifting, everything moving in slow motion, but only I can feel it.

How could this be happening? Everyone kept telling us we'd be safe. Detective Canavan had laughed when I asked if he thought it was a good idea for Tania to go through with the Rock Off.

"Hall is a thousand miles away by now," he'd said, the last time we spoke, "getting his ass bit by a million mosquitoes in Saskatchewan."

The head of Protection Services—what was his name? O'Malley? O'Brian?—had stood there with his shiny buttons and badge and his blue eyes filled with tears and said he'd have everyone—*everyone*—on duty, watching every door.

But all it takes is one door—one person looking away for one tiny second—and you realize how much everything can change, how fragile life is. This time I really am about to die, like I thought I was going to that night in Fischer Hall when Gavin hit me with the paintball.

Only this is real. This guy is going to kill me. I'll bet anything that even though Gary Hall gave a phony name at the door and may even have shown a phony ID, that's not a phony gun in his hand.

"What do you want?" I demand, my voice shaking. That's because of the fear I'm feeling, dancing and bubbling up and down my spine, like the water in the fountains outside in Washington Square Park. I have no idea how I'm still standing. I long to sit down, give my shaking knees a rest. But I have a feeling I'll be resting forever soon.

"Tatiana knows what I want," Gary Hall says, not unpleasantly. "Don't you, Tatiana?"

"What I want is for you to go, Gary," Tania says, her voice shaking as much as my knees. "*Now.* This is an invitation-only event, and *you*"—her eyes look crazy in the pink glow of the gels shining on the podium—"*were not invited.*"

I can't believe what I'm seeing, let alone hearing. Tania is actually standing up to her lunatic husband, and not in song.

"Yeah," I say to him, setting Baby on the ground, since he's begun to whine, not liking the fact that his mistress seems upset. Maybe he'll leap at Gary's throat, like a dog on TV. But he only wanders over to Tania's feet and cowers behind her. "Tania's right. I'm afraid you have to leave, Gary."

He looks at us both in disbelief. "I don't think you're

comprehending the situation, girls," he says. "*I am holding a loaded firearm*. I'm going to shoot one or both of you. I don't think you want that to happen. Tatiana, I've had enough of this nonsense. You're coming with me."

"No, I'm not, Gary," Tania says, her voice still shaking. But she holds her ground. "It's over. I told Jordan. He knows everything, and you know what? He says he loves me anyway, and you can tell the stupid story of how we never got divorced to the whole world for all he cares. He'll marry me again once you and I are divorced, after you've gone to jail for what you did to Bear and Jared and Bridget—"

"Then," Hall says, holding the revolver to the side of my head and pulling back the hammer, "I guess there's no reason for me not to shoot your friend, is there?"

I freeze. If I'd thought I felt like I was in my own private earthquake before, now I *really* feel that way, because I'm positive toy guns don't make that kind of noise when the hammer is pulled back. I know because Cooper, in an effort to familiarize me with firearms so I wouldn't feel so nervous around one, showed me how his Glock works (although he hasn't yet had a chance to take me to the firing range, since he's been busy guarding Tania). And every time a bullet snapped into the chamber, it made a noise similar to the one I just heard.

Now, I realize, I'll never get a chance to go to the target range with Cooper to learn how to shoot. Because I'm about to die.

"Is this what you want me to do, Tatiana?" Gary Hall demands in a voice hoarse with desperation. He reaches out to wrap a hand around my upper arm and drag me toward him. That's when I get a whiff of him. He smells of mothballs—the Mr. St. Clare costume has evidently been in storage—and sweat. The gun smells of oil and my imminent death. "Because this is what you've driven me to. *You're* making me do this. You made me hurt all those people."

I can't believe how clichéd he sounds. *Hey, buddy*, I want to say to him. *You need Stephanie to punch up your dialogue.*

But this scene from *Jordan Loves Tania* hasn't been prescripted. Gary Hall is deeply disturbed.

"If you'd just stayed with me and treated me with the respect I deserved after all the things I did for you," Gary goes on, "no one would have gotten hurt—"

"I am not responsible for the things *you* do, Gary," Tania says. "Only *you* can be responsible for your actions."

It occurs to me that Tania might actually have been getting some therapy behind my back. I only wish she'd have saved it for a time when Gary wasn't pointing a loaded gun at my head.

"You're making me do this, Tatiana!" he shouts, his fingers sinking into my skin as he jabs the muzzle of the gun into my updo, causing tendrils of it to fall from the many bobby pins that had been used to secure it. "I have nothing left to lose. Whether this woman lives or dies is entirely up to you."

Tania's expression changes. Maybe she's realized what I've already figured out—reasoning with Gary isn't going to work, because he isn't sane. He's never going to give up until he gets what he wants, which is Tania.

I watch the fight drain out of her . . . along with all hope. Her slender shoulders sag.

"All right," she says softly. "All right, Gary. I'll go with you. Let Heather go first, though."

He grins, triumphant, then shoves me away.

I'm not sure what makes me do it. I guess it's true that I don't want to die. But I know I can't let anyone else die either.

So as Tania moves past me, I snatch Miss Mexico from her limp fingers. Then I spin around and bury the pointy Spanish comb that's glued to the doll's head as hard as I can into the skin just below the bandage on Gary's hand . . . his gun hand.

Dolls are not meant to be used as weapons. Miss Mexico's head breaks off—along with the comb—in Gary's skin.

But Gary is startled enough—and in enough pain—that when he lowers the gun with a cry, he inadvertently pulls the trigger so that the revolver fires.

Fortunately, the bullet goes harmlessly into the auditorium stairwell.

Still, I hear people in the audience begin to murmur. I'm certain the NYPD and campus protection officers posted around the auditorium have heard the gunshot and are on their way backstage. I only hope they won't be too late.

I snatch Tania's hand and pull her behind the scrim, forcing her to duck with me beneath a table from one of the Drama Department's sets before Gary can pull Miss Mexico's head from the back of his trigger hand with his teeth.

As he's doing this, the stage door bursts open and Cooper strides out.

The bright white light thrown by the fluorescents behind Cooper temporarily blinds Gary Hall. But it allows Cooper to immediately recognize the man in the coat and tie from his photo on Tania's high school website. He sees the gun that Gary Hall raises in his direction. And without a word, Cooper shoots him three times in the chest, until Gary Hall drops the revolver, falls forward, and lies still.

So Sue Me

All those times you said
I'd never make it
All those times you said
I should quit

All those times you said
I'm nothing without you
The sad part is
I believed it too

Then you left and
What do you know
I made it on
My very own

So go ahead and sue me
You heard me
Go ahead and sue me

Now that I've made it
You say it's you I owe
Well, you owe me too
For the heart you stole

If I've got one regret
It's all the time I spent
All the tears I wept
Thinking you were worth the bet

Go ahead, go all the way
Take me to court
It'll make my day
So sue me

Go ahead and sue me

29

"So Sue Me"
Performed by Tania Trace
Written by Weinberger/Trace
So Sue Me album
Cartwright Records
Thirteen consecutive weeks in the Top 10
Billboard Hot 100, current number-one hit

"'Center mass,'" Cooper explains much later that evening when I climb into my bed beside him. "I wasn't aiming for his chest. I was shooting at whatever I was least likely to miss in order to avoid having him shoot back at me. That would be the largest part of him. They call that part 'center mass.' That's how you stay alive in a gunfight."

"Good to know," I say, passing him one of the drinks I've rustled up from the kitchen downstairs. "Anyway, you got him in the heart. I'd want you on my side in a gunfight anytime."

He takes a sip of the drink, then makes a face. "What *is* this?"

"Your sister Jessica's favorite drink, a pink greyhound."

He passes it back to me. "Never make this for me again, especially after I've just shot a man. They might take away my detective's license."

I put the drink on my nightstand. "I had a suspicion you were going to say that, so I made you a backup drink, just in case." I pass him a whiskey on the rocks.

"That's more like it," he says.

I lift the pink greyhound and clink the rim of his glass with mine. "*L'chaim.* It means 'to life.' I don't mean to be insensitive that someone is dead. I'm just happy it's not you or me."

"Me too," he says, after a sip. "And I know what *l'chaim* means."

"Well," I say, "at least with Gary dead, Tania won't have to deal with all the negative press if the police had caught him and word had got out that the two of them were still married. Now she and Jordan can quietly remarry somewhere and say it's a renewal of their vows or whatever." I wince. "Is *that* an insensitive thing to say?"

Cooper shrugs. "Not as insensitive as some of the things I've been thinking about those two. You nearly died tonight because of my idiot brother not telling anyone about that first letter—"

"That's a little harsh," I say. "Jordan's suffered enough, don't you think?"

"No," Cooper says flatly.

It had taken a little while for Tania and me to convince the dozens of NYPD and New York College protection officers who rushed backstage that Cooper was not the one who'd attacked us. That had been the man bleeding out on the floor. While all this was going on, Jordan was found unconscious in a stall in the lobby men's room. It turns out that just moments before Gary Hall let himself backstage, Jordan had encountered him at the urinals, recognized him, and attempted to perform a citizen's arrest. Sadly, this attempt was unsuccessful. Gary coldcocked him, propped Jordan up on a toilet, then shut the stall door, all as the auditorium lights were going down and everyone else was heading to their seats.

"But I tried, baby," Jordan said when he and Tania were reunited. "I really tried to get him for you."

"I know you did," Tania said, so overwhelmed with relief that Jordan had been found alive that she insisted on riding along to Beth Israel with him in the ambulance to make sure his CAT scans turned out normal. Four hours later, we got the call that the scans had, and that they were sending over Jordan's assistant to collect their things from our house.

"Thanks so much for everything, you guys," Jordan said into the phone. "But Tania doesn't feel like we need to stay with you anymore. She's ready to come home."

"Oh really?" I'd said, holding up my hand for Cooper to high-five. "That's too bad. We'll miss you both so much."

Now I stroke Lucy's head as she curls up on the bed beside us and gaze at Cooper's new Armani tuxedo, hanging from my closet door.

"You know," I say, "that paint is supposed to be washable."

"I don't want to talk about it," Cooper says and reaches into the drawer of the nightstand on his side of the bed for the remote. "What do you say we unwind by watching one of those shows you like, where the people eat weird things?"

"You shouldn't beat yourself up over it," I say with a smile. "I thought those girls were being attacked too."

"They *were* being attacked," Cooper reminds me.

"Right," I say. "Good thing you were there with your Glock to put a stop to it—"

He lifts one of the pillows and puts it over my face, pretending to smother me as I laugh and Lucy begins to bark and Owen, over on the dresser, looks away in disdain.

I don't blame the cat. Cassidy, in her nonstop quest to get as much on-camera time as possible on *Jordan Loves Tania*, had thought it would be highly amusing to pull a paintball gun from where she'd hidden it in the dressing room and ambush the competition as they were lined up in the hallway outside the stage door, waiting for the Rock Off to begin.

That turns out to have been what all the screaming was about right before Gary came upon Tania and me backstage . . . and why, because the paintball attack caused so much hysteria and chaos, it took Cooper a little while to wade through it and get back to us.

"What did I do that was so wrong?" Cassidy kept asking, her eyes widened innocently, when Mallory and the other girls, in tears, accused her of purposefully ruining their outfits. "Anyone can check out paintball stuff from the college sports complex. All you have to do is leave your ID. Don't be such bad sports, you guys. The show must go on, right?"

Only it turns out that in cases of shootings, the show does *not* go on. The Rock Off was canceled due to the real-life shooting, the film crew turned off their cameras, and the girls were told to go home with their families. Tania Trace Rock Camp was over, for good.

"This is *outrageous*," I overheard Mrs. Upton raging at Stephanie on the sidewalk outside the auditorium as I accompanied Cooper to Detective Canavan's car (because it turns out you can't shoot someone, not even a wanted suspect in multiple crimes, in self-defense and not have to go down to the station house to answer a lot of questions about it). "I demand that my daughter be given the opportunity that she was promised in the contract that she signed to compete for the $50,000 prize and recording contract with—"

"Mrs. Upton." Stephanie Brewer was leaning against the side of the building. She looked happier than I'd seen her in a while, but I'm pretty sure that was because the camp was officially over. "I've been wanting to say this to you for two weeks now. Shut. Up."

Mrs. Upton looked shocked. "*What* did you say to me?"

"I said, shut up," Stephanie said again. "Even if we did reschedule the Rock Off, there's no way your kid would win, because she's such a little bitch, no one at Cartwright Records can stand working with her. Okay? So take my advice and get out of here. No, wait . . . get out of show business."

Mrs. Upton blinked as if Stephanie had slapped her.

"I . . . I . . . I'll sue Cartwright Records for this!" she cried.

"That's right," Cassidy said, backing her mother up. "Cartwright Records and Tania Trace."

Emmanuella and a few of the other girls, including Mallory St. Clare, happened to be walking by with their parents as this happened.

"*What* did she say?" Emmanuella asked, coming to a halt beside Mrs. Upton.

"She said she's going to sue me," Stephanie said, dragging a hand through her hair. "And Tania. Like I care."

"That's what I *thought* she said." Emmanuella looked at the other girls, and then, in pitch-perfect harmony, they began to sing, "'Go ahead, go all the way, take me to court, it'll make my day!'"

Their exuberant voices lifted toward the night sky, causing people as far away as the dog park in Washington Square to turn their heads curiously to listen.

"'If I've got one regret,'" they sang, giggling in their paintball-streaked clothes, "'it's all the time I spent, all the tears I wept, thinking you were worth the bet . . . So sue me!'"

Christopher Allington walked over to where Stephanie was standing, tears in her eyes, as she watched the girls dance and sing as if they didn't have a care in the world.

He took out his camera phone to record the moment forever, but Stephanie put her hand on his arm and shook her head.

"No," she said. "Don't film it. Let's be in the moment, not view it through a lens."

Christopher smiled, lowered the camera, and put his arm around her.

Over by his car, Detective Canavan rolled his eyes. "Kids," he said as he unlocked the door. "Lord knows I love my own, but if I had to work with 'em all day, I'd shoot myself in the head." Then, with a glance at Cooper, he says, "Oh. Sorry. Aw, what am I apologizing for? You got the guy in the chest. Nice shot, by the way. Remind me to buy you a drink."

Back in my room, Cooper stops pretending to smother me, rolls over with a sigh, and looks up at the dolls from many nations. "It's nice to have your bed back."

"It is," I say. "Although I can't stop thinking about what they might have done in here."

"Like what?" he asks. "Besides pilfer your best doll? Gone through your diary? Is that the secret you're so worried I'm going to find out? Don't tell me Jordan knows it now and I don't. Although we all know even if he knows it, he probably put it in his Crazy File—"

"No," I say. "I meant what they did in here sexually."

Cooper looks appropriately disgusted. "Do we have to discuss my brother's sex life? I know you've been there and done that, but it's really not a subject I enjoy visit—"

"We've all made decisions that we're not so proud of," I interrupt quickly. "Even you. I've met some of your ex-girlfriends. And what Jordan lacks intellectually he makes up for in good intentions. He has a very kind heart. He also has a very big—"

Cooper picks up the pillow again and holds it threateningly over my face.

"—ego," I finish, laughing. "And I don't have a secret diary." I sit up, growing serious. "But there *is* something we need to talk about. I went to the doctor a couple of weeks ago, and she said . . ."

I don't know where I find the courage. Maybe from the same place where Tania found the courage to tell Gary Hall he wasn't on the invitation list to her Rock Off and so he needed to leave, even though he was pointing a gun in her face. In any case, somehow I manage to tell Cooper what the doctor said about how if we want to have a baby, we need to get busy . . . and how it probably isn't going to be that easy.

When I'm finished, he doesn't appear to understand.

"*Baby?*" he says, shaking his head. "Who said anything about wanting a *baby?*"

I'm confused. "Cooper. Don't you want kids someday?"

"We already *have* kids," he says, pointing toward Fischer Hall, though the windows of my room face the opposite direction so he ends up jerking his thumb at the wall behind my bed. "We have an entire *dorm* full of kids. Every time I turn around, you're rushing over there to help one of them out. Gavin, that Jamie girl, that one who was going to have to go back to India, the other one whose dad hates him because he's gay, not to mention an entire basketball team—"

"Those are *other people's* kids," I remind him.

"It doesn't seem like it to me," he says. "We see them more than their own parents do."

"Cooper," I say. "Most of them are in their early twenties. They hardly qualify as kids."

"Then why do I always have to pay for dinner whenever we go out with them?"

"Cooper—"

"Let's say the odds aren't really as bad as you think and you don't have to get this operation, or whatever it is," he says, growing serious. "Let's say you somehow end up with a baby. Are you going to quit working at Fischer Hall to stay home to take care of it?"

I have never thought of this before. In my fantasies, I always magically have three children, and they're five, seven, and ten, delightfully self-sufficient, and dressed in charming navy blue plaid school uniforms. "Well," I say, "I don't know—"

Quit working? I haven't even gotten a chance to look at Lisa's wedding binder yet. She's the first fun boss—aside from Tim, who doesn't count, because he was never officially my boss—I've ever had.

And what about Sarah? Even though she and Sebastian seem to have reconciled, I'm sure he's still going to Israel. Who's going to hold her hand through that? Not like I'm going to get pregnant and have Jack, Emily, and Charlotte right away—it will probably take years—but still, there's a lot of stuff I have to do, none of which involves staying home with a crying baby . . .

"Because," Cooper says, "and I don't mean this as an insult or anything, so don't get mad, but I don't really see you as the stay-at-home mom type. I know *I* am definitely not the stay-at-home dad type. I love my job . . . on the days when people aren't trying to kill one of us, that is."

"Most people can't afford to quit their jobs when they have a baby," I explain to him. I realize that many of Cooper's friends don't have children yet, because they're either incarcerated or famous rock stars, so it's possible he doesn't know these things. "They hire nannies or find day care. But yes, you're right, I do love my job, and I have to finish school. So I don't want to stay home to take care of a baby either. But—"

"Well," he says, "if neither one of us wants to take the time to stay home and take care of it, it seems to me like neither of us actually *wants* to have a baby yet. Or am I wrong on this point?"

I try to digest this, but it's extremely difficult, since everywhere I go, it seems, I'm bombarded with images of women my age pushing baby strollers or showing off their baby bump or telling interviewers that they never knew what true love was until they "looked into the eyes of their newborn."

"But if we don't try to have one now, we may never be able to have one. And doesn't *everyone* want a baby?" I ask. "Isn't it a primal urge?"

Even as the words are coming out of my mouth, however, I remember what Lisa said in our office. She doesn't want kids. I know Tom doesn't either. Is there really a chance Cooper feels the same way?

"Parenthood is the most difficult, demanding job in the entire world," Cooper says. "Even if you do it right, you could end up with a kid like . . . well, I think over the last

few weeks we've both seen plenty of evidence of the kind of
kids you could end up with. I think the worst thing anyone
can do is have a baby because they think it's what's expected
of them, or because it's what everyone else is doing, or because they don't know what else to do with their lives. If
you decide to have a baby, you've got to be 100 percent committed to the job. But if you ask me, Heather, you already
are committed to it." He points again in the direction of
Fischer Hall. "Whether you're willing to admit it or not,
you've already got a bunch of babies. They just came pre-
toilet-trained. And you didn't have to have an operation or
risk your health squeezing them out."

"Okay," I say. "Fair enough. But I can't really see Gavin
or any of those guys supporting us in our old age, can you?"

"Heather, *no one* should have a kid so it can support them
in their old age. That's one of the worst reasons in the world
to have a baby . . . almost as bad as having a baby to save
a broken marriage. People are supposed to support themselves. Are you and I going to support *our* parents in their
old age?"

"God no," I say, shocked at the idea.

Cooper reaches out to take my hand, then gives it a
squeeze. "So you see? There are no guarantees. We could
have kids, and they could turn out like Cassidy Upton or,
worse, Gary Hall."

This is another thing I had never before considered . . .
that Jack, Emily, and Charlotte might turn out to be total
and complete assholes.

"This is true," I say. "But they could also turn out to be
like us."

"Heather," he says, "need I remind you that we hate our parents' guts?"

I burst out laughing. "But our parents suck. We don't."

"Look." He squeezes my hand again. "I'm happy the way things are . . . happier than I've ever been in my life. If having a baby will make *you* happy, then that's fine, I'll have a baby with you. But I'm also fine—*more* than fine—with being . . . what do they call it again? Oh, yeah. Child free."

I narrow my eyes at him. "Are you only saying this to make me feel better, because the odds against me ever being able to conceive without medical intervention are so huge?"

" 'Never tell me the odds,' " he says.

Relieved, I squeeze his hand back. "That's the worst Han Solo imitation I've ever seen," I say. "But thank you."

A tightness I haven't even realized I've been feeling seems to lift from my shoulders, and tears have filled my eyes. I'm not sure if they're tears of joy, sorrow . . . or relief.

It doesn't mean I've turned my back on Jack, Emily, and Charlotte, I realize. If they happen someday, that's great. But the pressure of them *having* to happen someday or I'll somehow be incomplete or a failure is gone. And that feels almost as good as when Gary Hall took the muzzle of that gun away from my head.

"Don't thank me yet," Cooper says. "I think I have a pretty good idea how this is going to go, and if you think I'm going to let you adopt every misfit toy you meet in Fischer Hall, you're nuts."

"They aren't toys," I say, pulling my hand from his and furtively wiping the tears from my eyes. "They're young adults who only need positive role models and some guidance and direction in their lives. And room and board in exchange for twenty hours of work at the desk or in my office."

"Well, whatever they are," Cooper says, "we've got more pressing things to worry about right now. Like what are we going to do about Miss Mexico?"

"Oh, don't worry about her," I say. "I already checked online, and there are a million Spanish flamenco dolls like her that I can buy for about seven dollars. But I decided I'm not going to replace her."

"Oh yeah?" He's reaching into the nightstand drawer again—for the remote, I assume.

"I'm going to let Miss Ireland have a little breathing room," I say. "I think Miss Mexico was giving her an inferiority complex."

"I think they should do a docu-reality show about you," Cooper says, placing a small blue velvet box on my lap. "And call it *Freaky Doll Collectors*."

I stare down at the box. "What's this?" I ask suspiciously.

"Open it and see," he says.

I open it. It's an oval sapphire on a platinum band, with a cluster of tiny diamonds on either side.

I glance from the ring to his face and then back again in astonishment.

"I-it's . . . it's the ring from that antique store on Fifth Avenue," I stammer, feeling myself turning red. "H-how did you know I wanted it?"

"Sarah told me when I called the office one day looking for you," he says. He looks pleased with himself. "You weren't picking up on your cell. And it's *not* the ring from that store on Fifth Avenue. I went to the store on Fifth Avenue to look at that ring. Do you know how much it cost?"

I feel absurdly let down. "Oh. A lot, I'll bet."

"Three hundred and fifty dollars," he says. "That ring was fake, costume jewelry. I went to my friend Sid who works in the diamond district—*legally*, by the way—and I had him make you an exact replica, but with *real* jewels, on a *real* platinum band—"

I inhale, shocked. "Cooper," I say. "You shouldn't have. It's too much! It's too fancy."

"No, it isn't," he says firmly. "You should have more fancy things. Put that on and tell anyone who asks that we're engaged. I want everyone to know, especially my family. And we're not eloping, not anymore. After you get done billing the pants off Cartwright Records Television for my services, we're going to be able to afford a wedding at the Plaza. How many people do you want to invite? More important, where do you want to go for our honeymoon? What dolls do you need to add to your collection? Paris? What about Venice? How about—"

I fling my arms around his neck, holding him so tightly that he finally says in a strangled voice, "Heather, you're choking me," but I don't care, because I'm so happy, I never want to let go.

About the book

Read on

Insights,
Interviews
& More...

Five Questions for Meg Cabot
Creator of Heather Wells, the Heroine of *Size 12 and Ready to Rock*

1. First and foremost, will Cooper and Heather ever get married?

Yes, unless something goes terribly wrong. Read on for some hints.

2. Let's talk about Heather. Not very many authors write about plus-size . . . sorry, average-size heroines, since in the United States, 12 is the most common size. Why did you? Where did Heather come from?

I grew up in a super-size family. My brother is six feet eight inches tall, and by the time I was twelve, I was five feet eight inches, making me one of the tallest people (of either sex) in my middle school. It also caused one of the cutest boys in my class to loudly remark in the lunch line, "Cabot, if you get any bigger, they're going to have to bury you in a piano case, like Elvis." (Elvis was not buried in a piano case, FYI.)

  I immediately embarked on the first of what was to be many unhealthy crash diets. It was called the Sunshine Diet, and it involved eating only oranges and hard-boiled eggs. Although I lost ten pounds, I gained them all back, plus ten more.

Years later, I discovered that I had celiac disease and had to cut a substantial number of foods from my diet or else risk getting stomach cancer. This included all of Heather's favorites, such as beer, bagels, pizza, and anything fried. It sucks, but as a fellow celiac sufferer once told me, "Lady, stop complaining. You can still have nachos." (He was seven at the time.)

The reality is that most people who are considered "overweight" are not unhealthy, just like most people who are thin are not anorexic. These days, we see some average- and even plus-size female characters in books and film, but I wish we could see even more. It would be great if someday size 12s become the norm on our television screens just as they are in real life.

So, that's where Heather came from.

3. Size 12 and Ready to Rock *seems to explore slightly more serious issues than the previous books in the Heather Wells series, like intimate-partner violence and infertility issues. What's up with that?*

What could be more serious than murder? But I get where you're coming from. To be honest, incidents of teen dating abuse occurred a lot more often than murder in the residence hall where I worked for over ten years in New York City. Very rarely did the ▶

victim (usually female, but occasionally male) come forward herself. These incidents were nearly always reported by a roommate, and often accompanied by statements such as, "I don't understand why she stays with him. If my boyfriend ever hit *me*, I'd hit him back."

My bosses and I always wanted to tell them that if hitting someone back was really all you needed to do to end an abusive relationship, intimate-partner violence (also known as domestic abuse or domestic violence) wouldn't be the number-one cause of injury to women—which, sadly, it is. It's estimated that at least two-thirds of restraining orders filed due to sexual-partner abuse are violated. And one in three female murder victims is killed by her intimate partner.

The truth is, half of the female population will experience some form of violence from a partner during the course of a relationship. Domestic-partner abuse isn't something that occurs "only" to a single type of person belonging to a particular ethnic, cultural, or socioeconomic group. Statistically, you know someone who has been, or is being, abused. If you or someone you know needs help or more information, go to http://www.thehotline.org/ (but remember that if you are in an abusive relationship, computer use can be monitored and can never be completely cleared) or call **1-800-799-SAFE(7233)** or **TTY 1-800-787-3224**.

4. Infertility is a subplot of this book. Is this an issue with which you've struggled?

Yes . . . and no! Like Heather, I suffer from endometriosis, and a few years ago I underwent surgery to find out what was going on with a large, painful ovarian cyst that had been giving me trouble for nearly a year. Before the surgery, my doctor asked how important my reproductive organs were to me—meaning, if she went in there and found that she had no other choice but to remove them, would that be okay?

Up until that point, I'd honestly never given much thought to the matter! Like Lisa in *Size 12 and Ready to Rock*, I had spent so much time babysitting other people's kids when I was growing up, and I now have so many nieces and nephews thanks to my husband's and my own family (not to mention my literally millions of readers, many of whom write regularly to say they've grown up with my books), that I've always sort of felt like I already have kids.

So when my doctor asked if I'd be okay with her removing my reproductive organs if she had to, I didn't hesitate.

"Of course!" I said.

I've never been worried about not having a family. My husband and I already *have* our family, it simply isn't a traditional one comprised of a father, mother, and baby. Instead, it's made ▶

up of friends and neighbors, aunts and uncles, nieces and nephews, parents and grandparents, stepsisters and stepbrothers, cats and coworkers, bloggers and booksellers, readers and librarians, not to mention their wives, husbands, and partners, and an endless stream of children—so many children, frankly, that sometimes those of us who don't have kids full time wonder how those of you who do have the stamina to keep up with them.

Fortunately, my doctor ended up having to remove only one of my ovaries. She assures me that there are women in their forties who have endometriosis and are also missing one ovary who have still gotten pregnant. So if you fall into this category and do not have the energy to be a parent (like me), use birth control, for God's sake!

And always remember that on the path to happiness, sometimes there are unexpected twists and turns . . . but that doesn't mean they aren't the *perfect* twists and turns for you.

5. When will Heather be back?

Soon! Look for Heather in *Size 12 Is the New Black* in 2013.

Heather and Cooper can finally afford the wedding of their dreams . . . but it looks like that dream has a good chance of becoming a nightmare, and not just because, on the advice of her perky new boss, Heather's hired a wedding planner, and that wedding planner has turned out to be . . . well, less than reliable.

That's because he's missing and feared dead!

Heather doesn't have time to solve a missing-person case right now, not with seven hundred freshmen checking into Fischer Hall, hundreds of guests RSVPing to her wedding reception, and one out-of-towner who simply showed up without an invitation at all: Heather's long lost mother.

But with a runaway wedding planner to track down, a groom who's just about ready to call the whole thing off, and a residence hall to assistant direct, a mother-and-bride reunion is the last thing Heather wants—especially since there's a new RA who's doling out a lot more than advice to the incoming freshmen, which could mean that instead of wedding bells, Heather might be hearing wedding bullets . . . ⟶

Want More?
Keep reading to see where it all began.

Every time I see you
I get a Sugar Rush
You're like candy
You give me a Sugar Rush
Don't tell me stay on my diet
You have simply got to try it
Sugar Rush

"Sugar Rush"
Performed by Heather Wells
Written by Valdez/Caputo
From the album *Sugar Rush*
Cartwright Records

"Um, hello. Is anyone out there?" The girl in the dressing room next to mine has a voice like a chipmunk. "Hello?"

Exactly like a chipmunk.

I hear a sales clerk come over, his key chain clinking musically. "Yes, ma'am? Can I help you?"

"Yeah." The girl's disembodied— but still chipmunklike—voice floats over the partition between our cubicles. "Do you guys have these jeans in anything smaller than a size zero?"

I pause, one leg in and one leg out of the jeans I am squeezing myself into. Whoa. Is it just me, or was that really existential? Because what's smaller than a size zero? Negative something, right?

Okay, so it's been a while since sixth grade math. But I do remember there was this number line, with a zero in the middle, and—

"Because," Less Than Zero/Chipmunk

Voice is explaining to the sales clerk, "normally I'm a size two. But these zeros are completely baggy on me. Which is weird. I know I didn't lose weight since the last time I came in here."

Less Than Zero has a point, I realize as I pull up the jeans I'm trying on. I can't remember the last time I could fit into a size 8. Well, okay, I *can*. But it's not a period from my past that I particularly relish.

What gives? Normally I wear 12s . . . but I tried on the 12s, and I was swimming in them. Same with the 10s. Which is weird, because I haven't exactly been on any kind of diet lately—unless you count the Splenda I had in my latte at breakfast this morning.

But I'm sure the bagel with cream cheese and bacon I had with it pretty much canceled out the Splenda.

And it's not exactly like I've been to the gym recently. Not that I don't exercise, of course. I just don't do it, you know, in the gym. Because you can burn just as many calories walking as you can running. So why run? I figured out a long time ago that a walk to Murray's Cheese Shop on Bleecker to see what kind of sandwich they have on special for lunch takes ten minutes.

And a walk from Murray's over to Betsey Johnson on Wooster to see what's on sale (love her stretch velvet!): another ten minutes.

And a walk from Betsey's over to Dean & Deluca on Broadway for an after-lunch cappuccino and to see if ▶

they have those chocolate-covered orange peels I like so much: another ten minutes.

And so on, until before you know it, you've done a full sixty minutes of exercise. Who says it's hard to comply with the government's new fitness recommendations? If *I* can do it, anyone can.

But could all of that walking have caused me to drop *two whole* sizes since the last time I shopped for jeans? I know I've been cutting my daily fat intake by about half since I replaced the Hershey's Kisses in the candy jar on my desk with free condoms from the student health center. But still.

"Well, ma'am," the sales clerk is saying to Less Than Zero. "These jeans are *stretch* fit. That means that you've got to try two sizes lower than your true size."

"What?" Less Than Zero sounds confused.

I don't blame her. I feel the same way. It's like number lines all over again.

"What I mean is," the sales clerk says, patiently, "if you normally wear a size four, in stretch jeans, you would wear a size zero."

"Why don't you just put the real sizes on them, then?" Less Than Zero—quite sensibly, I think—asks. "Like if a zero is a really a four, why don't you just label it a four?"

"It's called vanity sizing," the sales clerk says, dropping his voice.

"*What* sizing?" Less Than Zero asks, dropping her voice, too. At least, as much as a chipmunk *can* drop her voice.

"You know." The sales clerk is whispering to Less Than Zero. But I can still hear him. "The *larger* customers like it when they can fit into an eight. But they're really a twelve, of course. See?"

Wait. *What?*

I fling open the door to my dressing room before I stop to think.

"I'm a size twelve," I hear myself saying to the sales clerk. Who looks startled. Understandably, I guess. But still. "What's wrong with being a size twelve?"

"Nothing!" cries the sales clerk, looking panicky. "Nothing at all. I just meant—"

"Are you saying size twelve is *fat*?" I ask him.

"No," the sales clerk insists. "You misunderstood me. I meant—"

"Because size twelve is the size of the average American woman," I point out to him. I know this because I just read it in *People* magazine. "Are you saying that instead of being average, we're all fat?"

"No," the sales clerk says. "No, that's not what I meant at all. I—"

The door to the dressing room next to mine opens, and I see the owner of the chipmunk voice for the first time. She's the same age as the kids I work with. She doesn't just *sound* like a chipmunk, I realize. She kind of looks like one, too. You know. Cute. Perky. Small enough to fit in a normal-sized girl's pocket.

"And what's up with not even *making* her size?" I ask the sales clerk, jerking a thumb at Less Than Zero. "I mean, I'd rather be average than not even *exist*."

Less Than Zero looks kind of taken aback. But then she goes, "Um. Yeah!" to the sales clerk.

The sales clerk swallows nervously. And audibly. You can tell he's having a bad day. After work, he'll probably go to some bar and be all "And then these women were just ON me about the vanity sizing. . . . It was awful!"

To us, he just says, "I, um, think I'll just go, um, check and see if we have those jeans you were interested in the, um, back."

Then he scurries away.

I look at Less Than Zero. She looks at me. She is maybe twenty-two, and very blond. I too am blond—with a little help from Lady Clairol—but I left my early twenties several years ago.

Still, it is clear that, age and size differences aside, Less Than Zero and I share a common bond that can never be broken:

We've both been dicked over by vanity sizing.

"Are you going to get those?" Less Than Zero asks, nodding at the jeans I have on.

"I guess," I say. "I mean, I need a new pair. My last pair got barfed on at work."

"God," Less Than Zero says, wrinkling her chipmunk nose. "Where do you work?" ▶

"Oh," I say. "A dorm. I mean, residence hall. I'm the assistant director."

"Rilly?" Less Than Zero looks interested. "At New York College?" When I nod, she cries, "I thought I knew you from somewhere! I graduated from New York College last year. Which dorm?"

"Um," I say awkwardly. "I just started there this summer."

"Rilly?" Less Than Zero looks confused. "That's weird. 'Cause you look so familiar . . ."

Before I have a chance to explain to her why she thinks she knows me, my cell phone lets out the first few notes of the chorus of the Go-Go's "Vacation" (chosen as a painful reminder that I don't get any—vacation days, that is—until I've passed my six months' probationary period at work, and that's still another three months off). I see from the caller ID that it is my boss. Calling me on a Saturday.

Which means it has to be important. Right?

Except that it probably isn't. I mean, I love my new job and all—working with college students is super fun because they're so enthusiastic about stuff a lot of people don't even think about, like freeing Tibet and getting paid maternity leave for sweatshop workers and all of that.

But a definite drawback about working at Fischer Hall is that I live right around the corner from it. Which makes me just a little more accessible to everyone there than I'm necessarily comfortable with. I mean, it is one thing to get calls at home from work because you are a doctor and one of your patients needs you.

But it is quite another thing to get calls at home from work because the soda machine ate someone's change and no one can find the refund request forms and they want you to come over to help look for them.

Although I do realize to some people, that might sound like a dream come true. You know, living close enough to where you work to be able to drop by if there's a small change crisis. Especially in New York. Because my commute is two minutes long, and I do it on foot (four more minutes to add to my daily exercise quota).

But people should realize that, as far as dreams coming true, this one's not the greatest, because I only get paid $23,500 a year (about $12,000 after city and state taxes), and in New York City, $12,000 buys you dinner, and maybe a pair of jeans like the ones I'm about to splurge on, vanity sized or not. I wouldn't be able to live in Manhattan on that kind of salary if it weren't for my second job, which pays my rent. I don't get to "live in" because at New York College, only residence hall directors, not assistant directors, get the "benefit" of living in the dorm—I mean, residence hall—they work in.

Still, I live close enough to Fischer Hall that my boss feels like she can call me all the time, and ask me to "pop in" whenever she needs me.

Like on a bright sunny Saturday afternoon in September, when I am shopping for jeans, because the day before, a freshman who'd had a few too many hard lemonades at the Stoned Crow chose to roll over and barf them on me while I was crouching beside him, feeling for his pulse.

I'm weighing the pros and cons of answering my cell—pro: maybe Rachel's calling to offer me a raise (unlikely); con: maybe Rachel's calling to ask me to take some semicomatose drunk twenty-year-old to the hospital (likely)—when Less Than Zero suddenly shrieks, "Oh my God! I know why you look so familiar! Has anyone ever told you that you look *exactly* like Heather Wells? You know, that singer?"

I decide, under the circumstances, to let my boss go to voice mail. I mean, things are going badly enough, considering the size 12 stuff, and now this. I totally should have just stayed home and bought new jeans online.

"You really think so?" I ask Less Than Zero, not very enthusiastically. Only she doesn't notice my lack of enthusiasm.

"Oh my God!" Less Than Zero shrieks again. "You even *sound* like her. That is so *random*. But," she adds, with a laugh, "what would Heather Wells be doing working in a dorm, right?"

"Residence hall," I correct her automatically. Because that's what we're supposed to call them, since calling it a residence hall allegedly fosters a feeling of warmth and unity among the residents, who might otherwise find living in something called a dorm too cold and institutional-like. ▶

Want More? *(continued)*

As if the fact that their refrigerators are bolted to the floor isn't a dead giveaway.

"Oh, hey," Less Than Zero says, sobering suddenly. "Not that there's anything wrong with it. Being assistant director of a dorm. And you're not, like, offended I said that you look like Heather Wells, are you? I mean, I totally had all her albums. And a big poster of her on my wall. When I was eleven."

"I am not," I say, "the least bit offended."

Less Than Zero looks relieved. "Good," she says. "Well, I guess I better go and find a store that actually carries my size."

"Yeah," I say, wanting to suggest Gap Kids, but restraining myself. Because it isn't her fault she's tiny. Any more than it is my fault that I am the size of the average American woman.

It isn't until I'm standing at the register that I check my voice mail to see what my boss, Rachel, wanted. I hear her voice, always so carefully controlled, saying in tones of barely repressed hysteria, "Heather, I'm calling to let you know that there has been a death in the building. When you get this message, please contact me as soon as possible."

I leave the size 8 jeans on the counter and use up another fifteen minutes of my recommended daily exercise by running—yes, *running*—from the store, and toward Fischer Hall. ◡

Don't miss the next book by your favorite author. Sign up now for AuthorTracker by visiting www.AuthorTracker.com.